"Impeccably written and well-researched, this is an atmospheric and haunting read. It takes the reader from languorous summer days by the lake on a country estate to the horror of the trenches with equal aplomb. . . . Judith Kinghorn skillfully navigates our journey through love and loss. . . . This is the perfect balance of romance and grit by a great new writer. Don't miss it!"   —The Riddle of Writing

THE

Last

Summer

JUDITH KINGHORN

**Doubleday Large Print
Home Library Edition**

NEW AMERICAN LIBRARY

NEW AMERICAN LIBRARY
Published by New American Library, a division of Penguin Group (USA) Inc., 375 Hudson Street, New York, New York 10014, USA

Penguin Books Ltd., Registered Offices: 80 Strand, London WC2R 0RL, England

Published by New American Library, a division of Penguin Group (USA) Inc. This is an authorized reprint of a trade paperback edition published by Headline Review, an imprint of Headline Publishing Group. For information address Headline Publishing Group, An Hachette UK Company, 338 Euston Road, London NW1 3BH, England.

ISBN 978-1-62090-948-5

Printed in the United States of America

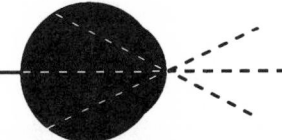

**This Large Print Book carries the
Seal of Approval of N.A.V.H.**

FOR JEREMY

What is this life if, full of care,
We have no time to stand and stare.
No time to stand beneath the boughs
And stare as long as sheep or cows.
No time to see, when woods we pass,
Where squirrels hide their nuts in grass.
No time to see, in broad daylight,
Streams full of stars, like skies at night.
No time to turn at Beauty's glance,
And watch her feet, how they can dance.
No time to wait till her mouth can
Enrich that smile her eyes began.
A poor life this if, full of care,
We have no time to stand and stare.

WILLIAM HENRY DAVIES

THE

Last

Summer

PART ONE

Chapter One

I was almost seventeen when the spell of my childhood was broken. There was no sudden jolt, no immediate awakening and no alteration, as far as I'm aware, in the earth's axis that day. But the vibration of change was upon us, and I sensed a shift: a realignment of my trajectory. It was the beginning of summer and, unbeknown to any of us then, the end of a belle epoque.

If I close my eyes I can still smell the day: the roses beyond the open casement doors; the lavender in the parterre as I ran through; and grass, lambent green, newly mown. I can feel the rain on my face; hear my voice as it once was.

I can't recall exactly who was there, but there were others: my three brothers, some of their friends from Cambridge, a few local people, I think. Our adolescent conversation was still devoid of any faltering uncertainty, and we didn't stand on the brink, we ran along it, unperturbed by tremulous skies, sure of our footing and certain of sunshine, hungry for the next chapter in our own unwritten stories. For lifetimes—lifetimes we had only just begun to imagine—stretched out before us crisscrossing and fading into a distant horizon. There was still time, you see. And the future, all of our futures, lay ahead, glistening with promise, eternal with possibility.

I can hear us now; hear us laughing.

That morning, as clouds gathered overhead, the earthbound colors of my world seemed to me more vibrant than ever. The gardens at Deyning were always at their best during June and early July. It was then, during those few precious weeks of midsummer, that the place came into its own. And though Mama had often looked anxious, complaining about the incessant battering of her roses, every well-tended bloom and leafy branch appeared to me luminous and fresh. From the flagstone terrace the lawns spread out in an undulating soft carpet, and on the mossy steps that led down to the grass wild strawberries grew in abundance.

I can taste their sweetness, even now.

Mama had predicted a storm. She'd informed us that our croquet tournament may have to be postponed, but not before people had arrived. So we'd all stood in the ballroom, which my brothers and I simply referred to as "the big-room," looking out upon the gardens through the open casement doors, debating whether to go ahead with our game or play cards instead. Henry, the eldest of my three older brothers, took charge as usual and voted that we go ahead in our already established teams. But no sooner had we arranged ourselves with mallets upon the lawn than the heavens opened with a reverberating boom, and we all ran back to the house, shrieking, soaking wet.

"Henry wishes tea to be served in the

big-room, Mrs. Cuthbert. We're all back inside now," I said, standing by the green baize door, wringing out my hair.

Mrs. Cuthbert had been our housekeeper for only a few weeks at that time. Years before she'd been employed by Earl Deyning himself, not only at Deyning Park—now our home—but also at his estate in Northamptonshire. It had been lucky for us that Mrs. Cuthbert had agreed to come back to Deyning after the old earl died, and my mother was delighted to have a housekeeper who knew the place so well. "Such pedigree," Mama had said, and I'd immediately imagined a little dog in an apron and mobcap.

"And how many of you are there, miss?" Mrs. Cuthbert asked, glancing over at me, smiling.

"Oh . . . fourteen, I think. Shall I go and count again?"

"No, that's quite all right, dear. I'll come through myself and see." She wiped her hands on her apron. "You've got my Tom with you today," she said.

"Tom? *Your* Tom?"

"Yes, he came home yesterday, and your mother kindly invited him to join today's little game. Have you not been introduced?"

"No. Well, I'm not sure. I don't think so . . ."

I followed Mrs. Cuthbert along the back passageway, toward the big-room, and I remember looking down at the red and black quarry-tiled floor, trying—as I'd done since childhood—not to step on the black ones. But now it was impossible. My feet were too big.

"He's not like your brothers, miss," she said, turning to look at me. "He's a gentle soul."

In the big-room, everyone had already seated themselves around the four card tables pushed up together. And suddenly I was aware of a new face, dark-eyed and solemn, staring directly at me. As Mrs. Cuthbert introduced me to her son, I smiled, but he didn't smile back, and I thought then how rude he was. "Hello," I said, and he stood up, still not smiling, and said, "Pleased to meet you," then looked away.

There was no thunderbolt, no quickening of the heart, but there was a sense of recognition. A familiarity about his face: the nose, the eyes; his stature.

I opted out of whist. All three of my

brothers were playing and I knew I stood no chance. Instead, I wandered to the other end of the room and sat down on the Persian rug in front of the fireplace. As I played with Caesar, Mama's Pekingese dog, I caught Tom Cuthbert looking at me. I didn't smile, but he knew I'd seen him. And, when I rose to my feet and walked back across the room, I was aware of him watching me. I sat down in an armchair, closer to the card tables, picked up a magazine and began to flick through its pages. I glanced over at him, caught his eye once more, and this time he smiled. And I knew it to be a special gesture, meant only for me. I didn't realize what it was like for him then, of course; had no idea of his discomfort as his mother served us all tea.

My upbringing had prepared me for a certain life, a life where I'd never question my role or the cast of players sharing my stage. It was a thoroughly modern idea, then, to educate a daughter, and, in my father's opinion, a pointless expense. So I'd studied at home, with Mademoiselle: a tiny bird of a woman, whose dislike of fresh air and susceptibility to drafts had rendered her pale and brittle. Her lessons in life had depended as much upon the temperature of her heart as the weather outside. Men, she had often told me—usually during arithmetic, and with a rug over her knees—were brutes; they had simply not evolved from animals, she said. However, Keats and Wordsworth appeared to bring out an entirely different side of Mademoiselle's compact and complex character, for then she would sometimes throw back the rug, rise to her feet, and tell me that life was *"nuzzeen"* at all if one had never loved. But by that summer Mademoiselle had left my life for good, for by then it was assumed I knew enough to be able to converse in polite society without appearing completely vacuous.

Like my mother's orchids, I had been nurtured in a controlled environment, an atmosphere maintained at a consistent temperature, protected from cold snaps, clumsy fingers and bitter frosts. My three brothers, on the other hand, had been allowed—even encouraged—to develop unruly tendrils, to thrive beyond the confines of any hothouse, to spread their roots, unrestrained, through that English earth they belonged to. It was different for a girl.

Marriage and children, a tidy home and a manicured garden were foregone conclusions. And a husband with money was always a prerequisite. For how else could that life be achieved? I was a Home Counties girl, happy to be part of a family who enjoyed a sensible, uninterrupted existence, no matter the weather, the visitors, or the events beyond the white gate: the boundary between my understanding and the rest of the universe. When I was young I'd sometimes nudged that boundary: I'd walked down the long avenue of beech trees to the gate, and perched myself there, on top of it. There was little traffic on the road that bordered our land then, but occasionally an omnibus or new motorcar would pass by and I would raise my hand to the unknown faces staring back at me. They were gone in an instant, but I always remembered those fleeting connections: new friends, all at once there, then gone again. Where did they go? What happened to them? Did they remember that moment too? Did they ever wonder what had become of me, the girl on the gate?

That evening, over dinner, I wanted to ask my mother about Tom Cuthbert, but she appeared abstracted. She gazed about the room with an unreadable expression on her face, and I wondered if she was thinking about the servants again. She'd returned from London the day before, festooned with packages, and with a new hairdo, but noticeably agitated. "It's simply *impossible*," she'd announced in the hallway, and in a voice much louder than usual, "to find any decent domestic staff these days. And when one does, one inevitably finds oneself replacing those months later." I couldn't blame her for her exasperation. She had traveled to London only the previous week to interview a prospective parlormaid, a butler, and a new chauffeur, and had stayed overnight—as she quite often did—in the comfort of her Piccadilly club. It was no wonder to me she knew the train timetable to the second and oft by heart, but so much to-ing and fro-ing had, she said, left her feeling *quite frazzled*.

"I met Mrs. Cuthbert's son today, Mama. He's called Tom, and he's been away . . . though I'm not sure where."

"He attends university, dear," she replied, without looking at me.

"But where?" I asked.

"Ha! Don't become too intrigued by Cuthbert, sis," Henry broke in. "Mama expects you to have your sights set *slightly* higher, I think," he added, and then laughed.

"I wondered about him, that's all. He's seems rather shy and . . . well, he has only his mother."

Henry looked across the table at me. "Shy, eh? I reckon Cuthbert's probably quite a rogue—underneath that aloof exterior."

"A rogue?" I repeated. "I don't think so. I think he probably prefers his own company to . . . to the likes of us."

"Aha! And she leaps to his defense! First sign, sister dear, first sign," Henry said, and George and William both sniggered.

"Enough teasing, thank you, Henry," said Mama, glancing to my father for reinforcement. My father cleared his throat, as though about to speak, but then said nothing.

"You're simply jealous," I said, looking back at Henry and forcing a smile. It was one of my stock replies to him when I didn't quite know what else to say.

"And why on earth would I be jealous? He's a servant, for God's sake."

"No, he's not. Mama's just informed us—he's at the university."

"Oh yes, learning to polish silver, no doubt," Henry replied.

"You're jealous because he's so much more handsome than you and isn't inclined to boastfulness," I said, staring down at my plate, and then added, "Mademoiselle says gentlemen who feel the need to boast almost always have unusually small *cerveaux*."

"Ha! Mademoiselle . . . hmm, well, she would know of course. And yes, that's right, I'm jealous of our housekeeper's son, for I shall never have what he has and I can never be the bastard son of—"

"Henry! That's enough," my father intervened. "I don't expect language like that from you or anyone else at this table. And I think you should leave your tittle-tattle and gossip at Cambridge. Do you understand?"

"Yes, sir," my brother answered.

And that was that.

I had no doubt that my eldest brother, Henry, knew a great deal of *tittle-tattle*. And more than that: I imagined there'd be idle gossip and tittle-tattle about him, too, somewhere. For of late he seemed to have acquired new friends, and spent more time in London than at home or Cambridge. Everyone knew Henry, and he, it appeared, knew everything about everyone. But his coterie had never been confined to Cambridge. Two of his closest friends from school had gone up to Oxford, another few straight into the army. He was the most outgoing of my three brothers, confident, popular, and extremely well connected. He liked to say he had his *ear to the ground* and I often imagined him lying prostrate upon some bustling city street.

Later that same evening I quizzed my brother, asked him what he'd meant by his remark, but he'd heeded my father's warning. "I was being flippant, dear. It meant nothing," he said to me. But I knew there was more, and something specific: something my father did not wish to have repeated, particularly not in front of me. There was no point in my pursuing it with Henry; he'd never go against Papa, no matter how full of bravado he appeared, and I was very much aware that to him I was still a child. But as I lay in my bed that night I pondered on it all again. I wondered who paid for Tom Cuthbert's education; and then I wondered if I'd heard Henry correctly. Had he actually used the word *bastard*?

Chapter Two

My father's inheritance, though by no means insubstantial, had been built upon and added to over the years, mainly through returns on investments in the railways. Five years before I was born he'd purchased Deyning Park from the impoverished earl, and commissioned one of England's finest architects to make it grander than ever. A ballroom and two entire wings were added to the main building, old windows and doors replaced; the old paneled library was refurbished, and an ornate carved staircase, Italian marble floor and Corinthian pillars were added to the main lobby. Almost five hundred tons of white Tuscan marble had been brought to Deyning to create my father's vision: a grand entrance hall with twenty-foot-high pillars. The oak-paneled dining room was easily big enough to comfortably seat thirty, and the sixteen bedrooms and four modern bathrooms ensured my parents could entertain *and* accommodate their houseguests in style.

Later, some five or six years after my birth, electric lights were installed in a few of the formal reception rooms, their twentieth-century brilliance altering Mama's color scheme, and causing much debate and consternation among the servants. At that time, a rumor drifted about the house that looking directly upon the electric light could blind a person, and one of the servants—Edna, I suspect now, though I have no evidence and it was a very long time ago—had told George this. My brother—in the midst of a scientific phase— had been determined to test this theory, and, as usual, appointed me his assistant. My role in this particular experiment was to stand guard as he climbed up on to the dining room table and then, once in position, beneath the new chandelier, and only when he gave me the code word *eureka,* to flick the wall-mounted switch. But as I stood on a chair, waiting for my cue, George became distracted by new possibilities, and as he flew along the highly polished mahogany table in his stocking feet he collided with Mama's oversized and elaborate crystal epergne, taking the thing with him on its final short journey. George and the epergne landed on the oak floor in a crash loud enough to wake the dead and within seconds half the servants and Mama were in the room. Luckily George wasn't injured, but the epergne—which, we were informed by Mama, was an *heirloom*—was pronounced unrepairable. Later on, in the library, George was tried: I was called to give evidence, and he was found guilty and sentenced by Papa to twenty-four hours' solitary confinement. And that marked the end of George's interest in electricity.

Parts of our home, I'd been told, dated back to the sixteenth century, but from the outside, at least, the place appeared resolutely Georgian: built in the neoclassical style from honey-hued stone with a pleasing symmetry, perfectly balanced lines, and a multitude of tall windows. At the front of the house, in the center, two Ionic columns framed the doorway, supporting a stone pediment with the words *Ubi bene, ibi patria* carved into it. To the east of the house, around a cobblestoned courtyard— always referred to as the stable yard—were the stables, coach house and a few servants' cottages. A warren of dark passage-ways and small interconnecting rooms led from the house to the coach house, where two motorcars now sat alongside the old wagonette and landau carriage of my child-hood. And there, too, the sleigh: still used occasionally in the depths of winter, when the lanes around us were white and thick with snow.

Father's penchant for the neoclassi-cal was a fitting backdrop to his and my mother's vast collection of artifacts and souvenirs from abroad: antiques, paintings, books, bronzes and sculptures from their continental tours. A delivery of crates and the unveiling of new works of art for Deyn-ing inevitably followed each return home. In his newly furbished library my father added to his burgeoning collection of rare books; books he would never read; books no one could read in any one lifetime. And while he indulged himself with his love of antiquities, Mama focused on our comfort, with new fitted carpets and expensive wall coverings from Harrods and Gamages. She'd taken advice, albeit paid for, from an old friend of hers who had an interior decorating business in London.

Sumptuous would best describe Mama's style. It was what she'd been accustomed to all her life; was what she knew. Consequently, our home was as lavishly furnished and decorated as any other fine country house: each window festooned, draped in richly colored silk brocades; looped back, tasseled and fringed; each vista—north, south, east and west—opulently framed in a color specifically chosen to match the light of that room, and the views beyond.

From my bedroom window I looked out across the formal gardens and lake, beyond the six hundred acres of landscaped parkland to the South Downs in the distance. It was the only point in my vision that my father did *not* own, and I sometimes wondered who lived there, beyond my world, beyond Deyning. As a child I'd rarely ventured farther than the ha-ha, which separated the park from the formal gardens. Terraces, ornamented with statues, urns and fountains, led down from the house's south façade to the striped lawns and broad herbaceous borders, extravagantly stocked with Mama's prize-winning roses and peonies.

A small army of gardeners and outdoor staff were employed at Deyning then. Even now, I see their faces, and their hands, my *outside friends*. Together, they managed the parkland, the home farm and the kitchen gardens; they maintained the formal gardens, and the tennis and croquet lawns, constantly rolling and trimming the grass to perfection. They pulled, planted, chopped, clipped and snipped, like defenders of a realm, for Deyning was a kingdom, guarded by acreage and entirely self-sufficient. The walled kitchen gardens produced all manner of fruit and vegetables: asparagus, strawberries, raspberries, loganberries, currants (white, red and black), gooseberries, plums, pears, apples, rhubarb, potatoes, cabbage, carrots, cauliflower and spinach. And in summer, up against the pink brick walls, peaches and nectarines. The home farm supplied us with all our milk, cream, eggs, butter and cheese, as well as our meat, poultry and game.

We knew no lack, experienced no want, and I knew no other way. I had never looked from the outside in; never thought about *how* we lived. Until that time: until Tom Cuthbert entered my life.

That summer we were all at home, still living a collective existence, still a family. At five years my senior, Henry had only just finished his studies at Cambridge, and William, two years younger than Henry, had completed his first year there, studying theology. George, my closest sibling—a year younger than William and two years my senior—was at Aldershot, training to be an officer. And, at sixteen years of age, it seemed my education was complete. Mama had been keen for me to attend a fashionable finishing school in Paris before coming out. It was what she had done, what everyone did, she said. But events on the continent had made my parents anxious, and so my sojourn in Paris was indefinitely postponed.

Strange though it may seem, I had no

desire at that time for a more eventful existence, or a broader vista. I filled my days with walks through the grounds, following the same paths, anticipating the same sights, content with familiarity. I lost myself in books, spent hours in my father's library, pulling out whichever title caught my eye. And it was there, in the library, that I had my first proper conversation with Tom Cuthbert. I'd seen him about the place: walking down the drive, disappearing into the distance; helping one of the under-gardeners cut logs in the stable yard; and a couple of times in the kitchen, when I'd been sent to query a menu for Mama. He'd been sitting at the table, reading a newspaper, doing nothing in particular, and he stood up and said "Hello," without any smile.

When he appeared in the library that day I was perched at the top of the library steps, reading a volume of Emily Brontë's poems, and I can't be sure, but I think I may have been reading aloud. He cleared his throat. "Excuse me," he said, "your father told me that I was welcome to borrow any books . . . I can come back later."

"No, please, I'm idling here. Do come

in," I said, looking down at him. He closed the door, and I had the faintest inkling of intimacy.

"I was reading a poem . . . Do you like poetry, Mr. Cuthbert?" I asked, filling the silence as he surveyed the shelves on the opposite side of the room, his back to me.

He pulled out a book. "Yes, I like poetry," he said, without turning to face me.

"I'm rather fond of the Brontë sisters myself . . . especially dear Emily," I said, trying desperately to sound grown up and worldly. He made no reply but continued his inspection of the volumes immediately in front of him, occasionally bending down or stretching up. And I watched him, surreptitiously, in case he should suddenly turn.

He was tall, taller than Henry, and his dark hair longer than my brothers' or anyone else's I'd seen. It hung down over his forehead in a wave he ran his hand through from time to time. He wore dark gray flannel trousers with navy braces, a plain pale blue shirt; no tie, no jacket.

"I imagine it's rather dull for you here," I said at last, uncomfortable with our lack of conversation and longing for a break in the deadlock.

He turned, smiled at me. "Dull? No, not at all. Why do you say that?"

"Well, it's somewhat quiet here, especially when my brothers aren't about the place, and not everyone's partial to the peace of the countryside."

He laughed. "I think I may very well be *dull* then, Miss Granville. I'm happy to be amidst this peacefulness. I get quite enough noise and bustle up at Oxford."

"Oxford?" I repeated, climbing carefully down the library steps.

"Yes, but only for another year, and then I'm done."

"And then what?" I asked.

"I shall go to the bar, become a practicing lawyer."

"Oh, so you'll live in London, I suppose . . ."

"Yes, that's my plan."

"Everyone seems to go to London, eventually, but I'm not so sure I shall. I rather think I prefer the country," I said.

He stared at me, half smiling, and I pushed my hair back from my face, glanced down at the book in my hand.

"Well, you're still quite young . . . you may change your mind yet."

"Oh no, I'll be seventeen in August. I'll

be coming out soon, and then I shall have to be in London," I said, and his smile broadened. He looked so handsome, so nonchalant at that moment, his hair hanging down over one eye. And as I felt myself blush I looked away once more. He was amused, quietly amused. I was still a child to him, naive and innocent; locked up in a modern-day fortress, talking nonsense.

"And I'm sure you'll have a gay time, and many suitors too," he said, still smiling, still staring. "But it's an odd ritual, is it not?" he continued, moving away from the shelves, a book gripped in his own hand now too. "Coming out? It's about finding a husband, isn't it?"

"No, not entirely," I said, unsure of what else to say, because I'd never really thought about it until that moment; what "coming out" meant, its purpose.

"Oh?"

"It's more about parties . . . meeting new people, that sort of thing. I think originally, historically, it was about finding a husband, but of course it's different now." I smiled. "After all, this is the twentieth century," I continued, feeling quite bold and modern, "things have changed." Then I added, "Look at the suffragettes . . ."

I wasn't quite sure what I meant by that last line, but I liked the sound of it. For despite Papa's misgivings (*hooligans*, he called them), I'd become deeply fascinated by the recent dramatic events I'd read about taking place in London. The window-smashing women, full of passion and fury, no matter how far from my own gilded cage, had captured my imagination.

He smiled at me, and I noticed his eyes: darkest mahogany, glinting with light. "Have times changed?" he asked. "Are you sure about that, Miss Granville?" He frowned, looking at me quizzically. And I knew he was being provocative. Like my brothers, I thought.

"I'm used to being teased, Mr. Cuthbert," I replied. "I have three older brothers—remember?"

"But I'm not teasing you. I'm curious, genuinely so. Do you really think times have changed? Do you truly believe that your own coming out and that of all the other debutantes isn't about finding a suitable husband?"

"Well, yes, I'll be introduced to society, and that society may well include my future husband, or not, as the case may be," I replied, perhaps a little too quickly. He said nothing, but tilted his head to one side and looked back at me through half-closed eyes. Then he shook his head and turned away.

"I amuse you," I said, without thinking.

"You do somewhat, but it's not so much you, it's the way . . . the way your sort operate," he replied, and I simply couldn't understand what he meant. Was he being rude? Was he playing? I couldn't be sure, so I shrugged and then laughed myself.

"Yes, we're a strange lot, aren't we?" I said.

"You're right, of course. Things are changing, and changing fast. Look at me: the son of a humble servant, at Oxford and bound for a career in the City."

"Yes indeed, your mother must be very proud of you," I replied, sounding like Mama.

He laughed again. He was so handsome when he laughed; so utterly uninhibited and free. It was not a joke, but he was free enough to laugh. To laugh out loud at me, pretending to be something.

"I'm sorry," he said. "I don't mean to be rude or disrespectful."

"No, I know that. I mean, I can see that."

He fixed his eyes on me. "Yes, yes I think you can . . . Clarissa."

And when he said my name, it was as though I'd heard it spoken for the very first time, as though he'd placed his hand upon my bare skin. No one other than my immediate family ever addressed me so directly, so honestly, using only my first name. *Clarissa*. He'd said my name, said it slowly, looking straight at me.

I'd been released from a cage and allowed to fly.

"I think I must go now," I said, not entirely sure of how to deal with his entrance into my life. "I need to dress for dinner."

"Of course," he replied, glancing over to the clock. "And I should get back to my studies."

"Really, Tom," I said, adopting his familiar style, "you don't need to go on my account. Stay here awhile. I'm quite sure no one will disturb you."

"No, I should go. But I'll come back tomorrow," he said, looking at me.

I smiled, nodded. "Yes. Yes, do that."

Chapter Three

The next day, when I awoke, I remember feeling quite different. In fact, everything seemed strangely altered. It was as though a door had finally opened on to my world, letting in light so every detail appeared sharper, more focused. And from that doorway I was able to look back on my life, my family, and begin to see us as others saw us: as Tom Cuthbert saw us.

I'd slept in that morning. By the time I went down to breakfast it was after nine, and yet the house seemed unusually quiet. Henry, I knew, was away, staying with friends in Salisbury, and my father, as usual, remained up in town, attending to business. But I wondered where my mother was.

As I sat at the dining room table, already cleared but for one setting, Mrs. Cuthbert emerged through the baize door with fresh tea. She asked if I'd like Edna to cook me something. And then she reminded me that my mother had caught the 7:38 to London—to attend a horticultural exhibition with Mr. Broughton, the head gardener—and wasn't expected back until late that evening. She told me that George and Will had also risen early; already set off to attend their old school Speech Day. And I felt momentarily angry that they'd all gone and left me there, alone. Why had Mama not invited me to accompany her? And why could my brothers not have taken me with them to their Speech Day reunion? It didn't seem fair. I was being treated like a child, I said to Mrs. Cuthbert.

"Oh, but you have all the time in the world, your whole life ahead of you. Don't wish it away too soon."

"I don't wish it away, Mrs. C, but I'd rather like *something* to happen."

Then I thought of Tom Cuthbert.

"And how is Tom?" I said. "It must be lovely for you to have him back with you."

She smiled. "Yes, it is. And he's a good boy . . . a gentle soul," she said, again, and then disappeared through the baize door.

For so many years, since George, the last of my brothers to be sent away to boarding school, had gone, I'd languished in a daydream at Deyning. Floating through the house and about the grounds, inventing people, places and events: a revered guest at so many glittering parties out on the lawn; an actress upon the stage of the ha-ha; an intrepid explorer cutting a swath through the Amazon jungle of long meadow grass. And though those desultory days of my childhood, when an hour had stretched to a lifetime and time itself was of no import, lingered on, they were in fact drawing to a close.

More latterly, the fantasies of my idle hours had taken on a different hue. For now it seemed I had to be *rescued*, and, perhaps inevitably, by a dashingly handsome—albeit slightly unkempt—young man. I was often confused, irritated by these unscripted interventions. I liked to imagine myself as one of those pioneering Victorian women

I'd read about: independent, brave, and resourceful. But no matter which way my dream unfolded, a swashbuckling-style hero inevitably marched in to lift me up into his arms. And, more recently, a struggle of sorts had usually ensued, which almost always resulted in a kiss.

The days of catching moths and butterflies were over. News of kittens in the stables or newly born lambs down at the farm no longer made my heart race. Though sometimes, particularly if Papa was present, I felt duty bound to feign that lost excitement.

But that day, I could think only of him, Tom Cuthbert. I wondered where he was, what he was doing. I floated about the house, intermittently looking in on the library hoping to find him there. I went to the kitchen three or four times on the pretext of needing to speak to Mrs. Cuthbert about some sewing. I walked out to the lake, through the stable yard, past Mrs. Cuthbert's cottage and back again the same way. I dawdled in the walled garden, distractedly helping a new kitchen maid pick raspberries, with one eye fixed on the gate to the yard, through which the door of

Mrs. Cuthbert's cottage was clearly visible. And then I dallied with Frank and John, the two youngest under-gardeners, as they sat on the bench by the greenhouse, eating the sandwiches Edna had sent out to them in a basket.

"Please, do sit down and enjoy your lunch," I said, as they rose simultaneously to their feet.

They took their orders from Mr. Broughton—a man whom I'd more than once heard described by Edna, our cook, as *a dark horse*—and were usually employed in what were still referred to as the "pleasure gardens": keeping the borders free of bindweed and ivy, cutting back and clipping the many and various shrubs, and attending to the pathways—so easily lost and overgrown. Up a ladder or down on their knees, they were always there, together, always smiling and laughing. Frank, short and squat, with freckles and bright red curls, and John, so immensely tall and gangly, with shorn jet black hair. Even to look at they made a comical pair, and Mama often said they should be on the stage.

That day, Frank, the same age as me and mad on cricket, blushed to the color of a ripe tomato when I inquired how his team was doing that season, and John said, "He wears the color of 'is 'eart on 'is face, miss," and then laughed. They had both worked in the gardens at Deyning since they were boys, both been part of every Christmas, birthday and celebration; and each summer, when Deyning played against the village team, Frank had no obvious conflict and always switched allegiance to bowl for Deyning Park.

The previous summer, when the days had been long, stretching late in to the evening, I'd taken it upon myself to teach Frank to read—and be able to write more than just his name. (Both he and John were too old to have benefited from my father's founding of the village school. They had, they said, for a while at least, on certain days, walked the three miles to the nearest school, but there were simply too many distractions on their route, and neither of them were suited to being kept indoors.) Each evening, after dinner, I sat with Frank outside on the veranda, teaching him the sounds of letters and familiar words, writing them out for him to copy and practice. I read passages from a few of my favorite books out loud to him, and some poems too. And we made progress. By the end of summer Frank was able to recognize any number of words, and confident enough to attempt the pronunciation of others. With a little help from me, he'd written a letter to his mother, even though she wouldn't be able to read it, he said; would need someone to read it for her. He joined the local lending library, and I gave him a list of books I thought he might enjoy. Then Mama intervened. She said she thought Frank was becoming a little *too attached*; that I had done enough, and that it was wrong—and possibly misleading— for me to continue my *sponsorship* of him. So I told him, reluctantly, that I'd taught him as much as I could, that he'd have to go on alone; go on reading, and continue with books until he could read as well as anyone else.

"I imagine you've both met Mrs. Cuthbert's son . . ." I said at last, leaning against a warm pane of the greenhouse.

"Tom?" John replied. "He were just out here, earlier. Weren't he, Frank?"

Frank, mouth bulging with bread, glanced up at me, blushing once more, and nodded.

"Well, he seems like a jolly nice sort," I said, looking from one to the other, and wondering if either of them knew any more than me. "But such a shame about his father . . ."

"What's that then?" John asked.

"Mr. Cuthbert," I replied, not sure what else to say.

"Mr. Cuthbert? Thought he'd been gone long since."

"Yes . . . yes, that's what I meant. Such a shame, for Mrs. Cuthbert I mean, and for Tom. I don't suppose he ever knew his father . . ."

John turned to Frank and—in a much quieter voice—said, "Aye, well, plenty like that 'round here." And they both laughed.

Finally, late in the afternoon, as I once again halfheartedly perused my father's bookshelves, I heard footsteps in the marble hallway coming toward the open library door. I grabbed a book, and sat down just in time.

He closed the door behind him and remained perfectly still for a moment, looking over at me.

"Oh, hello, Tom," I said, sounding surprised (even to myself).

"Hello, Clarissa. I was hoping I might find you here. And what are we reading today?" he asked, walking toward me. "More of the Brontës?"

I glanced down at the book, noticed it was covered in plain paper, and opened it quickly. "Ha! No, not today," I said, searching for the title. "No, today I'm quite lost in . . . *The Life and Adventures of* dear *Miss Fanny Hill.*"

"Really?"

He stood in front of me, his hands in his pockets, a quizzical look upon his face.

"Why so surprised?" I asked, looking up at him, smiling. "I don't limit myself to *just* the Brontë sisters, you know."

"Clarissa . . ."

"Yes?"

"Have you actually been *reading* that book?"

"Yes . . . yes, indeed I have." I opened the book at random. "I was somewhere . . . about here . . ." I flicked a page or two. "This page, I think . . . yes, this one. *She, no doubt, thought it was time to give up the argument, and that all further defense would be in vain . . .*"

I looked up again, blinking. He sat down

in the chair opposite me, leaned forward, resting his elbows on his knees, clasping his hands in front of him. His shirtsleeves were rolled back and I noticed the dark hair on his forearms.

"Yes, that's where I was up to."

"Do continue . . . please, read some more," he said.

"Are you sure? To be honest I was finding it rather dull."

He smiled. "No, please. I'd like to hear you read on."

I cleared my throat. *"And he, throwing her petticoats over her face . . ."*—I paused, slightly confused—*"which was now as red as scarlet, discovered . . . a pair of . . ."*—I paused again, then continued, slowly, quieter—*"stout, plump, substantial thighs . . . and tolerably white; he mounted them round his hips . . ."* My mind began to swim, my face grew hot, but I continued, my voice ever quieter. *"And coming out with his drawn weapon, stuck it in the cloven spot . . . where he seemed to find a less difficult entrance than perhaps he had flattered himself with . . ."*

I looked up at him, my face stinging. I wasn't entirely sure if what I'd read was the run-up to a grisly murder or some other act of wickedness. But by Tom's expression I could hazard a guess. He reached over, eased the book from my hand and closed it.

"I'm quite certain your father wouldn't want you to be reading that particular book."

"No," was all I could manage. I felt my lip quiver, and for a moment I thought I might cry.

"Are you feeling quite all right?" he asked.

"No, not terribly," I replied.

"Come, let's go outside. You look as though you need some air." He rose to his feet and walked ahead of me through the library, placing the book upon a shelf without a second glance. I followed him across the hallway and then outside, into the garden. *Perhaps he thought I read that sort of book. Perhaps he thought I'd picked it on purpose, wanted to read it to him . . .* I stopped, closed my eyes, and shivered.

"Do you need a shawl or something?" he asked.

"No, no thank you. I'm fine."

We walked in silence across the flagstones, past Mama's gaudy new swingchair, down the steps and onto the lawn. It had been another indifferent, overcast day, but now the garden glowed in the warmth of the early-evening sun. We walked under the drooping branches of the sycamore toward the bank of rhododendrons and the ha-ha just beyond.

"Feeling better?" he asked, turning to me.

"Mm, slightly," I said, not looking at him, a hullabaloo of unfamiliar words still echoing in my head.

I was neither able nor ready to put together a longer sentence. But I was aware that since reading about *his drawn weapon . . . in the cloven spot* I'd barely uttered a word.

"There's a bench over here," I managed at last. "One can see for miles."

"Perfect. All we need is a Singapore Sling," he said, as we sat down upon the wooden seat.

"Singapore what?"

"It's a cocktail, all the rage up at Oxford." He turned to me, smiling. "Have you ever had a cocktail?"

"I had a champagne cocktail once . . . at New Year."

"And did you enjoy it?"

"Yes. It made me feel quite . . . in love

with life," I replied, remembering my dance with Billy Robertson, a handsome under-gardener who'd since vanished from my father's employ.

He laughed. "Alcohol does that. It loos-ens folk up, makes them feel freer," he said, staring into the distance.

"Are there lots and lots of parties up at Oxford?" I asked, my equilibrium almost restored by the combination of air and conversation.

"Yes, there are. But I'm neither fashion-able enough nor rich enough to be invited to some. And"—he turned to me—"I need to work. I'm not like the other undergradu-ates who have a private income and are simply there because they have nothing better to do. Or want to have a wild few years before taking over the family estate. I have an opportunity, and I don't intend to throw it away."

"It must be difficult," I said, not sure what else to say.

"Difficult?"

"Yes, difficult for you—if you feel ex-cluded or perhaps on the outside of some-thing."

"Clarissa, you are sweet. But I'm not

remotely bothered about parties or social-
izing."

"I think all Henry does is gallivant
about—attending parties . . . and woman-
ize," I added, borrowing one of Mama's
words.

"Well, it's different for him. Look at this,"
he said, gesturing at everything in front of
us. "All this will be his one day. Whereas
I"—and he turned to me again—"I shall
inherit a shoebox of mementos, if I'm
lucky."

"But you may be like Papa . . . you might
make a fortune."

"Yes, I intend to do that. But what about
you, Clarissa? You may be married, and to
an earl—or even a duke—by this time next
year."

I tried to laugh. "I hope not. I don't wish
to be married *too* soon. And I'm not sure I
want to be married to either a duke *or* an
earl."

"Perhaps not, but your parents may." He
reached into his pocket, pulled out a packet
of cigarettes and offered me one.

"No, thank you. I don't."

I watched him light his cigarette, draw
heavily on it, sucking in his cheeks.

"I hope they want me to be happy more than anything else," I said. "And I intend to be ferociously happy."

He made no reply. But I watched him from the corner of my eye as he smoked his cigarette, staring into the distance through half-closed eyes, and I wondered what he was thinking. I longed to know his thoughts. I longed to know him. And, though it was much too warm an evening to be sitting outside in the sun, I didn't want that moment to end.

I noticed the tiny beads of perspiration glistening on the temple of his brow, above his mouth; the damp indigo patch under his arm. I watched him as he placed his lips around the cigarette, inhaled, and then blew a series of smoke rings into the sultry evening air. I fiddled with the lace on the ruffle of my high-necked blouse, pushed my fingers underneath the fabric onto my own hot skin; and I wished I'd done as Mama had repeatedly told me and worn my hair up.

"We'd better go. Your brothers will probably be back by now and no doubt wondering where you are," he said, flicking his cigarette over the ha-ha.

"I don't think so. They're not remotely interested in where I am. No one ever is."

He turned toward me. "If you were mine—I mean, if you were my sister—I'd be interested, and I don't suppose I'd be too happy to know you were idling with the housekeeper's son."

"It's up to me who I choose to idle with," I said, staring back at him, our eyes inches apart. I saw him glance to my lips, then back to my eyes, then back to my lips. *Kiss me. Kiss me now*, I begged silently.

He raised his hand to my face—as though about to touch it; then, in one swift movement, pulled away. "You know, you're quite dangerously beautiful, Clarissa Granville. Just as well you're kept locked away here," he said, and rose to his feet. "Come. I should take you back."

"But it's not late. I don't need to go back, not yet."

"I need to get back."

"Why? Will your mother be worried?"

"Clarissa . . . it's not right for us to stay out here—alone."

"Why ever not? What's going to happen? I hardly think you're about to seduce me,

Mr. Cuthbert. No, I feel quite safe here with you."

"Aha! But perhaps you shouldn't."

"Why? Do you plan on seducing me?" I asked, rising to my feet, looking back at him, into his eyes. "If so, do please tell me—as I'd like a moment to prepare."

He pulled me to him. "You really shouldn't say such things . . . you've no idea . . . have you?"

He held me tightly; his mouth so close I could feel the heat of his breath in short sharp bursts upon my face.

"No idea of what?" I asked, watching his eyes on my lips.

Kiss me. Kiss me now.

"No idea," he repeated, turning his face away, releasing his grip. He stepped back from me, thrust his hands into his pockets and looked up at the sky with a groan.

"I'm sorry . . ."

He sighed, turned to face me. "What are you sorry for? You've no reason to apologize. Come, let's walk back," he added, smiling at me once more.

We began to walk across the lawn in the direction of the house. "I'm sorry if . . . if I've made you feel uncomfortable in some way," I said. "I'm afraid my brothers' teasing has probably blunted my sensibilities . . . made me too flippant."

At the edge of the lawn, he stopped, looked down at the grass. "Perhaps I'll see you tomorrow . . ."

"Yes, perhaps," I replied, glancing away, toward the lake in the distance.

"I still need to look up a few books in your father's library . . ."

"Of course."

"Perhaps, later in the day . . . around four."

I turned to him. "Yes, around four. I'm sure that will be fine."

He smiled, and as he began to move away—walking backward—he said, "Oh, and Clarissa, promise me one thing . . ."

"What's that?" I asked, intrigued.

"Promise me you won't read another word of that book."

I laughed. "Of course not. I promise."

And then I went inside, to the library, pulled out the book and took it up to my room.

Chapter Four

I awoke early the following morning: catapulted back to my bed from Tom Cuthbert's arms. We'd been lying in an exotically decorated open-sided tent, on the lawn, under the sycamore tree. "*Clarissa . . . Clarissa*," he'd repeated, holding me tightly, gazing into my eyes. Then he'd kissed me, and the passion of his kiss had woken me. I closed my eyes and returned there, to languish once more in his arms. But as I felt his hands move over my body, I realized my state of dishabille; for I was in nothing more than my flimsy summer nightgown, which he appeared to have unbuttoned. And I leaped from my bed, still breathless and hot from that imagined kiss.

I was distracted over breakfast, and Mama, too, was unusually silent. She liked to check the menu for dinner each morning and almost always read it out loud, but not today. I stood by the sideboard, staring down at my reflection in a polished silver lid. *Perhaps I should wear my hair up . . .* As I lifted the lid from a dish of deviled kidneys, my mother sighed, loudly, and then informed me that she was going out to make calls later that afternoon. Did I wish to accompany her?

"Would you mind if I didn't today? I'm quite lost in my book . . . and determined to finish it this afternoon."

I sat down at the table next to her.

"Very well, but I think you should stay inside, out of the sun. And please do something with your hair, Clarissa," she said, and then she rose to her feet and left the room.

I was relieved she appeared so preoccupied, and I presumed she must be tired, for she'd returned home from London very late the previous evening. I'd been in my bed, reading, but when I'd heard her arrive back I'd gone to see her, in her dressing room. She'd been in one of her dreamy moods, and told me that she'd seen the most beautiful painting she'd ever seen in her life, *at a gallery in London.*

"But I thought you went to a horticultural exhibition . . ."

"Oh . . . no," she said, turning to me. "I left Broughton to do that. I met Venetia and we went to a gallery . . . and then out to dinner."

Later that day, as I watched her disappear down the driveway, I thought how remarkably brave and independent she was. Unwavering and indefatigable in her commitment to her many causes, she was happy to travel about the locality on her own in the dogcart; visiting people, delivering food parcels—eggs, butter, fruit and vegetables from the farm—ministering to those sick and needy, and attending to her many and various charitable causes. There seemed to be an inexhaustible list of charities with which she was affiliated, from the NSPCC to the League of Pity and the Mothers' Union; she attended drawing room meetings, and sat on the council of the

Primrose League, in my mind something to do with gardening: her one true passion.

Mama was obsessed with her garden, and not only in summer, but all year round. There was *always* something to be done, always something requiring her attention. In early summer her roses and peonies, in particular, inevitably scooped her a few first prizes at local flower shows. But sometimes she traveled further afield—to more out-of-the-way places, in order to exhibit a vividly colored orchid from the hothouse, or a new hybrid tea rose. She'd return from these trips with a ribbon or rosette, reinvigorated, and quite obviously elated.

I wondered if I'd be like Mama one day: as poised and controlled, as elegant. She seemed to me to inhabit an aura of ineffable loveliness, gliding about the place in a cloud of tuberose, exuding a soporific maternal balm upon our senses. Taller than most other women, she held her head high, for good posture and manners were, she said, the surest and most important indicator of character. She abhorred raised voices, or aggression of any kind, and had no time for wanton displays of emotion, or what she deemed self-indulgent outbursts.

Papa often said that when he looked at me he saw *the perfect vision* of my mother. And I never quite knew what he meant by that. For how could anyone be more perfect than Mama? But I was like her, in appearance, at least: I had her coloring, eyes and hair. And, as I'd grown up, others had inevitably commented: *Ah, yes, Edina's daughter through and through. Quite uncanny . . .*

As a child, I'd basked in that air of perpetual calm enveloping her, mesmerized by her beauty, the luminosity of her pale skin against her dark chestnut hair, the way she sometimes closed her eyes as she spoke. In the evenings—whenever she and Papa were at home—she'd come to the night nursery and I'd gaze up at her as she read to me: her dark blue eyes following the words on the page; her perfect lips moving with mellifluous sound. She was to me the stuff of fairy tales, the embodiment of all that was good and fine.

The granddaughter of the diplomat and financier Sir Montague Vincent, my mother's formative years had been divided between the palatial drawing rooms of London and her grandfather's vast estate in Hampshire. And there, waited on by liveried footmen in powdered wigs, she had spent some of *the happiest days* of her life. Before her own coming out, her mother had taken her to Paris to be fitted with gowns, a habit she had never outgrown. Each season she returned there—to be fitted with the latest fashions from Worth. Her jewelry drawer, my childhood treasure trove, included cuffs, collars and combs of diamonds, and endless ropes of pearls. She changed three—sometimes even four—times each day, aided by Wilson, her maid, and bathed in rose-scented bathwater. And her bedroom and dressing room—in the French style, all toile de jouy and soft fine lace, and scented with roses and orchids from the hothouse—were to me simply an extension of her.

But Mama had secrets. I could tell. For there was some unfathomable mystery lurking in those benevolent, smiling eyes; and tantalizing but as yet unspoken words on the very edge of her soft tongue. Oh yes, Mama had secrets, and I had had a glimpse of one of them, once, many years before.

"And what are my naughty cherubs up

to?" she'd asked, entering her dressing room.

We'd been playing with her jewels. And Georgie had spent a good hour dressing me up as the May Queen, with ropes of pearls around my head, tangled and fastened in my hair with brooches; diamonds galore about my neck and arms; and rings, slipping and sliding off my tiny fingers. He'd put powder and rouge on my face, though, and perhaps thankfully, I hadn't yet had a chance to check my appearance in the looking glass.

She moved toward me, slowly, and bent down, leveling her face with my own. "This one," she said, her eyes staring back into mine as she removed a heavy gold ring from the middle finger of my left hand, "is *not* for playing with."

"But that's the King's ring!" Georgie called out. "And she's the Queen . . . and she looks so beautiful," he added, rather appealingly.

She moved away and I watched her slip the King's ring back into the jewelry drawer, then lock it, and push the key into the top of her dress. It's a secret, I thought: the King's ring is Mama's secret. And I wondered if she'd told Papa. And if she had not, what a perfect secret it was.

When she left us to continue our game, I turned to my brother and put my finger to my lips.

"What?" he whispered. "What is it?"

I shook my head, for if he didn't know—I couldn't possibly tell him.

And I never did.

Sometimes I had been allowed to sit quietly and watch my mother prepare for a party or a ball. As she sat at her dressing table, straight-backed and head high, I'd looked on as Wilson brushed and then carefully pinned up Mama's waist-length hair, Mama lifting and turning her head this way and that, checking her profile, tucking in a curl here and there. I'd watch her select her jewels for the evening, running her fingers over the dark red velvet-lined tray; and though I'd looked for the King's ring, I'd never again seen it. I'd sat in silence and watched Wilson fasten my mother's jewels in place, and occasionally my mother would glance at me, my reflection in the looking glass in front of her. She'd tilt her head, smile at me. "These will be yours one day," she'd say, raising her hand to the gems glinting upon her décolleté. She was to me, then, the personification of romance, a dazzling celebration, like Christmas, and a luxurious gift to us all. But there were so many things, rituals and habits, too plebeian for my mother; for it was not how things *were* that mattered, but how they appeared. And idolatry such as mine could never be sustained, nor survive what lay ahead.

That afternoon, I timed my arrival in the library with perfection. And I'd taken a little more time with myself. I'd had Wilson pin up my hair, and wore a favorite blouse: one made from the softest white muslin, with hand-stitched pin-tucks. "You're a picture, Miss Clarissa, a perfect picture," Wilson said. "Such a shame there's no young gentlemen here to admire you."

Tom was already there, sitting in an armchair, his head bent, reading. And as soon as I entered, he closed his book and stood up.

"I do hope I'm not disturbing you," I said, standing inside the doorway, unsure of what to do.

"No, no of course not. I was hoping . . . hoping I might see you."

He remained on his feet, watching me as I ambled my way across the library, glancing to the shelves on my left. I quite wanted him to notice my hair, make a comment, compliment me, but of course he didn't.

"What are you reading?" I asked, standing opposite him, behind the other chair.

"Something very dull . . . much more dull, I think, than *dear* Fanny Hill," he said and smiled.

I looked away.

"It's a book about the principles of company law, Clarissa. And I'm quite sure you're not remotely interested in that."

"Hmm. Yes, that does sound awfully dull. Do you *have* to read it?"

His smile broadened. "I'm afraid I do, if I'm to pass my exams."

"Then I'm very pleased I shall never have to take exams."

"But now you're here I have a most welcome distraction," he said, putting the book down on the table beside him.

"Oh," I replied, not quite sure how to *be* a welcome distraction, and feeling the distinct pressure to be entertaining. "Well, I suppose we could have a game of cards . . ." I suggested.

He laughed, and I think he thought I was being funny.

"Are you allowed . . . I mean to say, would you care to take a stroll? Perhaps where we walked yesterday?"

I was a little shocked by his boldness, but it had turned into a glorious day and there was no harm in a walk.

We took a different direction to the one we'd taken the previous evening, this time venturing a little farther from the house, down through the meadow known as "lower meadow," toward the lake. It was my suggestion; I wanted to take him to my favorite place. He told me that he'd been helping out on the farm that morning, had woken early and been there by seven. I didn't mention that he couldn't possibly have been there at that hour, that we'd been lying on the lawn together, under the sycamore tree, kissing. But I imagined him walking to the farm in the early-morning sunshine as I'd been lying in my bed, and I wondered if he'd thought of me.

We stopped under the shade of the old chestnut tree.

"There should be a seat here," he said, staring out toward the lake.

"Exactly, and I've told Papa this so many times," I replied, staring in the same direction. "But he's promised me faithfully that he's going to find me an Arabian tent," I added.

He turned to me. "An Arabian tent?"

"Yes, so that I can sleep outside, under the stars."

"Would you really like that? Would you not be afraid?"

"Afraid? No, what's there to be afraid of? An owl, a fox, a badger . . . or perhaps a deer? No, there's nothing to be afraid of, other than the stars, the universe, and that sense of being infinitesimal . . ."

We stood side by side and the air hummed with the sound of summer. If I'd been on my own I'd have lain down upon the dry grass, as I'd done so many times before, squinting up at a mosaic sky through branches; searching for a cloud from which I would be able to see some far-off exotic country. When I was young George had told me that those very wispy, celestial clouds, the ones which appeared to me to have faces, were not really above us, even though they seemed to be so. No, he'd explained, those ones, those particular clouds, floated in the atmosphere *hundreds of thousands* of miles above another country. "So . . . which country is that one above?" I'd asked, pointing up to the blue yonder. "That one . . . that one," he'd said, scratching his head, and appearing to work out some immensely complicated mathematical equation, "that one, Issy, is above . . . the Sahara Desert." It was stupendous that he knew, that he was able to work this out at no more than ten years old; and the fact that I could see the cloud above the Sahara Desert enabled me to look down from it. I'd stare up at the white vapor and I was there. I could see the camels, the Arabian tents pitched next to a palm tree, an oasis.

I heard Tom's voice. "So, is this where you like to come?" But I was adrift; lost in a blissful trance and unable to come back to now, unable to answer. As though the universe for a moment held me to it, and that feeling of oneness—complete connectedness—had locked me in.

"Clarissa?"

I turned to him. He stepped toward me, raised his hand to my brow, where it hovered for a second or two. He ran his finger down the side of my face, along my jaw and onto my neck. I stared back into his dark, solemn eyes, felt my throat tighten. *Kiss me.* He glanced to my mouth, moved his head a little closer. I ran my tongue over my lips, half closed my eyes, waiting. He tilted his head toward me, his lips almost touching my own. Then he stepped back from me.

"I'm sorry, he said, looking down at the ground.

I didn't say anything. What was there for me to say?

"I'm not sure I *can* be trusted to be alone with you after all," he added.

"Oh, I think you can. In fact, I think you've just proved it," I said, and walked on toward the lake.

At first I thought he wasn't going to follow me. He loitered under the tree for a moment or two, and then I heard him: coming through the long grass, purposefully striding.

"You've every right to be angry," he began, walking alongside me, "and I can only apologize, Clarissa. I'm sorry, truly I am. I didn't mean to compromise you. It wasn't my intention to . . ."

I quickened my pace. "Tom, please don't

go on so. You're giving me a headache with all of your apologizing."

"You're cross. I knew you were."

"I'm not cross. Why should I be cross? You've done *nothing*."

"But I could have . . . and I very nearly did, which is why you're quite rightly angry."

"I'm *not* angry, Tom; I'm simply a little hot."

"Promise me you won't say anything, Clarissa . . . to your parents, your brothers."

I stopped. He stopped. I looked at him.

"Tom," I began, about to tell him, assure him, that I'd never breathe a word to anyone. What did he take me for? A silly girl who'd go running back to her mama as soon as the first boy made eyes at her? But then I saw his furrowed brow, his dark and anxious eyes, and I caught my breath. I reached out, placed my hand on his arm. "Really, it was my fault as much as yours. I encouraged you."

"You did no such thing, and now I feel even more wretched if that's what you think."

I walked on, slowly, for I wasn't about to insist that I had encouraged him. My hope had been silent, but nonetheless heartfelt.

I knew this and he did not, I reminded my-self. I stopped again, and he stopped.

"Think nothing of it. It's forgotten al-ready," I said, and smiled.

He took hold of my hand. "I don't want you to think of me as some hot-headed lout, Clarissa. I'm well aware that you're des-tined for greater things than . . . than me."

I eased my hand out of his. I knew where we stood was visible from the stable-yard gate. "Let's be friends then, and please believe me when I say the very last thing I think of you as is a lout, hot-headed or otherwise." And at last that worrisome look melted from his features.

Minutes later, as we sat upon the wooden steps of the boathouse, he asked me my impression of him, his character. "But I hardly know you," I replied.

"But you must have an impression by now, and tell me—I'm curious."

"Lonely, angry . . . determined," I said. They were the three words that sprung to my mind at that moment. He raised an eye-brow, and as he pulled out his cigarettes, I said, "So, now I've given you three adjec-tives, can you give me your three of me?"

He lit his cigarette, looking into the distance once more with half-closed eyes, then said, "Beautiful, desirable . . . unattainable."

"Unattainable?" I repeated. The first two words had made me smile as he'd said them each in turn, but that last one perplexed me.

He looked down. "Well, unattainable to . . . someone such as me."

I wanted to say, "No, no, I'm not, I'm not unattainable." But I did nothing, and I said nothing.

"Strange to think," he went on, "that by this time next year I'll have finished my studies, left Oxford . . . probably be living in some rather dismal lodgings in London. And you . . ."—he glanced at me—"you may be married, Clarissa, or engaged to be married, at least."

"Nothing is certain," I said.

"No, of course, nothing is certain, apart from a chasm which ensures our futures remain quite separate, I think." And then he turned to me, once again smiling. "Unless, of course, I go into domestic service, and then perhaps our paths may cross."

I tried to laugh. I knew it was a joke, but I wasn't altogether happy with his cynicism.

"None of us knows our destiny," I said. "And no one knows what the future holds. But I certainly don't wish to be married. Not yet."

"So will you marry for love?" he asked, sucking out the last dregs of his cigarette.

"Yes, of course. Why else would one marry?"

He shrugged. "Position; to maintain a status quo, perhaps; because one's parents deem it the right and proper thing to do. And the union of new money and old titles still seems to be very much in vogue."

I wasn't entirely sure what he meant by that, but his talk of futures being sold off made me feel nervous. I was out of my depth. Politics, social divides and the loveless marriages he alluded to were not my forte.

"I think there may be a thunderstorm later," I said, rising to my feet.

The air was stagnant and feverishly hot in that quiet hollow by the lake, and as I walked along the jetty I could feel the fine white muslin of my blouse sticking to my skin. I longed to be able to take off my shoes and stockings, to walk in bare feet and dip my toes into the cool, clear water. And for a moment, only a moment, I wished he wasn't there—so that I could remove my shoes, lift my skirt, and dangle my legs over the side of the little pier. I looked out across the water: I could hear a dog barking somewhere in the distance, and someone calling for it; a dragonfly hovered beside me, its wings iridescent in the early evening sun; and below me spiders skimmed across the lake's flat surface. A family of moorhens took to the water in front of me: a mother followed by half a dozen red-billed, fluffy black chicks. Late chicks, I thought. And as I watched them, I pondered once more on that word: *unattainable*. It didn't matter what he'd meant by it, I concluded, because the other two words I understood perfectly: *beautiful . . . desirable.*

I smiled to myself, glanced over to him. He was still on the steps, leaning back, watching me. "He desires me," I said out loud, as quietly as I could.

There are moments too sublime to be later conjured in words. Standing on the jetty that midsummer evening so long ago, the world was perfect and I felt invincible.

〜

My Darling T, your words made my hands shake, my heart sing out with joy, & I pray that no matter what the future holds those sentiments never change. Yesterday was heavenly, our perfect, perfect time, & I have spent the entire morning quite lost in my dream of it—& you. But today I cannot shirk my responsibilities, and oh how many I suddenly seem to have! In haste . . . YOD

Chapter Five

I met Tom the following afternoon at five, though I thought I'd spotted him earlier in the day, in the distance, by the lake, and for a moment I'd panicked, thinking one of us had confused our rendezvous. And later, when I approached the boathouse and couldn't see him, my heart sank. But he was there, beyond the trees, sitting at the end of the jetty. He stood up as I walked toward him. "Shall we take a stroll?" he asked. "It's much too hot here in the sun."

We walked slowly across the meadow, cutting a swath through knee-high grass filled with buttercups, cornflowers, daisies and cow parsley, and continued on—into the next field. At the far side of that field we came to the stile, beyond which lay two paths, one to the farm, the other back down to the lake. From the top of the stile I could see the farmhouse, a perfectly straight silver line rising up into the blue from the chimney on its red-tiled roof.

"Are you going to stay up there for long?" he asked, squinting up at me.

"If I jump will you catch me?"

He moved nearer to me. "Of course, but I wouldn't advise it."

I stayed exactly where I was, my hand to my brow as I surveyed and considered the options. I suggested to him that we follow the path down by the lake rather than take the path to the farm. I remembered a seat there, which Papa had often taken me to when I was younger. As I spoke, I felt something touch my ankle, and I stopped, looked down, and saw him pull away his hand. Then, as he helped me down from the stile, he turned away, as though he couldn't bear to look at me anymore. I began to walk but he didn't move.

"Is something the matter?"

"Let's not take that path," he said. "I really should be getting back."

"I see. Well then, you go back and I shall continue alone."

"No. You can't possibly walk so far from the house on your own. We need to go back, Clarissa."

I didn't say anything. He helped me back over the stile, looking away as I lifted my skirt, and we walked back through the fields in silence. As we neared the house, he said to me, "You're so innocent, Clarissa. Innocent and beautiful, and you know, it's really not a very safe combination."

"Oh. And what do you mean by that?"

"I mean you really shouldn't be suggesting we disappear off into the undergrowth on our own."

I stopped. "Ha! I did no such thing. I merely said we should take the path I know, the one I've taken with Papa."

He stopped, closed his eyes for a moment, as though I'd already exasperated him. And right then I felt a little bit furious.

"It's perfectly all right, Tom, I can see my way from here," I said, and marched on as fast as I could walk through the long grass.

"Clarissa . . . please, I'm telling you this

for your own good," he said, catching up with me, and sounding quite cross himself. "You need to understand . . . you need to appreciate that . . ."

I stopped again. "That *what*, Tom? That you're afraid you might one day lose control? Chance would be a fine thing!"

He stared at me, his jaw set, chewing his tongue.

"And I need to tell you," I continued, pulling off my hat, "that I shan't be able to meet you again. Ever."

"Well, that's probably a good thing too. We have nothing in common and it seems to me that all these walks you're so fond of are a completely pointless and time-consuming exercise."

"Good. Then we have nothing more to say to each other."

"It seems not."

"Good-bye then."

"Good-bye."

There was an awkward moment as I strode on up the hill, for I realized he, too, had to walk in that direction, but he hung back and let me walk on alone. When I reached the house I ran through the hallway, up the stairs and into my room. And as I slammed the door of my bedroom, a painted plate my godmother had given me fell from the wall and split in two.

For the next week or so I simmered quietly in a daydream, imagining Tom Cuthbert begging for my forgiveness, his declaration of undying love, and then . . . his kiss. I'd seen him about the place but had managed to avoid him, and once, when Mama invited him to play in a croquet match, I feigned a headache and stayed in my room.

I was sitting on the bench by the ha-ha, my unopened journal on my lap, when he walked up to me, eight days after our fracas. It was a glorious morning with no breath of wind and I'd been sitting there for some time, looking out into the distance, listening to the hum of bumblebees on the lavender close by. Perhaps it was the aroma of the lavender, soothing my senses, making me sleepy, but I felt unusually mellow: quite at peace with the world. And thus far I'd failed to record anything of the day in my journal.

"May I sit with you?" he asked.

I smiled. "But of course," I replied, looking up at him from under my hat.

He sat down next to me. "I need to talk to you." He leaned forward, fiddling with his hands. "You see . . . you see I like you, Clarissa. You're quite different from anyone I've known before, and really . . . well, I didn't mean those things I said."

"No, of course not. And neither did—"

"Please . . . please hear me out," he said. "What I was trying—trying very badly—to tell you that day was simply that I find it a little difficult, tricky, with you."

He turned, presumably to check my expression. I raised my eyebrows, expectantly.

"What I mean is . . . you know who you are, what you are; how your life will be. It makes it hard for someone like me. Do you understand?"

"Yes," I said, emphatically, but I had not a clue.

"I'm not really worthy of your attention or interest. And I have to remind myself of this all the time. I have to remember who I am and who you are. I have to remember that we will both be moving on . . . in quite different directions."

He stopped there, and I waited a moment before I spoke.

"Well then, let's be friends again," I said, and, instinctively, I reached out and placed my hand upon his arm.

He pulled his arm away. "But this is the crux; this is the problem. I'm not sure that I can be friends with you."

"Oh."

He ran his hands through his hair. "You see, I find myself . . . I find myself . . ." he went on, falteringly, then sighed.

"Tom, please. Can't we be friends? I promise that I shan't invite you on another walk," I said. And he laughed.

"Yes. Yes, let's be friends again." He tilted his head, looking at me sideways through a wave of almost black hair.

"Good, then it's settled, and you have nothing to fret about—and neither do I."

He pulled out his packet of cigarettes and lit one.

"I've missed seeing you," he said, leaning forward once more. "You weren't at the last croquet game, and I've not seen you for . . ."—he paused—"for a while. Are you well?"

"Yes, quite well."

He turned to me. "You do look well."

"Yes, I'm very well."

"Perhaps later, if you'd like, we can take a walk—down by the lake."

I smiled. It wasn't exactly begging for forgiveness, but it was enough.

I had never known my mother to look fretful or to frown. I'd grown up with her telling me "girls who frown shall never wear a crown," and it was enough, when I was small, for me to run my finger between my eyebrows to check my expression. That summer, whenever I came across my mother standing in contemplative pose, looking out through open windows, I took her hand in mine, assured her that all would be well . . . her roses would survive. But there was a new look in her eyes, the clear line of a frown between her brows, and when she smiled back at me I could see she didn't quite believe me. At mealtimes, whenever the conversation turned to events taking place in Europe, she'd look at me and give me that same smile. Of course, I'd seen the newspapers, and I'd heard my brothers and my father talking, but the crisis unfolding on another continent was so far from Deyning, so far from our lives.

Weeks before, the day after Henry returned home from Cambridge, the archduke had been assassinated, and I'd heard him say to Papa, "This'll surely mean war." At that time I had no notion of war, or death. God, I believed, created life, all of nature and beauty, and I had faith in Him. I loved Him. My father and brother were speaking of a strange-sounding, almost unpronounceable place, far away from us. These were modern times, civilized times; and wars—at least in my mind—belonged to history.

But events in Europe and talk of war began to take over *all* mealtime conversation. I tried to ignore these discussions, for I didn't understand them, didn't want to understand them, and they did not belong to summer. Instead, I continued to luxuriate in the reverie of the season. I walked through the walled garden, where even the curls of peeling paint upon the greenhouse door seemed unusually perfect to my eye. And where, inside, the heady aroma of ripening tomatoes and cucumbers fed my senses. I inhabited a profoundly fragrant world, where the scents of jasmine and honeysuckle mixed with sweet geranium, verbena and mint; where the incessant hum of bumblebees serenaded my thoughts and only butterflies caught my eye; where peaches and nectarines grew fat and ripe under a warm English sun. And when I looked out toward the cornfields in the distance, I saw only the glinting color of my future. There would be no war. How could there be? Certainly not in the midst of that summer.

But the cuckoo had already begun to change his tune, and a sudden, cruel westerly wind had scattered rose heads and petals about the lawns and pathways—like snow in summer. And I began to have the queerest feeling, a slipping-away sort of feeling. As though my material world was as ephemeral as the colors of that season, as though nothing was quite fixed anymore. You see, I wanted time to stand still; I wanted to fasten down those days and harness every color and shape in them.

I met Tom every evening, on what Mama referred to as my "solitary amble." And though we now spoke easily with each other, and had learned much of one another's characters in the preceding weeks, he seemed reluctant to move beyond a certain point. His reticence had made me bolder than I should have been. I knew this, and sometimes, alone in my room, replaying a conversation we'd had in my head, I'd find myself aghast at my own unscripted lines. There had been so many moments when he could have, should have, almost kissed me, I was beginning to wonder if perhaps he had some sort of problem—with me, or with girls. My cousin Edina (named after my mother) had explained to me the previous summer that some men simply *aren't that way inclined*. There are some men who *prefer* men, she'd told me. At that time I'd remained unconvinced; I needed evidence, I said. She'd picked on Broughton as an example, simply because he was, she estimated, over forty, and remained so very unmarried and unattached. And the idea of Broughton falling in love with another man had reduced me to a fit of giggles. But now I wondered if Tom fell into Edina's *disinclined* category, for he certainly seemed troubled.

It had been Edina who, four summers earlier, had educated me on *other matters* too. Sitting on our own in the summerhouse one afternoon she'd informed me, in her own inimitable way, how babies were conceived and born. We'd both sat in silence for a moment, each of us distracted by the image of any future husband attempting such a gross act upon us. Then, with immeasurable horror, I realized that Papa had done this to Mama—and not once, but four times!

"Oh my God! Papa . . . Mama . . ."

"I know. It's beyond belief, but I had to tell you, Issa. You need to know."

"And the baby?" I asked, my hands still over my mouth.

"The baby grows inside its mother until it's ready to be born and then . . . are you ready for this? Prepare yourself, please dear . . . it comes out of her bottom, ripping her in two!"

"Ugh! No . . . but it can't be so . . . Mama . . . she looks fine."

"I know. Mine too. But this is why so many women die, dear. And they bleed for up to ten years afterward. Can you imagine?"

"No! And I don't want to."

It had been a bittersweet moment in my life, for I'd made up my mind then that I— like Edina—would never have children. But four years had passed since that particular revelation, and now I merely smiled at my remembrance of it. And that twelfth summer, once the best and most cherished, had faded and blurred, fusing with all previous summers into a montage of shapes and colors, scents and sounds: the hot sun upon the unmoving sycamore, the dark coolness of the lawn beneath; the hum and grind of the mowing machine; the glistening water of the lake in the distance; white butterflies on lavender, sweet peas on wicker; sun-bleached red stripes, white lines painted upon green; the hearty clank of a croquet mallet, the soft bounce of a tennis ball upon the grass.

But summer hadn't yet ended.

I sat on the bank, alone, watching them play: Henry and George against Will and Tom. It was always toward the close of day that Henry took his competitive spirit out on to the tennis lawn, and one evening he inadvertently appropriated my rendezvous with Tom by inviting him to make up the numbers for *all-male* doubles. It was another sweet-smelling, balmy evening, the brightness of the day diffused to a liquid gold and poured out across the trees; everything languid and perfectly still, but for those white-clad figures in front of me. And in that soft westering light, a light tinged with the iridescence of early evening sun, they shone: dazzling, youthful beauty, immortal vigor and vitality.

Too perfect . . . too perfect.

Then, as though hearing my doubt, the chime of the church bell in the distance, calling out across the countryside, reverberated through that palette of overlapping color and texture and lullaby sounds. But this time interrupting, discordant, like a call to arms, stirring a sudden pang within me and reminding me once again how fleeting the moment of rapture. I lay back, flat against the earth's warm surface, listening to its rhythm, the bounce of the ball upon the grass, and those young male voices. I stared up at the empty sky and imagined myself floating up into it, higher and higher, and all the time looking down upon myself and Deyning: smaller and smaller. I could still hear the church bell, hear birds calling out from the tops of the trees, but I could no longer hear the voices from the tennis lawn. They had gone. Evaporated.

"Were you dozing?" he asked, standing over me.

I sat up. "No, I don't think so . . . I'm not sure . . . who won?"

"Henry, of course."

"Henry *and* George," I corrected him.

He sat down on the bank next to me, swatting at the grass with his racquet. He'd wanted to win, I thought.

"Henry—as I think you already know—rather likes winning. It makes him feel . . . complete."

He turned to me, smiling. "We all like to win."

"I've never won anything, ever," I said. "But it doesn't really matter."

"It's different for you," he said, looking away and pulling out his packet of cigarettes. "You don't need to win at anything."

"Oh, and you do?"

He shook his head, raised one side of his mouth. "No, I don't *need* to . . . but I want to. All men like to compete, I think, and win. And if I'm to make anything of my life . . ."

He didn't finish his sentence and we sat in silence for a few minutes, watching George and William knocking balls about on the tennis lawn below us.

"The Granvilles . . . all destined for greatness," he said, wistfully, still staring ahead at my brothers. I said nothing. I watched him once more from the corner of my eye. On the side of his clean-shaven face he'd missed a patch: a few dark hairs, a newly discovered imperfection, lending a perfect vulnerability.

"No . . . I think you're the one destined for greatness, Tom."

He turned to me, looking into my eyes with that now so familiar solemn, searching gaze. And reflected in those eyes the setting sun, picking out small flecks of gold in brown.

"I see it in you . . . I see it in you quite clearly," I added, staring back at him, anchored.

He glanced down at my hand, resting on the grass. "And of all people . . . of everyone, you're the one I'd most like to have believe that."

～

My Dearest T, did you really wait ALL night? I feel utterly wretched at the thought, but we are filled to the brim here & it's quite impossible for me to escape. Please tell me that you understand . . . Yr D

Chapter Six

On August the first we enjoyed a heavenly day of croquet, and we had almost a full house. Papa was in London once again, and Mama's dear friend, and my godmother, Venetia Cooper, had come down for a few days with her son, Jimmy, and Charlie Boyd, another old friend of Henry's from his school days. All four of my cousins—Edina, Lucy, Archie and Johnnie—were with us for the week, along with their mama, my mother's sister, Maude. And William, too, had a couple of friends staying. For me, everything was as it had always been, only better, because Tom was now with us. If only Henry and some of the others hadn't been so determined to talk about the possibility of war.

It was toward the end of the day when I yelled across the croquet lawn at Henry and Tom, "Please do stop discussing politics! You're spoiling our game!" And when I shouted that line at them for a second time, Henry immediately threw down his mallet and said, "Someone please help me throw my baby sister into the lake and then we can all have some peace!"

I saw him striding across the lawn toward me and I screamed, dropped my mallet and took off toward the woods. I heard Edina and Lucy shrieking, the boys cheering, and as I raced through the ferns, with Henry hot on my tail, I lost my shoe, tripped and fell.

"Please don't, Henry! Please don't!"

He laughed. "Oh, for goodness sake, Issa, do get up. Look at the state of you."

I could barely breathe. "I can't," I gasped. "I've hurt my ankle."

As Henry shook his head and walked away, Tom appeared, holding my shoe. He bent down. "Which ankle?" he asked.

"The left."

He placed his hand over my white stocking. "Here?"

I shook my head.

He moved his hand up over my ankle. "Here?"

"Yes . . . yes there," I replied, wiping away a tear.

"Are you able to stand?"

He took my hand and I let him pull me up. I stood on one foot as he slipped his arm about my waist. "Hold on to me," he said. I put my arm around his shoulder and tried to walk, but it was too painful and I cried out. "There's only one thing for it, I'm afraid. I shall have to carry you." He handed me my shoe, and then picked me up just as though I were a small child.

"I'm sorry," I said, as he strode back through the ferns toward the croquet lawn.

"Don't be sorry. Henry shouldn't have chased you like that. Anyway, I get the chance to have you in my arms," he replied, glancing down at me, smiling.

When we emerged from the woods Edina and Lucy came rushing over from the boys, who were standing in a huddle on the lawn with Henry.

Edina said, "Oh, darling! Are you very badly hurt?"

"She's twisted her ankle," Tom replied, in a perfectly calm and assured voice, and Edina looked up at me, raised her eyebrows, and smiled.

Then Will, George, Archie and all the others were around us, all wishing to look at my injured ankle. But Tom didn't stop. He continued walking across the lawn, then up the steps, onto the terrace, where my mother sat with Maude. When Mama saw us she stood up.

I remained silent in Tom's arms as he explained to Mama, with Maude standing next to her, exactly what had taken place, and I saw my mother look across the lawn in Henry's direction, narrowing her eyes. Maude looked at me, frowning with a tad too much concern, and then she scrunched her face up even more and said, "Such a brave Issa." Mama was examining my ankle, and as she rubbed her hand over it I cried out once more.

"Oh my poor child, you have hurt yourself, haven't you? He's such a beastly boy, that brother of yours." She looked at Tom. "Tom, would you be even more of an angel and take Clarissa up to her room? I shall fetch Mabel; she always knows exactly what's required with these sorts of injuries."

As he carried me into the house I felt faint, almost as though I were in a dream. I couldn't quite believe that Mama had asked Tom to take me to my room. And I suppose, looking back, it was a measure of her trust in him. I watched him, his face, as we moved through the hallway, past the jardinière, with its oversized palm, across the polished marble floor; his fingers spread out around my waist, his eyes fixed ahead. I studied the line of his jaw, the dark shadow of his clean-shaven chin, the curve of his mouth: a flicker of a smile playing upon his lips. We climbed the staircase in silence, through shafts of dust-filled light, and I could feel his heart, beating in perfect time with my own.

"You'll have to direct me from here," he said, standing at the top of the stairs.

I pointed. "Over there."

My door was ajar and as he carried me into the room he looked up and around, as though taking in its dimensions more than its detail: the walls, the windows, the ceiling, and then my bed.

"Beautiful room," he said, at last. "Strange, but it's exactly as I'd imagined."

"Are you going to put me down? I think you've more than done your bit, Tom."

He moved to the side of the bed, stopped and looked down at me, into my eyes, and then we finally relinquished our hold on each other as he placed me upon my bed. I shuffled up against the pillows, without thinking bent my leg and unbuttoned my other shoe. He moved over to the window, the one looking directly south over the terrace and the lake.

"Stunning view," he said. He turned and came toward me. "I should go. Mabel will be here in a moment and I'm sure she'll look after you." But he seemed awkward, almost reluctant to leave me.

I looked up at him. "Thank you, Tom. You've been most gallant."

He smiled at me, moved nearer. "You look like Titania," he said, pulling a piece of green fern from my hair.

At that moment Mama appeared in the doorway, shadowed by a stony-faced Mabel, carrying a small box and a bowl.

"Thank you so much, Tom," she said, moving past him.

He raised his hand to me and disappeared through the door.

That night I did not go down to dinner. My ankle had swollen to the size of a baby elephant's, despite Mabel bringing up towels filled with ice and insisting I rest it upon them. Edina and Lucy visited me in my room, as well as each of my brothers, and Henry apologized. Sitting on the side of my bed and taking my hand in his, he said, "You know, I really am sorry. I thought you were feigning, Issa—like you always used to."

Mama, too, came and fussed over me. Plumping up my pillows and straightening the bed, she said, "Tom Cuthbert was very considerate today, very charming and kind."

"Yes, he's a nice boy," I replied, knowing how much the term *nice boy* meant to Mama.

She glanced at me. "Yes, a very nice boy."

Some time after my eleventh birthday, I'd been relocated from the nursery floor to the vast expanse of my new "grown-up" bedroom, with its four tall windows looking out to the south and west. At first I'd hated it. The room seemed ridiculously large and much too formal with its matching wallpaper, curtains, upholstery and bedcover. I longed to return upstairs, to the gated confines of my childhood, to the sloping ceilings of my cozy attic life, and the dust and debris of a land far away from Mama's coordinated, plumped-up world. I longed for the toys I'd had to leave behind there: my brothers' toy soldiers and tattered fort; my dolls' house, my dolls; and those treasured books suddenly deemed "too immature." Miss Stephens, my nursemaid, departed, along with Miss Greaves—a governess (of sorts)—and Mademoiselle arrived. I'd resented these changes, was quietly angry with my mother. But by now, by this time, I had grown into my room and rarely ventured upstairs. I'd moved on.

The following morning, my ankle greatly improved, I went down to breakfast. When Mama entered the dining room, accompanied by Aunt Maude, they both looked unusually troubled, and then Mama announced to us all that Germany had declared war upon Russia. All day it was all anyone could speak of, and though we continued our croquet tournament, it wasn't the same. At four, play was suspended while Mabel and Mrs. Cuthbert once again brought out trays of fresh tea, jugs of lemonade and iced coffee, strawberries, cream and scones, and then served us from linen-covered tables set up on the edge of the lawn. For an hour or so we slumped in deck chairs on the grass under the sycamore tree, as Mama, Venetia and Aunt Maude looked on anxiously from the terrace. The boys all lay about on the lawn discussing whether and when they would enlist—if there were to be a war. And it seemed to me as though they were all set on it. From underneath my straw hat I watched Tom, even as I made conversation with Edina and Lucy. And from time to time he glanced at me, smiled, and then looked away.

Earlier that day, before our game started, when I'd been sitting on the grass with the others, Tom had sat down next to me. I'd had my hand behind me, resting flat upon the lawn, and I suddenly felt the tips of his fingers touching mine. I turned to him, but he did nothing; didn't look to me and didn't move his hand away from mine. I glanced at Edina, sitting directly opposite us, wondering if she could see, and when she smiled back at me I knew that she had, and I quickly pulled my hand away. Later, in the evening, Edina came to my room, asking if she could borrow a ribbon.

"I think you have an admirer, Issa," she said, her back to me, as she fiddled with my comb box.

"Oh really," I replied, with adroitly manufactured nonchalance.

"Yes, and I think you know too." She turned to me, smiling. "Tom Cuthbert?"

I laughed. "Edina, really . . . Tom is Mrs. Cuthbert's son."

"That may be, but he's extraordinarily handsome and, I believe, utterly preoccupied with you."

This, of course, was music to my ears. And I immediately recognized the potential benefit of an ally, a spy. For Edina was nothing if not an observer of people, and for as long as I could remember she'd been an unexploited expert on the subtle intricacies of character and human dynamics.

"Preoccupied with me? Do you really think so?" I asked, looking down, playing with the ribbon in my hands.

"Completely and utterly."

I looked up at her, unable not to smile. "He is rather gorgeous, isn't he?"

"Divine, darling. And you appear to have captured his heart *and* his mind."

"But how can you tell? What did you see?" I asked, eager for her to share her observations.

"Oh but, Clarissa, you hardly need me to tell you, dear heart. You must surely see yourself." She glanced at me, smiling. "He's completely enamored by you; in love, I'd say. And how do I know this? Because from the moment I arrived—or rather the moment he appeared, when we all sat on the terrace that very first evening—he seemed to be . . . a little too aware of you," she continued, moving about the room, as though conducting a talk to an audience far larger than one. "He'd simply fail to notice any other beauty fluttering her eyelashes at him. And even when he's talking, listening to someone else, he's so obviously distracted by you, dear." She looked at me, gave a little shiver. "Captivated . . . totally captivated."

It was tempting. I could have told her then that Tom Cuthbert and I had already begun a type of love affair, at least a love affair in my mind. But I decided not to. Although ten months older than me, which qualified her as indisputably worldly at that time, I knew Edina to be too easily flattered to be discreet. She'd be bound to want to disclose my secret to another, if only to be acknowledged in her role as confidante.

The following day, a little too self-conscious under Edina's scrutiny, I found myself avoiding Tom's gaze altogether. He and I seemed unable to converse in front of others, and so but for the occasional "yes" or "no" we usually said almost nothing at all to each other during those afternoon croquet games. But later, each evening, when we met in the meadow, we compared notes, dissecting the characters of Deyning's assorted houseguests.

"She's too uppity," he said, when I asked him about Edina. "And she watches you all the time. It's as though she's guarding you, or observing your every move for some in-depth study or other."

"How simply fascinating," I said. "She must be observing us both then . . ."

"How so?"

"Oh, nothing. Edina likes to watch people,

and I have to say she's really rather good at it."

"I hadn't realized it was an art."

"And what do you make of Lucy?" I asked.

"She's sweet. More like you . . . apart from that annoying habit of repeating the last line of everything anyone says."

I laughed. "She's only fifteen, Tom."

"I think Charlie Boyd rather likes you," he said, reaching down and pulling at a blade of grass.

"Charlie? Oh, Charlie's a dear, an absolute dear, and I've known him forever. He's like another cousin, that's all."

He made no reply and I wanted to tell him then that I wasn't in the least interested in Charlie, but instead I moved on, to my godmother.

"And what of Venetia?" I asked. I was curious to know what he thought of my godmother; curious to know if he was drawn to her in the same way other young men seemed to be. "Like moths to a flame," Mama had once said.

He turned to me. "Venetia?"

"Yes, what do you make of her? She's rather beautiful, isn't she?"

"Yes, I suppose she is rather . . . exotic," he replied, looking away from me.

I felt a twinge. I'd like to have been described as *exotic*; but it struck me that perhaps it was something one grew into.

"Voluptuous?" I asked, referring to Venetia's unmistakable and much renowned curves.

"Hmm, yes, voluptuous . . ." he said, dreamily.

And I could feel my face flush. "Well, you'll be pleased to know she rather likes *young* men, Tom," I said, rising to my feet.

He looked up at me, smiling. "And what do you mean by that?"

I hesitated. "Oh, nothing . . . nothing at all. I must get back now."

We walked back through the meadow in silence, maintaining our distance and separating at the stable-yard gate with a casual "good-bye." Aunt Maude—like her daughter, a keen observer—had asked me over dinner the previous evening whom she'd seen me with, walking back from the meadow. "Oh, possibly Tom Cuthbert, or perhaps Mr. Broughton," I replied. "I bumped into each of them on my walk. It was such a glorious evening, Aunt."

Then Mama said, "Clarissa does so love her solitary ambles," and I caught the tail end of Edina's knowing smile.

I couldn't sleep that night. It was hot—too hot. And despite every window in my room being open, the curtains tied back, the air was completely still. I heard Henry on the terrace beneath my bedroom, talking to our cousins, Archie and Johnnie. And I moved over to my window seat. "We've all got to do it," he was saying. "Those Huns are on the move now and they won't stop. They're after our empire . . ."

I returned to my bed and lay down upon the sheet. I thought of Tom; wondered if he was asleep. Was he dreaming of me? Henry's voice continued, and I tried to block it out and focus my mind on Tom: Tom and me under the sycamore tree. But Henry was gathering momentum, interrupting my scenes with his diatribe about whatever it was he was so impassioned about. I rose from my bed, walked over to the window and shut it, loudly and firmly.

I'm not entirely sure what woke me, or what time it was, but it was late, very late, and the voices on the terrace were much quieter. I heard giggling, female giggling, and I crept over to the window and peered down. At first I thought I must be dreaming, hallucinating, and as I looked away I could feel the sound of blood rushing through my brain. Venetia Cooper, Mama's friend, my godmother, was sitting on Henry's lap, and from what I could make out they were canoodling. I crouched down, peering over the padded cushion of the window seat. I saw Henry's hand move down her gown, then creep back up—onto her breast. I turned my head away. *I must have made a mistake . . .* I looked back, saw her stand up, take hold of his hand and lead him inside. I moved swiftly to my bedroom door, my heart pounding as I pressed my ear to it. I heard them coming up the stairs, heard them whispering as they passed by my door and headed toward the rose guest room. Then a door closed.

I sat down on my bed, contemplating the implications of what I'd just witnessed. I felt sick. Venetia must be almost forty, I thought, *and* she was the mother of his friend! Did Jimmy know? I wondered. And what would Mama and Papa say? I remembered Papa saying that Hughie, Venetia's husband, was an "exceptional shot," and I lay down and closed my eyes.

⌁

Your note did amuse me, not least your mention of the Grande Dame, but please don't be too hard on her. She has such innate charm, & I do so love her colorful displays, & her ways with "les garçons." Snob? I am not entirely sure what you mean. She certainly relishes her place with the "Smart Set," as you call it, but surely that's no crime? And indeed, how could it be otherwise? As for H's devotion, I make no comment . . . YOD

Chapter Seven

The following morning, over breakfast, Mama received a telegram, and I remember thinking, praying, *please don't let this be about Henry and Venetia*. There had been more telegrams than usual arriving at Deyning, but Papa was in London and I'd supposed them to be from him.

Mama looked up.

"I'm afraid it is as we've all feared," she began. And I looked down at my plate of kedgeree,* for I knew what was coming,

---

* An Anglo-Indian dish, served at breakfast, consisting of rice, fish and eggs.

and I could hear the next sentence: *Henry, my eldest, has been making love to my best friend, Venetia* . . . "Germany has invaded Belgium and declared war upon France."

My relief was immense, and I can't be sure now, but I think I looked up and smiled at Mama.

"We have given an ultimatum . . . all we can do now is wait, and pray," she added. Then she lifted her teacup. "God bless England."

"God bless England!" we all repeated, teacups in hand and in perfect unison.

I looked over at Venetia, who was staring at Henry. I glanced at Edina, who looked back at me solemnly and shook her head. And then I looked at Lucy, who—it has to be said—appeared quite mystified by the announcement.

Immediately after breakfast I walked in the grounds with Edina. And she seemed to me almost excited by the prospect of war.

"Can you believe it? We may be at war . . . at war, by this time tomorrow!" she exclaimed, wide eyed.

"No, I can't believe it . . . and I don't want

to believe it. I don't want my brothers to go and fight, Edina."

"But England is in danger, dear . . . we have to defend this island of ours," she said, marching slightly ahead of me across the lawn, her head high. And I wondered who she'd been talking to, where she'd learned that line.

"I hope that Germany sees sense," I said, not at all sure what *sense* I was referring to. "And that it doesn't come to a war. Because it will affect everything, won't it?"

"Well yes, I should say!"

"Do you suppose we'll still be able to go to Brighton?" I asked, for I was still thinking in terms of the days ahead, and our planned excursion to the coast. "I've been *so* looking forward to it."

"I'm not sure," she replied. "I suppose it all depends. Mama says if there's to be a war there'll need to be a great mobilization of troops . . . and we'll all have to do our bit."

"In what way? How can *we* do anything?"

"Well . . . if all the men go to war, I imagine we'll have to do all sorts of things." She stopped. I stopped. She stared over into the trees, tapping her finger on her lips, pondering, and so I waited; waited to hear what we'd all have to do. "Drive motor-cars," she began, "do gardening . . . that sort of thing."

It didn't sound like much to me, and as we moved on I said, "But Papa doesn't garden and neither do my brothers."

"No, but Broughton does, and think of the under-gardeners, all the outdoor servants you have here who may have to go."

"Really? You think they'll want servants as well?"

"Yes, of course, they'll all have to go and fight, dear."

It sounded slightly far-fetched to me. I wasn't convinced Edina had her facts right. I thought of Broughton: surely he'd not be much use. He was quite old and so gentle, only interested in flowers. And he wouldn't hurt a fly; was always rescuing injured animals. But if my cousin were right, how would we manage at Deyning without gardeners? I looked around me, across the manicured lawns to the neatly arranged borders where Frank and John were already on their knees and busy. It will all go to wrack and ruin, I thought. The whole place will become overgrown and lost in a wilderness. I looked up toward the house, the west side, and amidst a verdant tangle of Virginia creeper, jasmine and wisteria clinging to its stone façade, there was someone up a ladder there too. There were always people everywhere—attending to something.

That day no one seemed to want to do anything at all. We simply sat about watching the minutes and hours pass by, just as though we'd all received a death sentence. Telegrams were delivered, telegrams were dispatched; and Mrs. Cuthbert, Mabel, Wilson and Mr. Broughton wore funereal faces, as though they'd already received the bad news they had sworn to keep from us.

When I met Tom early that evening he was distracted, and as we sat upon the steps of the boathouse we had little to say to each other.

"Strange, isn't it? Summer seems to have ended already," he said, lighting another cigarette.

I turned to him, placed my hand upon his arm. I couldn't think of anything to say at that moment and somehow a touch seemed more voluble than any words. But he simply glanced at my hand and then looked away.

I don't know how long we sat there for, but long enough. And when we rose to our feet and I began to walk back toward the house, he called after me, said my name. I turned, expecting him to say something, but he simply stared at me, frowning.

"What is it?" I asked. And I so wanted to add to that, "my darling."

"Don't go back yet," he said.

"But I must go back. I have to."

"Clarissa . . ."

"Yes?"

He looked down at the grass. "Oh, nothing," he said.

When I arrived back at the house I bumped into Mama in the hallway.

"Have you seen Tom?" she asked.

I swallowed. "No, why?"

"I thought I'd invite him to join us for dinner. It's Edna's night off and Mrs. Cuthbert's cooking for us. He shouldn't be on his own at a time like this," she added, and walked off toward the servants' hall.

I stood still; I could hear Mama asking Mrs. Cuthbert if Tom would like to join us for dinner, but I couldn't quite hear Mrs. Cuthbert's reply; and then I heard Mama's footsteps coming back toward the hallway and I quickly turned and hurried off up the stairs.

Half an hour or so later, when I entered the drawing room, he was there, looking extraordinarily dapper, and sitting in front of the fire with Venetia and Jimmy. He glanced over at me, nervously, and I smiled. It was strange to see him there, in that room, dressed for dinner. There he was: one of us.

I wandered over to the boys, who were gathered by the window around George. He'd received a telegram requesting him to be back at Aldershot by midnight. They were asking him questions, talking about the war. I glanced across at Tom, wondered what he and Venetia were discussing. I could hear her saying something about Paris. She loved talking about Paris, slipping into French here and there. I looked ahead, out of the window. Nothing stirred. Every blade of grass, each stem and flower and leaf and shrub appeared perfectly still, as though all of nature held her breath, waiting; and the sun, still above the trees, more achingly golden than ever before. I'm not sure how long I stood there, transfixed, lost in that halcyon moment, but as I turned away I wondered what tomorrow would bring. Would it all be the same? *Will it be the same?*

I walked over to Maude, Edina and Lucy, who sat playing cards next to another window.

"Would you like to join us, dear?"

"No thank you, Aunt. I'm a little bored of cards . . . or rather, bored of losing at cards," I replied, and she laughed.

I moved on again, slowly, toward the fireplace. Above it hung the portrait of Mama by Philip de László. It had been commissioned by my father some years earlier, and was mesmerizingly beautiful. Venetia was speaking about Venice, another of her *most* favorite and yet-to-be-visited places. I caught Tom's eye, smiled. He didn't smile back at me, but I saw his gaze move from my face down over my body. And as I stood in front of the fireplace, running my finger over the contours of one of Mama's precious Meissen figurines, I sensed him watching me.

No fire had been lit that evening, which

struck me as odd, because Mama usually insisted on a fire in that room each evening, even in summer. *Lends the place atmosphere and warmth*, she said. But the polished steel grate remained empty, and the carved marble surround—with its acanthus scrolls, swags of husk and little putti—felt colder than usual to the touch. When I turned, the sky beyond the windows was changing, the last of the sun's rays shining low into the room, throwing pale mauve jets of light across the patterned carpet and silk furnishings.

"Clarissa, darling," Venetia began, her cigarette holder in hand, "you're such an ongoing distraction to these poor, poor boys . . . I'm surprised they can think of war—or anything else—with such a vision of beauty in their presence."

"Is there any news?"

She smiled. "No, dear child, not yet. We shan't know anything until much later tonight or perhaps tomorrow morning," she replied. "Do sit with us."

"You do look terribly beautiful tonight, Clarissa," Jimmy said, as I sat down next to him on the sofa.

"And it may not be fashionable for a

lady to have tanned skin, but it suits you, suits you very well," Venetia added. "Don't you agree, Tom?"

I looked at him. He was leaning forward in his chair, holding a glass of something. "Yes, it does," he replied, looking back at me, without any trace of a smile.

"Clarissa is going to be a sensation in London, an absolute sensation," Venetia continued, with a little shiver, and a shrug of lace. She reminded me of a box of chocolates that night. Confection, sealed in tight, perfectly wrapped and tied up in ribbons. The previous evening she'd come down to dinner in a purple-plumed silver turban and opera cloak. *Oh, is it fancy dress?* Lucy had asked.

"I've already warned your father, warned him that he'll have to keep a gun by his bed," she continued. "You'll be inundated, darling, inundated, but I'm hoping that Jimmy might be able to be your chaperone about town one day," she added, smiling at her son.

Jimmy turned to me. "I'd be more than delighted, anytime at all," he said, looking slightly awkward.

"Thank you, that's very kind, but I don't

know when that will be, at least not now. If there's to be a war, I don't suppose there'll be many parties or balls to attend."

"Oh but of course there'll be. Life must go on," Venetia said, and then she looked across at Tom. "And Tom, you must call on me next time you're up in town. I just *adore* having the young around me."

I felt my skin bristle. I hadn't told Tom— hadn't told anyone—about Henry's affair with Venetia, and it was definitely an affair. I'd been watching them, surreptitiously noting their furtive glances and private little jokes. Only that morning, when I'd walked around to the veranda, I'd found them there, almost entwined. They'd quickly moved away from one another and Henry had stuttered something to me about looking for a tennis racquet for Venetia, but Venetia didn't play tennis. I knew that. What did he take me for? And now she was trying to lure Tom to London.

"Yes, I shall do that," I heard him say.

I looked over to him. "Oh, and do you go to London very often, Mr. Cuthbert?"

He raised one side of his mouth. "No, I don't, but I'll be there soon enough and I'm sure I'll be grateful for a few friends."

I picked up one of Mama's magazines lying upon the ottoman in front of me and began flicking the pages, and then I glanced up and saw Venetia smiling at him with a worldly look about her. I glanced over at Tom. He was looking down but still smiling. I put down the magazine and stood up.

"I really must go and find Mama," I said, and left the room.

I didn't go in search of Mama. I went outside and stood on the terrace. He's going to have an affair with Venetia, I thought, wringing my hands and feeling utterly powerless. He's going to go up to London and embark on a torrid affair with that woman. I was pleased I'd broken her plate, and as I walked toward the window I wondered if its shattering had in fact been portentous. I peeked in through the glass: he was still sitting in the same place, listening to Mama, now seated on the sofa next to Jimmy. They all looked so serious, so worried. I marched back along the terrace toward the door into the house.

"Clarissa! I was wondering where you were. Can I get you a glass of lemonade or something?"

It was Charlie Boyd.

"No, no thank you, Charlie. I was taking some air. It's so stuffy inside and . . . and all of this waiting, waiting for news, it's altogether rather depressing."

"Hmm. Yes, it is somewhat. But you mustn't let it worry you too much, you know. You're much too pretty to wear a frown."

"So I've been told," I said, my head still full of Tom's impending trip to London. "I'm sorry, Charlie," I added, glancing back at the window. "I've recently discovered something quite . . . quite shocking, and I'm a little distracted."

"Oh dear, nothing sinister, I hope."

"Well, that's just it; it could be. But I really can't say any more."

"I see," he said, looking at me, smiling. And I immediately wondered if he knew something.

We walked back inside and as we entered the drawing room I took hold of his arm. I was determined not to look across at Tom or Venetia, but I heard her saying something to him about a hotel, and then the gong sounded and we all made our way through to the dining room.

I was seated at the opposite end of the

table to Tom, and on the same side, so that I couldn't, even if I'd wanted to—which I didn't—see his face. And after dinner, when Mama asked the ladies to retire to the drawing room for some cards and leave the boys to enjoy a glass of port, I excused myself, saying that I was tired. Edina seemed keen to come with me, and with a look of practiced concern on her face, she whispered, "Is it the war, dear? Or is it something else?"

"No, Edina, I'm simply tired."

I was in my bedroom, had unpinned my hair, when I realized that I hadn't bid my brother, George, good-bye, and he'd be leaving within the hour. I went back downstairs to the dining room, stood for a moment outside the door, and then opened it.

"Issa! Are you going to join us for a glass?" Henry asked and then laughed, the port decanter raised in one hand, a cigar in the other.

I looked over at Tom, who'd moved to the opposite side of the table. He smiled at me, wearily.

"I wanted to say good night, and good-bye to George," I said. "I'm going to my bed."

"Aha, beauty sleep, that's the secret, eh, Clarissa?" Charlie said, turning to me.

I moved over to George, who stood up and wrapped his arms around me.

"You're so brave, Issa, coming in here with all these obnoxious young men," he said to me quietly, and then he kissed my forehead.

I looked up at him. "When will you next be home?"

"I really don't know, but soon I hope."

"If you *have* to go and fight—will you be able to come home first?"

"That I also don't know," he said.

I put my head on his chest, held him tightly for a moment, then looked up at him and kissed him on both cheeks. "I love you, Georgie."

"I love you too, darling," he replied, to an echo of, "Aah!"

I moved toward the door.

"Do we each get a kiss?" Charlie asked. "Have pity, Clarissa. It may be our last chance."

I turned back to them, and—with a little affectation and perhaps rather dramati-cally—I blew them each a kiss. Tom smiled, and I allowed myself to look back at him for longer than the others.

"I say! That's not fair! That's cheating!" Jimmy shouted out.

"Yes, that doesn't count, doesn't count at all," Charlie said.

And as I turned to close the door, I glanced over once more at Tom, but he'd already turned away and was deep in conversation with Henry and Archie.

Oddly enough, I fell asleep very quickly that night. But I had a most peculiar and muddled dream, which I later recorded in my journal. I was in an enormous building, walking down a long corridor with doors on either side. I was searching for a particular door and when I found it, it had the letters VR painted upon it in purple. I opened it, and immediately inside, in a lobby area, Mama was standing clutching a telegram. "Clarissa, you shouldn't be here," she said. "Tom is performing an exam and he mustn't be disturbed." Then I heard Venetia's voice and I pushed past Mama to see Venetia lying on a bed with Tom bending over her. He looked up at me. "She's unattainable," he said. "You need to send for a doctor."

I shouted, "I know what you're doing, Tom!" And then Henry appeared and said, "But it's only a game, Clarissa," and when I looked back at Tom, he'd changed into Charlie Boyd and was dressed as a soldier.

I awoke early the following morning, stirred from my fretful dreams by the sounds of activity in the house: doors opening and closing; voices and footsteps in the hallway downstairs. I dressed hastily and went to find Mama. She was not in her room and so I rushed downstairs, where I found everyone sitting in the dining room, in a collective somber silence. Mama looked up at me and I knew immediately.

"We're going to war?"

She reached out, took hold of my hand. "We *are* at war, Clarissa," she replied.

. . . I was resting in the hammock, contemplating all of this, & what lies ahead. It's all too worrying & depressing. Lord K is asking for another 100,000, & H is determined to sign up . . . my very dearest dear, I fear our "plan" may have to wait. D

Chapter Eight

Over the next couple of days there was a flurry of activity at Deyning, but none of the activity any of us had hoped for or imagined that summer. My cousins and Aunt Maude left Deyning to return to their home in Devon, and Venetia, Jimmy and Charlie all returned to London. At the time I wondered why: why did they all have to cut short their stay with us? Surely it wasn't going to make any difference where *they* were. But almost immediately the fighting had begun; Kitchener was asking for volunteers; church was packed, special prayers said. It was upon us, and yet to me it all seemed to happen so quickly, so suddenly. By the end of the week Henry had been to Godalming to try for a commission in Kitchener's army and was waiting to hear. And Will was in a conundrum. He considered himself a pacifist and found the notion of war abhorrent, but he was also a patriotic Englishman.

I'd heard Mrs. Cuthbert and others say that the war would be over by Christmas, and the vicar, too, seemed to hold that belief. But my parents were not so optimistic. In the middle of August, barely two weeks after George returned to Aldershot, my parents received word that he'd arrived safely in France with the British Expeditionary Force. The very same day, Henry received his commission.

In Guildford, with Mama, I'd seen the billboards and the posters calling for volunteers: "There is still a place in the line for you . . ." they said, and I wondered which line, where? And on a trip to London, to visit Mama's dressmaker, we'd passed through Trafalgar Square and Piccadilly Circus and from the back of the taxicab I'd looked out at the smiling faces of pristine, uniformed young men. To me, their faces didn't appear to be troubled, worried or anxious; they looked excited, happy to be going off to war. Later, we'd intended on going to Lyons Corner House for tea, as we usually did before returning home, but the place was packed with soldiers, and with crowds outside on the pavement too. So we went straight to the station, where Mama held on to my hand tightly as we maneuvered our way through a chaotic, heaving mass of khaki. And as we headed back through the sleepy meadows and pastures, I could hear the soldiers bound for France and singing, farther down the train.

"How *can* they be so jolly?" I asked Mama.

"Because they're proud and patriotic," she said. "And now they know their purpose, and how noble it is."

My mother, like my father, believed and lived by noble principles: duty, sacrifice, and honor, truth and fidelity. And the war, still new and fresh, bound up in flags and bunting and patriotic rhetoric, offered her and others—including my brothers and all those other young men—an opportunity to truly live by and test those principles.

After all, was there anything nobler than self-sacrifice?

We were standing under the chestnut tree in lower meadow, sheltering from a shower, when Tom told me he was going to volunteer. I'd been expecting it, waiting for him to tell me. He didn't look at me as he spoke, but gazed ahead, across the field to the lake beyond, and there was an unfamiliar formality to his tone.

"Everyone should sign up," he said. "I'm going to go to Guildford tomorrow, and I intend to ask William to come with me."

I couldn't bring myself to say anything. What was there to say? "Don't go; stay here with me"? It would have been point-less. We'd already lost so many of the men on the estate and were left with only those who were too old or too frail to enlist. I'd heard Father repeating Kitchener's words, "Every man should do his duty." It was a mantra, spoken with a stern face. It was the Cause.

"I shall miss you," I said.

He turned to me, reached out and pushed my damp hair back from my face. "And I shall miss you, Clarissa."

I wanted him to kiss me then but, like all

those other moments before, he moved on and began speaking of something different, steering us away from that point. I didn't hear his words. All I could think was that he, too, was going to war; that he, too, was leaving Deyning, leaving my world. I'd only just found him, only just realized that the universe included someone named Tom Cuthbert and now he was about to disappear. It seemed already the war had found me. It had reached into my life, interrupting my summer and all those anticipated days of picnics, eating strawberries on the lawn, tennis and croquet tournaments. It had taken my brothers, and now it was taking him, Tom. And even then, in the slipping away, I sensed something more: an almost imperceptible queer tilting feeling. As though a magnet in the core of the earth was very gently, very slowly moving, and pulling me with it.

The rain stopped and we walked on in silence toward the lake. As we descended the bank I didn't bother to lift my skirt, and it clung about my ankles, wet and heavy. He offered me his hand, said my name: "Clarissa." I loved to hear him say my name; he said it so differently to anyone else: as though it was a question in itself. I took his hand, and as we walked on neither of us released our grip. We stood by the water's edge, side by side, hand in hand. It didn't matter anymore that anyone saw us; I no longer cared what the servants or anyone else thought. And I wanted to savor that moment, there, with him. A steam was rising from the water and the air already smelled of autumn. I had just turned seventeen.

From that day until the day he was called up we spent every possible moment we could together, as far away from the house and those prying eyes as we could. The night before he left I excused myself from the drawing room after dinner, saying I had a headache. I kissed my parents good night, climbed the stairs and went to my room. I arranged the pillows in my bed to look as best they could like a slumbering body, then I tiptoed back along the landing to the service lobby and down the stairs that led to the kitchen. I could hear Mrs. Cuthbert's voice in the servants' hall, along with Mabel and Edna, discussing the day's news: the Germans had taken Brussels. I crept along the passageway, through the scullery and stillroom into the garden room, and then out to the yard. There was little light outside and I had to feel my way ahead, but once away from the house I knew the pathway and the light from the moon became brighter. And standing in the moonlight, next to the boathouse, smoking a cigarette, there he was: my Tom.

I smoked my first cigarette that night, there, with him. We sat on the wooden steps of the boathouse for almost an hour, talking about things we might do one day, places we'd like to see. "I shall go to the desert one day and ride across it on a camel," I said, and when he laughed I felt so stupid.

He must have sensed my embarrassment, because he said to me, "I'm sorry . . . we all have our dreams, and yours are no more amusing than mine."

But he still made me feel like a child; he *and* my brothers. And then, as I looked down, wishing yet again that I'd thought before I'd spoken, he took my hand and said, "Clarissa, you must surely know by now . . . how very fond I am of you."

I looked up at him. "Yes," I answered. "Yes, thank you, Tom."

I wasn't sure what to say. What does one say? It was a compliment and I'd been taught to be gracious.

"You've made this summer so much more than I'd anticipated," he added.

"But I so wish you didn't have to go," I said, tearfully, unable to be like my mama, unable to hold back.

He turned to me. "Perhaps it's for the best that I shan't be able to see you, at least for a while. You'll be coming out soon enough, and I've no doubt, no doubt at all, that it'll be just as Venetia predicts . . . you'll be inundated with admirers, Clarissa . . . and I'm not sure I'd like that." He smiled. "You see, I'm very much aware that I've had you to myself these past few weeks." He lifted his hand to my face, ran his finger down my cheek. "And I've known you in a way that no one else will ever again be able to. Because I've seen you before . . . before life's touched you."

I smiled, even though I wasn't altogether sure what he meant.

"And please, Clarissa, promise me one thing. Promise me that you won't go and get married, not yet."

I tried to laugh. "Tom, I'm only *just* seventeen. Of course I'm not going to get married yet."

"Promise me . . ."

"I promise."

He'd never been overseas, never crossed the Channel, but if he was afraid of what lay ahead of him he never for one moment showed it. As we sat huddled together on the step, he played with my hands, threading them in and out of his own, turning them this way and that, holding them up to his lips, smelling the scent I'd dabbed on to my wrists before I'd left my room, laying my palm over his mouth. I longed for him to take me in his arms and kiss me. My entire body ached for him. I knew a clock was ticking, knew the moment had to be snatched.

"Tom . . ."

"Clarissa . . ."

"Why have you . . . why have you never kissed me?"

He looked down at my hand, held in his. "Because . . ." and he sighed, closed his eyes for a moment. "Because kissing *you*, Clarissa, would be dangerous."

"Dangerous?"

He turned to me. "You don't understand, do you?"

"Yes, I think I do, actually. You mean that you don't feel *that* way inclined. That you don't like kissing women."

And he laughed, laughed so loudly that I pulled my hand away from his.

"Clarissa . . . Clarissa, what on earth goes on in that beautiful head of yours?" he said. Then he put his arms around me and pulled me to him. "I've spent the last six weeks fighting with myself . . . six weeks trying to do the right thing, trying *not* to kiss you . . . and the reason kissing you, *you*, Clarissa, not anyone else, could be dangerous . . . is simply because I might not want to stop." He looked into my eyes. "Now do you understand?"

In the moonlight, and up close, his features had taken on the silver hue of a Greek god—chiseled from ancient stone. I looked from his eyes to his mouth, and then I placed my lips upon his. We kissed slowly, tenderly. He moved his face, pressed his nose against my mouth, ran his tongue across my lips, as though they were a flower whose scent he wished to taste and feel, and smell. He cupped my head in his hands, moved his lips back to mine, and I felt myself falling, sinking down into a place I'd only ever imagined. I wrapped my arms around him, pulling him closer and, as he moved his mouth down on to my neck, I heard him moan, say my name. Then, suddenly, he stopped and pulled away from me. He sat forward, his head in his hands, and I could hear his breathing, loud and fast.

"I'm not terribly good at kissing yet," I suggested, wondering if perhaps I'd been a disappointment to him.

He shook his head. "We can't, we mustn't . . ." he said, his voice strained, almost hoarse. And he didn't look up at me.

We sat there for a minute or two in complete silence, and I wondered if I should leave him, if he wanted me to go. But I couldn't leave him, not yet. I reached out, placed my hand upon his shoulder. And then I said, "I love you, Tom."

I hadn't planned to say it; I'd simply thought it out loud. But after I'd said it I realized it was what I'd gone to tell him that night. You see, I wanted him to know, wanted him to have something to hold on to, to come back for. And though I longed for him to say it back to me, he didn't. He said, "No, I don't want you to say that, not yet. Love me when the war is over. Love me when I come back, Clarissa."

I moved in front of him, crouching down, and when he raised his head and looked back at me his eyes were filled with tears. I took hold of his hand. "Can I not love you now *and* when the war is over? Because I'm not altogether sure that my heart is able to postpone what it feels."

He frowned, attempting a smile at the same time, and as we rose to our feet he wrapped his arms around me and held me, so tightly I could barely breathe. He released his grip a little, looked down at me. "I shall hold you to your promise, Clarissa, because my heart has to know that you're mine."

"I am yours. I'm yours."

"Then may I be so bold as to request another promise? Promise me that your lips belong to me too."

"My lips as well as my heart?"

"As well as your heart, and your mind . . . oh, and your body too," he added, smiling.

I think we said good-bye at least twenty

times before we finally released each other's hands. He made me walk back to the house ahead of him, but followed close enough that I could hear him, behind me. When I reached the stable-yard gate, I turned back to look for him, but he'd gone. I wanted to run back, find him, but as I stood there I heard Mr. Broughton's voice, somewhere beyond Mrs. Cuthbert's cottage, saying, "All ready for tomorrow then, Tom?" And I swiftly moved through the gate and back toward the house.

I'd intended on rising early the following morning. I wanted to wave Tom off with the others. But when I awoke it was already seven o'clock. I hurriedly dressed and raced downstairs to the kitchen, colliding with Mabel and a bucket of coal at the baize door.

"Oh, Miss Clarissa, you're up early this morning."

"Has Tom gone yet, Mabel?" I asked, breathlessly.

"You've missed him. He left for the station with Broughton about five minutes ago. He's going for the seven thirty-eight . . ."

I ran through the kitchen, through the servants' passage, out of the house, across the yard, and grabbed my bicycle. I can't remember the journey to the station that morning, but I remember arriving there, seeing the dogcart and dropping my bicycle to the ground. The train was just pulling up to the platform and at first I couldn't see him—didn't know which way to turn. Then I saw him, and I ran down the platform shouting out his name. He looked startled at first, quite panic-stricken, and then he smiled, walked toward me, and I literally fell into his arms. He held my face in his hands and kissed me.

And I have no idea what Broughton thought of the spectacle in front of him at that moment, how shocked he was or otherwise.

"I love you. I love you, Tom Cuthbert," I whispered in his ear, and I realized I was crying.

He stood back from me, holding my face in his hands. "Clarissa," he said, and then he turned, picked up his bag and climbed on board the train. He leaned out of the open window of the carriage door, reached for my hand and then the guard shouted something, blew his whistle and the train began to pull out of the station. I watched him go, never taking my eyes away from his, until he disappeared into a cloud of steam and out of sight.

I didn't hear Broughton at first; I'd quite forgotten he was there.

"Miss . . . Miss Clarissa? I think we should get you back home, don't you?"

Dazed, I followed Broughton out to the cart and climbed up at the front as he picked up my bicycle and placed it on the back. Then he climbed up, pulled on the reins, and we turned back toward Deyning. It was a beautiful morning, a morning that didn't go with war. The sky was pale and bright, completely cloudless, the countryside still asleep. And as we passed through the quiet lanes, I thought of Tom, on his train, bound for France, and of all the other young men heading out to the trenches. None of it made any sense to me. Life made no sense.

We said nothing, Broughton and I, on that journey home, until we reached the gate, and then he said, "God bless them all. We have to keep faith . . . pray for their safe return. All of them."

"Yes, we do," I said. But even then I wasn't sure.

Faith . . . Somehow it seemed a flimsy, insubstantial thing set against a war, like walking out in winter in a fine silken shawl meant only for summer months. Was it enough? Would it be enough? I wondered. I would test God, I decided: I would keep faith in Him—if He kept faith in me; kept Tom safe, and returned him to me, unharmed.

I cleared my throat. "Mr. Broughton, I don't wish to compromise you, but I'd prefer it if you kept my visit to the station this morning quiet."

"Of course, I understand," he replied.

I glanced at him. "Thank you."

He turned to me and smiled. And I remember thinking how handsome he was, despite his age. He had the look of Romany about him, with his dark butterscotch skin and chocolate eyes; his hands—scorched by sun, stained by earth—so different from my father's pale unblemished hands. He'd been with us for so long I couldn't remember a time when he hadn't been in my life. He was as much a part of Deyning as the old sycamore tree, as rooted and as timeless. And yet I knew so little about him.

I think Broughton kept his promise, but of course I'd forgotten about Mabel, and word of my hasty early-morning departure had been passed on to my mother's loyal maid, Wilson. As soon as I entered the house Mama appeared in the hallway.

"I wish to speak with you, Clarissa. Please go up to your room. I shall be along presently."

Minutes later, she appeared in my room and asked me to sit down. She picked my nightdress up from the floor, folded it and placed it under my pillow. Then she sat down on the chair by the fire.

"I understand that you cycled to the station this morning, Clarissa," she said, looking out through the window.

There was no point lying. "Yes, that's right. I did."

"And this was all to say good-bye to Tom Cuthbert?" she asked, looking directly at me.

"Yes, Mama."

"You do realize—you've made rather a fool of yourself, and very possibly tarnished your reputation?"

"I don't think so. I wanted to see him off

and I'd overslept. I don't think cycling to the station and bidding a friend adieu is a scandal. He's going off to war, Mama."

"Yes, I know that, and I wish him, your brothers, and all the other young men Godspeed and a safe return home. But . . . it doesn't alter the fact that you were seen by the servants, dashing off and in quite a state, as I understand. It's not right, Clarissa. Surely you can see that."

I made no comment. I no longer cared what the servants thought: what did it matter? But I needed to hear all she had to say. And I knew there was more to come, I could tell by the tone of her voice. I watched her as she lifted her hand to a stray curl, twisting and tucking it back in place; each movement slow and measured.

"You need to tell me what has taken place between you and Tom Cuthbert. You need to tell me the truth, Clarissa."

I hated the way she said his name: over-enunciating the vowels in that manner.

"I don't know what you mean. Nothing has taken place. We're simply friends, Mama, that's all. And I like him . . . enjoy his company. He's been one of us this summer."

She smiled, closed her eyes for a moment. "Clarissa . . . Clarissa, you're not a child, you're a young lady now. You know he's not one of us, nor can he ever be. I was happy for him to enjoy some tennis and croquet with you and the boys, but that's as far as it should have gone. I had no idea that you and he had . . . had forged a *friendship*," and she looked at me, narrowing her eyes, and added, "or become close."

"We have not become close, Mama. I told you, we're friends, nothing more."

"Well, I do hope you're being truthful with me. You see, it would be very sad for you if it were otherwise, because nothing could ever come of it. Do you understand?"

"Of course," I replied, looking away from her, my eyes stinging.

"It would be a truly *pointless* and impossible liaison, and only lead to heartache— for you, and for him."

"I know this, Mama."

"Good. I'm pleased that we've had this little chat. It's always good to clear the air."

She rose to her feet, came toward me, where I sat on the edge of my bed. "You know, you're infinitely precious to me, and to your father. You're our only daughter, our baby." She stroked my hair. "We want nothing but the very best for you, the very best," she said, and then she bent down and kissed my head. "Now, please tidy yourself up and come down to breakfast."

And then she disappeared through the door, leaving her words behind her.

Nothing could ever come of it . . . a truly pointless and impossible liaison . . . only lead to heartache—for you and for him . . .

✍

My Dear, no, I do not believe I have been "hasty" in my judgment (of that situation), but there is a war now, and tender hearts—even yrs—are NOT always innocent . . . which is precisely why I intervened. Yrs D

Chapter Nine

In a matter of days my world changed. And though the sun continued to shine, and the bumblebees and butterflies went about their business, oblivious to world events, the peaches and nectarines in the walled garden went unpicked and began to rot.

Haymakers disappeared from the fields, and the place was eerily quiet, with the air of somewhere after a party has perhaps suddenly and unexpectedly ended. People had gone but an echo of their presence lingered; their voices held in the atmosphere, passed on in the whisper of trees. Croquet mallets lay abandoned by the summerhouse, where Henry and Will had left them after our last game; their tennis racquets out on the veranda, along with Henry's battered Panama hat and George's cricket bat. And there, in a jar upon the table, the wildflowers Tom had picked for me in the meadow now drooped forlornly, wilting in the late summer sun. Sometimes I fancied I saw one of them—Tom, Henry, George or Will—out of the corner of my eye, walking across the lawn, toward me. Once I even thought I heard one of them calling out my name, and I called back across the terrace toward the trees, "Hello! I'm here! Where are you?"

I wandered in a daze, unable to comprehend the suddenness of so much departure. I walked along silent pathways, through lines of gigantic petal-less delphiniums and foxgloves, standing shoulder high, erect and perfectly still. They'll be back soon, I told myself; they'll all be back soon. Perhaps they'd be back before the end of summer . . . perhaps everyone could come back and we could resume our summer. But I knew, even then, that this was unlikely to happen. Too many had gone for them all to be able to return before the season's close. It would be autumn, autumn at the earliest, I concluded. And meanwhile, I had an important task to complete.

For my birthday Henry had given me a painter's case: a small square mahogany box with a brass handle, containing tiny tubes of watercolor, a small bottle for water, a folding palette and three brushes. It was old, secondhand, and I liked that. I liked the thought that it had traveled, been carried about over fields, perhaps beyond England; and the case alone was beautiful, a treasure even without its usefulness. The day after my birthday, Tom had presented me with what at first appeared to be a small leather-bound notebook, a new journal I thought; but it was an artist's notebook, containing proper watercolor paper. *The first thing I paint in it shall be for you,* I told him. And it was. I set myself up down at the boathouse one day and, after roughly sketching out the vista immediately ahead of me, more shapes than detail, I christened my new paints. When I showed Papa my effort later that day, in the library, he'd held it upside down and said, "Charming, my dear . . . what is it?"

I turned the book the correct way. "It's the lake and the island . . . and that's the sky," I said, pointing to the wash of pink and blue.

"Hmm, yes . . . now I see. But isn't it a little *too* blurred?"

I took the book from him. "It's meant to be. It's impressionistic, Papa."

I looked back at the painted paper. I'd planned on sending it out to Tom, but now I wondered what he'd see. Would he recognize what I'd tried so hard to capture? Or would he, too, hold it upside down and see only a blurred mess of pale colors?

"Perhaps you should work on it some more. Add a little more detail . . ." Papa suggested, smiling at me. And he was right. It needed more work.

"Yes, I think you're right . . . it's much too pale. I need to add darkness . . . give it more depth," I said, but he was distracted and had turned back to his map of Europe.

He'd recently pinned the map on the wall above his desk and had it marked with pins and little bits of red and blue ribbon. I suppose he thought he was doing his bit: keeping track, following events. Around the house all anyone spoke of was the war, and now I too was keen to hear about it, to join in. When I left Papa in the library that day I went to the kitchen, where Mabel and Edna sat peeling vegetables at the long pine table. It seemed to me that between them they knew everything, every figure and statistic. And their conversation, so different to the other side of the green baize door, was an endless stream of fascinating detail.

Edna had been with us for years, since before I was born, and Mabel, for at least five years. They were both unmarried and, along with the other female servants, had rooms on the east side of the house, above the kitchen and servants' hall, looking out over the stable yard. They were both younger than they appeared, and I only knew this because Mama had told me. She'd mentioned that Mabel was, surprisingly, *considerably younger* than Edna. So, I'd estimated, Edna was probably nearer to thirty than forty, despite her matronly appearance, and Mabel—a good few years younger.

I showed them both my painting, asked them what they thought.

"Oh yes," Edna said, squinting at it under

the light. "It's pretty . . . very pretty, miss. Is it the lake?"

And I think I yelled, "Yes! It is, it's the lake, and look, that's the island . . . it's not finished, of course, still needs more work."

"Very atmosphereful. Oh yes, you're artistic, Miss Clarissa. Always have been. Hasn't she, Mabel?"

Mabel wiped her hands, took hold of the book and studied it for a moment. She was always more reticent than Edna, and compliments were not easy for her.

"Yes . . ." she said, looking up at me with a tight smile. "Very good."

"Shall I . . . would you like me to paint something for you, Edna?" I asked, glancing over at her and smiling.

Her face lit up. "Ooh, yes, I should say. Yes, I'd like that. I don't have any paintings, you know? Not one."

"I'll do it then," I said. "I'll paint something for you next. But it might be . . . it might be more abstract."

"Abstract? That sounds lovely, dear," she said, as I took the book from Mabel and sat down at the table.

And as I pondered on my next "commission," they resumed their conversation:

the one I'd interrupted when I'd walked into the kitchen.

"And over twenty more gone last Friday—an' most of 'em from Monkswood too," Edna said, shaking her head. "How they'll cope there now I don't know . . ."

Monkswood Hall, the estate bordering ours, had twice or even three times as much land, a folly, its own chapel, and at least two farms. It also had three times as many servants. The Hamiltons, who owned it, had made their fortune building ships, and were rumored to be descendants of Emma Hamilton. This rumor seemed to be confirmed by their choice of name for their eldest son, Horatio (known to everyone as Harry). And they were obviously fond of alliteration, for the four younger children's names also began with H: Howard, Helena, Harriett and Hugo. We'd seen quite a bit of the Hamilton children growing up, and I'd attended the last hunt ball at Monkswood with my parents. Like my brothers, all three Hamilton boys had gone off to fight, and I was distracted for a moment by the mention of Monkswood, the memory of that ball, and my dance with Hugo Hamilton.

"But how many have *we* lost?" Mabel asked. "Got to be pushing a dozen now, countin' John and Frank, and them boys down at the farm. Mr. Broughton says at this rate there'll just be him and his barra' left."

"John and Frank . . . they've gone?" I repeated.

"Been gone since a week past Friday, and Frank's mother—beside herself," Mabel replied, staring at me, wide eyed.

"But . . . but Frank's not old enough, surely. He's only a few months older than me . . ."

"That's as may be, miss. But them young 'uns always finds a way."

I thought of Frank, immediately saw his sweet blushing face, and my heart sank. I hadn't said good-bye to him, or to John. And now they'd gone. I looked to Edna, who smiled back at me. "Don't you fret," she said, "the Lord'll keep the good 'uns safe."

"My cousin . . . she says we'll all have to do our bit . . . all have to do more," I offered.

Mabel raised her eyebrows. "Is that right, miss? Well, there ain't enough hours in the day to do what I have to do now—let alone *more*."

Edna shook her head again. "Things'll change, that's for sure."

"And when you think of poor Lottie Baverstock," Mabel said, looking up from her work for a moment and out through the window. "Her only just married . . . and him *over there* now."

"Well, at least she saw some action!" Edna said, and they both laughed, then glanced at me and back at each other.

Edna rose to her feet, the bowl of peeled potatoes tucked beneath her bosom. "We'll have to settle for dancing with each other at the harvest festival dance, I reckon. What do you say, Mabel?" And she wiggled her broad hips as she moved through the scullery door.

Mabel sighed. "And there was my Jack about to propose as well."

"You're to be married?" I asked.

She stared at me. "Well, yes, miss . . . eventually."

Growing up at Deyning, the kitchen had always been a place of extraordinary mystery to me, as well as mouthwatering delights. It was an intoxicating muddle of comforting shapes and smells, manpower and secrets, and I'd longed to taste more. For so many years I'd wanted to be part of that camaraderie, wanted to know where Mabel and Edna and all the others had come from, what their stories were. I wanted to understand their jokes and repartee. But by being there, within the warmth of the old range and their banter, I'd caught a glimpse of something: something quite different to the formality of my parents' world. They laughed, and loudly, at things I knew they shouldn't laugh at; they slapped each other's backs and danced without music; and for a while, at least, they had allowed me to join in: to giggle and sing with them, to eat with my fingers and lick spoons. But latterly these interludes had ceased. And now, it seemed, I was no longer allowed that glimpse.

During those first days and weeks of the war I suppose we were all stunned, all in shock. We'd had no time to think, no time to prepare, and almost immediately, even as we grappled with the very notion of war, the carnage had begun. Each day the ironed print of the newspaper delivered us straight to France, to strange-sounding, unknown villages; places we'd never heard of, and perhaps would never have known of, but places whose names we'd be unable to forget for the rest of our lives. By the start of September it was estimated that fifteen thousand British troops had already been killed. Fifteen thousand. Wiped out within a month of summer. And I thought once more of those men I'd heard singing on board the train; singing their way to death.

∽

. . . I cannot bear to leave this place, & the not knowing when or if we will return, whether it be months or years (as some now say) breaks my heart, & you know why . . . Today we had the Belgian soldiers (8 of them) here for tea at 3 & afterward took an excursion through the lanes in the Landau—for what I suspect will be the last time . . . I smiled the whole way, but inside I was screaming.

∽

The first time I heard them I thought it was thunder: a storm, sweeping in from the sea, over the hills. I lay in my bed listening to it, waiting for it to move in—or fade away. But it didn't. It continued. A dull, distant rumbling, punctuated every so often by something louder, a boom. Those were the *big guns*, Papa told me.

One particularly windy morning my father arrived back from the farm in a state of excitement. He came rushing into the morning room, where I was sitting quietly with Mama—reading the newspaper.

"You should hear it out there," he said, smoothing down his windswept hair. "From the bottom of long field woods you'd think the fighting was just beyond those hills. Remarkable," he added, shaking his head. "Quite remarkable . . ."

I raced outside and jumped into the dogcart to return there with him, but Mama refused to come. She had no desire, she said, to hear the distant barrage of warfare, particularly not one in which her sons were fighting. We sat in the dogcart on a track at the southernmost point of the estate; and we sat in silence for ten minutes or more, listening to the intermittent juddering and booms, swept across the Channel and into our fields.

"It seems so near . . ."

"It is near," my father replied. "Only a narrow channel of water separates us from that fighting, Clarissa."

And as we turned and headed home it suddenly hit me: *a narrow channel of water.* If the enemy could push forward, break through our lines, reach the coast of France . . . they could cross that channel of water. I wanted to ask my father questions; wanted to ask him the likelihood of that happening, for if anybody would know, I thought, he would. But I didn't want him to have to think about that possibility. I didn't want him to have to consider that. So I remained quiet. But as we headed back toward the house I couldn't stop this train of thought. For already I could picture the German soldiers arriving at Deyning, marauding about the place, pulling it apart and laughing loudly. And what would we do? What would I do? And what if it happened at night? Of course, of course it would happen at night, was bound to happen at night—under the cover of darkness. I'd have to have a gun, I thought . . . have to be able to defend myself. And I saw my-self in my room, my locked door being broken down by laughing German soldiers as I stood brandishing a pistol.

I took a deep breath. "Papa, I think I should have a gun," I said. "I think we should all have a gun by our beds."

He laughed. "A gun? But you don't know how to use a gun, Clarissa. And why ever do you need one?"

I didn't want to worry him, didn't want to have to explain to him how things *could* unfold.

"For reasons of safety, of course," I said. "To defend myself and Deyning."

He turned to me. "You're quite safe here, my dear. And you really don't need a gun. At least not yet."

I didn't notice August's end, or September's start. I was hungry only for news: news of the war. I read the newspaper, often from cover to cover and sometimes out loud, repeating entire paragraphs in order to try to comprehend them. As I read of battles, battalions and bombs, my world expanded and took on a different hue. I looked at fatality lists: incredulous, aghast. For how could so many be killed? They had only just gone. And though I tried to accept that my three brothers, along with Tom, were unseen players in that macabre daily news bulletin, it still seemed unreal. Life, our routines, continued at Deyning, but it was different. Everyone was already in some infinitesimal way altered by the sudden cessation of that summer.

My mother, ever resourceful and fervently patriotic, threw herself wholeheartedly into the war effort. She attended the Appeal to Women meetings at the local village hall, and returned full of plans and ideas for a working party, informing my father that we should offer up all of our young and healthy horses, and asking him if the middle meadow could be used as a rifle range. She had endless meetings with Mr. Broughton to discuss how best to utilize the kitchen gardens, and even toyed with the idea of digging up the parterre in order to increase Deyning's vegetable production. She briefed the servants on new rules concerning the running of the house, had the drawing room and ballroom shut up, and reassigned the usage of rooms in order to conserve coal. And she set about organizing all of us women at home to make war garments: balaclavas,* gloves, scarves and socks—anything deemed useful for *our boys* at the front.

She had George's new gramophone relocated to the morning room and, each evening after dinner, with the air of a colonel organizing his regiment, she rounded up her *knitting party*, which included Wilson, Mabel, Edna, Mrs. Cuthbert, and myself, fulfilling the role of a private, and delegated the unraveling and rewinding of balls of wool, and the sewing up of mittens. As we sat in a circle around the fire, serenaded by the crackling strains of Tchaikovsky or Beethoven, we seemed to knit and sew in time with the music. And I wondered who'd wear these things we'd made with so much fervor. Would they hear the music?

"I was thinking, Mama, wouldn't it be wonderful if these mittens were to end up on George or Henry or William's hands?" (Or on Tom's, I thought, glancing at Mrs. C.)

"Really, Clarissa, I do so wish you'd think

* Knitted headgear worn by soldiers, named after the Battle of Balaclava in the Crimean War.

less and try to be a little more industrious," she snapped back at me.

Her weekly trips to London had stopped, and without them she seemed to me to be unnecessarily short tempered. Could her incessant train journeys and interviews with parlormaids and the like really be so important to her? One evening she'd burst into tears when I asked her if she'd one day take me to stay with her at the Empress Club. And I wondered then if she simply enjoyed the hurly-burly of travel and if there was not some neglected Romany spirit lurking beneath that immaculate, pale exterior.

I wrote to Tom almost every day. And cycling to the end of the lane—where the road forks and the postbox stands in the middle of a triangle of grass—I felt the thrill of subterfuge: for I was having an *illicit* affair. Yes, it was a love affair, the beginning of a Great Love Affair, and the thought of him holding my letter in his hands, casting his eyes over my words, was intoxicating, heady stuff. When the weather became inclement I coerced Broughton into posting my letters for me. After all, he knew my secret, he'd seen me; seen us.

And I'd already told Tom to send his let-ters to me via Broughton, at his cottage. Broughton appeared quite untroubled by this arrangement and became used to me, I'm sure, appearing at his door or by his side somewhere in the garden. He'd pull the paper from the pocket of his apron and hand it to me with a curious, knowing smile. But quite often he'd be with Mama, and usually in the greenhouse or the hot-house, bent over some tiny specimen in a terra-cotta pot, examining its possibilities. And then I'd swiftly turn.

I sent Tom my watercolor of the lake, though I still wasn't at all happy with it. But it was home, I thought, something for him to remember and hold on to; and I'd painted it for him. I shall treasure it, always, he wrote to me, and I couldn't help but won-der if he knew what or where it was. But did it matter?

I told him of the magnificent white owl in the pine tree beyond my bedroom window; how I'd watched it fly off toward a huge sil-very moon one night and imagined it was flying straight to him, carrying a tiny rolled-up note from me. But what would that tiny rolled-up note say? he'd asked. "That my heart beats only for you," I replied. I told him about the enormous spider recently taken up residence outside my window-pane, its shimmering fly-filled web growing day by day. I like to think of that spider, he replied; I like to imagine I'm that spider, looking back at you through your window, watching you. I told him of my solitary afternoon excursions, rowing across the lake to the island: the water murky, the air damp and filled with smoke from bonfires. I shall row you there one day . . . I shall take you there, and spend the whole day listening to your voice, studying your face, he wrote. Do you think of me? Do you think of me now? I asked, hungry for more. Always, he replied. *You're my vision, Clarissa, my beacon of hope.*

I found myself seeking out Mrs. Cuthbert more and more; being with her made me feel closer to Tom, and I often had to stop myself from blurting out her son's news, having received a more up-to-date letter than she. I sat at the table in the kitchen, chatting to her, asking her questions, gathering whatever snippets I could: stories and anecdotes about his childhood, which I later recorded in my journal. There was never any mention of Mr. Cuthbert, and I'd long since dismissed Henry's queer remark in the dining room that day. And Tom had told me anyway, told me what he knew: that his father had died shortly before he was born, that there'd only ever been him and his mother. But he must have been a tall man, I thought, a handsome man; and quite different to Tom's mother, who, sweet as she was, was a diminutive woman with no obvious beauty. They looked so different, and Tom had such an entirely different demeanor to that of his mother. Sometimes it was hard for me to imagine that Mrs. Cuthbert had actually given birth to *my* Tom.

We were still counting the war in days then. Sunday, November the first, was the ninetieth day, and in church we all prayed once again for a swift end to the fighting. Could it end by Christmas? Would my brothers and Tom be home by then? I imagined us all singing carols under the tree in the hallway, the war already in the past, already a memory.

In one of his letters to me Tom quoted some lines from Blake, I think: *To see the world in a grain of sand, And a heaven in a wild flower, Hold infinity in the palm of your hand, And eternity in an hour . . .*

But I could tell by the tone, by the words he chose not to write, that he was living through something too awful to speak of. He never mentioned love, never mentioned the future, but he told me that he thought of me upon waking and when he closed his eyes and tried to sleep. I prayed for him in church, and for my brothers too. I thought of him as I walked through the grounds, had conversations with him in my head; I pictured him smiling; imagined his hand in mine, his lips touching mine; and each night I dreamed of him.

I played games with myself, handing out questions for the universe to answer: if this pebble lands beyond the jetty, he'll come back to me; if *that* leaf blows down from the roof, it means he'll marry me; if the owl hoots once more it means I shall receive a letter from him in the morning post.

I had to be careful to rein in my ecstasy after receiving any letter from him. This was certainly not the time to be wandering about the place singing or whistling a jolly tune. And so I tutored myself in the art of solemnity, kept my euphoria private, and adopted a serious demeanor in keeping with everyone else and the general ambience of the house. I continued my solitary daily walks about the estate, carefully choreographing scenes and conversations yet to happen. I returned to those places of our clandestine moments together, replaying them in my head, languishing in his treasured words . . . and sometimes adding more. I stood under frosty sunsets, my warm breath mingling with the cold evening air as I watched the silent flight of birds across the sky. And even in those twilit autumnal days I felt a light shine down upon my path. For though he was no longer at Deyning, no longer in England, the fact that he lived and breathed had already altered my vision; and nothing, not even a war, could quell my faith in the inevitability of his presence in my life.

❧

. . . I am close to our front line now, not far from Neuve Chapelle, & close enough to hear the fighting. It's been rather warm here of late, and the roads—all

cobblestoned—are hell to march on, particularly in the heat, but the Route Nationale is as straight as a die & one can see for miles & miles across the countryside. Did I tell you, we're not allowed to have white handker-chiefs? In case we're tempted to raise them up into the air and wave them about like a white flag. Those who knew absolutely no French now know "Mouchoir rouge"! In fact, we seem to be inventing new French words by the day, Franglais. I'm compiling a list (of those suitable for your eyes) and will send them on to you soon . . . I know you'll be amused.

Chapter Ten

～

MDD, Yes, he knows . . . he knows that which I crave is the very thing he is quite unable to give me . . . but I fulfill my role, and this is what matters to him. It is futile . . . & yet to give up on the dream is like killing off a part of oneself. That part which was once everything, a guiding light, a promise, a hope. Life is NOT simple, but it is to be LIVED. Yr D

～

Christmas came, but it was not the same, and there was no end to the war. We read about the ceasefire, the Christmas truce on the Western Front, and then we heard about it from Henry, and from William too. In separate letters and in different words they told us how they'd sung carols and exchanged gifts with the Germans. They'd shaken hands with the enemy in no-man's-land and, Henry told us, played football with them. And I found it more than a little confusing to reconcile these images of bonhomie and fellowship with the subsequent and ongoing killing. How could they sing and be joyful, thankful, together, then kill each other? And why? I pondered on this and then asked my father, but he could offer me no satisfactory answers, nothing that made any sense.

Early the following year my parents and I decamped to our house in London: a tall, stucco-fronted Georgian building overlooking Berkeley Square. The place had been shut up since the previous spring, for though Mrs. Watson, our cook and housekeeper, and Mr. Dunne, the elderly butler, remained in situ there, my parents preferred to use their respective clubs for short excursions up to town rather than open up the house. The added complication of the transference of servants from Deyning to London always caused my mother some consternation, and with Deyning running with less than its full complement of staff, this had become even more of a headache to her. Prior to our departure there had ensued a great deal of debate about who, exactly, was to come with us to London and who should remain at Deyning. In the end, only Wilson and Mabel came with us, and my mother yet again faced the prospect of trying to re-cruit servants.

Our London home was, I suppose, simply a smaller, more compact version of Deyn-ing, with rooms situated in a less predict-able order. Here, the servants were based belowground, in a warren of basement rooms, including the kitchen and servants' hall; at ground level, my father's study, with a connecting door to his billiards room, and a smoking room; on the first floor, the for-mal reception rooms—including the draw-ing room and dining room; immediately above, and taking up the whole of the sec-ond floor, Mama's suite of rooms, with its Chippendale Chinoiserie furniture and hand-painted Chinese silk walls. My fa-ther's bedroom and dressing room, as well as my brothers' bedrooms were situated on the third floor, while my room and three spacious guest rooms occupied the fourth floor; and, at the very top of the house, the servants' attic bedrooms.

The view from my bedroom window in London was quite different from that at Deyning. Facing westward, not south, it looked out upon the back of town houses like ours, across slate rooftops, stables and small courtyards. Unlike ours, few of the houses appeared to have any garden, and but for the occasional ornamental tree, rising up tantalizingly from a moss-covered brick wall, my view was devoid of Mother Nature's soft curves. But when the sun slipped down behind the rooftops, and the sky turned from a smoky gray haze to a brilliant pink, everything in my room took on that luminous blush: the dark brown wood of polished mahogany transformed to a fiery coral; the cream silk of my bed-cover to a shimmering rose.

However, I was not to witness many sunsets that particular season, for despite the lack of eligible dance partners my mother was determined that I should still have some sort of coming out, and sooner rather than later. And so, after being outfitted with new gowns, we began the somewhat muted merry-go-round of tea dances, entertainments and *At Homes*. At that time, I had no idea that my mother's determination to get me up to London—away from Deyning—was in any way linked to Tom. Fate, I thought, seemed to be conspiring against us. For without Broughton, without anyone to attend to the actual postage and receipt of letters, it was impossible for me to correspond with him.

It was my father, still commuting between London and Deyning at that time, who informed us that Tom had been home, on leave, and that he'd seen him, spoken with him. I was bereft. He'd been home for two nights, Papa said, and the morning before my father left he'd saddled up his horse for him, and politely inquired after me.

"Decent chap, young Cuthbert," my father said. "He'll make his mother proud of him yet."

I wanted to ask my father so many questions; I wanted to say, how did he look? What else did he say? Where is he now? When will he return? But Mama's eyes were already upon me and so I said nothing.

But I wrote to him later that evening, determined to get a letter to him if only to explain my absence, and my silence.

The following morning I asked Mama if I could take Caesar for a walk across the square. It was frosty and cold, but the sun was shining. Yes, she said; yes, do that. And so I marched out across Berkeley Square, and then scuttled off in the direction of Bond Street, with Caesar, and the letter, hidden inside my coat, tucked into my dress, next to my heart. In that letter, I explained that I was stuck in London, that I'd had no choice in the matter, and that I was devastated to have missed him at Deyning. I told him that the parties and tea dances were all a crashing bore, littered with silly giggling girls and awkward boys with weak chins. I told him that none of it meant anything to me. I told him that I'd write to him whenever I could, and that he should continue to write to me via Mr. Broughton, and I'd be able to collect his letters when I returned to Deyning:

. . . And I'll wait for you, my darling. Even if it means waiting until I'm old and gray, I'll wait for you. Because I love you

with all my heart and everything I am. And nothing anyone can say shall ever alter that . . . So know that I am yours, and will only ever be yours: heart, mind, lips and body, yours, always,

Clarissa

I walked back to the house deliriously happy, and even Caesar must have picked up on my mood because he yapped excitedly all the way home.

It was not impossible. It was my life, and he was My Love.

The following week Mama hosted a party for me: *Mrs. Granville, At Home . . . Dancing 9:30.* But I had no interest in that party, or in any of the other rather somber dances and parties we attended. When the band played the national anthem at the end of each event (each ordeal), I felt relief. I hated the endless introductions, the pointless conversations, and those stupid, fawning boys. All I could think about was Tom, and his letters—waiting for me with Broughton. And I longed to get back to Deyning. I wanted to tell the other girls, "This is not really me. I'm only doing this to please my mother; I've already met the man I shall marry . . ." But of course I didn't. I danced with young officers and played the game, under my mother's watchful eye.

"So-and-so seemed awfully keen, Clarissa," she would say, always encouraging, steering me toward a particular young man she'd spotted, taken a shine to. And I was always vague and non-committal in my response. "You really do need to give a little more of yourself, dear," she said to me after one particular ball. And I couldn't say to her, "But, Mama, I have nothing to give. My heart is taken," so I pretended that I didn't understand what she meant and inadvertently allowed her the opportunity to coach me in the art of flirting.

"You need to smile more," she said. "Perhaps giggle at their jokes, *even* if you don't find them amusing . . . look at them when you speak . . . and accept their compliments graciously."

It was all so tedious, so unnecessary. I watched the other girls and thought how ridiculous they seemed, for their mamas, too, had obviously coached them, and seeing them put into practice everything my own mother had tried to teach me made me determined not to fall in line. Somehow my defiance, my aloof demeanor, appeared to have the opposite effect, and I was inundated with dance partners and overtly keen suitors. And Mama, forgetting her previous advice, said, "Of course, the other gels are much too keen and far too flirtatious. The reason you're so popular, my dear, is not simply because of your beauty, but because you hold back a little, and that's always quite intoxicating to a man."

Tea, it seemed, was a much bigger, grander occasion in London than in the country. And everyone dressed for it. In gowns of sable-trimmed silk, satin brocade and velvet, and gathered around white linen-covered tables piled high with sandwiches, scones, muffins, crumpets and cake, they passed on the latest gossip. But none of it, no matter how sensational or titillating, was of any real interest to me. You see, in my head I'd begun to write the story of my life: the story of my life with Tom, how it could be, how it *would* be. I was stranded between two worlds, lost in a twilight place of never-ending possibilities. Occasionally, and often in the clatter of real conversation, I'd find myself mouthing the words of an imaginary conversation, one yet to take place. And once or twice Mama had felt the need to surreptitiously tip me out of my reverie with a little kick or a sharp nudge. Then, usually en route home, she'd pour forth. "Really, Clarissa, you seem to be growing more distracted by the month! Gels are supposed to grow out of daydreaming when they become young ladies, otherwise they appear . . . well, simple." She'd sigh, turn and look out of the window. "I'm tempted to take you to Doctor Riley . . . truly I am."

Once, after Venetia had hosted a tea dance for me, I'd overheard a conversation between her and Mama. The two of them had removed themselves upstairs, to Venetia's boudoir, and I'd gone up to tell them that people were beginning to leave. I could hear Venetia's voice beyond the door, slightly ajar, and I stopped.

"I'm quite certain you've no cause to worry . . . she may be dreamy, but weren't we all once? And she's a sensible girl."

"Sensible?" Mama repeated. "It's not a word I would necessarily use to describe Clarissa . . ."

"But she's growing up, dear. Working

her way through that filtering process. I remember it well, and it is somewhat daunting. Especially for a girl who has had such a sheltered life . . . perhaps you should have had her up to London more often."

"Yes, you're right, and I realize that now. She's spent far too much time down at Deyning . . . on her own . . . traipsing about the fields, reading poetry . . . talking to the trees . . ."

Venetia laughed. "Ah, but she's beautiful . . . and the boys do seem to fall at her feet, not that she notices—as you say—but then that in itself is *très charmant*. I'm sure she'll forget about him in time. Truly, I shouldn't fret; these sorts of crushes do fade, and if we're honest, haven't we all fallen afoul of them—at some stage or another?"

I heard Mama sigh, then Venetia added, "We need to steer her in the right direction, my dear, that's all. And perhaps the sooner we can have her engaged the better."

I didn't want to hear anymore. I coughed, opened the door.

"People are leaving," I said flatly, staring at my mother.

"Oh gracious, and we were just about to

come down, my dear," Venetia replied quickly, moving forward. She stopped, ran the back of her hand down my cheek. "Such a beautiful goddaughter."

I was furious: angry with my mother for talking about me in that way, and for discussing Tom with Venetia. Venetia who had been seducing Henry for goodness knows how long. But perhaps Mama knew, perhaps she condoned that sort of behavior. Perhaps that sort of behavior was acceptable within the confines of her tight circle of friends, for it seemed to me as though there were distinctly different rules for different people.

As we walked home from Venetia's that day I was quiet, monosyllabic in my replies to her. I half wondered if she'd say something to me about her conversation with Venetia, if she'd realized that I might have overheard. But she was distracted; worried she was late for a meeting. Her latest rallying cry was for the Belgian refugees. She'd become involved with the Red Cross, attending endless meetings—trying to arrange housing for them. She had also recently been assigned a "district" and visited the workhouse in Marylebone each week. But the plight of the Belgian refugees seemed to have come between her and her wits, and having already proposed that the parkland at Deyning be handed over to the army for training purposes, she'd suggested to Papa that we offer up the house to the homeless Belgians. She was a patriot, determined to do her bit, stalwart in her defense of her world.

When Mama and I returned to Deyning, briefly, and with Papa, I could barely contain myself. There would be at least twenty letters, I thought, waiting for me with Broughton, and all I had to do was get to him, to think of a pretext to get out of the house and meander toward his cottage. I felt dizzy and sick with excitement. And I was becoming cunning in my duplicity.

"Shall we go for a long walk, Mama? To deep dene* perhaps, and then back by the lake?" I suggested, as our motorcar passed through the white gate. I knew that the very last thing my mother would feel like was a long walk after the journey from London. And I was right.

"Oh, Clarissa, I think you'll have to take

---

* Old English term for valley.

your walk alone, dear. I'm much too tired
and I need to speak with Mrs. Cuthbert
and the servants . . ."

I couldn't understand it. There were no letters. None at all, he said.

"But are you quite sure? You see, it simply doesn't make sense, Mr. Broughton."

We were standing by the greenhouse in
the walled garden, and he didn't look at
me. As he spoke he kept his eyes down,
looking into the wooden barrow in front of
him, piled to a peak with darkest earth.

"Yes, I'm quite sure. There've been no
letters . . . none at all."

"I see." I turned and walked away.

No letters, no letters . . .

I wasn't ready to go back inside the
house, to face Mama, who'd immediately
notice the change in my mood. I wandered down the pathway, toward the gate
I'd skipped through only minutes earlier,
and as I turned to close it I paused and
looked back at Broughton. He was standing in the same spot, staring back at me,
folding his hat in his hands. But then he
looked away, put his hat back upon his
head, picked up the long handles of the

barrow and disappeared inside the green-house.

I walked through the stable yard, past Mrs. Cuthbert's cottage. He'd been there, quite recently, I thought, glancing up at the small window poking out from the red tiled roof. He'd been back and I wasn't there. I stopped at the gate, ran my hand over the gnarled oak of the thick gatepost. His hand had touched that: had he thought of me? Then I lifted the iron latch and walked on into the field. The grass was long, heavy with dew and shimmering with gossamer. In my haste, I hadn't changed my shoes, hadn't supposed I'd be walking far.

No letters, no words . . .

When I reached the boathouse I sat down upon the damp steps and looked out across the lake. The day had a lifeless feel to it: the countryside silent and per-fectly still, the water colorless and flat, and the air cooler than I'd anticipated. The sky hung low, so close to the earth it seemed to almost touch the water in front of me. I looked down at my feet, began to pick off the blades of wet grass clinging to the leather of my shoes. We'd made a pact, I thought; and I'd risked so much to get one

letter to him. And I'd copied out a poem for
him, by Emily Brontë.

In summer's mellow midnight
A cloudless moon shone through
Our open parlour window
And rosetrees wet with dew.
I sat in silent musing
The soft wind waved my hair
It told me Heaven was glorious
And sleeping Earth was fair . . .

∾

. . . Yesterday we marched some 20
miles, stopping for tea and rum, & then
on again, but the rum keeps us warm—&
morale is quite high. Some of the men
who joined us have gone for weeks
without any real sleep or respite, & have
not removed their boots in as long.
They've had no proper meals, nothing
hot, and the temperature has suddenly
plummeted. When they fell out of line
we tried to pick them up, but the CO
came along with his stick. He had to.
He couldn't leave them there—they'd
have frozen to death . . .

Chapter Eleven

Dearest T, I do what I believe is best for ALL of us, which is not always easy, & my responsibilities—to everyone—weigh heavily on me. I too cannot bear this reality, but what choice do we have? We must nurture brave hearts, & pray for peace & for all that is noble, and good and fine. I neither know nor understand what "might lie ahead," but I do know that without US my life would be devoid of all hope and beauty. It makes me utterly and unbearably miserable to think of you lonely and sad, & to know also that it is beyond

my power to ease your suffering, but I want to remind you how very close you are to my heart, now & always . . . and ever in my thoughts . . . in haste, Yr D

⌁

We remained at Deyning for only three days before returning to London, and for me it was a thoroughly miserable time. The house had been requisitioned and my parents and Mrs. Cuthbert were preoccupied with inventories, organizing the removal of paintings and any items of value. Mrs. Cuthbert, Mr. Broughton and a few others were to remain at the house, as caretakers, but my father was upset and agitated at the prospect of army personnel trampling through his precious home. "It'll be wrecked," he said, shaking his head. Huts for soldiers were going up on the grounds, and the whole place had already taken on a somewhat gloomy, neglected look. Windows now stood bare, their views somehow altered and made ordinary by their lack of lavish frame. Stripped of its furniture and glorious interior colors, Deyning had become like a museum emptied of its exhibits. Certain rooms were to be used for storage and would remain locked, their ghostly contents shrouded in dust sheets. Other things were to be transported to London. The rooms I'd known since childhood now stood bare of family treasures and personal memorabilia. The curtains, carpets, rugs and tapestries, which had for so long cushioned our existence, lending the place softness and warmth, had been taken down to be put away for the duration of the war, and the whole place echoed with an unfamiliar sadness.

"But what if the war ends soon?" I asked my mother. "What if we wish to come back here?"

"Sadly, I don't think that will happen, Clarissa. People are saying that this war may go on for years."

I sat upon the staircase, watching Broughton and the few remaining men from the estate carrying endless tea chests and crates, furniture and carpets. Back and forth, and back and forth across the marble floor, directing each other as they maneuvered larger pieces through doorways.

"Steady there . . . a little to the left . . . that's it. Careful now . . ."

I felt as though I was watching the dismantling of a stage set; theater in itself. I watched as they carefully carried Mama's portrait—covered in a blanket—from the drawing room through the front door and out to a waiting wagon. It was moving to London along with us. I watched them carefully take down the chandelier in the hallway, for that, too, was moving up to London. I shuffled along the step as Wilson and Mrs. Cuthbert trudged up and down the staircase carrying hatboxes, bags, and tied bundles of linens and towels.

I remembered all the Christmases we'd celebrated, always with a huge tree situated next to the staircase where I now sat. As a child, I'd sat upon that same step, huddled up against the balusters, studying the tree, its shape and decorations; enthralled by the magical light and shadows upon the walls around me. Dancing. Over Christmas the only light in the hallway had come from the silver candelabra burning on the hallway table. But on Christmas Eve and Christmas Day night small candles were attached to the branches of the tree, their soft light reflected in the vast chandelier suspended high above and thrown back across the walls like stars across the universe. I remembered the smell, that mingling of pine and wax and burning logs: the smell of home, the smell of happiness. I'd sat there in my nightgown, listening to the chime of crystal; the laughter, music and voices emanating from another room, an adult world I could only imagine. And always hoping for a glimpse of Mama, as she whooshed across the marble floor, beautiful, resplendent . . . invincible.

It was nearly always Stephens, my nursemaid, who'd find me there and march me back up to the nursery floor. "But I only wanted to see Mama," I'd plead, as she secured the gate at the top of the stairs.

"Your mama is busy, Miss Clarissa; you know that. And she wouldn't be pleased to see you running about the place in your nightgown, now would she?"

I wasn't sure. Would she be so displeased? Mama loved me. She told me so. *More than anything in the world*, she said. Stephens didn't know this of course. Stephens didn't understand. How could she? She didn't have a mama like mine.

Quite often Stephens found me hiding behind the jardinière in the corner of the hallway, trying desperately to align myself with its narrow stand, trying to be invisible; but my usual hiding place had been inside the dumbwaiter, which carried Mama's breakfast tray and meals up to the nursery floor each day. Oh, how much fun my brothers and I had had playing in that! We'd sent each other up and down and up and down, with Henry inevitably in charge of the pulley, as the rest of us gathered intelligence, spying on Mama and the servants . . . and hiding from Stephens and the dreaded Miss Greaves. And only once did it get stuck: with poor Georgie inside it. The ropes had become tangled—from overuse, Stephens later said. We could hear his desperate cries for help echoing throughout the house, as though he were trapped down a very deep well. And then, when I became somewhat hysterical and began to cry, because I really did wonder if we'd ever get him back, Henry had shouted at me to shut up, which had only made me cry all the more.

Of course those childhood games and adventures had long since ceased, but they remained a part of Deyning, a part of the world I was leaving.

"You all right there, miss? Not too cold?" Wilson asked as she passed me on the stairs.

I was freezing. Without carpets and furniture the house was cold, and colder still from every door standing open to the elements, and the air had a dusty, acrid smell to it. But I continued to sit there, lost in the warmth of my memories. Occasionally Mama appeared, directing operations with a slight frown but a steady, calm voice. My father remained in his library, among his last remaining boxes of books. Later, in her boudoir, Mama told me how hard it was for him.

"This place is everything to him . . . everything," she said, tearfully. "We must rally him, Clarissa. You mustn't allow him to see you looking so miserable . . . otherwise he will feel even sadder." But I realized at that moment that she was speaking of herself. Though my father was unsettled by the upheaval and chaos around him, he was essentially a pragmatic man. It seemed to me that it was Mama who was shaken and sad. And I was surprised, and wondered why, because she'd been the one who'd wanted to hand the place over to the army, and to the Belgian refugees; and because I was unused to seeing my mother upset or agitated by anything. And it still seemed so unnecessary. Why did our home have to be packed away? Why could Papa not have said "no" to the army? It was *his* home after all.

My parents' grim acceptance of a long war shocked me. It seemed defeatist in itself; a blindly pessimistic acquiescence in something which had for me, up until that point, at least, been a temporary state; something which *could* be endured and lived through, and then, at its end, normality restored. But their quiet acknowledgment of a long struggle ahead and the sight of our home, our lives, being dismantled and packed away for an indefinite period shook me out of that dream. And it made me begin to realize that perhaps I hadn't fully come to terms with what was taking place across Europe.

∽

. . . I don't understand why you haven't written, and now my heart is fit to burst & I feel even more desperate,

because we are leaving here, leaving Deyning, & I shan't be here when you return (there is no IF, only WHEN). To-day I walked down through the meadow to the lake & I thought only of you, I thought of you all day, & all day yester-day, and the day before that . . . If this reaches you, please write to me . . . write to me in London. Everything here is truly awful, but nothing compared to what you're going through . . . Oh my darling, I love you, I do love you, & I don't care what you say about waiting until this thing is over . . . I know only what I FEEL.

On our last night at Deyning we retired to our beds early. With nothing of comfort to sit upon—and nothing much to look upon—it seemed the only thing to do. In my bedroom I stood for a while in my night-gown looking out of the window. But there was little to see or bid adieu to. The moon lay on its back, slumped in the distance beyond the trees: a bright white sliver of a crescent rocking low in the blackness, like a deflated balloon, which had shrivelled and then slipped.

Perhaps not surprisingly, I slept badly that night, my dreams filled with Deyning, and angst-ridden conversations with a whole array of people about its future. And for the first time in years another dream came back to me.

When I was young I'd had a recurring dream about an invisible door, a kind of opening in the ceiling of the drawing room, through which all sorts of strange children were able to enter the house. Literally, dropped in from above. That night I dreamed I was standing in that place once again, and this time the sun shone down through the invisible hole in the ceiling. I felt its heat, and an utterly sublime sense of peace. Then, through the sunshine, it began to rain, and as I stood there, my arms outstretched under that heavenly shower, and looking up into the light, a tiny girl fell through the hole to my feet. She was a child, but so very, very small, with black hair and the brightest blue eyes. She smiled up at me with perfect white teeth.

"He's always here," she said, pointing. I turned, and looked into darkness. And when I turned back to her—she'd gone.

Early the following morning, before setting off for London, I stood on the terrace with Papa watching armored biplanes fly over the house. Like a swarm of tiny toy flying machines they buzzed high above us, moving in and out of mist and low cloud.

Will . . .

My brother William, by now attached to the Royal Flying Corps, had been taught to fly in a matter of weeks, and had only recently been deployed to the war zone, piloting one of those tiny wooden biplanes over the muddy fields of France and Flanders. I turned to my father, and when I saw his face he looked so different to the Papa of my childhood: anxious and, suddenly, old.

I took his hand in mine. "Don't worry, Papa, God will keep William safe."

He looked down, shook his head. "I'm not so sure . . . no, I'm not so sure God can keep them safe."

"Don't say that," I said, gripping his hand. "We have to keep faith . . . we have to. The war will end one day soon," I went on determinedly, and despite knowing that no one, least of all my father, believed this. "Then things will go back to normal. All will be as it was."

I'd never heard my father talk like that, never seen him look so troubled.

He sighed, looked skywards again. "Yes, yes, the war will end one day, Clarissa—it has to—but England will be a different place, the world will be a different place . . ." He turned to me. "And you know, I rather liked things as they were. I've never wished for change . . . and I'm too old for it now," he added, releasing my hand and walking away.

I took one last look across the ragged, uncut lawns. The air smelled of decay and rotting vegetation, and a chilled gray mist hung over the place, almost but not quite obliterating color and shape, but blurring lines, rendering everything in front of me gloomy and drab: a ghost of what she once was, I thought.

Minutes later, as our motorcar pulled away, I turned and looked back at the house. In front of it stood Mrs. Cuthbert, Mr. Broughton and the handful of servants who'd helped to pack the place up. And as we moved away, down the long avenue of beech trees, I watched them become smaller and smaller, and smaller still, until they disappeared into the stone façade of Deyning, and then, finally, it disappeared too. As we passed by the white gate and turned out on to the road I wondered if we'd ever again live at Deyning, if life would ever be the way it used to be. And I thought of *him*, somewhere in France. He'd return there, God willing, but I'd no longer be there. Deyning was not part of my life any more, and, it seemed, neither was he.

∼

. . . When we finally arrived in the town we simply flooded the place, & then lay about in the streets waiting to find out where we were to be billeted. A few of the chaps here seem to think the worst is over, & we're all praying, hoping that this is the case, and that by the time our turn comes we'll have had some good news . . . but in truth I know this is unlikely. Anyway, I am in a small farm cottage with five others, and a fire! So for now, at least, I am warm, and able to think . . . think of you.

PART TWO

Chapter Twelve

We regret to inform you . . . the telegram began. *Seen to fall . . . shot down over enemy lines.*

I didn't and couldn't believe the words, though I saw them for myself. For how could my brother William be dead? He'd only just learned to fly, only just gone. And the war would surely be over soon. It was a mistake, it had to be. There'd be another telegram, I told Mama; another one to tell us that they'd made a mistake. He was twenty years old. People didn't die at that age, didn't get killed. His face flashed before me, animated, laughing; alive. It was a mistake, it had to be; a dreadful mistake. But I saw the line in my mother's brow, an ever-deepening line. I saw my parents' grief. And the sight of them sobbing into each other's arms told me that the only mistake was my heart's inability to accept my brother's fate. William *had* been killed. And I kept saying it to myself: *William is dead . . . William is dead.*

Weeks after we'd learned of Will's death Papa took ill with pneumonia, and my mother's grief was postponed while she focused her attention and energy on him. The doctor came to the house each morning, and as I stood on the landing, straining to hear the hushed conversation below me, I heard him repeat one word: *grief.* I wondered then if Papa felt guilty, for he'd been the one who had persuaded William, eventually, to go and fight. I'd heard them arguing in the library, days before William signed up. "No son of mine will be a shirker!" Papa had said, and in an unusually loud and angry voice.

Of course, there could be no funeral for Will: like so many others, his body, what—if anything—was left of him, could never be recovered. All that had been returned to us were a few items of uniform, two books and some letters. I pondered on that, and on those words, *seen to fall*. But I could not bear to think of my brother falling from the sky; hurtling toward the ground, on fire, knowing he was about to die. It was too much. And without a body, without evidence, how could they know for sure that he'd been killed? Could he have survived? Was it possible? Sometimes this train of thought offered me a glinting light of hope. I imagined Will arriving back at home, laughing at us for thinking him dead, and then explaining that he'd been on some secret mission: undercover, behind enemy lines. It *was* possible. It could happen. At other times it made sense to me that my brother, the theology student, the one closest to God, had been plucked from this life in the heavens. I'd close my eyes. Of course! William didn't spiral back down to earth; he simply cast off that reluctant soldier's body . . . his soul remains up there, in the sky. William: an angel.

I thought of Tom, wondered where he was. Did he think of me still? Did he remember me? I tried to recall our conversations, but fact and fiction had muddled themselves, and I couldn't now be sure if some of the lines I credited him with were mine and not his. I tried to picture his face, those dark solemn eyes, but already his image had begun to fade. Sometimes his face would come to me, in all its beauty, and then slip away again. And I'd struggle, struggle so hard to conjure it back, focusing on a specific moment . . . that evening by the ha-ha, when I'd watched him as he smoked his cigarette; and I could *almost* picture his profile. But like every other cherished memory of that last summer, it too had faded. I tried to remember his kiss, the feel of his lips upon mine, but it seemed as though that memory, too, was slipping away from me.

Don't leave me; never leave me.

My mother forgot all about parties and balls. She spent her days scouring the newspaper for names she knew, searching through the Roll of Honour, tracking the movement of regiments, battalions, and events *over there*. Henry was mentioned in dispatches, and so too was Jimmy Cooper. But a son's fearlessness on a battlefield in another country only exacerbated the sense of fear and dread at home. And, rather than an end in sight, we appeared to be going further and further away from *the beginning*, from that point of faith and hope and optimism.

Long numbers, numbers with more zeroes than I'd ever seen before, were printed each day: 500,000 men to Romania; 300,000 more men needed; 70,000 more men dispatched 126,000 men taken prisoner, 258,000 casualties . . . endless numbers, printed in heavy black ink. We read of the German prisoners transported to Frimley, where crowds had gone to see them—only to discover they'd already been transported to the Isle of Man. We read of the German submarines off the coast, torpedoes and air raids; bombs dropped on familiar seaside resorts up and down the country. And we read of the continuing struggle at Ypres. We read about asphyxiating gases and pulled out the encyclopedia; of the events in Basra, the Dardanelles and Gallipoli—and pulled out the atlas. We read of the sinking of the *Lusitania* and of more airship raids on the coast. And in the early hours of the morning of May the thirty-first the Zeppelin arrived, and we heard the bombs fall on London.

Together and separately we surveyed the endless daily images of war published in the *Illustrated London News:* double-page black and white photographs straight from the front; drawings of scenes of carnage, our troops and the fighting. I studied these pictures with a morbid fascination, for the churned-up, charred landscape they depicted was unlike any I had ever seen or could ever—even in my worst nightmares—have imagined. It was the landscape of Hell. And the notion that Tom or my brothers could be one of the murky figures in the foreground was too horrendous to contemplate.

Somehow, amidst all of this, life continued. Father slowly recovered and began to come downstairs in the evenings. He listened to me play my new pianola, and we played bridge and piquet. We read *The Gates of Doom*, and then *From China to Peru*, with my mother and I taking it in turn to read a chapter out loud. When Papa was stronger we went out to the pictures and to the theater. London hadn't shut down.

We saw *The Flag Lieutenant* at the Haymarket and *A Girl Like Me* at His Majesty's. We joined in the fervor of patriotism, celebrating our troops' victories and sending parcels out to *our boys* taken prisoner in Germany. Each evening in London there was an atmosphere of camaraderie and defiance; we were stalwart, ready for anything, we thought. If our sons and brothers at the front could cope, so could we.

❧

. . . Why have you not written? Why have you not replied to my letters? I know that you're out there, I know in my heart that you're alive, & I pray to God every single night to keep you safe. Please, please, if this reaches you, get word to me—somehow, let me know that you are still mine, for I am yours, & shall always be YOURS.

❧

I'd known Charlie Boyd almost all of my life. He'd been at school and at Cambridge with Henry; was one of the Set, as Henry called it. In physical appearance he was the opposite of Tom: shorter, broader and fair, with freckles, blue eyes and strawberry-blond hair. He was without doubt the funniest of Henry's friends and took delight in sending himself up. I liked that about him more than anything else. I thought, underneath all that bluff and bravado there was something very decent and, perhaps, rather vulnerable too.

My parents knew the Boyds well, and Mama adored Charlie. He'd written to her about Will, assuring her that his death would have been instantaneous; that it was far better for him to have died a valiant hero's death than to have been left disfigured, traumatized or disabled for life. He succeeded in making Mama believe that Will's life had not been in vain, that she must be proud of her son's sacrifice and, though I remained unconvinced, I was grateful for the comfort his words gave my parents.

✑

. . . **We are all in shock & utterly bereft at our loss, and though I feel the aching void in his passing, a part of me**

feels equal to the country now in my suffering. And yet what strange justification—to offer up our sons & align ourselves in grief, as though our sacrifice were all the more noble by its magnitude. But I hold steadfast & will not succumb to self-pity, and I could not have lived through these past few weeks without your words, so wise, so considered, & so true. He was, as you say, a radiant force for good . . .

I can't remember when I began to write to Charlie, but I imagine it was shortly after Will died, after he'd written to me. I began to look forward to his letters, they were always upbeat, and there was always something reassuring in the words he chose to write. He'd been in our lives for so long, was a part of a continuum; part of our family, I suppose. At first our letters were the letters between dear friends, or brother and sister, but they quickly became something more. It was inevitable. The war heightened all emotion, every sentiment was amplified, every longing accompanied by a sense of urgency. There was no time to ponder, to reason or to speculate; each thought and feeling had to be recorded and passed on. It was our duty as women, we were told, to keep our boys' morale high: to let them know that they were missed, that they were loved; that someone was waiting for them back at home. And in a way I think I truly believed that my letters and thoughts would keep Charlie safe, keep him alive.

It had been almost a year since I'd last heard from Tom, and though I still thought of him, wondered where he was and included him in my prayers, I'd begun to wonder if I'd ever see him again. And the thought that I might not, the thought that we might never again know each other, had slowly begun to reduce me, eroding my hopes, and the potential of my life. I knew I could survive without him—yes, I would survive—but the thought of a lifetime without him made the path ahead narrower, dimmer.

Over the course of one year my life had been irrevocably altered. I had changed and I knew he would be changed too. We would never again be the sweethearts who'd sat upon the steps of the boathouse looking up at the stars. And even if we did, if we could return to that place, if we could recapture that moment, would we see the same stars? Would he look at me that same way: tilting his head to one side, staring at me sideways through a wave of almost black hair, smiling? We could never again be who we were; and we would never be the people we'd once been destined to be. He would always have a special place in my heart, but he no longer held it, I reasoned. And I could not allow him to. I could not have that breadth and brightness back—only for it to disappear once more. For that, I knew, would surely kill me.

～

...He is raging about the newspapers & says it will be a bad thing for us if America declares war on Germany, but—after the Lusitania—I'm not so sure. The feeling in America seems to be very strong, but at least the newspaper editors here are being restrained—for once . . . In the meantime, I am v busy with my district, the refugees have been moved and now we have POWs in their place, and all sorts of criminals! And London continues to stand tall.

Chapter Thirteen

⚘

. . . I have no wish to describe this place to you . . . except to say it is Hell, a squalid, sickening & rancid Hell, inhabited by brave-hearted lunatics. I close my eyes & try to imagine you, so perfect, so beautiful. You remain my vision, my beacon of hope . . .

⚘

It was just after Christmas, the second Christmas of the war. Charlie had had one week's leave and was returning to the front. He'd come to stay overnight with us in London, and had already asked if I'd see him off the next day, and it was the thing to do. That evening, after dinner, my parents retired to bed unusually early, leaving Charlie and me alone in the drawing room. We'd been sitting side by side on the sofa when he took my hand in his and said, "You must know, I think, how terribly fond I am of you, Clarissa."

"Yes, yes, I think I do," I replied, looking down at my hand in his and wondering what was to come.

He cleared his throat, turned toward me. "I'd like to think that perhaps you feel the same way . . ."

"Oh yes, of course. I'm very fond of you too, Charlie."

He smiled, his pale blue eyes suddenly quite misty. "Thing is, Clarissa, I think I'm more than fond of you. Thing is, I . . . well, I love you."

For a moment I thought he was going to cry. He looked down, squeezed my hand tightly. "You see, I've always rather liked you, but it's grown into something more . . . and your letters, well, they've kept me going, you know. A letter from you, your name, it somehow makes me feel invincible." He looked up at me. "You mean the world to me, Clarissa, the world . . ."

I pulled my hand from his, lifted it to his face, and ran my finger down his cheek. "Dear Charlie, you are adorable."

And then he leaned forward and kissed me.

His kiss was different to Tom's: tentative, gentler; less passionate, but perhaps kinder. He wrapped his arms around me and pulled me to him. And then, in a playful and overly effusive way, he began to cover my face in kisses, telling me, between each one, that he loved me. The way Papa used to do when I was a child. I began to laugh and then he did too. "I'm so happy," he said, looking at me and smiling. "If I die, I shall die a happy man."

"No! Don't say that. You're not going to die, Charlie Boyd, do you hear me? You are not going to be killed in this wretched war. Otherwise I shall be very, very cross with you."

He laughed again. I loved to see him laughing like that. There'd been so little laughter in our home for so long and Charlie had brought it back.

We sat in silence for a moment, and he

held my hand once more. Then he moved from the sofa down to the floor, and on to one knee. He took hold of my hand again, looked up at me with newly serious eyes.

"Clarissa . . ." he began, and I knew what was coming. "This may be a little premature, may not be the perfect time, but I have to ask you . . . will you do me the honor . . . will you marry me?"

I wasn't prepared. I hadn't expected a proposal that evening. And what could I say? I couldn't say "no." I couldn't let him return to war burdened further by my rejection. I thought of Tom, and I heard my mother's words: *Nothing could ever come of it . . . a truly pointless and impossible liaison . . . only lead to heartache—for you and for him* . . . I stared back at Charlie, into those kind blue eyes.

"Yes, Charlie . . . yes, I will marry you."

The foyer of Waterloo station that evening was chock-a-block: parents seeing off sons, wives clinging to husbands, children wrapped around the legs of their fathers.

"This is a bloody nightmare," Charlie said. "Let's get a cup of tea or something."

We walked arm in arm across the heaving concourse to the station restaurant, and inside we managed to find a table tucked away in a corner. As Charlie summoned over a waiter and ordered a pot of tea for two, I removed my gloves and unbuttoned my coat. When I looked up, there he was, sitting a few tables away from us, with a girl.

I didn't quite know what to do. Charlie had his arm around me, was busy saying something about his train and without thinking I moved my chair away from his and looked in the opposite direction. I felt sick. I didn't want to see him with that girl; didn't want him to see me with Charlie.

A moment later he was standing in front of us.

"Oh, hello, Tom," I said, as though we'd seen each other quite recently; as though I didn't really care. "I think you may have met Charlie at Deyning. Charlie, you remember Tom, Tom Cuthbert . . ."

Within a minute the four of us were huddled around the small table: Tom; his girl, Gloria; Charlie and me; looking for all the world like reunited old friends.

"I'm so sorry about William," he said. I nodded but said nothing. I still wasn't able to talk about Will in the past tense. In fact, I didn't like to speak about him at all.

"You know the trains are all cock-a-hoop, old boy? With a bit of luck we may find ourselves stuck here for some time," Charlie said, and then he turned to me and added, "But poor Clarissa so hates these wretched good-byes. Don't you, darling?" And he pulled me to him in an overly tight embrace.

He and Charlie would be traveling on the same train to Dover and as they discussed the journey ahead of them, what time their crossing was likely to be, Gloria leaned toward me. Wide eyed and smiling, she said, "Tom's only had a few days. But we've made the most of it—if you know what I mean," and I felt my face tingle. I glanced over to him, caught his eye.

"Yes," I said. "Yes, of course." I didn't know what else to say to her, didn't want to talk to her.

"You haven't seen him in a while, have you?" she asked, quietly.

"No, it's been . . . been some time," I said, pretending to look for something in my bag. It had been sixteen months.

"I could tell. He looked like he'd seen a

ghost when you walked in here," she whispered.

"So, what have you two lovebirds been up to?" Charlie asked, smiling at Gloria, who giggled. "Making up for lost time, I'll bet!" he added.

I glanced at Tom again, who looked awkward and attempted to smile back at me. And then I stood up and excused myself. In the ladies room I lit a cigarette and smoked it slowly. I was in no hurry to return to our impromptu little tea party and Charlie was irritating me with his bon vivant manner. As I sat in front of the mirror, swaddled in my new fur-collared coat, smoking, I pondered on Tom and his girl: they'd quite obviously spent his entire leave *making up for lost time,* as Charlie had so succinctly put it. What on earth did he see in her? She wasn't his type at all, I thought, and then, as I stubbed out my cigarette, she appeared.

"I do so like your coat, Clarissa," she said. "And I bet it cost a bob or two."

"Thank you," I said, rising to my feet, picking up my bag.

She was short, a good few inches shorter than me, and curvy in a way that was no longer fashionable. Perhaps he liked that shape. Perhaps I was not his type after all.

"Have you and Tom known each other long, Gloria?" I asked, glancing at the mirror and tucking an imaginary curl back in place.

"Oh no, not long at all. But you know how it is—when you feel as though you've known someone forever? That's how it is with us." And then she disappeared behind the lavatory door.

When I returned to the table, Charlie and Tom were drinking glasses of beer.

"You'd better not let anyone see you drinking," I said as I sat down.

The king, along with various members of the government, had recently vowed to abstain from alcohol for the duration of the war, to set an example and encourage others to do the same.

"Ha! I hardly think one beer's going to lead to ruin. And apparently we've another hour, darling. I'm sorry, I know how much you hate these places," he said.

"No, not at all," I replied. And then I leaned over and kissed him on his cheek.

He looked quite bashful for a moment,

glanced at Tom, and said, "Golly, what it is to be loved, eh, Tom?"

Tom said nothing, and I didn't look at him; I continued to stare at Charlie with what I imagined to be love-struck devotion. And even when Gloria sat back down at the table, I kept my gaze resolutely upon Charlie, who glanced back at me with a look I can only describe as muted excitement.

"Would either of you girls like a little something?" Charlie asked, beginning to seem agitated by my continued gazing. "Clarissa? A cocktail, perhaps? I'm sure they'll be able rustle you up *something . . ."*

"Not for me, thanks, Charlie. I don't on Sundays," Gloria said.

"Darling?" Charlie asked again.

"Yes, why not. A glass of champagne, please," I replied.

Gloria giggled again.

"I'm not sure they'll have champagne here, sweetheart . . ." Charlie said, looking about for our waiter. "But I shall go and inquire."

I watched Charlie get up from the table, kept my eyes on him as he moved through the crowd toward the bar, as though mesmerized by some vision just beyond the khaki uniforms. I heard Tom say my name, "Clarissa . . ." but I continued staring in Charlie's direction. I don't know why. But I couldn't bear to turn and look into his eyes.

Then she spoke. "Clarissa . . ."

I turned to her, smiling.

"I think Tom was trying to talk to you, Clarissa."

"Oh, I'm sorry. Yes, Tom?" I said, finally looking directly at him, into his solemn, unsmiling eyes. And for a moment, as he held me there, in silence, I knew that we both wished away our sweethearts. I knew that we were both in agony.

"How is your father? I heard he's been quite ill," he said.

"He's much better now, thank you."

"And your mother? Is she well?"

"She's quite well, thank you. And yours?"

"Yes, she's also well."

He glanced down at my hand, resting on the table, moved his own toward it, and then looked up into my eyes. "And you, Clarissa . . . how are you?"

I stared at him, unable to speak. From the corner of my eye I could see Gloria glancing from me to him then back to me.

"Sorry, darling, no champagne, I'm afraid, so I've ordered you a sherry . . ."

I wrenched my gaze away from Tom to Charlie. "That's perfectly fine," I said. "And perhaps more appropriate. After all, we have nothing to celebrate. Not yet."

Charlie turned to me, smiling, took hold of my hand and said, "Or perhaps we do . . ."

I shook my head, mouthed the word "no." We'd agreed to keep our engagement quiet, at least for the time being, and so no one apart from our respective parents knew. He squeezed my hand, nodded. I glanced over at Tom; he was watching us and I wondered what he'd seen, if he knew.

We sat there for what seemed to me an interminable time. I hardly uttered a word, but Charlie and Gloria chatted animatedly, and Tom managed the situation with a quiet calm. I was aware of him watching me as I sipped my drink, as I glanced about the place, as I smiled from time to time at Charlie and at Gloria, feigning interest in the conversation. I tried not to look at him. I tried but I couldn't. And when I did, when

I finally allowed myself to look back into his eyes, I could barely breathe. My longing for him simply overwhelmed my senses, blocking out all other sight and sound.

"I imagine Clarissa's changed somewhat since you last saw her, eh, Tom?" Charlie said, and I realized he must have noticed Tom staring at me.

"Yes. Yes . . . she's quite grown up," he replied, still looking at me.

Charlie picked up my hand, kissed it. "And you know what? I think I'm the luckiest chap in all of England."

Gloria laughed. "Aah, isn't that lovely," she said, addressing me. "You're a lucky duckie and a half. I wish someone would say that about me," she added, winking at me, and then she glanced at Tom, who'd turned away and was looking across the restaurant.

I pulled my hand away from Charlie and said, "I think we'd best get going now, dear."

And as Charlie finished his drink and summoned the waiter for the bill, he said, "Allow me to get this, Tom." Then he turned to Gloria and said, "It's been a rather pleasant surprise to have had this little seeing-off party to ourselves, has it not?" and she laughed again.

I glanced once more at Tom as Charlie settled the bill, but he didn't look at me. He stared out of a window behind me, frowning, his jaw set. I wondered what he was thinking, and I yearned to touch him: to reach out and take hold of his hand. When we stood up and moved outside to say good-bye, before those final, private adieus on the platform, he simply shook my gloved hand.

"Good-bye, Tom. And good luck," I said, forcing a smile.

He stared at me, into my eyes. "Good-bye, Clarissa."

My heart lurched as he turned and walked away, his girl on his arm, and Charlie must have seen something in my expression, because he said, "Is everything all right, darling? You've been acting a little peculiar all evening."

"These good-byes . . . they're just so wretched," I said.

On the platform, as Charlie held me, I looked for Tom. But I couldn't see him, or his girl.

"You best go now, get yourself a seat," I said.

"So long as you're sure you're fine."

"I'm fine, Charlie, really I am. Bon voyage, sweetheart." He held me, kissed me, but I was distracted—and I know he sensed it. And as he climbed on board the train, I felt my heart shiver. "And Charlie . . . please, do look after yourself."

I stood there for some moments, and then, as the guard passed by, I asked how long until the train departed. He pulled out his pocket watch: "Three minutes, miss," he replied. I moved down the platform, searching the packed carriages, excusing myself as I weaved my way through uniformed soldiers, embracing couples and bags. I know it sounds awful now, as though I didn't care about Charlie—and I did, I really did care—but I had to see Tom again. I knew I'd hear a whistle blow at any moment and that would be it. I knew that I might be making a fool of myself but I didn't care. I knew he had his girl with him but it didn't matter. Nothing mattered. I was almost at the end of the platform when I stopped and glanced through a window, and there he was.

As soon as he saw me we smiled at each other and in a way that would have been enough: enough for me to hold on to and perhaps enough for him too. But he leaped up, disappeared for a moment and then reappeared at the open window of the carriage door. And I was already there, of course. We had seconds.

He reached out and took hold of my hand as I climbed up on to the footboard. He pulled off my glove, held my palm over his mouth; his eyes closed. And I couldn't speak. I wanted to say so much but the words wouldn't come.

Then he looked at me. "Clarissa," he said. And that was all he said: my name. The whistle blew, he let go of my hand and I stepped down. As the carriage lurched and began to pull away I stood perfectly still, my eyes fixed on him: his eyes, his face, and then his outline; until the front of the train curved away, and he disappeared from view.

I stood there for some time watching the packed carriages as they moved along the platform, a blur of khaki and smoke, and unknown smiling faces. And even after the light at the end of the train had vanished I continued to stand there, staring down the empty track into the blackness. I can't recall anyone else on the platform, yet I know it was crowded, that I was surrounded by people. I thought: my heart is on board that train; my heart is bound for France. It wasn't over. It would never be over.

In the taxicab, heading home, I realized I was missing one glove.

Chapter Fourteen

My father died on September the seventh, 1916. He was fifty-eight years old and for me, at least, his death was sudden and premature. He'd never completely regained his former health or vitality after his bout of pneumonia the previous year, and when he became ill for a second time, my mother had feared the worst and tried to prepare me. He was laid to rest in the mausoleum he'd had built at the churchyard close to Deyning.

Three weeks after my father's death, late one evening, we received a telegram. Mama read it outloud. And for an indeterminable time everything stopped, and I was there and not there.

Then I screamed.

A scream so loud it shattered and splintered into a dreadful chorus that rattled and shook my brain and bones and cells and soul. I grabbed the telegram from Mama's hand, threw it on the fire, ran out of the room into the hallway, and then outside, into the square; and I continued running, zigzagging down streets, through mews, on and on, as though I could escape from that moment; escape my brother's death and run back through time.

Eventually, I stopped running. I stood in the darkness on a street corner and looked up at the sky. It's a mistake, I whispered; it's mistaken identity. *Mistaken identity . . . identity mistaken . . . not George . . . would never let himself get killed . . . professional soldier . . . mistake.* Then, shivering, my head pounding, numb with shock and the cold night air, I turned and began to walk home.

When Mama led me upstairs, holding on to my hand, she said to me, "We have to be strong . . . we have to be brave; we have to be heroic, like George and William."

Oh yes, Mama, they're all heroes . . . they're dying by the thousand to be heroes.

She made me take a pill, told me it would help me sleep, calm me. But I didn't need a pill, for there was nothing left in me; no sound to make, nothing to say.

The telegram I'd destroyed had informed us that George had been badly wounded at Flers-Courcelette, and that he'd been taken to a casualty clearing station, where he'd died from his wounds, hours later, on September the seventeenth. George had died exactly ten days after Papa's death, and I wondered if he'd known, and I hoped he had not. Mama had of course written to both him and Henry, but she'd refused to send either of them a telegram and had delayed her letters to each of them until after Papa's funeral.

Still in the depths of a very private grief, my mother was plunged further. And though she'd spoken of bravery and strength, it was then, immediately after this unspeakably cruel coincidence, that I saw her character momentarily crumble. For days after we learned of George's death she remained within her room, in her bed, unable to speak, unable to eat, unable to cry. In the space of twenty-four months she'd lost two of her sons, her husband, and her home.

Unlike Will, George was returned to us. Mama arranged for his body to be collected from Waterloo station and taken to a nearby undertaker. On the evening of his return she finally rose from her bed. She asked me to accompany her to the chapel of rest, but I couldn't bear the thought of seeing George dead, so I waited in the motorcar while she went inside. When she finally emerged from the building and stepped back inside the car, she looked even more fragile, and unspeakably pale. I took hold of her hand, and she turned to me and smiled.

"He's at peace now," she said. "He's with William, and Papa."

The following morning we returned to the chapel of rest, and I watched as my brother's coffin was carefully placed inside the hearse, our wreath of white lilies laid on top. Mama had been adamant that we should accompany him, that he should have every honor befitting a beloved son, a fallen hero. She'd shuddered when the undertaker had visited us and spoken about train times to Guildford and onward connections. "I shall take him," she'd said, as though she planned on driving him there herself.

We followed the hearse slowly and in silence through soot-blackened streets, through the wide leafy avenues of newly built suburbs, and then out on to the meandering country lanes. It had rained heavily overnight and the roads were awash with mud, fallen branches and debris from the fields and hedgerows. A few miles from the churchyard, where the road forks in two and the postbox stands on a grassy triangle, there had been a landslide, forcing us to take a different route: the road past the entrance to Deyning. And I remember thinking, it's meant to be, we have to take George this way. And as we came around the bend in the road, over the brow of the hill, I could see the chimneys, the rooftops in the distance.

I said, "There it is, Mama. There's Deyning." But she didn't look. And even as we passed by the white gate she didn't turn her head.

At the church there were a few of the

staff from the house, including Mrs. Cuthbert, Mr. Broughton and some of the servants from London. Mabel and Edna—both now employed at a factory near Croydon—Stephens and Wilson, Venetia, Aunt Maude and a handful of Mama's friends made up the small gathering of mourners. Inside the tiny church, we prayed for George's soul. We prayed for peace. And we sang. We followed the coffin out of the church, down the muddy pathway toward the mausoleum. And there, I watched my brother's journey end. Weeks away from his twenty-first birthday, his life was over.

. . . ashes to ashes, dust to dust; in sure and certain hope of the Resurrection to eternal life, through our Lord Jesus Christ . . .

I felt my eyes sting, my lip begin to quiver. I turned to Mama, standing next to me. She held her gloved hands firmly in front of her, her heavy black veil concealing any private agony. I heard the iron door close. I glanced over at Maude, who looked to Mama and then moved toward her. I bit my lip, clutched on to my purse. And as I closed my eyes I heard myself whisper my brother's name: *Georgie*.

A few days later a brown paper parcel containing my brother's uniform arrived at our home in London. I unpacked it myself, in the hallway. It stank, was stiff with mud and blood: George's blood. I stood holding it, looking at it, unsure of what to do with it. It wasn't until Mrs. Watson appeared and placed her arms around me that I realized I was crying.

"But what will you do with it?" I asked, as she tried to take it from me.

"It'll have to be burned, miss . . . you can't keep something like that, now can you? And if you ask me, it's not right it's been sent back here, not right at all." She pulled the last remnants of George from my hands. "Should never have been sent here," she repeated. "I'll get Mr. Dunne to deal with it. Now don't you worry . . . you go upstairs and Mrs. Watson'll bring you a nice cup of tea."

I saw them do it. Saw them burn it, in the garden outside. I watched from my bedroom window. George's blood, posted back to us for old times' sake, rose up in a plume of dark gray smoke and disappeared into the London dusk. And Mama knew nothing about it.

In the weeks that followed, ever mindful of her own decorum, my mother struggled to regain her former equilibrium, but she appeared unsure of herself and, I suppose, of the events taking place around her—over which she had no control. She became needy of me, reluctant to leave the house, and she fretted endlessly about Henry, the last of her boys. Her boys: her three boys, now one. Looking back, I realize it was also around this time that she began to worry about money.

I comforted myself with the knowledge that George, a born soldier, had died as he would have wished: in battle, fighting for his country. Unlike Will, and a professional soldier, George had never had any doubt about his duty; never been tortured by any moral dilemma about the notion of war or, it seemed, of killing men. I remembered the debates my brothers had had in those tense days immediately before war was declared. George had been resolute, uncompromising in his views, while Will had prevaricated, and Henry been somewhat flippant.

Without Papa, and with Henry away, I had to be strong. I heard my father's voice in my head: "You must be strong, Clarissa . . . stay strong for your mama." And so for a number of weeks, perhaps even months, I ran my mother's home. I dealt with the servants, handled the accounts and tried to keep the place looking as it always had. I wrote to friends and family, and I wrote to Henry, informing him of George's death. I mourned my brother, cried in private, and I wondered not if, but when another telegram would arrive. What then would we do?

The intoxication of youth, snuffed out, extinguished in a matter of months, left in its place only a numbing sobriety. For too many young souls had already been sacrificed, too many lives shattered. And to those of us left standing, impotent, on the sideline, with splintered hearts and broken dreams, light had all but vanished from our lives. No matter what happened in the future, things could not be undone. George and William, and thousands upon thousands of other young men would never be coming home. None of us could return to that briefest of moments before the war, when the heady anticipation of a life unfulfilled lay before us. It had gone forever.

Each day I had studied the casualty list published in the newspaper, running my finger down it, quietly saying the names out loud and all the time silently pleading with God for there not to be a Granville, a Boyd or a Cuthbert on the list. But after George's death I stopped looking. I no longer wished to see that ever-growing list of names. I even suggested to Mama that we cancel our daily newspaper delivery. But she was insistent upon following events. As long as Henry and others she knew were out there in the trenches, she could not abandon her vigil.

Like me, the newspaper editors appeared to be growing demoralized and losing their patriotic fervor. They were preoccupied by the country's grievances, and the outcry against the food shortage seemed to outweigh the outcry against the guns and munitions shortage. A "Food Controller" was hastily appointed by the government, but with German submarines increasing in number almost daily, there was little for him to control. There were complaints, too, that too many shirkers had evaded the "call-up," that Mr. Asquith and his government had not been forceful enough, and the whole country seemed to be in an angry, malevolent mood.

Night raids had become more frequent. The maroons* sounded and I'd head down the four flights of stairs, from plain carpet to patterned carpet to marble and then, finally, to the linoleum of the cellar steps, along with Mama, Mrs. Watson, Mr. Dunne, and whomever else was in the house at that time. There, we'd all sit around an old pine table, trying to play cards by candlelight, once or twice to a juddering vibration, and the tinkling of the chandelier in the hallway above us. I'd watch Mama fix her gaze upon the ceiling, concentrating, willing the monstrous thing not to fall. But I can't recall any hysteria or melodramatic outburst. When the all-clear eventually sounded, there was never a rush, never an immediate departure back up the linoleum-covered steps. We'd all invariably sigh, sit in silence for a few minutes, then, slowly, collect ourselves and begin the move back upstairs by candlelight: Mama to her Chippendale Chinoiserie and hand-painted silk walls; me to my rosebuds.

---

* Commonly used term for alarms during World War I.

Mama continued going to church and, though I usually accompanied her, I'd begun to feel ambivalent about a god who presided over so much death and destruction. I no longer wished to take Holy Communion, though I did, simply to keep Mama happy. The body and the blood of Christ: what did it mean anymore? I mimed the words of hymns; *all things bright and beautiful* and England's *green and pleasant land* no longer resonated with the times. And I found myself questioning the words of our prayers. *He that believeth in me, though he were dead, yet shall he live: and whosoever liveth and believeth in me, shall never die.* But there could be no resurrection, I thought; no bugle would ever herald *their* return. The dead were dead and would never be coming home. They lay buried in the bloodred mud of another country for all eternity. How serene could peace be after this? How sweet would any victory be?

Even though I walk through the valley of the shadow of death, I will fear no evil . . .

The valley of the shadow of death . . . it seemed to me a fittingly concise description of our country. For though we weren't living in those squalid trenches, though we weren't facing that endless barrage, we were living through a time of extraordinary darkness, when life seemed only to be about death.

I had heard nothing from Tom, nothing at all, but Mama had been kind enough to tell me that Mrs. Cuthbert was well, and still at Deyning. Then, one evening, as we sat playing piquet, she said, "I hear Tom Cuthbert's an officer now . . . a captain. He was mentioned in dispatches . . ."

And there he was again.

I imagine she thought it safe to mention him, now that I was engaged to be married. Both she and Papa had been delighted by my engagement. She'd told me that I'd made my father very proud, and happy; that it was the one good piece of news in years.

"Oh really?" I replied, without looking up.

"I know you quite liked him, Clarissa. I know you and he had a . . . a friendship," she continued, arranging the cards in her hand, "but it could never have worked, never. You must realize that by now," she added.

I glanced up from my cards. For a moment I contemplated saying something; telling her that I hadn't *liked* him, I'd loved him, and always would; that it wasn't a friendship, it was a love affair. But then I thought better of it. After all, she'd been through so much.

I looked back at my cards. "Mrs. Cuthbert must be very proud of him," I said.

"I'm sure. He was a nice enough chap. Your father always said that, had a great deal of time for him."

I looked up at her. "Yes, I think he rather liked him."

She smiled, closed her eyes for a moment. "I'm sure he did, but he was a servant, dear. I don't suppose your father would have liked the idea of him as your suitor."

"He was not a servant, Mama. He was studying, studying law . . . and he may yet end up practicing it."

"And good luck to him. I hope that he survives this wretched war and makes something of his life. But you, my dear . . . well, your life was always destined to be *quite* different than his. And still will be. Quite different."

I stared at her. "All our lives will be different after this war, Mama. Look at us: our lives have already changed."

I felt irritated by the way my mother was talking. How was I so different now? How were we so different? Her sons had been as fallible as any others on the battlefield.

She looked down at her cards, sighed. "Clarissa, Clarissa . . . your head's always so full of romantic notions. We must accept the life we're born into, my dear, no matter how irksome or dull we find it at times. The war will end . . . one day, hopefully soon, and then you shall resume your life. You'll marry; have a family, a home of your own. And Charlie will make a fine husband. A very fine husband."

I said nothing more. Mama still had her dreams for me: an eligible husband, Charlie; a big society wedding; a town house and a country house; children. But I was already having doubts: doubts about marrying Charlie, doubts about everything. Nothing seemed certain, and I wasn't sure what, exactly, I wanted in my life any more; wasn't even entirely sure who *I* was anymore. The girl I'd once been, the girl who'd been able to imagine the future—glistening with promise—had gone. I could no longer see ahead, no longer see the possibilities. And if Tom Cuthbert wasn't to be part of my future, what was there? For he had starred in every fantasy, each and every dream.

I still thought of him, dreamed of him, but so much had changed, and my life in London had propelled me down a path he was not on. I had no idea where he was, how he felt or what he was thinking. I knew nothing other than the fact he was alive, somewhere. For news of any death traveled quickly and my mother's continued obsession with the daily fatality list ensured an up-to-date, albeit grim, knowledge of our ever-diminishing circle of friends and acquaintances. He may have met someone, may be engaged; may even have married Gloria, I thought.

If I'd received one letter, a note, anything at all, I'd have stopped my progression down that path. But there was nothing. He'd never written to me after our meeting at the station that day, and though I'd hoped, even prayed, that our paths might cross again, somewhere, anywhere, they had not. I'd half expected to see him at some party or other; there were always so many army personnel and officers, and I'd gone to any number searching for him among the uniforms. I'd scan rooms looking for his face, and occasionally my eyes would pick out a tall, dark-haired man in the crowd and my heart skipped a beat. But it was never him. Why would it be? He was not part of the crowd I mixed with in London. His life wasn't there and never had been. And I was weary from longing, exhausted by my imaginings, and all those anticipated meetings and reconciliations. So I began to tell myself that Tom Cuthbert would never be part of my life again; that he was a memory.

When Henry had come home on leave, he'd done his best to be like Papa. He'd sat in Papa's place, assured Mama and me that all would be well. But things were changing, and changing rapidly. Unbeknown to any of us, Deyning had been mortgaged. My father, ever the entrepreneur, had taken risks on the stock market and his losses, which he'd kept from almost everyone, had in all likelihood contributed toward his ailing health. Now death duties coupled with those losses meant that Deyning would probably have to be sold. Henry had done the sums, with a lawyer, of course. It was simply too expensive to run, he said, and, with the servant problem, much too much of a headache. He'd sat down with Mama and me to try to explain this to us.

"No," Mama said, quite emphatically, "Deyning is your birthright, your inheritance, Henry. Things will get better once this wretched war ends . . . and then, then our lives will resume. Things will return to normal *and* we shall return to Deyning."

"I agree with Mama," I said. "We can't possibly sell Deyning, Henry . . . it's our home."

Henry sighed, shook his head. "I don't believe things will be the same, and, as much as it saddens me, I don't in all honesty believe that we'll be able to keep Deyning."

Mama laughed. "Rubbish! This country has survived many a war. One doesn't start reinventing oneself simply because of a war, dear. We have to stand firm and together, and we have to hold on to all that we believe in, all that we are. Papa would turn in his grave to hear you speaking this way. Deyning was everything to him, you know that . . . and the costs, the servants, well, perhaps we shall have to do what they call *economize* . . . run with fewer servants, though for the life of me I can't imagine how. But . . . if it has to be so, then it has to be so."

I saw Henry shake his head again, but he left it at that. There was no point in trying to convince Mama, certainly not at that time. Later, I wrote to Charlie: "Everything is changing. Nothing is fixed or certain anymore."

Ƨ

. . . **Can you believe they sent his uniform home to us? Mr. D set fire to it outside in the garden, and I watched it as it burned . . . I still can't believe he is gone, that both of them are gone, & in so short a space of time. I keep expecting one of them—both of them—to appear here, on the doorstep, in the hallway, poking a head around my door, just as they always did, bright-eyed** little boys smiling back at me. And this is what I dream of, night after night. . . . I try to comfort myself with the knowledge that they were loved, and enjoyed a supremely happy childhood & youth, but yes, a part of me is angry. And, in my darkest and most private moments, & though I know it's hideous and selfish, and that others have suffered just as much, I find myself wishing that He could have taken another, another two, and spared mine. And I wonder, am I culpable? For I let them go . . . encouraged them, and despite knowing how cruel it would be. And now I keep thinking if W hadn't joined the RFC—hadn't gone up in one of those wretched machines—he might still be here, & if G hadn't been so very brave & hadn't gone back to get that boy—he'd still be here . . . but people tell me how noble their (& my) sacrifice, and speak so poetically of Heroism. And though at first I thought I might not live, & felt all my courage slip away, & so much so that I was unable to move or feel or speak or think, it has slowly returned, enough for me to continue living. And of course,

I owe it to them, and to those still here. But life will never be the same, & I shall never be the same, for something in me is broken and can never now be mended.

Chapter Fifteen

∽

. . . They played a searchlight on us all through the night & then at dawn the bombardment started—the very worst I have experienced so far, with shells raining down all around us . . . it lasted an hour perhaps, no more, but so intense that my ears, head, hands and heart continued to ring & tremble & vibrate for hours afterward. Three of our horses were killed, and later, we had to load the mutilated carcasses onto a wagon and then bury them in a ready-made ditch close by. I hate this place. Hate all of it, & with every part of

my being, and yet I know this hatred might very well help keep me alive . . .

∽

I didn't particularly feel like going out to a party that night, but both Henry and Charlie were home on leave, and Henry was keen to be out and about "on the circuit," as he called it. Food rationing had begun to affect everything, and though restaurants remained open, most had cut down to one or two courses, and—like the theaters—closed early. But behind shuttered windows the whoopla of a party and thumping of a piano could be heard most nights. Nightclubs had arrived in London and bands played on until the small hours; for those boys home on leave were determined to have a good time. We were all determined to have a Good Time.

I spent longer than usual getting ready that evening. I think I almost preferred the anticipation to any actual event. Those idle hours languishing in my bath, listening to music from the gramophone next door; then selecting a gown, and jewelry. Perhaps it was because the evening still lay ahead, uncharted and unknown. It could be anything I wished for it to be. And I loved my room. Mama had allowed me to select new wallpaper and furnishings when we'd moved up permanently from Deyning, and I'd created a rosebudded sanctuary, with matching wall coverings, curtains and bedspread. It was a girlish symphony of pink, and it reminded me of the old rose garden at Deyning.

That evening I chose to wear a navy blue satin gown, one I'd worn before, the previous week, but one Charlie hadn't yet seen and one I knew he'd like. It suited me well, and Henry had told me I'd be "sure to capture any man's heart in that dress." I'd borrowed Mama's diamond choker, again, and wore her blue fox stole over my shoulders. The three of us—Henry, Charlie and I—drove only two streets away, to drinks at the Millingtons' before heading on to Venetia's son Jimmy's party on South Audley Street. Although Jimmy had been at school with Henry and Charlie, he had gone on to Oxford, not Cambridge, and he was the only one of Henry's friends, apart from Charlie, whom I genuinely liked. I wondered then if Henry's affair with Venetia had ended, or if it was still going on. I'd never mentioned it to anyone, and now it didn't seem important. I no longer cared whom my elder brother was sleeping with, just so long as he was alive.

We could hear the revelry as soon as we pulled up outside Jimmy's. "Sounds promising," Henry said, rubbing his hands together. Inside, the place was heaving; the hallway jam-packed with people, noise and smoke; faces I knew and a few I didn't. Almost all of the men were in uniform and everyone seemed exuberant, over-animated. I think back now and realize there was an air of desperation at those parties; as though each one had to be better than the last; as though each one was the last.

We'd been there a little while when Charlie and Henry disappeared off together in search of a bottle and I found myself ensconced in a corner of the hallway with Rose Millington—whom I'd just seen at her parents' house—and a few others. I was laughing at Rose's impersonation of her mother—she was so funny, a brilliant mimic—and as I turned away, as I turned away from her, laughing, I glanced up and saw him: sitting on the staircase, watching me. And I looked away quickly, I'm not sure why, perhaps because it had happened before; because I'd been to any number of parties where I thought I'd spotted him, only to realize it wasn't him. I thought I'd imagined it. So, I turned again, slowly, and looked back.

I felt my stomach tighten, couldn't move; couldn't even smile. And I can't recall him moving down the staircase, but a moment later he was standing in front of me.

"Hello, Clarissa," he said, so close we were almost touching.

"Tom . . . what are you doing here?"

I didn't mean it as it sounded. I was shocked, unprepared.

He raised one side of his mouth, half smiling in that way I remembered. "I bumped into Jimmy on the boat train yesterday," he said. "I saw you arrive, was on the stairs . . . thought you'd seen me."

I shook my head. "No . . . no, I didn't see you."

His face had changed: older, thinner, and so very pale, as though he had not been out in the sun for years. Like most of the others he'd grown a mustache, and that wave of almost black hair, which had once hung down over his eyes, had gone. And those eyes—staring back into mine—seemed darker, with a new intensity, a new depth and vulnerability to them.

"I've three days' leave. I'm heading down to Deyning tomorrow," he said, and then he frowned. "I was so sorry to hear about your father . . ."

"And I imagine . . . I imagine you know about George," I said.

He nodded. "Yes, I heard. You've been through such an awful time, Clarissa . . . awful."

"No different than anyone else really. Life's not exactly turned out the way we all expected, has it?"

He looked down, shook his head.

"But you're here," I added, desperate to lighten the ambience, "and that . . . that *is* good."

He bit his lip, looked back at me, his head tilted to one side, and I placed my hand upon his arm. "I can't begin to imagine what's it been like for you, Tom . . . what it must be like out there."

And because he didn't speak, didn't reply, and because I thought I needed to fill that silence with words, I continued. "And I've thought of you . . . I've wondered about you, how you are, where you are . . . and wondered if our paths would cross . . . and now . . . now they have."

But he said nothing. And then, for what seemed to me an interminable time, but may have only been seconds, we held each other's gaze; and in that time, in that look, we said everything. And without any sound, without any words spoken, I heard him think my name, over and over.

"Are you going to introduce us, Clarissa?"

I turned. Rose was standing at my side, her eyes fixed on Tom.

"Yes, of course . . . Rose, this is Tom . . . Tom Cuthbert, an old friend of mine, from Deyning."

"How do you do," she said, extending her hand, and no doubt expecting him to take it to his lips. But he didn't. He glanced at her, shook her hand and smiled politely, then looked back to me.

"You must forgive me, Rose. I haven't seen Clarissa for some time and I'm keen to hear her news . . ."

"Oh. Oh, I see. Yes, of course, don't

mind me," she replied, and turned back toward the others.

It was so crowded in that hallway, with people arriving all the time, calling out to friends they recognized and loudly pushing forward. And forced even closer by the crush of that revelry, I grabbed hold of his shoulder to steady myself, and he put his arm around me and held me to him. In that great swell of bodies no one could see the firmness of his hold, my arms around him, our bodies pressed together. Neither of us spoke, we simply stood there, looking at each other, dazed by our sudden reconciliation.

"Is Gloria here?"

"It was nothing, Clarissa. It meant nothing."

"I rather think it did to her."

"Perhaps, but it's the way of the war," he said.

"You never wrote to me."

He shook his head. "I wrote. Please, can we go somewhere? I think we need to talk."

"Yes, but I need to—" I began, but he took hold of my hand, and gripping it as though his life depended on it, he led me through that merry chaos and out of the front door.

Outside, people loitered on the steps, smoking, and leaned against the railings in intense, intimate conversation. And it felt strange, almost illicit, to be out there, alone—with him.

"I can't stay out here," I said, pulling my hand from his. "Henry's here and he'll—"

"And he'll tell your mama? Let me have a moment with you, please? Just a moment, Clarissa."

"But I'm cold," I said, shivering, and he took off his regimental jacket, placed it around my shoulders, then lit us both a cigarette.

"I wrote to you . . ." he said, and then sighed. "I wanted to tell you, wanted to tell you that day at the station. The reason you didn't receive my letters, Clarissa, is because your mother intercepted them. She found out—don't ask me how—about your arrangement with Broughton. And she spoke to my mother." He paused. "She asked my mother to inform me that I was, under no circumstances, to correspond with her daughter again," he added, imitating Mama's voice, and pulling his jacket around me more tightly. "I wanted to write to you," he continued. "I longed to write to you. I wanted to tell you all of this, but there was no way I could. I knew you were here, in London, but I knew that if I wrote to you here your mother would simply take my letters."

I didn't say anything. I was piecing things together, running over what he'd told me in my mind. Mama had taken his letters; his letters to *me*.

"Clarissa . . ."

"Let's walk," I said.

"But . . . Henry?"

"He'll not notice. Has he seen you? Does he know you're here?"

"No, I'm not sure . . . I don't think so."

"Come along then," I said, taking hold of his arm.

We walked down the street slowly, in silence. Then, a little faster, we crossed Park Lane and entered Hyde Park. It was black and it was cold, but all I wanted was some time alone with him. All I wanted was to feel his arms around me once more and know that he was mine.

We moved quickly across the grass, under the low branches, and then up against the damp bark, he pulled me to him. "Clarissa . . ." he whispered, taking my head in his hands, and then his mouth was over mine, his tongue wrapping itself around my own. He moved his lips down my neck on to my shoulder, murmuring my name again. And as I lifted his head I traced the contours of his face with my fingers. I found his mouth with my own, pushed my tongue into it as his hands moved up through my hair, cradling my head as we kissed. And as I sank further into a state of bliss, I heard myself say his name and drew him closer, wrapping him into me, into his jacket, so that we were cocooned, melting into the ancient tree; invisible to the world, lost in the blackness.

And as his kisses became harder, more desperate, I felt his hands move over my breasts, down my gown to my hips; his breath quickening as he lifted folds of satin, his open mouth pressed to my neck. I heard him moan as his fingers strayed above my stockings, caressing my bare flesh. And I was lost; I was nowhere. Nothing existed other than him, his touch. I moved my hands down his back, on to his buttocks, pulling him to me. All I knew was my own desire. He was there; he was real. I couldn't see him but I could hear him, taste him, smell him. And lost in that blindness—in the heart of a city at war—we had found each other again.

He moved, tugging at the belt of his trousers, and then I felt his fingers: pulling aside silk, probing; pushing gently. I heard myself say his name again, and I didn't care. I was conscious only of my need, his need, our hunger for each other; and then him, inside me; his hands easing me up to him, on to him; my legs wrapped around him, his mouth over mine. And all at once I was rising on a great swell; floating away from him, away from myself, up, up into the ether. I was the night, I was the darkness; I was the universe. I heard myself cry out as his body tensed, and then I heard my name, in one long, breathless shudder.

When I opened my eyes I could see. I could see the lights of the city glinting through the trees; hear the traffic in the distance.

"Please . . ." he whispered. "Wait for me, Clarissa. Tell me you'll wait for me . . ."

"I'll wait for you, my darling. I promise I'll wait for you."

We walked back across the park, hand in hand, stopping to kiss each other with every few steps. And then, as we neared the house, we pulled away. Once inside, I excused myself and went upstairs to the bathroom. I looked at myself in the mirror: I appeared quite different, I thought. I was pink cheeked, yes, and a little disheveled. But there was something altogether changed about me. I smiled at my reflection, splashed cold water on to my face and then pressed it into the soft white hand towel. I checked my dress, pulled off my new silk camiknickers and pushed them into my evening bag. I took out my tiny hairbrush, tidied my hair; dabbed my nose with powder.

I loved Tom Cuthbert and after the war was over we would be married. I had no doubts. Even if we had to elope, it *would* happen.

Tom was waiting for me at the bottom of the stairs, and as I descended, sidestepping people and glasses, he watched me intently, smiling. We had a new secret now. As I reached his side he slipped his hand around mine and squeezed it tightly. And then he turned in toward me. "You're *so* beautiful," he whispered. "I want you . . . again."

I turned to look at him. He was the most handsome man there, I thought. And soon we'd have to part again; for how long, I wasn't sure. I wanted to give him something, wanted him to have something of mine, but what? I reached inside my bag, pulled out the tiny roll of flimsy silk and pushed it into his pocket.

"What's that?" he asked.

"Something for you. Something for you to remember me by," I said, looking into his eyes, smiling.

"As long as I know you're mine—I don't need anything else."

"I'm yours. You must know that by now."

"Yes," he said. "Yes, I think I know that."

"Ah! There you are! And look who you've found. I'll be damned . . . Tom Cuthbert!" It was Henry, worse the wear from drink, and unsteady on his feet. I let go of Tom's hand. "Charlie's been looking for you, sis . . . Tom, my man! How the hell are you?"

"Really? We've been here all the time," I said, without flinching, as Tom took hold of Henry's outstretched hand.

Henry swayed, his eyes half closed, and

then turned and shouted over to Charlie, who wound his way over to us.

"Clarissa . . . I've been looking all over for you . . ."

"Then you need to get your eyes tested, Charlie Boyd. I've been here with Tom, catching up . . . remembering old times."

I said good-bye to him that night without a kiss, or a handshake, without any sign at all. I walked away. I had to. What else could I do? At the door, as we said good night to Jimmy and a few others, I looked back for him but he wasn't there. He'd disappeared, as if he'd been part of a dream.

Later, in my bed, I closed my eyes and relived each second of our time together. I could still feel his hands; still taste him in my mouth. And beyond my window, somewhere in the city, I knew he was thinking of me, dreaming of me. I had no idea where, what street or under which roof, but it didn't matter. Out there in the ether our spirits remained entwined.

Despite everything, despite everything that happened afterward, I've never for one moment regretted that night in the park. I wanted Tom to be my first. I wanted Tom. It was our moment and I knew it may never come again, and if it didn't, if we hadn't made love then and there, I'd have regretted it for the rest of my life. It had to be, was meant to be. Some things are.

Chapter Sixteen

. . . The landscape here is quite blown to pieces: farms, churches, villages and towns simply reduced to piles of stone & rubble, & the trees—entirely stripped, no more than charred stumps, protruding from the churned-up earth like ghosts. And the guns go on and on . . . But I think I have become immune to it all, the horror. Unimaginable sights, which not so very long ago would have made me ill, have little impact now. The dysentery is possibly the worst thing, truly awful, & robs the men of what little dignity they have left—before it kills

them . . . The stench & the noise are enough to make a man insane. We are all desensitized, completely brutalized, but it seems to me the only way to survive . . .

∽

Outside my window there was a tree. I watched its leaves turn from palest gold to burnished copper. I watched them fall, fluttering against my windowpane, tumbling through damp air to the sodden path beneath. I looked out through naked branches to an unknown, opaque sky, heard the sighs of time with each tick of the clock. And as my belly grew, daylight dwindled.

Emily Cuthbert Granville was born on Monday, November the twelfth 1917, with a mop of dark hair and brilliant blue eyes, at St. Anne's, a convent and a type of nursing home, in Plymouth, Devon. She weighed almost eight pounds at birth and she was, the sisters told me, one of the healthiest and most robust babies they'd had in a long while. We weren't Catholic, but it was the place my mother had chosen for me to stay for the duration of my confinement. Aunt Maude lived in Taunton, and it was, Mama had said, perfectly feasible that I should have gone to stay there for a while, with family, and quite enough to tell people. There could be no further communication with Tom Cuthbert, she said, not now, not ever. And she would make sure that no one knew anything, for *no one* could know: not him, his mother, or even Henry . . . no one.

"I hardly know what to say to you, Clarissa," she'd said to me, after Dr. Riley left the house that day; the day he confirmed what I already knew and what Mama had undoubtedly suspected. I had just confessed, only just told her the name. And as I'd spoken his name, I'd seen her wince. There was a sharp intake of breath as she raised her hand to her chest and then closed her eyes, as though at that very same moment she'd experienced a sudden and acute pain. For some minutes she did not speak, and then she said, "I never want to hear you speak his name again." She opened her eyes. "And I hope we never—either of us—set eyes on him again."

She sat in the armchair by the window

in my room, looking anywhere except at me, still lying upon my bed, fully clothed; for Dr. Riley hadn't taken long to deliver his prognosis. He'd asked me a few simple questions, in his usual quiet and kindly way, and smiling at me all the while: could I recall when I had last menstruated? Did my breasts feel somewhat tender, larger? Had my waist thickened . . . were my clothes a little tighter? Then he'd asked me to lift my blouse and unbutton my skirt. He pressed his hand down upon my distended abdomen. "Hmm, yes," he said, and then turned to Mama and nodded.

Mama did not visit me in Plymouth. It was much too complicated, she said, and anyway, she needed to be in London for Henry. Aunt Maude was my only visitor during my stay at St. Anne's. She came each week, on Wednesday afternoon: the only day we were allowed visitors. Charlie continued to write to me, care of Maude, and she brought his letters, along with any from Mama, and took away my replies. I pretended to Charlie that I was having a splendid time in Taunton; that life was gay and all was well. I invented excursions, events, even conversations. And in his letters he told me how very sensible it was for Mama to have sent me there, and how much he longed to see me. He told me that he loved me and that when the war was over we would be married. And, if I still loved Devon, he'd buy a cottage for me there.

My mother's letters to me were measured, formal, and always without any reference to the circumstances. I could easily have been a friend, an acquaintance even, on holiday in Devon. She updated me on the weather in London, her visitors, and on Henry's movements and news. And she always included a précis of her recent correspondence: who was where, with whom and doing what. Each letter ended, "You are ever in my prayers . . ."

But Mama and our house in Berkeley Square felt so far away, so long ago; for days in Devon lasted longer, much longer than days in London. And I inhabited a dimly lit world. A world, it seems to me now, without any dawn or sunset; a place adrift, almost outside of time. Minutes flattened, stretching into shapeless hours; days merged with nights, weeks with months. I used my voice little, and my eyes

even less. I retreated to that place of imagined warmth and light, breathed in the
scents of lavender, jasmine and rose; I
stood under a Sussex sky, the clouds high
above, the cornfields in the distance, and
Tom—watching me.

Kiss me . . . kiss me now . . .

I made only one friend at St. Anne's: her
name was Edith Collins. Edith was a year
younger than me, though she could easily
have passed for five years older. I can't
recall where, exactly, she came from, but
she'd been working as a kitchen maid in a
large house somewhere in the West Country and had "fallen"—as she put it—to the
son of her employer. I don't think I saw her
shed a tear once. Her approach was pragmatic, her attitude one of defiant optimism;
she would put this behind her and move
on, she said, although she wasn't entirely
confident that it wouldn't happen again.
"What would I do with a baby?" she said.
"Far better for him to have a life with a
proper family than be stuck with me."

At first I didn't tell Edith too much about
myself, or my circumstances, and she, still
mindful of her place, didn't ask. Mama
had made me swear never to tell a living

soul of my predicament; had made me promise to never again mention the name *Tom Cuthbert*, to anyone. But after knowing Edith for a few weeks, and realizing that I'd probably never again see her, I decided to tell her my story. Unlike her, I cried the whole way through my shameful confession.

"But what's the problem? You love him, he loves you—you could get married . . ." she said, putting her arm around me.

"No, no," I said, shaking my head, still crying. "You don't understand. It's impossible . . . would never be allowed."

"Says who, your mother? You could elope . . . you could, you know. Plenty have."

I tried to explain. I told her that Tom wasn't even aware I was having his child, and then, through my sobs, that he may not even be alive. "It's hopeless, Edith . . ."

For nineteen days I nursed my baby. And each day, as I held her, I watched the dusk descend earlier and earlier: a damp, colorless blanket enshrouding that unfamiliar place. For nineteen days I watched her feed and sleep and grow. Her tiny pink fingers curled tightly around my own as she suckled at my breast, a silent drizzle weeping at my window. I sat by her crib, studying her features, memorizing her perfect face, listening to the sound of her breathing. For nineteen days she belonged to me.

I told her all about her father, and about Deyning. I described the gardens, the house, each room, my bedroom, reminding myself of who I'd once been. I took her for walks through my memory; following all those familiar paths to secret places. I carried her through the fields, walked down through the lower meadow and stood with her by the lake. I showed her off and introduced her to people she'd never meet, a life she'd never know, and that place called home.

⌒

. . . **Home, it has become an ideal, like heaven, inhabited by angels. A place we dream about & speak of & long for. And all those things we once complained about, found irritating & annoying, those people we disliked & avoided, those places so dull and dreary to our untired, untrained eyes, we now long**

for, & would surely welcome with joy & open arms. Out here, the next best thing to Home is Heaven, and so each day hundreds gallantly march across that threshold, like a doorway back to safety . . .

⁓

I wrote to Tom: *I wonder where you are now, if these words will ever be read . . . and if you will ever come back to me. We have a baby, my darling, a beautiful baby girl, but I can't keep her . . . I'm not allowed to keep her.*

And then I tore up my words.

The night before they came, Edith handed me a small green bottle. She instructed me to mix its contents with a little of the quinine, in a separate bottle. It would help me sleep and, she said, soothe my nerves. The sisters had told me that Emily would, eventually, go to a good home; to a childless couple who'd prayed for a perfect little baby girl just like mine. There was nothing for me to fret about, all would be well; and once I'd recovered I could make a new start. It would take time, they said, but my baby would be loved and cherished, and surely that was what mattered. I must pray, they said; pray to the Good Lord for his forgiveness and for his blessings upon my poor illegitimate daughter.

When they lifted her from my arms I was in a laudanum haze, scarcely stirring and conscious of nothing but the vaguest sense of being alive. And then, for some reason, came the words of the twenty-third psalm: *Even though I walk through the valley of the shadow of death, I will fear no evil . . .*

Later, I did pray, but not for God's forgiveness: I prayed for my daughter's forgiveness. I prayed that one day she would find it in her heart to know and understand my actions. And I prayed that one day we'd find each other; that I'd be able to hold her and love her again. I don't remember much about that time now, and in the years that have since passed I've tried to understand why my mother did what she did. I tell myself, she did what she believed was right; she did what she thought was best. It was different then.

It was different then . . .

Two days after Emily left St. Anne's, I

did too. I said good-bye to Edith, whose own baby was due any day, and I returned to London on the train, accompanied by Aunt Maude. I stared up out of the carriage window at the bruised sky hanging over England: all black, blue, pale purple, gray and yellow. Beneath it, a dark patchwork of meadows and pastures, sewn together by hedgerow and thicket; then a farm, a cottage; and every so often the huddled stone and steeple of a village. I thought of the people inside those farms and houses and cottages, gathered around a fire, or perhaps in the kitchen by the range, and I wondered if Emily would soon be carried into one of those homes; if she'd be held and made warm.

Maude tried hard not to mention her. She spoke of trivial things, chitchat, and gossip. Edina was living in London, working as a nurse at one of the general hospitals, and had recently become engaged to a doctor. Lucy remained at home with her parents. Maude had already lost both of her sons, my cousins. Archie had been dead for over a year, and Johnnie killed that June. And she spoke about the war: the war, the war, the bloody war. At that moment it was a background noise in my life. An irritation I didn't need; something I didn't want to think about or hear about. And then, when she finally said, "It'll all come good, Clarissa. It's for the best," I began to cry again, and so did she.

It was dusk when we arrived at Paddington, and as I stepped off the train onto the platform, I remembered the girl with the swollen belly who'd passed through that same station months before, and I stopped, and placed my hand upon my stomach. Maude took hold of my arm, but for a moment I could neither move nor speak. "Come along, dear," she said. "Your mother will be waiting." And I contemplated running, where to I don't know; perhaps back on to the train, back to Plymouth.

"I don't want to go home," I said.

"Oh now, don't be silly, dear. Your mama is longing to see you . . . longing to see you."

As we passed through the streets of London, heading from the station toward my mother's home, I noticed the shop windows, ablaze with twinkling lights and tinsel, festooned Christmas trees and garlands. I hadn't thought of Christmas, hadn't realized it was upon us. I felt as though I was returning from a long exile in another country, as though I'd been away for years.

At the house, as the cab driver lifted our bags out onto the pavement, my mother appeared at the door. She never opened her own front door and, looking back, I suppose that in itself was a gesture. But it meant nothing to me at the time. She took me in her arms and held me. I remember her perfume, so familiar; my lips touching the pearls of the choker she wore around her neck. She looked as she always did: immaculate and in control. And I felt nothing. Nothing at all.

Inside, the house looked exactly the same. And it struck me then how queer that while my life had been turned upside down, nothing in my mother's home was in any way altered. There were flowers, a winter arrangement, I think, of berried holly and white roses on the hallway table; a fire burned there and another in the drawing room, where a maid I'd never met before brought in the tea tray. As Mama and Maude discussed the journey and our timings, the maid served tea, offering me milk and sugar, as though I were a new caller. I watched my mother as she spoke with Maude; saw her glance across at me once or twice, then lift her hand, trying to find a curl she could twist and tuck back in place.

"We've already had so many heavy frosts," she said to Maude, "the pavements have been lethal, quite lethal. Only this morning I had to ask Dunne to put down more salt on the steps outside."

I sat in silent numbness, felt myself disappearing, shrinking in front of them: a fallen woman, a disgraced daughter, indelibly stained. When, eventually, I rose to my feet and asked to excuse myself—to unpack, I said—Mama looked at me anxiously and said, "Yes, you do look a little pale, dear. Perhaps you need to rest after your journey."

My journey, my journey . . . the one you sent me on.

That night I did not go down to dinner and I have no idea what Mama and her sister spoke of. Did they mention me? Did they talk about my baby, the baby I'd given away for Christmas? I don't know, and at the time I didn't care. I never wanted to leave my room again. I wanted to disappear, forever. Later, she came to my room, sat down upon my bed and took my hand in hers.

"My darling, what you need is a good night's sleep in your own bed. Everything will seem so much better once you're properly rested."

I looked up into her eyes, those beautiful, doleful eyes. She pushed my hair back from my brow. "Perhaps you'd like me to get Antoine over to do your hair tomorrow, hmm?" she asked, referring to her hairdresser.

I stared at her, felt my eyes sting, but said nothing.

"Well, perhaps later in the week," she said, rising to her feet. She stood still for a moment, her back to me, her hands clasped in front of her, as though she wasn't quite ready to leave the room; as though there was something more she wished to say to me.

"The gels are so looking forward to seeing you again. Rose in particular . . . she's missed you."

Then she left the room.

I heard her footsteps descend the staircase, her door close as she disappeared into her suite of rooms on the lower floor. I rolled onto my side, took hold of a pillow, wrapped my arms around it and held it to me. I closed my eyes, felt the sun on my face, the grass against my legs, and I could see him, there, in the distance: waiting for me.

Maude stayed with us for three days, during which time neither she nor my mother ever mentioned the baby or my time at St. Anne's. After Maude left I wondered if my mother would talk to me, ask me about Emily, her granddaughter, but she did not, and I quickly realized that it was not and never would be a subject for discussion between us.

ᥴᨆ

. . . **The fighting raged on for three days and nights, & yesterday young Norton was struck. I somehow managed to drag him through the mud and back to the trench, but he'd been hit in the stomach and for almost an hour he lay in my arms—crying for his mother. He'd**

told them he was eighteen, but I very much doubt he was even sixteen . . .

⁓

I remember a white moth among the pink rosebuds of my bedroom wall. A small white moth. The only one. It came one day and seemed reluctant to leave, even when I held open the window and tried to coax it out to freedom. Sometimes it moved to another rosebud, another wall, but it was never drawn to the open window. Then, perhaps two days after it first appeared, I could no longer find it amidst the buds upon my wall. I searched the pattern, searched the floor, and then, finally, I found it on the window sill. I picked it up, held it in the palm of my hand. And I wondered again why God created so many beautiful but infinitely fragile things.

I stretched my arm out through the open window, willing it to live. *Fly . . . fly . . .* I watched it as the breeze swept it from my hand. Watched it fall through the air and land upon the roof below. And there it lay, completely still.

The next morning it had gone. I couldn't

be sure if the wind hadn't picked up that tiny white moth, carrying it further across the rooftops of London. But I like to think it had flown.

Strange, the things we remember.

༄

. . . Last night five of us went out on a listening patrol. We crawled on our bellies through a gap in the wire—through the mud into no-man's-land—and tried to get as close as we could. We couldn't hear anything, nothing at all, and no one speaks or even understands German anyway—so it was a hopeless, pointless exercise &—in my opinion—v badly thought through . . . but then so much is here. I suppose the COs are desperate, we're all desperate.

༄

It was Henry who said it, and at the time I was grateful.

Tom.

Hearing his name spoken out loud broke a spell, made him real, and released me from a promise; a solemn but unsigned agreement that had become a burden to my conscience. He said he'd seen him with her at a party; that it was quite obvious they were "at it."

Rose and Tom . . .

"Jeepers, do you remember when you had such a crush on him, Issa?"

"No, not really," I said. "We were friends, Henry, that's all."

We were friends . . . that's all.

"Rubbish. You had the hots for him—and in a big way, as I recall. And you know? I think he rather liked you too."

. . . He rather liked me.

"So, did you speak to him?" I asked, without looking up from my book.

"Yes, of course I spoke to him. I quite like him actually. Doesn't seem to care too much what people think, which is . . . really rather refreshing."

"And so . . . what did he say?"

"Oh, this and that. Where he'd been . . . he's an officer now."

. . . Captain Tom Cuthbert.

"Yes, I know. Did he ask after Mama?"

"He asked me about you. Said he'd heard of your engagement, asked when the wedding was," he replied, removing his shoes, putting his feet up on the ottoman.

"And what did you say?"

"Said I didn't know, that it would all depend on when Charlie was next home and when you both deemed it necessary, ha!"

"And how long . . . how long has he been seeing Rose?" I asked, closing my book, looking up at him.

"Haven't the foggiest. But I can't imagine her parents know. If they did they'd be livid. Anyway, what is it with him? I mean, I know he's handsome and all, but he *has* nothing."

. . . He has nothing; he is no one; can never be one of us.

"It's not his wealth then, is it?" I replied. "But you know, people don't select who to fall in love with according to their wealth or lineage, Henry."

He narrowed his eyes and looked at me quizzically for a moment; opened his mouth as if about to say something, then thought the better of it and said nothing.

"It may be the case with who they choose to marry, but not where love's concerned," I added.

"Hark you, my wise sister. And where, pray tell, does this newfound knowledge come from? Or are you thinking back with regret and longing to dear old Cuthie?"

I managed a smile. "Not at all. And I'm quite sure Rose Millington shan't marry Tom Cuthbert. She's much too ambitious. But she'll enjoy his attention. He's . . . quite intense, and women like that—for a while at least."

I looked away, saw Tom staring into Rose's pale eyes, his lips moving toward hers.

"You're all the same: fickle," Henry continued. "You want everything . . ." He paused, sighed. "The promise of eternal love and adoration, and then, when you think you have it, when you think you have it all, you no longer want it. Isn't that true?"

I didn't answer.

"Well? Isn't it?"

"Perhaps, but I don't believe men are any different. You all long for what you don't own and can't afford, and as soon as you own it, as soon as you're sure of it—it loses its appeal. So, perhaps it's a human trait and not specific to either sex."

"Ha! Yes, but it's the unattainable that's always the most desirable."

"The unattainable . . ." I repeated. And the poignancy of that word hit me like another blow.

He stretched out in his chair and sighed. "Have you noticed how old and cynical we sound now, dear?" he said.

"I suppose that's what the war has done to us," I replied.

Later, I sat at my dressing table, staring at my reflection in the looking glass. I would soon be twenty-one; I would soon be married. I hadn't heard his name in so long, and Henry's blasé mention of him had thrown me more than I'd realized. One syllable, one syllable was all it took. He had been a moment in my life, a wonderful reckless moment, nothing more. *Nothing more,* I told myself out loud. I picked up my hairbrush, moved it slowly through my hair. An unsmiling face stared back at me, beseeching me. And when I closed my eyes it was still there. "He used you," Mama had said, but I knew he hadn't used me any more than I had used him. My heart ached for him and for our baby, the child whose existence he knew nothing of; the child I'd given away, handed over to a stranger like an unwanted parcel. I clutched my stomach, felt myself begin to shake, and somewhere—somewhere in the distance—I could hear someone crying: great convulsing, breathless sobs. I put my hands to my mouth; heard his name, muffled, desperate; and then a shout, followed by another, and then another. I saw a girl sitting on a pink carpet in my white nightgown, swaying to and fro, rocking empty arms. And the sadness I felt for her was overwhelming.

I don't remember Mama entering my room. In fact, I can't recall anything that happened in the subsequent days and weeks.

∽

. . . **Four men were shot for desertion this morning. They'd been here for 3 or 4 months, & without any break . . . Every few days the names are read out to us—as a warning, but some would rather face a firing squad than stay here another day. Last week another** young boy in my battalion was shot. He'd become hysterical, lost his nerve and couldn't face going back into the line. He was tied to what was once a tree, in his civilian clothes, a piece of white cloth pinned over his heart. Now, rumor has it, his father and uncle are joining up to avenge his death on the Germans . . . What are we doing? Why are Englishmen shooting Englishmen? Best to suspend all thought & reason.

Chapter Seventeen

Dearest T, I have delayed my response to your last simply because it was (to me) incomprehensible. There is no hypocrisy on my part, is there on yours? I endeavor to do what I believe is right for each of us, and this in itself is a burden to me, and yes, to my conscience, which I now realize is that part of me you neither understand nor have any desire to understand . . . and I am deeply sorry if I have failed you. Do not for one moment think I am untouched or untroubled by this, I have given it a great deal of thought, but it is the only way, &

nothing to do with being part of any "smart set." Dearest, you speak of love as though it were a thing beyond morality—or what is decent—and yet didn't you also once tell me how inherently noble and good Love is? Can you not see how it would be otherwise? I'm afraid there was no alternative. Yrs, D

Was it some sort of nervous breakdown? I'm not sure. I'm not sure I'd heard that phrase then, or even if it had been invented. But weeks slipped by and I rarely left my room; I didn't want to, couldn't face anyone, couldn't face life. Dr. Riley came to call once or twice, but he spoke to my mother and not to me. He prescribed tablets; to help me sleep, Mama said. But I didn't need tablets to help me sleep; I needed tablets to help me wake up, to help me wake up from my nightmare. The only person I saw, apart from Mama and the doctor, was Venetia, once, when she came up to my room to see me. She brought me a silk scarf from Liberty's and was as effervescent as ever.

"Your mama's told me you've been a

little off color, dear; not quite yourself since you returned from Devon . . ."

I tried to smile.

"Well, really, it was always a bad idea. I told your Mama that at the time . . . I said to her, 'Edina, Devon is so terribly, terribly damp, and so very far away!'" She reached out, stroked my cheek. "Poor child, I'm not surprised, not surprised in the least that you've returned here lackluster and depressed. I should too, I'd imagine—had I been sent there!"

She went on to give me her summary of news, a catalog of backdated events I'd missed, and snippets of gossip, punctuated every so often by a roll of the eyes, a sigh or a shrug.

But I didn't hear any of it. I watched her as though I was watching someone on a stage, a character from a play; I even saw myself upon the same stage: the sickly girl in the bed. And I found myself wondering about Venetia and her life. Had she ever known heartache or loss? Perhaps she had. But it struck me that day how childlike she was, the extraordinary result of a life spent in a rarefied, cosseted world. The world I'd once been destined for. And suddenly I felt years older than my god-mother, a woman who had only ever ventured beyond Mayfair to attend the theater or the opera, or to stay in a grand country house. But I was different, I realized. And, though Venetia saw the same Clarissa, lying next to her, albeit pale and *lackluster*, I was already changed, already altered by the path of my life. I would never be the person I'd once been destined to become.

I wondered who her latest lover was, which young officer was dedicating poetry to her from the trenches, and what she said to them. Did she speak to them of love? Is that what it was that drew them to her? Or was it something else? Yes, she was beautiful, and yes, she was voluptuous, but was that enough to sustain them? And then it dawned on me: perhaps it was. Perhaps Venetia, with her love of all things frivolous and gay, and her tactile maternal ways, offered them a backward glance; reminding them of that other time, what they had left behind; what we had all of us left behind.

Later, I heard them on the landing, talking. "Well, you know Clarissa. She's always been a sensitive creature . . . always felt life a little *too* much. And this blasted war . . . our own losses have hit her hard," Mama said, and I smiled, as much at her ingenuity as her disingenuousness.

When I remembered the time before the war, it was the light I remembered most of all. As though the killing fields of France and Flanders had released tiny particles into the atmosphere, filtering out the sun's rays, absorbing that brightness I remembered. And with each year the air had grown thicker and darker still. And with each year my memories of that time had intensified in their luminosity; cherished snapshots now phosphorescent beacons.

Can it really be three summers since we all sat about on the lawn, like children, drinking lemonade, the boys full of bravado and desperate to impress the girls? Has it only been three years?

At night I'd pull back the curtains of my bedroom window and stare out across the darkened city. I'd follow the searchlight's nervous beam up, up, up through the clouds into the inky black sky, staring into heaven, seeking out the enemy. Like a wound healing, there was a nerve in me slowly coming back to life. The ache for my baby had lessened; now only occasionally did I experience that gnawing agony, that wrench. And I'd learned to live with it. I had to. I'd limited my thoughts of her to the abstract. She was a name, and though she was my baby, in my mind she had to become *a* baby. I could not bear to think of anything specific as to her situation or her whereabouts; whether she was lying in a cot of some far-flung orphanage, alone, or in someone else's arms, looking up into their eyes. I simply couldn't follow her path, either in reality or in my imagination. I'd handed her over, I'd given her away, and in doing so I had no rights to any imagined smile or gurgle. But sometimes, alone in my room, I said her name out loud.

"Emily . . . Emily Cuthbert."

"There'll be another. There'll be more babies for you. You'll see, when the time is right . . . when you're a little older, married," one of the sisters had said to me, shortly before I left Plymouth, as though my grief was for a misplaced favorite hat.

I'm sure that Mama, and Charlie too, thought that planning our wedding would give me something to look forward to, something to help me recover from whatever it was I was suffering from. But I had no interest in any wedding, least of all my own. So, as Mama brought swatches of duchesse satin and silks to my room for me to hold and compare, I feigned preferences for this one or that. She sat patiently with her notebook in hand, listing guests we'd need to invite: a depressing task in itself, due to the names of those absent from that list or any future list. She made a point of being cheery, talking of the future, never the past. And she never mentioned Papa, or Will, or George. She never mentioned Deyning, or Tom Cuthbert, and of course she never mentioned my baby.

"When the war is over," she said to me one day, "I shall take you to Paris, darling. You never had your time there, I'm quite aware of that. I'll take an apartment . . . and we'll do all the things you always wished to do. We'll shop on the rue St. Honore . . . visit Worth . . . go to the Louvre. Would you like that?"

"Yes, Mama. That would be nice."

Sometimes she'd look into my eyes with such sadness in her own that I wondered what, exactly, she wanted to say; for I sensed her burden, the weight of words unspoken, still longing to be said. But my mother had never allowed herself such freedom. Truth was something one held tight, like honor and sacrifice, and all those other now tattered ideals she hung on to. And I wondered how many words she'd never uttered; how many tears she'd never shed; how many secrets she held in her heart, and all those words, all those words she'd never allowed herself to say.

But I knew three of them, at least. Three words she'd never utter, no matter what. Because speaking them would mean admitting a mistake; and Mama *never* made a mistake. And yet, already, I knew that I had: I'd made a mistake in agreeing to marry Charlie. I was fond of him, I loved him—loved him like a brother, but I could not marry him; I could not lie, say "I do" and become his wife.

I decided not to speak to my mother about this. It was between me and Charlie, and no one else. For a while I contemplated writing to him, to try to explain. I composed a few different versions of a letter to him in my head. But it seemed so cruel, so uncaring, to put those words of rejection—no matter how dressed up— down on paper, and then post them out to him, with a "love from Clarissa" at the end. I imagined him in some dark and muddy trench, leaning against a pile of filthy sandbags, reading my letter, his heart aching . . . his heart breaking. And I couldn't do it. It would have to wait. I'd tell him in person.

～

. . . I too am sorry. I do not speak about it because I do not wish to, and, I imagine, neither does she. She is fine, a little fragile, and—as ever—somewhat distracted, but she is moving on with her life, and this is good. I try so very hard to be brave, to keep faith, but I am severely tested. I am weary of writing letters of condolence, of trying to find words—which no longer seem to carry any meaning or weight. What can one say? We have all suffered, & too much for any words of sympathy . . . and the sight of more weeping mothers in the street—preceded by yet another Union Jack–covered coffin, cause me to question everything I once believed in, & all that I am.

Chapter Eighteen

...I am not sure where to send this letter, or even if I will post it, but I want you to know that I forgive you. I forgive you for not writing to me, I forgive you for abandoning me, & I forgive you for not caring about what has become of me. Shall I tell you? Shall I let you in on the secret? Well, for a while I went quite doolally, oh yes, quite doolally-lally. In fact, I may even still be, in which case you can ignore everything I write here and resume normal duties. You see, I'm not altogether sure that I'm equipped to deal with this war, this bloody bloody

bloody stupid bloody war, & this awful life. No one issued me with a tin hat, or a uniform, or any armor, and I shall never be awarded anything. I shall receive no badge or medals, and no one is allowed to know . . . will ever know. Oh, but I forgot, it's different for me, isn't it? I don't need to "win" anything. I must be content with loss, & losing . . .

For me there was no beginning, no middle and no end, there was just one long and bloody war. I tried to imagine a time when there would be no war, but that great well of optimism, like my sense of patriotism, had almost run dry. I tried to remember that summer, the summer before the war, but it seemed to me a lifetime ago. And it was. It was hundreds of thousands of lifetimes ago. For how many had gone? Everyone I knew had lost brothers, cousins, lovers, fiancés, and friends. And yet we, the young still living, browbeaten by numbers and anesthetized by grief, clung to our stale dreams and shriveled hopes, and that fine silver thread, the future.

Sometimes I smiled when I wanted to cry, and cried when I should have been laughing. We all did. I can recall so many occasions when repressed, muddled emotions resulted in someone inadvertently laughing at a piece of tragic news, or bursting into tears at a joke. We spoke of death the way one speaks of the weather: "Did you hear so-and-so had been killed?" had become a standard point in any conversation, usually immediately after a "How are you?"

When my mother walked into my room, clutching an envelope, I knew as soon as I saw her face that it was more bad news.

"No, not Henry . . ." I said, sitting up in my bed, putting down my book.

"No, darling, not Henry," she said, taking hold of my hand. "I'm afraid it's Charlie . . ."

The telegram was from Henry: Charlie had been badly injured.

My mother telephoned the Boyds immediately. Charlie had been injured in an ambush on a night patrol. Nine of his men had been killed. He'd already been returned home and admitted to one of the London general hospitals.

The next day Mama and I went to visit

him. He lay in a small bed curtained off from the rest of the ward—his torso and arms bandaged like an Egyptian mummy, his legs under some sort of cage, covered by a sheet—in an open-eyed state of coma, seemingly deaf and dumb. I looked on in silence, stood at the end of the bed and watched my mother as she spoke to him. But he couldn't see her, couldn't hear her. I glanced about the ward—at the other injured servicemen, but none of it was real, none of it touched me. That small green glass bottle had continued to be my comforter, nullifying my senses, and, like Charlie, I was locked in a dream. Only I could hear and move and speak, and sometimes even smile.

We visited Charlie almost daily for two months before he was transferred to Craiglockhart, a military hospital near Edinburgh, specializing in the treatment and care of shell-shocked servicemen. A friend of Mama's, a doctor, had told us that the rate of war neurosis was much higher among officers than among regular soldiers, simply because their positions required them to repress their emotions and set an example. These men were often ashamed of their fear, he said, and, in his opinion, it was no coincidence that the most severe cases occurred in officers who'd also made a name for themselves as heroes, performing daredevil acts to prove to their men that they were not afraid. It made sense. And at that moment I could imagine Charlie, my ever-cheerful ebullient fiancé, at the front. At Craiglockhart, we were told, Charlie would be able to have the new electric shock treatment, he would learn how to walk and speak properly again.

I watched him slowly begin to recover from his physical injuries, but he was not as he should have been. He walked badly, dragging one leg, and putting together even the simplest of sentences seemed to be a struggle. At first he'd been unable to control both the pronunciation of words and the loudness of his voice, often shouting out in such a way that I'd jump. And he looked different too: wide eyed and haunted, and so very tired. He told me that he was afraid to sleep, afraid of the nightmares that delivered him straight back to the trenches. But sometimes these nightmares came to him in the middle of a sentence; and then he'd shriek, cry out a name, or begin whimpering like a wounded dog. He suffered appalling headaches, heart palpitations, dizziness, and sweats; and once, in front of Mama and me, he had what appeared to be some sort of fit—his whole body jerking violently upon the bed, shaking its tiny frame. He'd burst into tears a few times when we were there, and I knew, I knew then that Charlie believed he, too, should have been killed; that he wished for death, not life.

Perhaps it was seeing Charlie in that state, or perhaps it was watching the nurses who attended him, but I finally decided that I needed to do something, something useful. I'd heard that the hospitals were still desperate for volunteers, albeit for menial work, and so, the same day Charlie was transferred, I walked to the Russian Hospital for Officers on South Audley Street, and asked if they could use me.

The sister who interviewed me—a solid, fearsome woman with tiny blue eyes and a Scottish accent—told me that I'd need to be there by seven each morning, "bright eyed and bushy tailed. You'll be working down in the basement kitchens," she said.

"It's by no means glamorous, so I suggest you come attired a little differently."

I looked down at what I was wearing. "Yes, of course."

"From time to time you may be needed to help out on a ward . . . cleaning, stripping beds, that sort of thing. Is that acceptable to you, Miss Granville?"

"Yes, yes," I replied eagerly.

"Good. But I should warn you, many of the men we have here are traumatized . . . incontinent of mind *and* body. It's not pleasant—not nice for any of us, or for them—but it has to be done, and we're all run ragged . . ." She paused, smiled at me. "Unfortunately we don't have time for the manners and courtesies you're no doubt accustomed to, Miss Granville. You'll have to get used to that. You'll have to think on your toes and look sharp. But I'm sure if you can do that and keep your head, you'll be fine."

"I am a pantry maid!" I declared to my mother when I returned home.

"But are you quite sure? Are you certain you're able to cope?"

"Yes of course. And I have to do *something*, Mama."

It was mindless work, and no one really spoke to me. When they did I was simply addressed as "Granville." But I was happy to be doing something, happy to be useful at last. And I had no time to think, no time to dwell on Tom Cuthbert, my baby, or Charlie. I worked in a small, windowless pantry in the hospital's basement, next to the kitchen. In a long white apron, thick hairnet and white cap, it was my job to set the breakfast trays each morning, stack the trays on a trolley and wheel it through to the kitchen. There, I helped the kitchen maids—working from a list—to add food to the trays. Some were bestowed with nothing more than a plastic cup of yellowish milky liquid and a straw, a blue note placed next to it, with a name and a number; crockery and cutlery removed—for me to return to the pantry. Others, soft food—porridge, stoned prunes or scrambled eggs—served in a bowl, never on a plate, with a spoon and never a fork, and a pink note. And a few received something more substantial, with the full complement of cutlery, and no note. Then I took the trolley up to the wards with one of the kitchen maids, leaving her there to help the nurses hand them out, while I returned to the kitchen. By the time I'd finished clearing the kitchen, the trays had arrived back and I had to wash, dry and stack everything away for the next day. Sometimes I was asked to stay on for an hour, to do extra cleaning or mop out the kitchens, but I never saw inside the wards, never really saw the men, though I heard them, once or twice. The *blue notes*.

It was around this time, shortly after Charlie had been sent to Edinburgh, that Jimmy Cooper called on me. He was home on leave and took me to dinner at the Savoy. We drank champagne, ate caviar, foie gras, and lobster, and later, that same evening, we went to a party at the Millingtons. I was apprehensive. I hadn't seen Rose in a while, and I wondered if Tom would be there, home on leave, and if they were still seeing each other. He wasn't there and I was pleased. I don't think I could have borne it if he'd been there, been with her.

"Darling!" Rose said, kissing the air to both sides of my head. "I simply love the new you!"

Much to my mother's horror, I'd had my hair cut in the new "short" style. I'd had

Antoine cut it. It was, he told me, all the rage in Paris. Times, fashions, and everything else seemed to be changing, and I noted that Rose, like me, was wearing a new, rather daring, shorter gown.

Rose had always been a city girl: her vista happily confined to the angles of streets and pavements and rooftops. On her occasional visits to Deyning, I remembered, she'd always preferred to stay on the terrace or flagstoned pathways rather than walk on the grass or among the trees. She had a morbid fear of mud and didn't like the weather, any weather it seemed to me: summers made her sneeze and she found winters in the countryside *too, too depressing*. But in London, among the shops and cafés and theaters, she thrived. And though we were the same age she'd always seemed to me to be years older: more sophisticated, more knowing. Mama had once called her a flibbertigibbet sort, and perhaps she was.

"We never seem to cross paths these days . . . but I'm so, so pleased that dear Jimmy's brought you along. Oh darling, we simply must have a good old catch-up.

And . . . I've a little treat for us upstairs," she added in a whisper.

Among my ever-diminishing group of friends in London there was a new craze: injecting morphia. The drug not only worked on physical pain, its effects produced a pause long enough to obliterate reality, suspending thought and reason. It removed those light-absorbing particles and made things shine once more; made *us* shine once more. And life just seemed too short not to burn brightly.

At that time it wasn't fashionable, certainly not among those I knew, to drink. To appear in any way inebriated—by alcohol, at least—was considered quite vulgar and rather louche. And, under pressure from the temperance movement, and then the newspapers, the government had severely restricted the sale and consumption of alcohol anyhow. Shortly after the war began, hotels, restaurants, bars and public houses had had what was known as the "Beauty Sleep Order" imposed on them, and sometime later, this lights-out rule had been brought forward, from ten thirty to nine thirty. I'd heard of a few places, certain dubious Soho nightclubs and bars, which somehow managed to stay open into the small hours, but most of the people I knew entertained at home. It was easier. And, I suppose, it allowed us to do whatever we wished in private.

My mother, like so many others, caught in the grip of a xenophobic obsession about spies and foreigners in the city, had once asked me if I'd come across drugs at any of the parties I went to. She'd read in the newspaper that itinerant immigrants and foreign soldiers were targeting young English women—to sell into prostitution and white slavery. She mentioned opium and cocaine, and I was shocked. Shocked that she knew these words. Of course I'd lied to her, told her I knew nothing; said I hadn't seen anything.

But the craze for these things had been around for a few years by then, and the war, the never-ending news about it and about death, served only to accelerate the need for escape. All of us had friends working in one or other of the London hospitals, and with so many doctors, nurses and VADs about, the drugs were easy enough to obtain. Even our local Mayfair chemist, the place my mother liked to patronize, advertised their gelatine sheets impregnated with morphine and cocaine as *useful presents for friends at the front*. And a few very fashionable London girls I knew carried the most exquisite, beautifully enamelled silver *bonbonnières* of morphia grains or cocaine in their handbags.

Later that evening, as we sat side by side on her bed, Rose took my arm. "Now don't worry, darling. It doesn't really hurt," she said, examining my flesh, tapping at it. And it didn't. I felt nothing. For what's a pinprick? She disappeared to the bathroom, to sterilize the needle, she said, and when she returned I watched her inject herself. She pulled out the needle with a sigh, turned to me and smiled. And we sat there for a while, sharing a cigarette, chatting about who was seeing whom, and who'd died. Then, with a queer sort of drifting feeling, as though I wasn't completely there, I heard myself ask her about Tom: was she still seeing him, writing to him? And I heard my voice, slightly slurred and slow.

"Good grief, Clarissa, I was never *seeing*

him as such. It was just a thing, you know? He's hardly one of us, is he?"

"But I thought . . . Henry said you were . . ."

"Well, strictly between you and me, I was with him . . ." She got up, walked over to the window. "He is rather handsome . . . and quite compelling, but can you imagine what my parents would say? No, no, it was a momentary thing."

"And . . ." I heard myself say, egging her on for the detail of their *thing*, ". . . tell me more." And then I lay back against her pillows, a blissful mellowness creeping into my senses.

For a moment I thought she wasn't going to divulge anything further; then she came and sat down on the bed next to me.

"Come along, Rose," I said, half closing my eyes, ready to test the pain. "Tell me . . ."

"It was here," she said, looking above me, above my head, remembering. "He made love to me here. Oh, I know how preposterous it sounds, darling . . . but it was a moment of complete abandon."

And in my blissful haze, through the morphia, I felt a twinge in the pit of my stomach.

"Yes," I said, "a moment of complete abandon . . . how wonderful."

"I suppose if his circumstances were different I might fall in love with him," she said, still staring at a patch of wall above my head. "And truly, it was sublime. But I know—I know what you're thinking. You're thinking I'm a little tart to go with such a person, but he's altogether different from other men. There's something unusual . . . rather extraordinary about him . . . It's hard to explain, but I think you know what I mean, don't you?"

"Yes," I said, "I can imagine."

"He's so passionate . . ."

"Really?"

"So desperate . . ."

"Yes . . ."

"And quite obviously experienced with women," she said, looking at me with a wicked grin.

"Oh?"

She sighed. "To be honest, I'd be more than happy to have him as a lover for the rest of my life." She moved closer. "The things he knows, Clarissa . . . seriously, darling, it would make your hair curl. I said to him, 'I don't know where you've learnt about women, but surely it can't have been in the trenches.'"

"And what did he say?"

"I can't quite recall now. I think he said it was Paris. You know they all go there, don't you?"

"No, I didn't know. You mean they go there to pick up women?"

She laughed. "Oh, Clarissa, really. They don't need to pick them up, they pay for it, darling. And you know what they say about French prostitutes . . ."

"No," I said, beginning to feel dizzy. "What do they say?"

"Well, that they invented everything. Every debauchery known to man . . . or woman, ha! And they're everywhere at the front, brothels all over the place. Apparently there are more cases of syphilis and gonorrhea there than anything else. Isn't that just so horrendously . . ."—she glanced about the room, searching for the word—"sad," she said at last.

Suddenly I felt sick. "Must be the morphia," she said, and showed me to the bathroom.

I looked at myself in the mirror. He'd made love to her. He'd said her name and made love to her. I closed my eyes. *He made love to her as I had his baby.* I saw myself back in my room at St. Anne's in Plymouth; saw them together on her bed. And then I vomited.

"Are you all right in there, darling?" Rose asked through the door.

"Yes . . . yes, I'm fine," I said, staring back at the girl in the mirror. "You go down. I'll see you there."

"Are you sure? I can wait, dear."

"No, Rose. You go back down. I'm fine . . . I'll be along in a jiffy."

I heard the bedroom door close, and stood staring at my reflection. My eyes appeared unusually large and dark; my complexion a luminous ivory. I picked up the tablet of rouge on the marble wash-stand in front of me and applied it to my cheeks. A touch of color: *a mask; theater; a beautiful, sad creature from a Greek tragedy.* I lifted a tortoiseshell hairbrush, pushed it through my shorn hair, away from my face.

"You're not Clarissa," I whispered. "Clarissa doesn't look like that."

I walked slowly down the staircase, moving my hand along the polished wood of the handrail, and then on, through a small sea of vaguely familiar faces.

"Clarissa!"

"Are you quite all right, dear? You look a little pale . . ."

"Clarissa?"

I smiled, kept moving, looking ahead of me all the time, and then on into the Millingtons' ballroom, into the crowd. I closed my eyes, lifted my arms, swaying in time with the music: *this is good; this is fine . . . I am good, I am fine.*

I opened my eyes; saw Jimmy standing in front of me.

"Clarissa?" He sounded strange, quite far away.

"I think I need to go home now, Jimmy," I said.

Later, in my room, I lay on my bed, staring at rosebuds, drifting. I smiled. I was home now. I was safe. He was gone. All I needed to do was bury him. I had to extinguish every sensation I associated with him. But how? How do you kill everything you've ever felt to be good without killing some of yourself?

I rose from my bed, walked across to

my desk, opened the drawer and pulled out my journal and pen . . .

You may survive this war, but from today you are dead to me.

I climbed back into my bed and pulled the covers up. I wanted to be lost; I wanted to be found: found by him. I wanted him to feel my pain and beg for my forgiveness. I wanted to give myself to someone, anyone, and for him to know. For him to *feel* each touch, each and every kiss, like small shards of glass pressed into his flesh.

I would do it. I would.

I would make him feel the pain.

I stared at pink rosebuds between slow blinks, and I hated them. I'd never again be the girl on the gate, longing, and waiting for friends. I'd never again be the girl he'd made love to in the park. I'd never walk across a meadow and hear a lark or a cuckoo with that same sense of wonder. I'd never watch the sun set and feel at one with the universe or gaze up at the moon and stars and feel that same sense of awe. And I'd never again look at a baby and smile.

Chapter Nineteen

Oddly enough, it was around this time I began to see more of Rose. I couldn't and didn't blame her for what had taken place between her and Tom. After all, she had no idea, knew nothing at all of my seemingly doomed relationship with Tom Cuthbert, or the child I'd given birth to months earlier. But then neither did he. And in reminding myself of that, in reminding myself of that pertinent fact, and knowing that he had been with Rose *after* he'd learned of my engagement to Charlie, offered me a degree of comfort.

Rose was a socialite, a true Mayfair girl.

The only child of indulgent parents, and with a healthy trust fund, she always seemed to carry notes, not coins. She was the one who arranged and hosted tea parties and soirees; the one who picked up the bills at the Ritz and other places, and then, afterward, paid for the ridiculously short taxicab rides home for us all. She liked to visit fortune-tellers, and would quite often take a taxicab all the way to the outer suburbs, only to hear, yet again, that *a tall dark stranger in uniform* was on his way into her life.

But, and even aside from Tom, even before I learned of their "thing," I'd always been confused by my feelings for her. I admired her bravado, her joie de vivre and her generosity, and yet, in a way, those were the very same qualities I disliked about her, and viewed as shallow and insensitive. She seemed to me to be a girl without poetry in her blood, someone who'd never looked up and noticed the sky; someone who'd simply fail to see the full spectrum, or the differing hues and tones of any single color. But that was Rose. And Rose was Rose.

For a short while our friendship was

quite intense. We saw each other most evenings after work and sometimes, at her house, in her room, we took morphia; and then lay about trying to imagine the future, our future. *A future.* Perhaps that's the reason it became intense: the morphia, or "morphy" as she called it.

She said to me, "You know, dear, I keep thinking, and really . . . the thing is, soon there'll be no one left to marry . . . we'll all end up old maids . . . childless and unloved." She turned to me. "Doesn't it worry you, darling? I mean to say, I know you're engaged and all that, and poor Charlie's invalided, but what if he has to go back . . . what if something happens to him? It must cross your mind, dear . . . must cross your mind all the time."

We were lying on her bed, side by side, and as I turned to her I noticed the flecks of red in her hair—Titian red—spread out over the pillow.

"I don't think about it."

She turned toward me, on to her side. "Really? Never?"

"No. What's the point? Whatever will be will be."

"Clarissa! But you love him—don't you?"

I closed my eyes. "I suppose so. Sort of."

She lay back, and for a while we lay in silence, the only noise the rumble of traffic going up and down the wet street outside. Then she said, "But has he made love to you? You don't have to tell me, of course . . . but I was wondering, wondering if you're still a virgin."

I didn't answer her immediately. The morphia made me drift, made my thoughts loose and shapeless; and it was a difficult question to answer.

"No," I said, after a while, "he hasn't made love to me, Rose."

I didn't say any more, and neither did she.

And I have no idea who or what she was thinking of, where she was inside of herself, but I was with *him*.

For a while, I'm not altogether sure how long, but perhaps no more than a few weeks—and I know that it was spring, because I vividly recall the blossoms on the trees as I walked home—we took *morphy* quite often; most days, I think. It made everything infinitely better, made the world . . . kinder, softer, warmer. And it took away all of my pain and heartache, all of my loneliness, and replaced it with the most sublime sense of peace.

Sometimes, its effects literally transported us to another place. And once, when Rose and I attended a private exhibition of paintings—and had taken only the smallest dose, hours earlier—we both fancied we'd seen the colors change and move about the canvases. Another time, when we read poetry out loud to each other, it was as though I was able go inside the poem, able to see and *feel* the vibration of every single word.

My mother never noticed a thing. Oh, she'd comment from time to time that I looked a tad pale or tired, but she'd always considered me dreamy, distracted and, I suppose, particularly at that time, fragile. If she thought something was amiss she never voiced it, but that was her character: she'd rather arrange flowers than deal with reality. But I was becoming needy, greedy for my share of grains, and I'd begun to pay Rose, because as she'd quite rightly said, she shouldn't have to pay for *everyone else's fun*.

———

It was Rose who asked me if I'd help out at the kiosk: a small buffet for soldiers arriving back from the trenches, situated on one of the platforms at Waterloo station. She and a few other girls from our neighborhood ran it together, working on a rotation so that it was open around the clock, day and night. We served tea, buns and cigarettes, all paid for by donations, but mainly by Lady Astley, a friend of Mama's, who'd set it up. So, I continued to work at the Russian Hospital each morning and cycled to Waterloo station each afternoon. There were always at least three of us working there, a few more if we knew it was going to be frantic, when the boat trains were due in. But the time of arrival of any trains was always a matter of conjecture. If they were late in the evening, as they quite often were, we'd all be there until the small hours, and then I'd leave my bicycle chained up at the station and share a taxicab home with the other girls.

Lady Astley came down to see us all at least twice each week, bringing supplies from Fortnum and Mason and often staying for a good few hours, helping to serve tea and chatting with the men. She liked us to look our best, said it mattered to the men. "They need to see smiles and pretty faces when they step off those trains," she said. And we weren't just to serve them: we were to greet them, she said; to cheer them up, chat to them and listen to them. After all, they were heroes, each and every one of them, she told us. And so, with a smile on my face, I handed out tea to Tommies and to officers. I chatted to the walking wounded and to the seemingly fit and able, and I sat with those badly injured on stretchers, limbless bodies with boyish faces, holding a teacup to their parched lips, placing a cigarette to their mouths, and then lifting it away as they exhaled. In that miasma of putrid flesh and seeping wounds, blood, dirt, sweat and vomit, I held hands and stared into black-ringed eyes. I smiled at their generosity, their never-ending compliments and propositions of marriage, and sometimes I winked back at them. Yes, I flirted, we all did; even Lady Astley, I think.

And to them all, I was Clarissa.

"'Ere, Clarissa, Arthur says he's in love with you, already!"

"Clarissa! Another cuppa over here, love, and bring them lips with you, ha!"

The station was always pandemonium when the trains came in, especially at night: filled with volunteers like us, Red Cross workers, nurses and ambulance men waiting to collect the injured. Depending on the time of day, there would sometimes be a crowd of fervently patriotic members of the public to welcome their returning troops with a song, as well as a few vividly painted ladies.

All of the men were exhausted and, not surprisingly, dazed; startled by their welcome, and perhaps the recognition of something near to normality, near to a memory. Many were suffering from the effects of mustard gas: half blind, skin blistered, eyes weeping, stuck together, or covered by a bandage; they moved along the platform in a long automated line, hands upon the shoulders of the man in front, zombie-like.

In the hut, for that's all it really was, we had an iron boiler, an enormous tea urn, three old jugs and a pail for washing up. But somehow we managed. More than that, we did it all with gusto. Lady Astley's two daughters, Flavia and Lily, were there almost every day, and Rose too.

I don't think I'd ever felt as alive or, bizarrely, laughed as much. And this was perhaps what struck me more than anything else: that these men, men who'd been living on their wits, fighting for survival, and in such appalling conditions— for by then we all knew about life in the trenches—could still laugh, and sing; still flirt and smile. My vocabulary expanded, and I learned a few new songs. None of them Mama would have liked, all of them I loved.

"You're a looker and a half mind, ain't ya? Gotta sweetheart, love?"

"Here! Bert! Come and meet me new fiancée, Clarissa . . ."

Of course I looked out for Tom, and for Henry too. And once, during my first few weeks, Jimmy Cooper appeared; astounded and delighted to find me there, thinking I'd somehow anticipated his arrival as I ran toward him shouting out his name. But I never saw Tom. Oh, occasionally there'd be a man down the platform, emerging through the steam, half lost in

the sea of pale, thin faces and khaki uniforms, and yes, for a moment, I'd think, *it's
him, it's him*. I'd catch my breath, forget
what I was doing as I tried to follow that
face. And then I'd lose it. *It wasn't him . . .
it can't have been him.*

Then, one day, when I arrived to take
over from Rose, she said, "You'll never
guess whom I've just been talking to,
literally—just gone on the last train."

"Who?" I asked, hanging up my coat on
the inside of the door.

"Tom Cuthbert!"

I turned. "Really? Just now?"

"Yes . . . minutes ago, dear," she replied.
"He had a three-day pass, said he'd been
down to Deyning."

She must have seen something, sensed
something. "You all right, dear?" she
asked, reaching out and touching my arm.

"Yes, fine," I said, raising my hand to my
head. "Just a headache, that's all."

"Do you want Flavia to stay? Do your
turn, dear? She can, you know . . . she's
already said that. She said she can stay
until later."

Flavia was hovering beside her, the two
other girls standing further back.

"No, I'm fine. Truly, it's nothing."

Rose lit a cigarette, picked up her handbag.

"Right-o then, see you tomorrow, dear. Don't expect it'll be too busy tonight. Nothing much seems to be happening, but you never know."

She turned to go.

"Rose!"

"Yes, darling?"

"Tom . . . Tom Cuthbert, how did he seem?"

"He looked exhausted, like the rest of them . . . said it was his first leave in ten months . . . said he'd slept for three whole days."

"Did he . . . did he mention me?" I couldn't help it; I had to ask.

She looked at me, perplexed for a moment. "No, darling, he didn't. And do you know I completely forgot to tell him that you were helping here too, completely forgot. How silly of me."

"Oh well," I replied, smiling back at her, "not to worry. See you tomorrow then."

I watched her go. Watched her and Flavia move off down the platform, their arms linked, their heads leaning inward, already deep in conversation. And I stood there completely still. Frozen on that spot. *He was here . . . moments ago he was here.* I closed my eyes, tried to imagine him standing where I now stood. I breathed in the dusty station air as though inhaling the echo of his energy, his breath. I took myself back through the preceding minutes. I'd been on my bicycle, cycling down the Strand . . . and then over Waterloo Bridge . . . and he'd been there. And I had that feeling once again: the queerest feeling of being out of kilter with the rest of the universe.

He was here.

We had missed each other by seconds.

I turned, went inside the hut, and began stacking the clean cups on to a shelf. Then I unstacked them, and put them into lines. I noticed one was chipped at its rim. A strange, perfectly formed chip, in the shape of a *V.* I stood there for some time, staring at that chipped cup, running my finger around and around its imperfect rim, until my flesh finally caught its sharp edge, and tore.

I was lying on my back, stretched out on the pale pink velvet chaise longue at the end of her bed, and she said, "You know, dear, you'll ruin your hair, lying like that."

We should have been at Flavia Astley's twenty-first birthday party, or at least on our way. But by now it was after nine.

"Do you really want to go, Rose? I'm not sure I can be bothered . . . think I'd rather stay here."

"Hmm. I think we should . . . don't you? We'll have missed the dinner by now, of course, but if we don't turn up . . . and there's my parents, your mother . . . we did say we'd follow on."

An hour earlier, as the front door had slammed shut, and Rose's parents—along with my mother—had headed off to the Astleys' party, two streets away, I'd once again taken a needle to my arm, after I'd injected Rose. She only wanted a light dose, she said. She'd taken a sixth of a grain. I had a quarter, I think, or perhaps a little more.

I said to her, "Tell me about your thing with Tom again . . . Tom Cuthbert."

I don't know why, but some dark, perverse part of me, my brain, wanted to hear her speak about it. It was a scrap, of something, sustenance, and—no matter how unappetizing—I was famished, my heart desperate. And I thought just to say his name, hear another speak his name, might somehow satiate those splintered molecules of my being.

She lay on the bed next to me, her feet on the pillow, her head propped in her hands.

"Tom Cuthbert," she said slowly, slurring the syllables, "is really . . . *quite* . . . delicious."

I turned on to my side, looked up into her eyes: tiny black pinprick pupils swimming in a watery gray.

"You know, Rose, your eyes are the color of the sea."

She looked down and smiled at me.

"I think I need to tell you something," she said. She moved on the bed, pulled a pillow down and rested her chin upon it. "In fact . . . I need to tell you two things, darling."

"Hmm, and so," I said, watching her.

"Well, that night with Tom, the time I said I was with him . . . I sort of lied."

I stared at her. "Sort of?"

"I didn't mean to . . . he did kiss me . . . but nothing more. I made up the rest."

I didn't say anything. I wondered if I'd heard her correctly.

Did she just say she made it up?

After a minute or two I came up with one word to say to her: why?

"Oh . . . I don't know," she said, sounding quite angry and burying her face in the pillow.

Then she lifted her head. "You asked me, you egged me on, and I wanted to be able to tell you something . . . something more than the fact that he'd kissed me when he was drunk." She paused, sighed, and then turned over, on to her back. "You don't understand," she said, staring up at the ceiling. "Nothing exciting ever happens to me. No one's ever been in love with me . . . desired *me*."

"But Henry said you were seeing him."

"Yes, because that's what I told him. I wanted Henry to think that . . . I wanted to make him jealous. Oh really, Clarissa, I've been in love with your brother for years . . . and I don't think he's even noticed me."

"That's not true. He really does rather like you, Rose, I know that." I sat up, slowly. There was a quivering sort of glow about the room and I could feel my heart palpitating, my whole body trembling, as though everything were caught in the same vibration. I said, "Tell me the truth, Rose. What happened between you and Tom Cuthbert?"

She rolled on to her stomach, lifted her head and looked back at me. "Nothing, really, that's just it. Oh, we kissed, but . . ."

"Yes?"

She frowned, began to fiddle with the lace on the pillow. "He was drunk, and it was dark . . . and he seemed to think I was you, dear. You see, he said your name; he kept on calling me *Clarissa*."

Chapter Twenty

～

Charlie and I were married in October 1918, at the church around the corner from our home in Mayfair. He'd told me, and more than once, that it was all he was living for, to marry me. In the end, there seemed little point in waiting. Both Mama and the Boyds had said so. "The sooner you marry the better," Mama had said. "It will give poor Charlie the motivation he needs to pull through and make a full recovery."

In the weeks leading up to my wedding Mama had repeatedly told me that I was a little too thin, a little *too* pale. But I had no appetite for food, and no appetite for marriage. On the day, an hour or so before the service, and sitting on my bed with Rose, I pushed a needle into my vein, and she said, "I'm really not sure it's a good thing for you to be doing this at this moment in time . . ." Minutes later, she stood with me, holding back my veil, as I'd retched over the lavatory, and then she held me as I cried silently on her shoulder. It was the last time I ever took morphia.

Henry had managed to secure two days' leave and came home to give me away, and after the wedding we had a small reception at Claridges. Our wedding photograph appeared in *The Times*, the *Tatler* and *Country Life* magazines: Charlie in his uniform, stern faced and minus his walking stick, and me, looking serene and wan in my gown of ivory duchesse satin and Mama's long lace veil, staring back—unsmiling—at the camera with peculiarly dark eyes. Of course, it was not the wedding my mother had once hoped for, not the wedding she'd planned for me for so many years. There were simply too many missing for it to be a fulfillment of that dream. And there could be no honeymoon.

The war was not yet over, and Charlie had to return to Craiglockhart to continue his convalescence and treatment. So we had only one night together, our wedding night, in the honeymoon suite at Claridges.

We were both nervous, and the combination of champagne and pills had made Charlie even more emotional. When I emerged from the dressing room, wearing the long silk negligee I'd selected at Selfridges only the week before, he smiled. "You're so beautiful," he said, and then burst into tears. He was sitting on the edge of the bed in his pajamas, and I immediately moved over to him, sat down next to him and held him in my arms. I wasn't sure if it was wedding-night nerves or something else. But he told me then, through his tears, that I'd made him so happy; that our life together would be good. "We're going to be so happy together, Clarissa," he said, looking down at my hand, held in his.

We lay in each other's arms for quite some time, talking about the future, where we might buy a house, how we'd like it to be. And we talked about the war, the likelihood of it ending in the coming months.

"I don't want you to get better too

soon . . . not if means you have to go back and fight. Not now," I said, looking up at him.

He stared up at the ornate cornicing on the ceiling. "And I don't want to go back there. Ever."

I think I realized that night that he would never be the Charlie I'd known before. The witty quips, the jesting and teasing I'd always associated with him seemed to have gone from his character forever. There was a new intensity to him, which frightened and excited me at the same time. And he seemed so much older than the other Charlie.

He said, "I want you to know I'm not a virgin, Clarissa."

I didn't say anything. I wasn't sure why he had told me this, what he expected me to say, but I didn't want to ask questions, and I didn't want him to ask me any. He reached over to his side, switched off the lamp, then he moved down the bed, alongside me, and took me in his arms. "I shall be very gentle with you, darling."

"Yes."

We kissed slowly, and as his hands moved over my body, following its lines and curves, I could hear his breathing, becoming heavier, quicker. "I love you . . . love you so much," he murmured. He pulled up my nightgown, moved his hand up my leg to the inside of my thigh. I felt him against me, felt his hardness. He pushed my legs apart with his own, pulled my nightgown up further still. I was beginning a descent, slowly moving through the blackness to a memory. I wrapped my arms around his neck, placed my lips upon his shoulder. "I'll be gentle," he said again, in a whisper, and moving himself between my legs. I could hear the rumble of traffic in the distance, feel *his* lips upon my neck, *his* hands exploring . . . And then, as he entered me, and moaned loudly, I came back into the room.

"I'm sorry, darling. I don't think that was quite as pleasurable for you as it was for me," he said, moments later. "It'll get better though, I promise. First time's never very enjoyable for the lady."

I felt a tear escape. "Don't worry, it's been a long day . . . we're both tired."

"I didn't hurt you, did I?"

"No, no," I said, "you were gentle, very gentle."

We lay in each other's arms in silence, and as his breathing slowed I quietly moved away. I lay on my back, my eyes wide open to the darkness, and I pondered on that momentous day, my wedding day. None of it was as I'd once imagined. This is my new life, I thought, I am married: for I had said *I do*.

I rewound the events of the preceding twelve hours: arriving at the church with my dashing elder brother; walking down the aisle on his arm, and seeing Charlie, standing there in his uniform, smiling nervously, leaning heavily on his stick; the small sea of ostentatious hats and plumage; the oversized arrangements of white roses, eucalyptus and ivy; Mama, turning to look at me with a queer, sad smile.

I do . . .

I whispered those words once more. I had married Charlie, for better, for worse, for richer, for poorer, in sickness and in health.

I do . . .

The following morning, after breakfast, Charlie delivered me back to my mother's house, and then went to catch his train. He'd been in a strange mood that morning, distracted and monosyllabic. When he bid me good-bye, kissing me on my cheek, his manner was brusque. But I put this down to the fact that he didn't wish to leave me, didn't wish to go back to hospital.

Venetia was already at the house that morning, and she and Mama both fussed over me. I was a new bride; I had just had my wedding night.

"Aha! Well, you look radiant, dear. And you were an absolute vision yesterday . . . stunning, wasn't she, Edina?"

"Yes, beautiful, very beautiful," Mama said, looking up at me from where she sat and taking hold of my hand. "Your father would have been so proud . . . so proud."

My mother had never once asked me if I loved Charlie. And, to be honest, the idea of marrying for love, per se, seemed . . . indulgent, outdated, and unrealistic, like another prewar luxury that didn't fit with the times; didn't fit with austerity. Marrying for love belonged to another era, an era when there had been enough time to dream. For now it was enough to be married; to have someone still alive and in one piece to claim as one's own. And I imagine that Mama was relieved. Relieved to have me married, respectable, and in safe hands.

In the weeks that followed, the weeks between my marriage and the end of the war, I tried to focus on my new life, on being healthy and happy. I told myself it was a new beginning, and when I began to tremble and shake, I repeated the phrase Mama had used—*a fresh start*—in my head, and sometimes out loud.

For a while I avoided seeing Rose. I continued my work, and I played bridge— with girls who liked playing bridge; I went to matinees at the Gaiety cinema and to the theater with Mama and Venetia, and for dinner to Kettners, Scotts and the Carlton Grill. Of course it felt no different to be married. I was still living with Mama, still sleeping in my rosebudded sanctuary; only my name had changed. I was now Clarissa Boyd, and I practiced my new signature endlessly. I found myself talking about "my husband" and planning a future, our future. And soon, I'd have my own home. The plan was for us to live with Mama once Charlie had been discharged, or when the war was over, and from there, to look for something of our own.

There was an end and a beginning in sight, and I sensed it within every pore of my being. There was a future, a future without a war.

On November the eleventh, the day we'd all prayed for finally arrived. At 11 a.m. the maroons sounded across London—and this time for the armistice and not an air raid. The war was over. Within minutes celebrations erupted across the city, and I heard the shouting, the jubilant crowds making their way to Trafalgar Square and Piccadilly, but it was a bittersweet moment, tinged with the most profound sadness. For Mama and I, like so many others, could only think of those we'd lost, those unable to share in that victory and national euphoria.

Mama appeared quite calm, almost subdued as she poured us each a glass of sherry, and then, with a shaky hand and tears in her eyes, she made a toast: "To our long-awaited victory . . . and to my brave, brave boys, William and George, and all the others who can't be here today."

The war is over.

I held the tiny glass out, clinked it against Mama's, and as I raised it to my lips I thought of Tom. Was he on his way home?

Or was he already back, and in London? I knew he had to be alive, had to have survived, otherwise I'd have heard; I'd have sensed something. I'd have known.

As Mama disappeared from the room, to go below stairs and tell the servants they could all have the day off, I walked over to the window and looked down on to the square. Already there were crowds of people, shouting, dancing, linking arms, and some even kissing. One young chap had managed to climb up one of the trees and waved a flag there; another, immediately below him, stood on a bench, his hat clutched to his chest, singing; and in the midst of this riotous frenzy were cars and taxicabs, spilling over with people, hooting loudly as they headed through the square.

And I began to laugh. "The war is over," I said out loud, and then I unlocked and opened the door on to the balcony.

"The war is over! The war is over!" I shouted out across Berkeley Square.

A uniformed man shouted back up to me, "God save the King!"

"God save the King!"

"And to France!" another called up.

"Vive la France!" I called back, laughing.

And another voice: "To victory!"

"To victory!"

Then Rose and Flavia and Lily Astley appeared below me.

"Come down! Come down! We're going to celebrate. Come down now!" Rose shouted up.

Minutes later, I was on the top of a bus, crammed to capacity with girls and soldiers, everyone shouting and singing, and crowds cheering back at us as we passed by. We got off the bus at the Ritz and drank champagne with friends in the packed bar, and then we headed on—to the Carlton—to meet more friends. From there, and with an opened bottle of *free* champagne, we traveled on the roof of a taxicab to Trafalgar Square, where it seemed to me the entire country had gathered, and where we sang songs, made toasts, and vowed eternal loyalty and love to everyone we saw. And later still, we followed the throng to Buckingham Palace, and there, with aching throats and ragged voices, and linking arms with those around us, we cheered our King and Queen. That night and all through the night London continued to celebrate. Out on the streets people sang, laughed and wept; cars, buses and taxicabs hooted, and we all waved, blew kisses and shouted back. Each and every house opened its doors, welcoming strangers like long-lost relatives.

It seemed to me as though order had been restored and then rapidly magnified; the world was once again a place of peace and goodwill, and love. How could we *ever* have been at war? People like us, so reasonable, so just; so magnanimous? And walking home down Curzon Street, with my heart fit to burst, I noticed the moon, winking and blinking at me between clouds. That sweet heavenly face, still promising light and dawn. And I whispered to her once again.

You see, it was a moment; one of those moments you never, ever forget.

"The war is *over*," I said, as I climbed into my bed, elated, exhausted.

The war is over . . .

Then, at the very edge of wakefulness, it hit me: the sheer magnitude and permanence of our loss. How could we forget them—those missing from the party? How could we dance and sing and celebrate? And as I lay there, I tried to count up all the boys I'd known who'd been killed in the war: my brothers, their schoolmates and friends, the brothers of my own friends, my cousins, all three of the Hamilton boys from Monkswood, so many of the men from the estate, and Frank and John.

"Frank and John," I said out loud.

I hadn't thought of them in such a long time, and at that moment they came to me so clearly, so vividly—those two young under-gardeners—as though I'd seen them both only days before. But Frank had been killed in the very early days of the war, his nimble cricketer's feet stepping on a mine within days of arriving at the front. John had survived almost two years, been invalided home, only to return to the trenches to be killed. No garden would ever again know their toiling hands, no girls the color of their hearts. No village green would ever again see Frank's white figure run forward, his arms encircling the air, spinning a ball toward the wickets.

Good night, sweet boys, good night.

The following morning Mama handed me the newspaper, saying, "You may well see yourself in one of those photographs." And as I glanced over the front page I noticed the date, November the twelfth. Emily's first birthday. Amidst the Forgotten, she'd been forgotten too.

A few days after the armistice we received a letter from Henry. He told us that there were no celebrations at the front. Many there believed that the armistice was temporary and that the war would soon resume. After so many months and years of living under intense strain, in mortal danger and thinking only in terms of war and the enemy, the abrupt release was physical and psychological agony. Some, he said, suffered total collapse, and some could only think of their dead friends, while others fell into an exhausted sleep. All of them were stunned by the sudden meaninglessness of their existence as soldiers; their minds numbed by the sudden silence, the shock of peace. Those of us back at home continued to read about death in the newspapers: the soldiers killed by stray bullets after the ceasefire; and those already in oblivion, unaware of peace, who'd later died from their wounds.

It would be weeks before Henry could return home. He had to see to it that arrangements for the transportation of his men and others were in place and then managed. It was "chaos," he told us in another letter. The logistics of demobilizing our troops—trying to get them all back home in time for Christmas—was nigh on impossible, and, as an officer, he would have to stay until all of the men under his command were on their way. He wasn't sure when he'd be back, but soon, he hoped.

Those days, the days immediately after the armistice, were strange for us too. For once the euphoria of victory slowly ebbed, I sensed a queer sort of atmosphere and awkwardness about the city, and with people I knew. How did we begin to pick up the pieces of our lives? And what were we left with? How could we look each other in the eye again, smile, and say, "How do you do!" in that cheery, universally acknowledged British way? And how *did* we do? Those of us who had not been in the trenches, who'd not lived in squalor—with mud and rats, discarded limbs and rotting bodies, that deafening barrage and stench of death—could never pretend to know or understand. We had no visible injuries, no scars, no tattered uniform or medal, but we too were damaged: damaged by grief and loss, damaged through association; and associated through guilt.

The demobilization of five million men was upon us, and as disoriented men in mud-caked uniforms began to appear on the streets—unsure of what to do or where to go—the mood in London changed, and we seemed to be grappling with a new dilemma. For suddenly the horror of the war was there, on display in front of us, as hundreds of thousands of men arrived back from the trenches. Delivered back into the bright lights of normality, they flooded the city's streets, stations and squares, and assembled in parks, where temporary camps had been set up as holding stations for them. They loitered by tube stations, and on the corners of Oxford Street, Regent Street, in Leicester Square and Piccadilly: traumatized, bewildered souls, often drunk, and sometimes begging. So very different to those pristine uniformed young men I'd seen there years before. And those wretched scraps of men, the ones who'd been disfigured, their bodies chewed up and spat out for their country, were there too: limbless, and in freakishly painted tin masks to hide their missing faces. There was no escape, we had to see what we had done, had to confront the conse-quence of our actions. And here they were: our valiant young heroes.

There could be no return. None of us, no matter our situation or circumstances, could pick up the pieces of life as it had once been, before the war. We had all been changed, and our lives as we'd known them had gone, and gone forever.

. . . We will undoubtedly have to sell off the land, but I am praying we might somehow be able to save the house (and the garden), despite the rather desper-ate need for funds, and so I try to be optimistic for H's sake, for this is all such a dreadful worry to him, & he is in no fit state to deal with it. Everything seems adrift, unstable, and I feel as though with each passing day we are nearing another calamity—not another war, God forbid, but an exhausted collapse of our ragged economy. It is inevitable, I believe. And what a life for those who fought for their country! What meager life their reward. Sometimes I can't help but wonder if it wouldn't have been better for the Germans to have arrived on these shores . . . for perhaps then the men would have work, a sense of pride, & my boys still here . . .

Chapter Twenty-one

I finally returned to Deyning late in the spring of 1919. Some weeks before, Henry had had a lawyer come to the house in London to explain things to Mama, and to me. It was impossible, financially impossible, for us to keep it. The entire estate—the house, the land and the farm—would have to be sold, he said. It would be divided up and auctioned as separate lots, allowing interested parties to buy some or all of the estate, and ensuring, he hoped, that we got the best price.

My mother had been stoical, nodding her head as she cast her eyes over the pages of numbers laid out upon the dining room table. But I couldn't believe it. Those numbers meant nothing to me, and Deyning— everything.

Henry was already at the house when Mama and I arrived. He'd gone down a couple of weeks before, taking two friends with him for company, and was supposed to be working through the inventory, making a list of repairs to submit to the army. Mama and I were to oversee the packing up before the auction, which was to be held the following month. He had telephoned the week before, warning me, and telling me to prepare Mama about the state of the place. But nothing could have prepared us.

When we motored up the driveway that day we were stunned by what we saw. The gardens, only five years before so lovingly tended and well kept, were lost, hidden under giant thistles and waist-high weeds; cows roamed about, grazing on what had once been the tennis lawn, and the whole place was littered with debris: dilapidated huts, piles of wood, rolls of barbed wire, abandoned wheels and oil drums. "Like a gypsy encampment," Mama said, staring out of the car window as we approached the house. Tank tire tracks had slewed up the earth where manicured lawns and neatly arranged flower beds had been; and great clumps of grass, dandelions and rampant ivy clung to every ornamental wall and flagstone pathway. Without Mama, without the gardeners, the wilderness had finally marched in on the place, exactly as I'd once imagined.

I wondered then if Tom Cuthbert might be about. I knew Mrs. Cuthbert still lived at Deyning, in the same cottage, but I'd never once heard Tom's name mentioned. In fact, I had no idea where he was or what he was doing with his life. And though I still dreamed of him from time to time, I hadn't actually thought of him in a while. I'd been busy, looking after Charlie and seeing to our new home. We'd recently moved into a house not far from Mama's, and she and I had spent the preceding weeks selecting wallpapers, fabrics and new furnishings. The move had distracted me, and perhaps Mama too, from the impending loss of Deyning. And she seemed to have finally accepted that Deyning, like

William and George and Papa, belonged to the past and not the future.

As our car came to a standstill I felt a sense of dread, and wondered what awaited us inside. But my father had been right: the house *had* been wrecked. Spindles—and even some of the balusters—had disappeared from the staircase; shelves and paneling—gone; a number of doors were missing, others, hung splintered from shattered hinges; and broken windowpanes, crudely boarded over, made the place appear even more dark and gloomy. My mother quietly wept, shaking her head in dismay as she walked about the place, moving slowly from room to room, unable to comprehend the decimation.

"I can't believe it," I said. "It's only been five years."

"But a long five years," Henry replied.

"Yes. A very, very long five years," my mother whispered.

"Mrs. Cuthbert's been wonderful, and Mabel's come back to help too. She's in the kitchen, I think. We've all worked jolly hard. You should've seen the place when we arrived here . . . it was bloody filthy,"

Henry said and then laughed, but his laugh was forced and shrill.

My mother moved toward him, lifted her hand to his face, and stroked his cheek. She said, "Henry, my darling boy, your father would be so proud of you. This is not what he would have wished for, not what he would have wished to see happening, but he would be proud of you, my dear."

But the atmosphere was strange, and Henry's mood odd and unpredictable. He pulled away from her, began to rub the place she'd touched, as though wiping away something, as though in pain.

"It's all right, Henry," she said, in a barely audible monotone. "Everything is fine. All will be well."

I suppose she knew the signs, even then; knew when Henry was about to have an attack.

"Clarissa, could you please ask Mabel to serve tea now. Henry and I will be in the morning room."

I walked away, down the passageway toward the kitchen, and at the door I stopped and turned back to look at them. Henry's head rested upon Mama's shoulder, and I thought he looked as though he was crying. She was stroking his hair, whispering to him. It was the first time I'd seen what my mother would later refer to as Henry's "panic attacks."

The following morning I rose early. I'd decided to have a final ride across what was still our land, on Father's old horse, Brandy. We'd always kept livestock at Deyning, always had horses. Before the war, before our younger horses went off to the front, I think we'd had over a dozen. But now there was only Brandy; and he, too, despite all my pleadings, was going to auction.

It was a bright morning, the stable yard filled with sunshine and the warm smell of manure. I saddled up Brandy myself, and as I stood in the shadows—on the mounting block—I was vaguely aware of someone out of the corner of my eye. I took no notice, thinking it to be one of the men from the village Henry had brought in to help clear the place up.

I mounted Brandy, gathered up the reins. "Hello, Clarissa."

It took me a moment to realize it was him. He looked so different: unshaven, shabby. And for a split second I thought I might be dreaming, that perhaps he wasn't real, was a vision. I'd heard that sometimes—even when we're least expecting it—we're able to conjure up absent loved ones, like ghosts. He must have sensed my shock, because he grimaced as he turned away from me.

"Tom . . . I didn't know . . . didn't know you were here. No one said."

He stood with his hands in his pockets, looking down at the ground. Then he raised his head and without turning to look at me, he said, "I think my congratulations are a little late, Mrs. Boyd."

I didn't say anything because I didn't know what to say.

He moved across the cobblestones toward me, and I could feel my heart, pounding so violently I thought I might faint.

"I saw your wedding photograph, of course . . . in *some* magazine or other," he said, standing in front of me, reaching out to stroke the horse's nose. "And I wish you both well. Charlie's a decent chap . . . and a lucky man," he added.

He leaned forward, rubbing the side of his face against Brandy's jaw. And I wanted to reach down, touch him; run my hand through his hair.

I said, "So, how are you? You look . . . a little different."

He didn't look up, but kept his face pressed against the horse.

"I am different," he said. "And you are too, Clarissa."

"Yes, we're all changed, Tom. Life's changed."

He stepped back, raised his eyes to me. "It is. And times move on."

"Yes, times move on . . . they have to," I said, feeling that tug: a pull in my solar plexus. "And doesn't it seem like a lifetime ago," I continued, trying to sound like an old friend, "that we were all last here, all of us together?"

He stared at me. "Yes, a lifetime. It's a different world."

"A different world," I repeated.

"But a lovely morning for a ride," he added. Then he turned, walked across to the stable-yard gate and opened it for me. I pulled on the reins, moved across the cobblestoned courtyard, and as I passed through the gate I looked down at him and simply said, "Thank you," the way I would to anyone. As I entered the meadow, looking out upon that place which had once been ours, I shut my eyes. Then I heard the clunk of the gate behind me—like a latch dropping on my heart—and I turned back, but he'd already disappeared.

My ride was not the ride I'd anticipated. All I could think of was him. Each point along the way led me back to him: every tree and field, each fence and gate and stile. Every familiar point on the horizon, memorized and cherished for the moments I'd spent there with him, or thinking of him; each landmark and vista reminding me of him. A white veil of mist hung over the lake, and beyond it, a windless, serene landscape: dreamlike and out of reach.

When I returned to the stables, an hour or so later, a young boy helped me to dismount and took Brandy from me. And I contemplated going to Mrs. Cuthbert's cottage and knocking on the door. I wasn't sure what I'd say, or even if he'd be there, but I wanted to see him, wanted to say so much. But how could I? And what was there to say now? I was married. I was Mrs. Boyd.

Over breakfast, and before Mama came down, I asked Henry what was to become of Mrs. Cuthbert. He told me she'd be fine; she'd stay on in her cottage, he thought; probably continue as housekeeper at Deyning. It wasn't the right time to ask too many questions, and Henry didn't seem to cope well with questions—so I tried to leave it at that. I tried but I couldn't.

"I saw Tom Cuthbert this morning," I said, as I buttered my toast.

"Oh yes," Henry replied, from behind the newspaper.

"Has he been here for long?"

He lowered the paper, stared across the table at me. "He's been here for years, Issa. You know that."

"Yes, yes . . . I know he's lived here for some years, but he went away to war too," I said, wondering if Henry had somehow momentarily forgotten about the war. "What I meant was has he been back here long?"

"Oh, I've no idea. He's certainly been around for the last couple of weeks, but how long before that I'm really not sure." He shuffled the newspaper, folding it and laying it down next to him, then added,

"Yes, now I come to think of it, he did ask after you." He looked across at me and smiled. "You know I always had a hunch that he . . . rather liked you. Even looked a tad despondent when I told him you *and* your husband would be coming down."

"Charlie had to stay in London . . . he's still having treatment. And, anyway, he wouldn't have been able to cope with the chaos and upheaval here."

Mama had already informed me that our day was to be spent listing all of the items that were to be sent to London, and those that were to remain at the house to be auctioned. *A full day's work*, she'd said to me the previous evening. I couldn't disappear, and I knew that she would not be pleased to know Tom Cuthbert was about, back at Deyning. And, though I was worried about how she would react to that news, I decided I had to tell her I'd seen him; explain to her, prepare her. But the thought of uttering his name to her made me shake so much that when I lifted a slice of toast to my mouth I noticed my hand already trembling.

In the end it was easier than I'd anticipated. We were sitting in what was once her boudoir, ticking off items on Henry's scrawled inventory.

"Yes, I knew he was here," she said, without looking up at me. "How is he?"

"He's . . . fine. Older, of course," I said, surprised by her lack of reaction, her calmness.

"How was he with you?" she asked, moving papers about.

"Perfectly fine. It was brief, Mama. We said very little, but he wished me well on my marriage."

"Good," she said, and then she looked up at me. "Do you still love him?"

I couldn't quite believe she'd asked me that question, so boldly, so openly. And even now, I find it hard to believe that she did. For in those five words she finally acknowledged something: that I had loved Tom Cuthbert.

"I don't know," I answered, honestly.

"I do what I think is best for each of you . . . both of you," she said, lowering her eyes again. "It could never have come to anything. But I think you realize that now." She peered at me, over her spectacles, and I could tell she wasn't quite finished. "You've been through a great deal,

Clarissa, but it's all in the past now. Leave it there. Don't be tempted to revisit those dark days."

At first I wondered what she meant. Was she referring to my baby? Was she worried I'd tell Tom?

"I have no intention of revisiting them, Mama," I replied, looking away from her to the list in front of me.

It had been two years. Two years since I'd discovered I was pregnant with Tom's child, and yet it felt to me more like ten. So much had happened in that short space of time: I'd been sent away, given birth to my daughter and given her away; and now I was married. But of course only my mother knew all of this. A piece of my history, those *dark days*—that indelible part of my story—could never be acknowledged; never be spoken of. Some losses, it seemed to me, particularly in wartime, were noble sacrifices, but the loss of an unplanned, illegitimate child was beyond shameful; it was, quite simply, unmentionable. Later, upon reflection, I knew exactly why my mother was so concerned. She was worried that my seeing Tom Cuthbert again would reopen what had once appeared to her to be a gaping, messy wound. After all, it had tidied up nicely, left no visible scars.

That evening, having our before-dinner drinks in the dismantled drawing room, he appeared; dressed for dinner, shaven and dapper. I was shocked. I half expected my mother to ask him to leave, but instead she moved toward him, asked him how he was, spoke to him kindly, even tenderly, and he was nothing less than a gentleman in his demeanor and replies to her. Henry was in the mood for a party and played "I Wonder Who's Kissing Her Now" on the gramophone.

"Come along, Issa . . ." he shouted, tugging at my hand, already half drunk. He sang the words of the song, pulling me across the bare floorboards, a cigarette hanging from his dry lips, as Mama looked on, smiling nervously, her head slightly lowered—ready, expectant of anything. He would peak early and collapse, I thought, and I'm sure she thought that too.

Julian Carter and Michael Deighton had been in the same year at school with my brother. They were Henry's only surviving friends—along with Charlie and Jimmy—

from what he'd once called the Set. Almost their entire class had been killed in action. Michael had been a patient at the same hospital in Edinburgh as Charlie for a while and was a gentle, fragile soul, with a nervous smile and quiet manner. Julian had once been like Henry: handsome, loud, and full of fun; but all arrogance had been knocked out of him. He'd served in the Royal Flying Corps and had been badly burned and blinded when his airplane crashed returning from a night mission. No girls would ever again be rushing to kiss his mauled lips and badly grafted face.

As Henry pulled me across the drawing room floor in an attempt to dance, these two damaged boys, for that's really all they were, sat together quietly like old men, watching—or in Julian's case, listening—to the young at play. And then the gong sounded, and we all marched into the dining room, overly gay, overly animated. I hadn't spoken to Tom in the drawing room, but at dinner we were seated opposite each other, and I felt a little too aware of his presence, especially in front of Mama. He and Henry, now seated in Father's place, smoked incessantly, and, I noticed, drank more than they ate. The conversation was mainly politics, with a few ridiculous and highly implausible stories from Henry, who was in dangerously sparkling form. I saw my mother watching Henry, and then saw her whisper something to Tom, seated on her right. And I suddenly realized why she'd wanted him there: to keep an eye on Henry, to look after him. She knew he would, you see.

After dinner, I noticed Mama whispering to Tom once again, in the hallway, before she excused herself and bid everyone good night. The rest of us, four war-torn damaged young men and me, returned to the drawing room. We'd been drinking champagne, the last of the good stuff from my father's cellar. "Let's celebrate," Henry said, returning from the kitchen with two of the young girls Mrs. Cuthbert had hired from the village, *and* another bottle. "Let's bloody well celebrate being alive, eh?" he said, smiling at Tom, and passing him the hand of one of the girls. And in a way it almost seemed like the old days. For there we were, celebrating, and dancing to George's gramophone records. It was a party, a party at Deyning, and but for the missing furniture and carpets, and the absence of two of my brothers, it could have been . . . how it should have been.

"I say, Issa, Georgie would have loved this," Henry called out to me as he whirled around the young blonde, and it was true: George always loved an impromptu party.

I stood on my own, sipping champagne, swaying in time to the music, watching Tom and his partner. I couldn't recall ever having seen him dance before, and he moved well, his feet keeping perfect time. I watched him guide her over to where Michael and Julian sat, and a beaming Michael rose to his feet and eagerly took her hand. Tom glanced over at me, then sat down and lit a cigarette. No, he won't dance with me, I thought; we can't dance together. Not now. I looked at Julian and my heart ached for him. I wasn't sure if he wanted to dance, or even if he was able, but I walked over to where he sat with Tom.

"Julian . . ." I said, putting down my glass and placing my hand upon his, "will you dance with me?"

"Ah, Mrs. Boyd, I thought you'd never ask," he replied, rising unsteadily from his chair.

As I led him to the middle of the room, slowly, he said, "Do you remember the last time we danced together, Clarissa?"

"No, I don't," I said, taking his hand and placing it on my waist. "When was it?"

"It was here. Henry's twenty-first birthday party, the year before . . . before the war broke out," he said, trying to smile, stretching the tight skin of his new, colorless mouth.

"Yes, of course it was, of course. I remember now . . . you told me that you were waiting until I was eighteen, and then . . . then you were going to ask for Papa's permission to marry me. You really were such a flirt."

He laughed. "Those were the days. I don't suppose I'll be doing much flirting now, do you? More likely scare the girls off."

"Don't say that."

"Just as well I can't see myself really. But I want to know, do I . . . do I look particularly gruesome? Tell me, Clarissa; tell me the truth. Do you think anyone might see beyond this face . . . might love me?"

He'd stopped shuffling; we'd stopped moving.

"Well," I began, looking back at him,

almost wanting to cry, "you're not quite as handsome as you were, Julian, which at least means you give the others a chance now . . . and you're certainly not going to win any dancing competitions . . ." He laughed. "And if all you'd ever wished for was someone to love you for your good looks, then you may well be disappointed. But if you let someone see inside your soul . . . see who you really are, then yes, you'll be loved, darling, and she'll be a very lucky lady too," I added. And then, quite spontaneously, for I certainly hadn't planned on kissing Julian Carter that night, and I'm still not sure what came over me or why I did it, I took his head in my hands, placed my lips where his had once been and held them there for a moment. As I stepped back from him, I heard Henry clap and then shout, "Encore! Encore!"

I turned to Tom, and he stared back at me—his head lowered, as though he'd meant to look away.

Julian said, "My God, Clarissa . . . I wasn't expecting that. You're the first person to kiss me since . . . in years."

Minutes later, I led Julian back to his chair.

Tom stood up. "I suppose if I ask you to dance *now*, it might seem like I want a kiss too," he said. And Julian laughed.

I placed my hand upon his shoulder, felt the warmth of his flat against my back, and I let him guide me across the floor. I didn't, couldn't look into his eyes. I stared at his tie, his shirt collar, the line of his jaw, his mouth. Then, as Henry disappeared—twirling his dance partner through the open French doors—he pulled me closer, and I felt his breath on my face, his fingers spread out over my spine. A woman's voice sang out forlornly, "I ain't got no-body," and as he moved his hand in mine, interlinking our fingers, I looked up at him, into his eyes. He didn't smile, or speak, he simply held my gaze.

But I'd begun to feel light-headed. I'd drunk far more than I was used to that night, and my physical proximity to him—his touch—seemed to have exacerbated the effects of the champagne. So, as the record finished, and with my head slightly spinning, I said, "Please excuse me. I need some air."

There was a full moon that night, a long shadow stretching across the driveway in front of the house. I don't know how far I walked, but I remember standing against a fence, trying to light a cigarette, when he appeared by my side. I knew he'd come. I knew he'd follow me. He took my cigarette, lit it and handed it back to me, and we stood there for a while, smoking, without saying a word.

"You hate me," I said at last, without looking at him.

I heard him sigh. "No, I don't hate you, Clarissa."

"Did you ever love me?"

"Do you want me to have loved you? Is that what you want?"

"I want you to tell me the truth. I want you to be honest with me. I need to know."

"But you belong to someone else now."

I looked at him and I wished away the world; wished away Deyning, my mother, my brother, Charlie and everything else I knew.

He reached out, stroked my cheek. "Beautiful Clarissa," he said. But as I moved toward him he stepped back from me. "You said you'd wait for me. You promised."

"I did wait . . . I waited so long."

"I can't stand the thought of you with him . . . with anyone else."

"I don't want to be with anyone else. I've only ever wanted you."

He stood holding on to the fence, staring out across the moonlit field.

"I think I should go away, leave here; leave England."

"But you've only just come back . . . no, no, don't say that. Please . . ."

He turned to me. "Clarissa, you're married. You have a life now . . . a life with Charlie. What do you suggest I do? Wait for you to one day fit me into your diary, so that we can meet for tea and reminisce about *old times*? Wait in the hope of one day being invited to your home for dinner— so that I can see you, so that I can watch him with you, watch him love you . . ." He turned away, ran his hands through his hair. "We have to move on. I have to move on."

"No. I won't let you," I said, and I reached out but he pulled away again.

"What do you want from me, Clarissa? Do you want us to have an affair? Is that what you want?"

"No! Oh, I don't know . . . but I can't—"

"I could be your butler, eh? Or perhaps Charlie's valet . . . polish his shoes for him, service his wife when he's not about. Is that the idea? Am I getting a little warmer?"

"Tom!"

He closed his eyes, shook his head. "We can't, Clarissa, we can't . . ." He turned to me. "Look at me. I have nothing." He shrugged. "I'm nobody. How could I ever take care of you?"

"But I love you, Tom."

"Forget about me; love your husband, Clarissa."

And then he jumped over the fence, and walked off through the paddock toward the light of his mother's cottage.

Chapter Twenty-two

I didn't want to go back to London, but I knew Mama would. She didn't want to stay and watch what was left of her home be dismantled, packed into crates. She'd said to me the previous day, "I shouldn't have to do this . . . I shouldn't have to see this." And she was right, I thought.

"I've been thinking, Mama, perhaps I should stay here with Henry," I suggested over breakfast. "It seems wrong for us to leave him, for him to be here on his own—sorting everything."

"But what about Charlie?" she asked.

"He'll be fine. We have Sonia now," I

said, referring to our new maid. "She'll look after him. I can stay here until the end of the week, and get Charlie to come down and fetch me then."

She looked at me quizzically, and I saw the thought flash through her mind: Tom Cuthbert. Then she said, "You're right, of course, I would feel better if one of us were to stay here with him. But are you quite certain that Charlie shan't mind?"

"Quite. I'll telephone him now.

"Mama would prefer it if I were to stay here with Henry. Would you mind awfully if I did?"

"Yes, I jolly well would. Do you really have to? There's no doubt a bloody army of helpers there—*and* those two friends of his."

"There's not an army of helpers here, Charlie. And Julian certainly can't do anything," I added. "I think Henry only brought him down for a break. And to be honest, Henry's not much use either. He's simply not able to cope with it all on his own."

"Really, Clarissa, I need you here . . . I need you here with me."

"But it'd only be for the week."

"The week! You mean I shan't see you all week?"

"I'll call you. Every day. I promise. And on Friday, you can drive down here."

He muttered something, then said, "Well, it doesn't seem as though I have any choice in the matter. But it's really not on, you know. You're my wife . . . you're meant to be here for *me*."

"You'll be fine, dear. And they do say absence makes the heart grow fonder . . ."

It wasn't as though I was planning anything sinister. I simply wanted to stay a little while longer at Deyning. And even if Tom Cuthbert hadn't been there, I'd have elected to stay and help Henry. But yes, I wanted to see Tom again too. I couldn't leave him. Not yet.

After waving off Mama, I spent the morning sorting china and crockery with Mabel in the dining room, listing each dinner and tea service, checking for chips and cracks before she wrapped them in newspaper and placed them into a crate. Henry had gone down to the farm, where there was to be an auction of livestock the following week, and I wasn't altogether sure where Michael and Julian were, or even if they were still at Deyning.

"I think we'll make that do for now, Mabel. I'd quite like to take a walk, have some fresh air. Perhaps we can finish off later this afternoon."

I saw her roll her eyes. "Right you are, miss. Well, I'll be helping Mrs. C if you need me," she said, and then she picked up another box and carried it from the room.

I wandered outside, on to the terrace. It was a warm day, already humid, and I wondered whether to walk to the lake, take a swim. I wondered where Tom was. He could be anywhere, I thought.

I walked back into the house and headed for the kitchen.

I poked my head around the baize door. "Mrs. Cuthbert?"

She appeared in the scullery doorway, wiping her hands on her apron. "Oh, hello, Miss Clarissa. Can I get you something?"

"Actually, I need Tom. I wondered if he'd help me move some boxes."

"Oh, Mabel and I can do that for you, dear."

"No, these are very heavy boxes. Books."

"Ah. Well, I imagine he's still at home, I'll go and fetch him for you."

"No, no, it's quite all right, I'll go," I said, and then I disappeared before she could say anything else.

I knocked on the cottage door, waited a moment and then turned the handle and stepped into the small hallway. "Hello!"

I glanced into the room on my left: a tiny room with a low beamed ceiling and crammed with furniture. I stepped back over the hallway and opened another door: a kitchen, even smaller. Ahead of me, a steep, narrow staircase. I climbed it, quietly, not sure what I'd find, but wondering if Tom would be there, in his bed, asleep. At the top of the staircase I opened the door immediately on my right. Mrs. Cuthbert's bedroom: immaculately tidy, with a pink bedspread on a small single bed. I stepped back out of the room, gently closing the door, turned to the other the door and lifted its latch. The room was in semidarkness, the curtains still closed. And there he was: lying facedown, sleeping.

I could have left. I could have descended that narrow staircase and left the cottage, but I didn't. I entered the small sloping roofed room closing the door behind me, and then I slipped off my shoes, went over to his bed and knelt down on the floor next to him. I didn't touch him; I sat listening to his breathing, watching him. A faded blue curtain gently swayed by the open window next to me, and but for the sound of birds outside, the place was perfectly silent. I closed my eyes for a moment: *thank you for keeping him alive . . . thank you for keeping him safe.*

A white sheet wrapped tangled around his midriff; two legs, so perfectly formed, sprawled out across another; and an arm hung listlessly from the edge of the bed.

I studied that forearm, dangling in front of me, noting its shape, its dark hairs and scars; and then I lifted it, and pressed my lips to his flesh. He stirred, pulled his arm away, moved on to his side and opened his eyes, blinking at me.

"Am I dreaming?" he asked, in a thick, sleepy voice. A voice I'd never heard before.

"Yes," I replied, rising to my feet, "this is a dream, Tom . . . just a dream."

I unfastened the buttons down the front of my dress, stepped out of it and laid it over a chair, on top of his clothes. I rolled down my stockings, one by one, and placed them carefully over the same chair. I untied my camisole, lifted it up over my head and placed that too upon the chair. And then I pulled the comb from my hair, and placed it upon a chest of drawers. I turned to him, watched his eyes pass over my body, saw him swallow, his mouth open slightly, and then I climbed into his bed, next to him, naked.

We made love without uttering any coherent word. And afterward, I dressed in silence and left the cottage. I remember walking back to the house feeling the most sublime sense of peace. Had I no shame? No, not with him; never with him.

A little while later, I walked to the lake. I changed into my bathing costume at the boathouse and then swam across to the island. And as I sat on the jetty looking back at Deyning in the distance, I remembered all the summers and all the picnics I'd shared there—on that island—with my brothers. I saw them rowing over the water toward me, calling out my name, laughing. And then I saw a figure, standing by the boathouse, completely still, looking back across the lake at me. I watched him strip off his clothes, dive into the water and swim toward me. And I watched him emerge from the water.

"Miss Clarissa, will you be needin' anything . . . anything at all?" he asked, standing in front of me, naked.

"Hmm. That depends what you had in mind, Cuthbert," I replied, looking up at him, squinting into the sun.

"Can I be gettin' yer summit to drink, p'raps?"

"Yes . . . that would be rather nice. A glass of champagne, I think . . ."

"Very well, m'lady."

And he turned, and dived back into the water.

"Tom! No! Come back!"

A few minutes later I saw him emerge at the other side of the lake. And I giggled out loud as I watched him pull on his clothes and then run up through the field, toward the house. *What on earth is he up to?*

I lay back against the warm timber and looked up at a never-ending blueness. How perfect some moments are: there was not a cloud between heaven and me. And as I languished there in the sunshine, I could hear the unabashed joy of young birds in the trees behind me, the rumbling of a distant motor. I closed my eyes, remembering our lovemaking of earlier that morning. And then I thought of Charlie. *Dear Charlie.* I didn't want to hurt him, didn't want to deceive him. But somehow it didn't feel wrong to be with Tom. You see, I'd given *him* my heart, promised it to him so many years before.

When I sat up, there he was, rowing toward me this time, fully clothed, a cigarette in his mouth. He climbed out of the boat, lifted out a large basket and a rug, and walked toward me.

"You were quick."

"Time is of the essence, ma'am."

"Oh God, I do hope you're not stuck in character for the whole afternoon."

"Why? Do you not like it? I thought it might excite you . . . me playing that part."

"I don't need you to play any part," I said, as he spread the rug out next to me. "Though I do rather like having you wait on me."

"Aha! I knew it. Well then, m'lady, I'll be applyin' for yer position as lady's maid."

"Gosh, that would be novel," I replied,

and giggled. "And I can just see you in the uniform."

"Yes, and it shall be my job to see to it that you're properly dressed . . . and un-dressed, each day, of course," he contin-ued, sitting down, and pulling a bottle of champagne from the basket. "But there may be more undressing than dressing," he added, glancing at me.

I rolled on to the rug and lay on my stomach.

"But you can't undress me more than once."

"Yes, I can," he said, glancing at me again with a wicked grin. "I could spend all day dressing and undressing you."

He popped the champagne, pulled a glass from the basket and poured it, lick-ing the spillage from his hand and handing me the glass.

"Where did this come from? Papa's cel-lar?"

"Of course."

"I thought we'd finished that."

"Not the bottles I'd purloined."

"You're shameless!"

"I know. But I happen to know this very gorgeous creature," he said, lying down next to me, "who rather likes champagne. It was an act of mercy, really."

I laughed. "You think champagne will keep her alive and gorgeous?"

"Absolutely. Champagne and me. Lots and lots of me."

I rolled on to my side and looked up at him. "You're right. Lots and lots of you will keep me alive."

He turned to face me, his head propped in his hand. "I think we should build a house here . . . and shoot anyone who comes across the water."

"That's not very friendly," I said, smiling at him, his humor.

"I don't feel like being friendly with anyone apart from you."

I reached out, stroked his face. "We'd have to have some friends . . . we'd get bored of each other, cooped up here on an island, day in, day out."

"No we wouldn't. We could simply pretend to be other people when we got bored of our real selves."

I laughed again. "Ah, you mean you play lady's maid to Miss Clarissa."

"Yes, that sort of thing. And I'm sure I can come up with a few more."

"Such as?"

"Let me think . . . Groom to Miss Clarissa—or rather to her horse?"

"*Horses*, please. I'd have more than one."

"Gardener to Miss Clarissa?"

"Broughton!"

He raised an eyebrow. "And then we'd have to spend an awful lot of time in the hothouse . . ."

I smiled. "You do seem bent on domestic service."

He ran a finger down my nose. "But of course. It's my family's line of business."

"Perhaps I could be Issie, the extraordinarily well-endowed parlormaid to Lord Cuthbert," I suggested.

He looked up at the sky and shook his head. "No. I'm afraid I can't see you being very convincing in that part." He turned to me, "You can only ever be Clarissa."

We lay there for a while staring at each other, smiling. We'd already finished our glasses of champagne when he rose to his feet.

"Come," he said, offering me his hand.

"But where?" I asked.

He placed the bottle and glasses back

into the basket, threw the rug over his shoulder, and then led me away from the jetty, into the trees.

"But where are we going?" I asked again, carefully dodging nettles, ducking branches, but happy enough for him to lead me on.

"Away from eyes," he replied.

When we emerged from the shadows, at the other side of the island, he stood on the bank looking about; surveying the landscape for *eyes* I presumed. Then he put down the basket and spread the rug out once more. I was cold, shivering.

"You really need to take that off . . . let it dry," he said, sitting down. "Here, take my shirt." He pulled it off, over his head, and handed it to me, then turned away as I rolled down my bathing suit and put on his shirt. I hung the damp costume over a branch and sat down next to him on the rug. Ahead of us was nothing but water and empty cornfields, the hazy outline of hills in the distance. He took hold of my hand and for a while we sat in complete silence, staring out in front of us.

"I did wait, Tom," I said at last.

"No, let's not speak of it, not now," he

said, and then he took hold of me, pulled me down onto the rug and kissed me.

We made love again, there, under that bright Sussex sky, and afterward we swam in the lake; moving through the water separately then coming together once more, our bodies entwined under its dark wetness. When we emerged from the water, teeth chattering, he wrapped the rug around us both and held me in his arms. We spent the remainder of that afternoon lying on the bank, cocooned and naked inside the rug. We talked about his plans for the future. He said he simply wanted to get on with his life now and wouldn't be returning to Oxford.

"But what about the bar?" I asked.

"I don't want to go into law, not now. I couldn't go back to all that now."

"What will you do?"

"I'm not entirely sure." He turned to me. "But I've been thinking about America . . ."

"America?"

"Yes. There are opportunities there. Opportunities to make a lot of money." He paused, staring at me. "You could come with me."

"Come with you?"

"Yes, come with me. Come with me, Clarissa."

"But what about Charlie, and Mama?"

"Leave Charlie and come with me."

My head was swimming. "Leave Charlie?" I repeated. "But it would kill him. He loves me. I'm everything to him . . . all he has."

He looked away, closed his eyes.

"I have to see you, Clarissa. I can't stand the thought of living in the same city, the same country, and not being able to see you . . . be with you."

I pressed my lips against his neck. "But you've lived without me for quite a while . . . and survived."

"That was different. There was a war on. I wasn't free, wasn't able to see you." He sighed. "And now I've seen you"—he tightened his grip around me—"held you, tasted you . . . I can't bear to let you go again."

"And Charlie?" I asked, again.

"What about him? Were you thinking of him when we made love this morning?"

"No! Of course not. But it's different here. You belong to me here . . . and I belong to you here."

"Here," he repeated, wistfully. "And *here* is about to disappear. Deyning is about to be sold. So, after these few days, is that it?"

"Please, don't make it sound so brutal."

"Well, it is, isn't it?"

"No, it's not. But I can't see any other way," I said, sitting up, putting my head in my hands. "America . . . it's just not possible."

He grabbed hold of my wrist, pulled me back down to him, and wrapped his arms around me. "I want to make love to you for the rest of my life," he said, kissing my face. "And when I breathe my last I want you there. I want the last word I utter to be your name, the last face I look upon to be yours . . ."

And I began to cry, for I too couldn't bear the thought of a future without him in it.

"Don't go to America. Please, Tom, don't go to America," I said through tears. "Stay here, in England. There are jobs here . . . opportunities here . . ."

"Clarissa . . ."

"Promise me, promise me you won't go."

"I can't, I can't make that promise," he

said, lifting his hand to my face, wiping away the wetness. "I can't make that promise," he said again, kissing my forehead. "But I shall try, for a while at least, not to go."

We didn't leave the island until early evening. He rowed us across the water slowly and in silence, and then he sat on the jetty as I changed back into my clothes in the boathouse. We walked through the pink blush of the meadow and stopped by the tree—"Our tree," he said—and looked back at the lake. It had been a perfect day. One etched on to my memory forever.

Of course, I'd entirely forgotten about any arrangement with Mabel, or the fact that Henry had had no idea where I was. And as I walked across the hallway, toward the stairs, Henry's voice boomed at me from the doorway of the drawing room. "Issa, thank God! Where the hell have you been?"

I stopped in my tracks. "Oh, hello," I said, calmly. "Where've I been? I've been having a wander about the estate, and I rowed out to the island."

He moved toward me, and I immediately saw from his face how frightened he'd been.

"You can't just disappear off like that, for hours on end and on your own; don't you realize? Don't you realize anything could happen to you?" He was shouting, in a state.

"I'm so sorry, Henry. I forgot the time," I said, reaching out and touching his arm. "But I'm here now, darling, and as you can see I'm perfectly safe and unharmed," I added, looking up into his anxious eyes.

For a moment I thought he might cry. I could feel the tension in his body; see the strain in his face. And I felt immeasurably guilty to have caused him such distress.

"Bloody stupid . . . bloody stupid . . ." he muttered, as he turned and walked away.

Later that evening, before dinner, I telephoned Charlie.

"Yes, it's been a heavenly day here too, though I haven't seen much of it," I lied. "Mabel and I have been so busy packing up the place."

Chapter Twenty-three

⟆

I'd already decided that I wanted to spend all the available time I had that week with Tom. I knew that our time was limited, and I also knew that though it would be unbearable to say good-bye to him, I had no choice; I had to. Somehow, in my mind, there seemed to be a degree of absolution for my sins, my infidelity with Tom, if I returned to my husband. My unfaithfulness was finite. I would, ultimately, do the right thing, I thought.

I'd invited Tom to join us for dinner that evening. Henry was drinking heavily again, and he, Michael and Julian were reminiscing about the war—about the brothels at the front. Tom and I barely spoke. Instead, we conducted a conversation with our eyes, knowing the others would not notice. After dinner the five of us retired to the drawing room and played gramophone records once again. And I danced with him once more as the other three sat around smoking, watching us. I'm really not sure what they saw, but they must have seen, must have known. While we were dancing, holding each other, I whispered to him to come back to the house later, through the servants hall and up the back staircase. I knew Henry would soon be out for the count. And, perhaps sadly, Michael and Julian didn't really matter.

"Good night, all," I said, when I left the room, leaving all four men there, and blowing them each a kiss.

As I climbed into my bed I heard Henry and the other two singing their way up the staircase, followed by an attempt—by Henry, I presumed—to play "The Last Post" on his bugle. Tom, I thought, must have gone home but would be back shortly. Then my door opened, and there he was.

"Tom! Henry has only just gone to bed."

"Clarissa, they barely know what day of the week it is let alone where I am or what *we* may be up to," he replied, pulling off his tie.

"Are you absolutely sure? If he finds out he's bound to tell Mama."

He didn't answer me. He took off his clothes, leaving them scattered across the floor and climbed into bed with me. Then he said, "If we're going to have an affair, Clarissa, can you please stop mentioning your mama?"

"I'm sorry."

"And that's another thing—you must stop apologizing to me."

He took hold of me, kissed me passionately.

"I've been longing to do that all evening," he said, and then he reached over and turned out the lamp.

The next few days were blissful. We spent every afternoon together, usually on the island with a picnic. Once, when it rained, we rowed back across the lake and spent the remainder of the afternoon locked inside the boathouse. We scripted and acted out a play all about life at Deyning, with each of us playing a multitude of different parts. Tom, of course, proved to be the better mimic, adding something more—"a soupçon of wickedness," he said—to each familiar figure: an unsurprising but ridiculously lascivious Mr. Broughton, with a penchant for being naked while gardening; a lusty Edna, with a preference for women; and an acutely observed spoilsport called Mabel. And as I rolled about the wooden floor, half naked and crying with laughter, I didn't think about tomorrow or next week. I didn't think about the future, or the past.

But sometimes, in our quiet moments, I'd watched a frown creep into his brow. I'd felt him wince, his whole body tense, seen him shut his eyes. And I knew in those moments that he was remembering the war. Not inviting it back, but having it forced forward in his memory. And I didn't want to ask him about it, because I didn't want him to have to go back there, to remember. And the one time I had asked him, when I'd said, "Tell me. What is it? You can tell me . . . I want you to know you can talk to me about it," he'd turned to me and said,

"No. I don't want to talk about it. I'll never talk about it." He'd looked at me with such intensity, such fear and pain in his eyes. "I don't want you to know," he said. "I don't want you to know what I've seen . . . what I've done."

Each evening, after dinner, we danced; and later, upstairs in my bed, we made love. On our last night he said to me, "We will be together, one day; I know it. And if I thought for a moment it wasn't to be, I think . . . I think I might stop breathing."

I wanted to tell him then about Emily. I wanted to but I didn't know how to. I hadn't uttered her name to a living soul, and I'd buried her so deep inside my own that it was almost impossible for me to think of her as being real. Had I actually had a child? Was there really a little girl somewhere looking out on to the world with those same serious dark eyes?

Emily.

She'd be two years of age: walking, speaking, part of another family. And that was my comfort, the one thing I'd held on to: that she *belonged* to someone, somewhere. For if I wasn't able to love her, the idea that she belonged, that she was held close, loved and cherished, offered a degree of assuagement.

But if I spoke her name—what would happen?

On our last night together I did speak her name. As we lay in bed, wrapped in each other's arms, I said her name out loud.

"Emily . . ."

He turned on to his side. "Emily? And who, exactly, is Emily?"

I closed my eyes. *He said her name.*

"A little girl. She's a little girl," I said.

He laughed. "And *where*, pray tell, does Emily live?" he asked. "Or is she one of your imaginary friends?"

"Yes, I suppose she is."

I couldn't tell him. I couldn't tell him we had a child, one I'd misplaced, given away, and then, after telling him that, leave him myself. So I played a game with him; a game dictated by him.

"And what does she look like?"

"Oh, she's very small . . . with dark hair and very dark eyes. Serious eyes."

"Hmm. And is she kind?"

"Oh yes, she's very kind, but quite shy."

He reached out, stroked my hair. "Is she here now?" he asked.

I stared up into the blackness. "Yes and no . . . I like to think she's here."

"Well, perhaps you can leave little Emily here with me tomorrow. And perhaps . . . perhaps occasionally I shall send her back to you with a message."

I swallowed, closed my eyes again. "Yes, I think she'd like that," I said, beginning to cry. "I think she'd like that very much."

He took me in his arms and held me tightly. "You'll know when I'm thinking of you now, because Emily will be there," he said.

The following morning Charlie arrived. I hadn't expected him until later in the day, and, luckily, I was still at the house, attending to another list with Mabel.

"Charlie!"

He stood in the doorway for a moment, smiling, then came toward me. "Hello, darling, I thought I might as well take the day off—come down here early and surprise you."

"Thank you, Mabel," I said, and then I whispered, "Oh, and Mabel, would you be so kind and let Mr. Cuthbert know that my husband has arrived, and I shan't be need-ing his help with the boxes."

I'm not sure what Mabel thought. She must have known that Tom hadn't lifted a box all week. But she nodded at me and said, "Yes, miss. I'll let him know."

That evening Tom declined my invitation to join us for dinner and sent a message via his mother that he was "otherwise engaged." I sat in the dining room with the men, but I hardly spoke, and I couldn't eat a thing. I looked down at the food on my plate, glanced up at Henry and the others as they spoke; and I tried to smile back at Charlie. I stared at the bare walls, felt each and every minute as it slipped away; and I longed for him. I wanted to run to the cottage, find him and hold him once more. And when Charlie climbed into my bed later that evening and reached over to me, I finally felt the shame of infidelity. For I *was* being unfaithful: I was being unfaithful to my heart.

Early the next morning, as we said our good-byes, Tom was nowhere to be seen. Looking back, it was probably better that way. I couldn't have coped with a farewell, or even a polite adieu, and I knew he didn't want to see me with Charlie.

As we drove away I felt physically sick. And I didn't look back. I didn't want to see my world disappearing from view. I wanted to stop the car, get out and run back up the driveway, home, and to him. I wanted to tell Charlie. I wanted to say to him, "I'm sorry. I'm so very, very sorry, but I love someone else . . ." And then he spoke. He said, "I know how hard this must be for you, Clarissa. I know you feel as though you're leaving behind everything you've ever loved. But you have a new life now, a life with me. And I know we're going to be happy." He reached over, placed his hand upon mine. "So happy."

∽

. . . Yes, the sale of the place is sad, very sad. It is a loss, the end of an era—as you say, but in truth that era ended for me when William and George died. It is all gone now, that life, & those halcyon days; it went with them, & belonged to them . . . and in my dreams I see them in the Elysian Fields . . . at Deyning.

PART THREE

Chapter Twenty-four

॰

. . . What worries me most is not the financial struggle, but H's increasing alcohol addiction and fragile state of mind. He was once so full of life & ambition—easily the most ambitious of the three—but that aspect of his character has completely gone, & now all he does is sit & stare, lost in a trance, and often quite unable to hear me. He continues to suffer from nightmares, & is prone to weeping, about what he cannot tell me.

॰

Had I known, that morning in the spring of 1919, how my life was to unfold, had I known how infinitely precious love is, I would have told Charlie everything and run back to Tom. But the war had just ended and I was still young and craved some semblance of the life I'd been brought up to live. I was neither mature enough nor strong enough to cope with any estrangement from the remnants of my shattered family. My mother had suffered such loss, and Charlie, mentally as well as physically fragile, was dependent upon me. It seemed to be up to me to try to restore a sense of normality to our lives, to be the Granville who lived happily ever after. My marriage to Charlie—our future together—was the foundation of that, I thought.

When I left Deyning that day I hadn't allowed myself to dwell upon a future without Tom. At that time I still lived from day to day, week to week. I simply didn't think about the years ahead. And, apart from those few weeks we'd shared before the war, and that final week at Deyning, Tom and I had never spent any time together. Not really. He was not and had never been a part of my life. Oh, in my head, in my heart, he'd been everything, but that remained a secret, my secret. So, I followed a path through muted seasons, occasionally allowing myself to think of him, wonder about him, but I was resigned to the separateness of our lives; resigned to that sensation of *loss* as being part and parcel of life. Brothers, cousins and friends didn't grow old, but remained childhood memories; fathers passed on; homes changed; and babies, too, could be taken. Why would the man I'd fallen in love with not disappear from my life too? It was part of a pattern. It seemed to me that anything, everything, I loved and held dear, I would be estranged from.

One month slid into another, and then into another, and I moved on with my new life: my life in London as Charlie's wife. I'd already lived in the city for a number of years, already become acquainted with its many and various tones of gray, accustomed to—and even admired—its hard lines: the almost black shiny new roads and smooth slate rooftops; the murky shape of skeletal trees through smog, and those glinting, hot summer pavements. But now

I felt only its weight, and that weight deep and heavy in my heart, as though I was holding in my breath, not fully exhaling. As though I was waiting. Waiting.

But waiting for what?

It had all gone, everything. There would be no dawns or sunsets like those I'd known at Deyning; no early-morning mists to watch rise up from a lake, and no moonlit-drenched trees to wish upon. And there was no Tom. No Tom. He and everything I'd cherished had gone and could never come back. Yes, I'd lost all I held dear. I'd lost everything. And so I began to go back there, quietly, in my mind. I began to measure time—days, weeks and months—against that place: against the past.

But all of us were burdened, none of us free. For we'd been the children destined for a *great war*. The ones who'd run at it, into it, singing, and shouting happy adieus; now tormented souls, haunted by our stolen youth and absent friends, and our memories of another time. And peace, peace of mind and heart, was not God-given, not our birthright. Instead, it floated around us, teasingly. Peace. We all spoke of it, liked the sound of it, but it was a word already worn thin. And that other time, like a half-forgotten dream, came in flashes of color, light and shade; vaguely familiar shapes and fragmented images. Silence took me back, and stillness too. The scents of summer, its sounds: the whisper of the giant beeches in the park, the distant hum of a mowing machine; the sight of children picnicking, or out in boats on the lake; a lone butterfly, dancing amidst the geraniums and lavender of a window box. Yes, all of these carried me back.

I had no idea then that grief is never entirely spent. No idea that it can be suspended, frozen, sometimes for years. War had anesthetized us, numbed our senses, and even the warmth of summer could not thaw that chill around our hearts. Birthdays, Christmases, high days and holidays; family celebrations and simple pleasures, once so treasured for their languid, perfect moments were irrevocably altered by those missing: those forever young, smiling faces. And so my life was not the life I'd once imagined for myself. How could it be? My cast of players had gone; Deyning had gone; and my heart had been displaced. My marriage to Charlie was not what it should have been, for I wasn't able to give myself fully, or to love him the way I knew I could. And we were both haunted. Haunted by the memory of how we'd once been, who we had once been, and that childish notion of unfettered happiness.

Charlie's love was of a different nature. Our relationship had not been founded on physical attraction, or chemistry, though—initially, at least—it had flickered. I had married him to do the right thing, and, perhaps, to be safe, secure: to be *married*. And he'd probably married me for the same reasons: to have a wife, someone he could call his own, look upon and feel proud of, the way one would anything one deemed valuable, and perhaps rare and pleasing to the eye. To Charlie, our marriage, I knew, was something of an achievement.

During those early days, I didn't allow myself to ponder on our relationship. I embraced my role as best I could and distracted myself perfecting the part. There were people to see and entertain, a husband to amuse and look after. And we tried, I think, in those early years, to be happy together, to be in love. We both wanted children, wanted that cushion around us, and it was my fault, I thought, my fault no children came. My body seemed unwilling to produce that seal of approval without my heart's agreement. And it seemed a fitting punishment.

I went to see doctors, specialists, and, unbeknown to Charlie, tried any number of remedies and potions from women in far-flung parts of London promising me a baby. I'd lied, of course, when doctors had asked questions. I'd pleaded ignorance to the workings of my body and never said, "But I know I can do it; I've done it before." Perhaps it was that. Perhaps it was simply the tedium and disappointment of living with that longing for a child, but the complexion of our marriage changed. We stopped discussing possibilities, the future, and children. And then, three years into our marriage, we stopped sleeping together.

Of course I'd known from the start that my marriage to Charlie was a mistake. But I had *promised* to marry him, and I'd made him that promise when he was a fit and able-bodied man, fighting for his country, for all of us. I couldn't have abandoned him when he returned home, invalided; as though a war-damaged fiancé was somehow not quite up to scratch. And so, though I was lonely, hungry for love and physical intimacy, there was no way out. Happiness, I realized, was an ideal as elusive as peace.

I once tried to talk to Mama about my marriage, but she stopped me almost as soon as I began. "Clarissa, Clarissa," she said, her eyes fluttering closed, smiling, "a successful marriage is not about physical love, or passion. That type of love—however intoxicating—simply doesn't endure. A successful marriage is founded upon a partnership; it is an *alliance*, an understanding. And it is about companionship and, sometimes, forgiveness and tolerance too . . ."

I didn't tell her how much I'd already tolerated, how often I forgave Charlie. I'd never spoken to her about his black moods or his unreasonable and increasingly volatile behavior: the rages about something being out of place or dinner not served at the correct time. I'd never mentioned the silences, the evenings when he refused to speak or even look at me, and then, later, disappeared off into the night.

"But I'm still young, Mama. I need to be loved."

"You are loved, my dear. Charlie adores you."

"I don't want that . . . adoration. I want *real* love."

She sighed, looked at me, narrowing her eyes, as though trying to tune into my thoughts. "Life is about compromise, Clarissa. We all have to make sacrifices; all of us . . . even me."

I looked up at her. "But you had a perfect marriage. You and Papa loved each other . . . had children and were together until . . . until he died."

She smiled, closed her eyes again for a moment. "Yes, I loved your father, not least because we shared four children. We shared a life. And it was a good marriage, but no marriage is perfect." She sighed again. "And my marriage was not *always* perfect."

I stared at her. I'd never heard my mother speak of her marriage before, never known her admit to imperfection in any area of her life. All at once a door had opened, and I wanted to know more. I wanted to know who my mother was; what she'd known, how she'd felt. Had she, too, known grand passion? Had she ever been forced to question her life, her marriage to my father? Had someone come between her and Papa?

"Have you . . . have you ever loved anyone apart from Papa?" I asked.

There was a pause. She looked away from me, and I knew there was something.

"Yes . . . there was someone, once; many years ago now." She raised her hand to her chest, searching for her pearls. "But it was not to be."

"Before you married Papa?" I asked, silently willing her to tell me, to say more.

She stared at me.

"After you married Papa?"

She closed her eyes, momentarily, and I knew that to be a *yes*.

I wanted to ask her more questions, but I wasn't sure how, *or* if she was prepared to tell me any more. Then she said, quite calmly, in a matter-of-fact voice, "It was a long time ago, and it was impossible." She smiled at me. "I had you, your brothers—

and, of course, there was Papa. And it was . . ."—she twisted the long strand of pearls through her fingers—". . . could never have come to anything."

"I had no idea."

"Of course not. Why would you? You were still a child."

"Did Papa know?"

"No, he did not. Oh, he may have had his suspicions, and we went through a few . . . a few difficult years. But I loved your father, Clarissa. And I have no regrets."

This was all my mother was prepared to tell me at that time. It was another lesson in compromise and sacrifice.

My life in London was quite different to that time during the war, and my circle of friends had changed too. Charlie was working in the city and we saw more of his friends and work colleagues than we did of my old crowd. A number of them had moved on anyhow, were married and living in the country. But occasionally, at a party, we crossed paths with one or other of them.

Jimmy Cooper had remained in the army

after the war. He'd been out in India for two years and had only recently returned when we bumped into him at a charity dance at the Hyde Park Hotel. I knew Jimmy, like his mother, to be a diligent correspondent. He always seemed to keep track of everyone, knew who had married whom and where they were living. And as I stood chatting with him that night, he did indeed seem to know more—was more up to date on everyone's movements—than me, despite having been away for two years.

"I can't believe you've been away for two whole years, Jimmy Cooper, and yet *you* have all the gossip!" I said to him, and he laughed.

"I have to admit, most of it's passed on to me from Mama. You know how much she loves to know *everything*," he said with a smile.

"Yes, and hand it on. I think that's the part she likes best, don't you? She'd have won a medal during the war—for reconnaissance!"

"Ha! You're right. She'd have been a superb spy . . . though perhaps a little too conspicuous behind enemy lines."

I laughed. The thought of Venetia,

trussed up in all her finery, crawling through no-man's-land, was a bizarre but highly amusing image. And while it was good to be laughing, to be able to make jokes about that time, I had a sudden stab of guilt: guilt that we were standing there, at a dance, laughing about the war. And I felt a twinge of guilt about Venetia too. I hadn't seen her in a while. In fact, if truth be told, I'd been avoiding her. The last time I'd called upon her she'd asked me too many questions: questions about my marriage and about Charlie. "You and Charlie . . . you're happy?" she'd asked, staring at me with those piercing violet eyes.

"Yes," I'd replied, "yes, of course."

"It's just that . . . well, you sometimes seem a little distracted, dear, a little lost."

I'd shrugged, shaken my head, unsure what to say. "I'm fine, it's fine," I said, looking away from her.

"*Fine?* Fine does not make my heart sing, Clarissa. Fine does not evoke that flutter of happiness I so wish to feel when I look at you. And you know, you can tell me . . . you can. I'm always here for you. You're the daughter I never had . . . as dear and as precious to me as my own."

"Mama says that marriage is about compromise . . . and sacrifice. She says passion does not endure."

She smiled. "Ah, I see. And you . . . you've known passion?"

I hesitated, and then I said, "Yes, yes I have."

"But not with your husband, not with Charlie?"

I looked down, shook my head.

She sighed. "You're still in love with him, aren't you? You're still in love with Tom Cuthbert."

At that moment I was relieved to hear her say his name. She knew, and I was pleased she knew. I wanted someone to know the truth. When I began to cry she moved over to me and took me in her arms.

"Please, please promise me that you shan't say anything to Mama."

"Of course I shan't. I wouldn't dream of it . . . there are many things I don't tell your mama, Clarissa." She took my head in her hands and looked at me. "But you have to try and make your marriage work, my dear. Otherwise . . ." She stared at me, unsmiling, with tears in her eyes now too. "Otherwise you have years of loneliness ahead of you, and I simply can't bear the thought of you lonely and unhappy."

Even later that same day I'd regretted telling her. I wasn't convinced that she wouldn't report back to Mama or inadvertently say something. And so, for the next few weeks, I'd purposefully avoided her, hoping to put a distance between that sad outburst and myself. Hoping we'd both forget. But weeks had turned into months, and now I felt guilty.

"I must visit your mother," I said to Jimmy. "I've been a little lax in my calling of late."

"Yes, you must. You know how much she adores seeing you . . . adores seeing you both."

I glanced over at Charlie. He'd moved farther away from us, was talking with a group of people I didn't recognize, and so, with practiced nonchalance, I took the plunge.

"And do you ever hear anything of Tom Cuthbert?"

"Ha! Now there's a name that doesn't often crop up," he said, stopping a waiter and grabbing us each another glass of champagne. "But Cuthbert was never the best correspondent. Bloody unreliable, I'd say."

"But now that you're back—will you be seeing him?"

"Good grief, didn't you know? He's in America."

"America? No, no . . . I didn't know."

"Yes, been there for almost two years now, I think," he said, sipping his champagne. "And doing quite well for himself too, from what I understand."

"Really . . . I had no idea."

And it struck me then, the separateness of our lives. For Tom had been living on the other side of the world, living on another continent, for almost as long as I'd been living my new married life in London.

"How strange," I said, thinking out loud.

"Why's that?" Jimmy asked.

"Oh, nothing. I just thought . . . thought he would be living here in London . . . thought he would be in the city."

He laughed. "No, not Cuthbert. He was always restless, even at Oxford. Never quite . . . fit in. And I suppose he's gone *to make his fortune*." He laughed again, and for some reason I did too.

And then I said, "But you know . . . he probably will, Jimmy."

"Ha! Yes, you're right, he probably will. And he'll no doubt return here one day waving his crisp American dollars in all our faces!"

"No, he'd never do that. He'd never be arrogant or ostentatious in that way."

He looked at me curiously. "You rather liked him, didn't you?"

"Yes," I said, smiling, "yes I did."

That same night, back at our home, Charlie had come to my room. I was tired, told him I wanted to sleep. He was drunk, and more unsteady on his feet than usual. He hated his walking stick, hated his disability and, perhaps, hated himself. He was in an angry, belligerent mood, and when he stumbled and I climbed from my bed to help him, he turned and shouted, "No! I don't need your help! I don't need a bloody nurse, I need a wife."

"You have a wife, Charlie. I'm your wife."

He moved over to me, his face inches from mine. "Yes, you're my wife and you're *stuck* with me, Clarissa. And I'm *stuck* with you!"

"Is that what you think?" I asked quietly. "Is that how you feel?"

"What do you care how I feel? What do you know? You know nothing . . . nothing at all about suffering and pain, real pain. Oh yes, yes, you lost your brothers—and you never let us forget that, but you've never had to give up anything, anything of yourself, never had to sacrifice anything. You don't know what it's like . . . you have no idea. And look at you . . . you can't even produce a baby."

I closed my eyes, waited a moment before I spoke. "I know it's difficult for you, and I try to understand . . . really I do." I reached out, touched his arm. "I'm sorry."

He turned to me. "But you're always bloody sorry!" he shouted. And then he pushed me back on to the bed. "And if you're really sorry," he continued, unbuckling his belt, "you'll fulfill your obligations . . . as my *wife*."

I didn't protest, didn't say anything. And I didn't push him away. I didn't move. I lay on the bed, exactly where I'd fallen. I looked away from his contorted face, closed my eyes and tried to shut out the pain; tried to imagine I was somewhere else: . . . *the lower meadow . . . the lower meadow; under the tree . . . look up, see the sky . . . see the clouds . . .*

When he'd finished, he struggled up from the bed, picked up his stick, and then left the room. He didn't say anything, didn't speak. What could he have said? What was there to say? I was his wife. He was my husband.

Minutes later, I heard him leave the house.

I'm not sure how long I lay there. All I remember is a burning pain, and the *tick-tock . . . tick-tock . . . tick-tock . . .* of the clock. I didn't want to cry. I didn't want to acknowledge what had just taken place in any sob or sound of anguish. Even then, I knew it had to be locked away. Forgotten.

"America," I whispered. "America . . ." I said again, louder. I wanted to hear myself speak, to shatter the silence, break through the hideous echo. And as I spoke the name of that faraway continent I imagined Tom, standing, looking out from one of those very tall buildings; so tall and so high he could see across the curve of the earth's surface to England, to London, to the light of my room, to me.

"Tom . . ."

Was that to be it? I wondered. Were my snatched moments with him to be the sum total of my experience of passion and real love in this life? Were they already spent? Had I already and unknowingly passed through my zenith: that moment of unutterable perfection, when everything is the very best it can be, will ever be?

Oh, but you had it, you had it, Clarissa, and you knew it . . .

And at that moment I thought of William, hurtling toward the ground in a burning airplane. I thought of him *and* George. They had both died so young; had either of them ever known *real* passion, passionate love? And I so hoped that they had. I hoped that each of them had known at least one moment, one splendid, unforgettable moment; one that in the hour of their death they'd been able to return to; to know that they had lived, truly lived.

I felt a solitary tear slide down my temple into my hair.

No self-pity, Clarissa, no self-pity . . . think of them; think of all of them.

And I did.

I saw Frank's whitened cricket shoes,

Hugo Hamilton's bow tie; Julian's pale lips, and Archie's smile; I saw hands waving back at me from a train carriage window, and boys in uniform—standing proud and tall. I saw my father, his map and his pins and his bits of ribbon, and the men at the station, tattered and frayed and caked in mud; and the men in red coats, and the posters and words; the words, and the gloves . . . the gloves, the balaclavas, the socks; the socks and the gloves, and the uniforms sent home . . . the mud and blood and the uniforms sent home. Home.

Chapter Twenty-five

⁓

. . . I am quite well, & continue to distract myself with the social merry-go-round here, and my friend V's (who's quite the Bohemian now) new interest in Spiritualism. She's rather keen for me to attend one of her séances, telling me that G or W may well "come through," and though it's tempting, I'm not sure . . . Of course, there was a time when I would never have entertained such an idea, but V assures me that no HARM can be done, & that her Madam Zelda (apparently the very best & most

**fashionable in all of London) never fails
to bring Them through . . .**

∽

When I recall the winters of my childhood they're inevitably bathed in a pure white light, the reflection of a frozen landscape. I remember awakening to that brilliance, seeping into my room through the heavy winter drapes; the rush of chilled air as I threw back the eiderdown and climbed from my bed; the ice on the inside of the windowpanes; and the world beyond, a place of strange new shapes and alabaster stillness.

Once, when I was still quite young and my parents away in London, we awoke at Deyning to find the thickest blanket of snow I'd ever seen. It was over a foot deep. "A right rare dumping," Edna had called it. We were cut off, completely stranded for the best part of a week, the servants and me. And Mr. Broughton had to walk five miles through the snow-covered fields to the village to send a telegram to my parents. For the first few days normal routines and lessons were suspended, but conditions were so bad that Miss Greaves forbade me to venture outside. So I'd sat at the nursery window looking out upon that still, eerie landscape: the skeletal trees and frozen lake; the dark shapes of the deer moving slowly across the white parkland in the distance; and that low-hanging sky, so full of snow it seemed to billow with the weight. Each evening I ate downstairs, in the kitchen, with Miss Greaves and the others. I was allowed to stay up late, and we sang songs and hymns—with Miss Greaves at the piano—in the servants' hall. And one night, terribly late, ready for bed and in my nightgown, Edna took my hand, led me through to the scullery, and then lifted me up on to the slate bench.

I stood there transfixed, watching tiny white crystals spiraling out of the blackness, sliding down the skylight above me. And when I turned to her, for her to lift me down, she wrapped her arms around me, kissed me and held me to her so tightly, and then she carried me all the way back to the servants' hall just as though I were a baby, her own baby. I used to tell her all the time that I loved her, and I did.

I didn't want the snow to melt, didn't want things to return to normal. But as soon as my parents returned home, and despite more snow, everything changed. Evenings of song beyond the green baize door stopped, routines and order resumed, and even Miss Greaves appeared less than enthusiastic at the resumption of lessons on the nursery floor.

I can't recall another winter as severe as that, and I certainly never again experienced the warmth of that *snowed-in* camaraderie, but for a few weeks during January 1925 snow fell steadily over London. Frozen days gave way to nights of glistening, moonlit frosts. No number of blazing fires could keep us warm, and no number of clothes could stop us from shivering. And it was then, in the depths of that particularly hostile month, that my brother Henry slipped further from us. It had been a gradual sink into the abyss, a slow dance into oblivion. The hedonistic mix of parties, pills and whisky, which had once alleviated his anguish, had become increasingly ineffective. And that keyhole in his memory, that small glinting light of who he'd once been, finally faded.

Unlike Charlie, who, despite his disability, had managed to pick up the pieces of his life and had gained employment working at a city-based firm of solicitors, Henry was still without a job, and without any wife. He lived in a rented flat in Marylebone, spent his nights at bars and parties, and gambling, and his days sleeping. I don't think he'd ever expected to have to work and, after the war ended, though he'd toyed with the idea of staying in the army, and at one stage had even talked of going out to India, he'd slowly drifted into a malaise.

Henry had always been extravagant; it was part of him, his character. He'd been indulged, brought up to have certain standards, expectations, and he enjoyed life too much to embrace or understand any need for financial planning or frugality. He'd inherited some money, of course, after the sale of Deyning, but our home had been sold at the worst time, and for a ridiculous sum. And my father's debts—coupled with taxes and death duties—had eroded my brother's inheritance to no more than enough to live on adequately for a few years, not a lifetime. By that winter he'd run out of money and, it seemed, energy.

Mama was of independent means, with an income derived from a trust set up by her father for her and her siblings. But in the years immediately after the war that income had fallen, and fallen dramatically. And, though entitled to some of the proceeds from the sale of Deyning, she'd forfeited her share in favor of Henry. She'd felt guilty about Henry's *shabby inheritance*, and she said it would, at the very least, give him a start. But whatever monies Henry had received from the sale of our home had long gone and, more latterly, Mama had had to bail him out: paying off the arrears on his rent and clearing his gambling debts. She'd tried talking to him, told him that it couldn't go on, that she couldn't afford to fund his precarious lifestyle any longer. And I'd talked to him too, or I'd tried; but he'd stopped making sense, and appeared neither willing nor able to listen.

"It's not fair on Mama, Henry," I said. "She can't be expected to support you now, at this stage . . . it's simply not fair on her."

We were sitting in my drawing room. He'd called on me unexpectedly, wanting money, telling me he'd be able to repay me in a few days. But he looked dreadful: pale, disheveled and exhausted, his hair uncut and unwashed, his coat threadbare.

"That's why I've come to you," he said, running his hands through his hair. "And I hate myself for doing this to you, Issa, really I do . . ."

It was snowing outside, already dark. I noticed he was shivering, and I rose to my feet and placed another log upon the fire.

"But I have no money, Henry. Nothing apart from the pin money Charlie gives me," I said, standing in front of the fire, my back to him.

"I'll pay you back in a few days, I promise. Anything . . . anything's a help. I've just got myself rather stuck, you see."

I turned to him. "But you're always rather stuck, dear. And it can't go on . . . you know that. You know Mama has limited funds now."

He stared at the fire. "Yes," he said, "I know that. And I intend to find myself a job, but I just need to sort a few things first."

I walked out to the hallway table and picked up my purse.

"I can only give you two pounds, I'm afraid. It's all I have," I said, returning to the room. He was standing by the fireplace, his back to me, and when he turned to face me he looked so wretched.

"I'm sorry, Henry, but it's all I have," I said again.

He turned away, leaned his head upon the mantelshelf. "You know, Issa, I sometimes wish I'd not come back . . . wish I'd joined the others."

"No, don't say that. You must never think that."

I moved over to where he stood, placed my hand upon his shoulder. "You just need to pick yourself up, dear, get a job . . . sort yourself out. Look at Charlie, and Jimmy too. If they can do it, you can."

He sighed, and then turned to face me. "Yes, you're right, of course. I need to sort myself out . . . I'm a bit of a mess at the moment, I know that." He smiled down at me, wearily.

I put my arms around him. "Don't worry, Henry," I said. "It'll be fine. It'll all be fine."

When I walked him to the door, he said to me again, "I'll pay you back, I promise."

"Don't worry about the money, Henry. Just promise me, please promise me you'll get yourself sorted."

I watched him walk off down the deserted snow-covered street, holding his collar up around his face, and my heart ached for him.

About a week later, early one evening, Mama telephoned. Henry's landlord had called on her, only minutes before, demanding money, she said, and telling her that Henry had not been at his flat in over a week. My mother wanted Charlie to try to find him. She thought Charlie might know where he was. Yes, Charlie said, he'd see what he could do; he'd go out immediately and make inquiries. So, as Charlie disappeared in a taxicab, in search of Henry, I headed on foot to my mother's house.

Had he made a decision? I wondered. Had he finally decided to join *the others*? Would his body wash up on the muddy banks of the Thames? And I prayed that he hadn't taken his own life. That he was somewhere, drunk and perhaps lost, but not dead.

Charlie was unable to find out anything that evening. He'd been to his club, asked the doorman, and others there, when they'd last seen Henry: not for some time, weeks at least, they'd told him. He'd been to a few bars and to the public house near Charlie's flat; yes, they knew who Henry Granville was, but no one could recall having seen him of late. Charlie did his best to reassure Mama. He said it wasn't unheard of for men . . . those who had survived the trenches, to do this sort of thing. He'd heard of such cases before, and usually these men turned up again, safe and unharmed. He would resume his search the next day, and he'd make a few calls, put a few people on to it.

"But he can't just disappear," I said to Charlie, as we walked home from Mama's later that evening.

"Yes, he can," he replied, lighting a cigarette. "And to be honest, Clarissa, I'm not entirely surprised."

"What do you mean? Do you think he's taken his own life?"

"Well, that can't be ruled out, but no, I don't think so. Your brother may be many things, but he's not a coward. No, I think he's gone. I think he's fled London, for the time being at least."

I stopped. "Fled? Fled London? But to where? And with what? He has no money, Charlie."

"Yes, he's certainly left a trail of debts behind him, and I didn't want to say in front of your mother, but a lot of rather angry people too." He took my arm and led me on. "His debts are more substantial than we'd supposed. Only last week he cashed a rather sizable check with the landlord at his local public house."

"But how? Mama says he has no money . . . nothing in his bank account. Nothing at all."

"He doesn't. The check was not honoured by the bank."

"So he owes this man money as well?"

"He did, and a considerable amount too. Tonight has been a rather costly evening in more ways than one . . ."

I stopped again. "You mean to say you've had to clear all these debts? You've had to give people money?"

He laughed. "I do indeed, and I did. And I'm now rather keen to catch up with your errant brother myself."

We continued walking, and then I asked

Charlie, "And do you really think he's gone, gone away somewhere?"

"It would make sense, wouldn't it? Leave all his troubles behind. And I went to his flat, went through his things . . . his passport's nowhere to be found."

"You went through *his things*?" I said, slightly aghast, and knowing how Henry would feel.

"Yes, of course I did. I was trying to find out *where* he might be. Oh really, I don't know, Clarissa. Perhaps he'll appear tomorrow . . . or next week, or next month, but I've a feeling we shan't be seeing him for some time."

Over the next few weeks Charlie and I played a rather duplicitous game with my mother. We had no choice. At first, when it became apparent that Charlie wasn't able to locate my brother, she'd wanted to go to the police, even though the last thing she wished for was a scandal, or any publicity. But Charlie very swiftly advised her against taking that course of action. He told her that it would only expose Henry's sad situation, the circumstances surrounding his disappearance. He said as soon as Henry's name appeared in the newspapers, which undoubtedly it would, all sorts of unscrupulous people would come forward to sell their tawdry tales.

At that time, the newspapers, and certain magazines, were filled with stories of society figures embroiled in scandal—having affairs, or lost to drug addiction or alcohol. In the absence of war they'd had to find something else, I suppose, to secure their readership. But it seemed to me unnecessarily cruel that those viewed in any way privileged, no matter their circumstances, or how browbeaten, damaged or lost, had been so viciously exposed and held up as examples. And it had made people paranoid: paranoid that even the most off-the-cuff remark—let alone a conversation—would be sold and appear in the next day's news.

No, Mama said, there must be no publicity. So more weeks passed, and then Mama spoke of hiring a private detective. She'd seen advertisements in the newspaper, had even cut some out, and she showed them to Charlie and me. It appeared not altogether unusual, she said, sounding reassured and quite motivated, for people to disappear. She was right, of course, and, in a way, hiring a private detective made perfect sense. But it would be costly, and though my mother was by no means poor, she no longer had the income she'd once enjoyed. Charlie suggested that we wait a while. And so we did. We waited for my brother to contact us, to write or telephone, but months passed by and no letter or telephone call came.

I never told my mother the extent of Henry's debts, or of the sad state of his tiny flat, which I'd had to clear; nor did I tell her of his missing passport. But I eventually explained the likelihood of him no longer being in London, that he may well have fled the country.

"But why? Why on earth would he do such a thing? Really, it simply doesn't make any sense . . . none whatsoever."

"But if he wasn't happy, had no money, felt his life here was . . . worthless, going nowhere, then perhaps it does make sense."

She shook her head. "No, I'm sorry, I still don't understand why he'd choose to disappear . . . after *everything* we've gone through, Clarissa."

"Maybe he thought it would be easier this way, Mama. Perhaps he couldn't face telling us how he really felt . . . couldn't tell us the truth. And by disappearing, going some place where no one knows who he is, where no one knows anything about him at all, he can be whoever he wants to be."

She stared at me, wide eyed. "*Whoever he wants to be?* You mean change his identity . . . his name?"

I said nothing.

"Thank the Lord your father's not alive to witness this."

"I'm sure he'll turn up, Mama, sooner or later. He has to. He'll get in touch with us eventually. Charlie's quite certain of that."

This, too, was a lie. And it was to be years before we found out what had happened to my brother Henry.

Chapter Twenty-six

No one other than the very rich lived the way we once had at Deyning. The lack of an heir, extortionate death duties and the absence of anyone willing to go into domestic service made it nigh on impossible to run such places. Large country houses had been abandoned, left to wrack and ruin, or razed to the ground in order to avoid paying taxes, and almost inevitable bankruptcy.

I knew that Deyning had been standing empty for a couple of years. The American family we'd sold it to had lost a fortune and been unable to sell it, and I'd recently seen it advertised across a whole page in *Country Life*. I'd gasped at the bargain price, and at the state of the gardens. It looked like a relic of a bygone era, a ghostly place. I'd peered through a magnifying glass at the hazy photographs, and there it was, that place I knew so well. Where each pathway, tree and rotting stump had meant so much; where every hollow and incline, each fence and stile and gate had once been so eagerly anticipated. But how different it now looked.

It had been photographed in winter, the trees stark and black against a gloomy sky; the house, bereft, and suitably gray; the terrace, empty of its detail, and statues and urns; the lawns, overgrown, shrunken by rampant rhododendron and shapeless shrubs. And those broad herbaceous borders, once exuberant drifts of vibrant color, gone, lost in the tangled undergrowth. There, too, was the view: the lake, a dark expanse in the foreground, the fields beyond, strangely colorless, and the South Downs, reduced to a murky smudge.

"Looks no different to the last time I saw it," Charlie said, dismissively, when I showed him the photographs.

"No, it looks worse . . . much worse," I said, looking once more at the photograph of the house's southern façade, and my old bedroom window. I could almost see myself there, peering out at that forlorn landscape, waiting for someone to come and rescue the place and, perhaps, me.

"Someone will buy it . . . bound to. It's going for a song," Charlie said. "You wait and see. It'll go to one of these new property developer types."

And it was through Charlie that the news came to me. He'd been sitting alone in a quiet corner of the bar at his club when he heard the name, Deyning. He didn't recognize the voice with a hint of an American accent, he said, and remained where he was, his back to the gentleman, listening. The man was busy explaining to another that he'd purchased the place at a severely knocked-down price. "Yes, yes, it's been on the market for some time, and in a dreadful state too. The army was there through the war, absolutely trashed the place, and the people who took it on never lived there . . . did nothing with it."

"And what will you do with it?" the other gentleman asked.

"Return it to its former glory, I hope."

"And then what?"

"And then . . . I'm not entirely sure."

As Charlie relayed the story to me, relishing its tiny details, I listened, unaware of what was to come but knowing there was something, something that had to be told. He'd stood up, he said, turned, and looked across the room. He didn't recognize either of the men at first, supposed them both to be new members, and so he focused his attention once more on the voice he'd listened to, the one who'd spoken about Deyning, the one who had just bought Deyning. Tall and dark, and dressed in a well-cut suit, he looked *almost* like any other gentleman in the club that evening, "but perhaps a little too suave . . . a little too handsome," Charlie added, and then laughed. Yet there was something, something about him so familiar, he continued. He'd moved toward him, and as he neared, as he approached the two men, he suddenly recognized him. He looked so different out of uniform, Charlie said.

Tom Cuthbert.

I could no longer hear Charlie. He continued to speak but the definition of his words was lost, distant and muffled, as though an invisible wall had sprung up between us. I looked away from him, tried to focus on something, anything, but my head felt heavy, too large for my body, and awash with his image. *Tom.* I focused on my breathing, trying to slow my heart. Charlie moved toward me, handed me a drink, and as I took the glass from his hand I smiled up at him, or at least I think I did. You see, I was drowning, drowning in the moment, in the mention of his name.

I quietly sipped my drink, looking down into the glass, holding on to it tightly with both hands; and as my heart slowed and the room began to stop spinning, I heard my husband's voice once more.

They had spoken at some length, he said, had had a drink together. Neither one could recall the last time they'd seen each other, but they thought it had been at Jimmy Cooper's, at a party there during the war. Yes, I thought, yes, it was then, it was that night, for they'd never come face-to-face during that last week at Deyning. Tom had only recently returned from America, Charlie said, had been away over six years. And then he told me, told me I'd be able to speak to Tom myself, for he and his fiancée would also be at a party at our American friends, the Blanches, the following evening.

I could barely breathe. Not only was Tom back, and in London, but also I was to see him the very next day. Charlie sat down, lit a cigarette, and continued to muse aloud about Tom Cuthbert, his good looks *and* his new fortune.

I wasn't able to ask Charlie the pertinent questions I'd have liked to ask. I'd been blasé, told him, yes, of course I remembered Tom Cuthbert. And I could tell already that Charlie was intrigued, almost captivated by Tom's charm and obvious success. He sat opposite me, clutching his glass upon the arm of his chair, staring at the floor through half-closed bleary eyes, smiling to himself. And every so often I'd see another flash of their conversation ricochet through his memory, and he'd lift his head, smiling to himself; half laughing.

"And he asked after you, dear," he said. "He said, 'And how is your *wife*, Charlie? How is Clarissa?'"

"Oh, really . . . and what did you say?"

He turned to me with a queer, sad sort of smile. "That you were well, of course."

For a few minutes we sat in silence. Charlie lost in his impressions, me in my memories.

"I do wonder where all his money's come from," I said, at last, rising to my feet.

"Haven't the foggiest. Done very well for himself though . . . made a pile and bought a pile, ha!"

"He was always destined to go far," I said, as I left the room.

Of course I wasn't really surprised to hear how well Tom had done for himself. Even before the war, when he was still studying, he had been determined to succeed, driven by something neither my brothers nor most other young men I knew possessed: ambition. I'd heard mention of him only once of late, from Jimmy Cooper once more. He'd recently attended a college reunion dinner at Oxford and had heard from a mutual acquaintance that Tom was *doing very well* in New York, and making *a packet*. The mention of his name at that time had rocked me, and for a while I'd had vivid dreams about him. In those dreams I was always searching for him, always in a crowd trying to find him. I'd wake up and feel that same desperate longing, as though I'd only just left him. Eventually, but for the odd occasion, I'd stopped dreaming of him, and I concluded that it was probably for the best that an ocean separated us.

But now the circle was closing: Tom Cuthbert was in my orbit once more.

That night, after Charlie had come home and told me about Tom buying Deyning, I couldn't sleep. And when I did, when I finally fell into an exhausted, nervous sleep, just before dawn, I dreamed of him once more: him and me back at Deyning— together. The following morning I awoke long after Charlie had left the house and gone to work, and I lay in my bed for quite some time pondering on the evening ahead. I contemplated falling ill: feigning a headache or the symptoms of a mysterious virus. I hadn't seen him since our last night together at Deyning, just after the war, and I wasn't sure what to expect, or even if I'd cope. Would he be the same? Would we be the same?

Later, over coffee with my mother, I wondered whether to tell her the news. The names Deyning and Tom Cuthbert had for so long been synonymous in my mind but, I knew, were mutually exclusive in hers. Occasionally she'd mention Deyning, referring back to that time when all of us were together, but such memories only brought pain. Our lives had changed, and Tom's name—no longer uttered by either one of us.

That day, as she spoke, I imagined her reaction, the look upon her face: first, the horror at the mention of the name, Tom Cuthbert; that I could still utter these three syllables after so many years; and then, as the news sank in, the realization of a new order. For where did that leave us? And where did that place her judgment? Tom Cuthbert, who had not been good enough for her daughter to look at, let alone marry, now presided over all that had once been hers, all that she'd once held dear. Like a stain burnished on our souls, his name was in our lives forever.

I decided not to tell her. She'd know soon enough.

Chapter Twenty-seven

∽

. . . No one is able to tell us anything, or give us any answers. We have tried, interviewed everyone we can think of, but it really is as though he's evaporated into the ether. C assures me that he will turn up—eventually, she tells me that he may well have taken on "another name," a new identity, & that this might actually be something good (for him, at least). What perilous & decidedly queer times we live in.

∽

After much deliberation I chose to wear a new silver-blue silk chiffon dress, one I'd had made that season. It was short, daringly short, and sleeveless too, with an asymmetrical hem just below the knee, a broad sash at the hips and a deep V neckline.

The fashion continued for a boyish shape and I had taken to wearing one of the new-style brassieres, which laced up at the sides to flatten one's chest. It was a look quite the opposite of my mother's and Venetia's day, when curves had been accentuated, even worshipped, when women had been held in by whalebone, heavily upholstered like an item of furniture. Now it was all the rage to look shapeless, and *bare*, with uncovered arms, and legs revealed in flesh-colored silk stockings. It was a bold, modern look for a bold, modern world. But it was a step too far for Mama, who loathed the new fashions, and considered them hideously unfeminine and quite immoral. She blamed alcohol, cocktails, the new jazz music, the craze for dancing—particularly the Charleston—and even the suffragettes, for what she perceived to be an unstoppable moral decline. The day she'd spotted a lady *wearing trousers* outside her home in Berkeley Square, she'd used the telephone—which she insisted should only ever be used in emergencies—to call me up and tell me. "I don't know what the world's coming to," she said. "And where will it all end? With gentlemen in tea gowns?"

That evening, Charlie and I arrived at the Blanches' late. After handing our coats to the butler we made our way up the staircase to the first-floor drawing room. I was nervous, more nervous than I could remember ever having been, and it was my fault we were late. I'd had something of a panic attack before we'd left home, and had locked myself in the bathroom with a large brandy, telling Charlie—through the door—that I had what I thought was the onset of a migraine. Even in his ignorance he'd not made my ordeal any easier, and had simply lectured me on punctuality and the importance of timekeeping—in what I now thought of as his *army voice*. I'd sat perched on the edge of my bathtub, listening to him as he paced about the room, waiting for me to emerge, giving minute-by-minute time checks as though we had an appointment with the King. When, eventually, I opened the door, ready for him to continue his diatribe about my hideously sloppy timekeeping, he'd simply stared at me and smiled, as though he'd suddenly recognized a long-lost friend; as though he hadn't seen me in years.

"Good God, Clarissa . . ." he said, "are you out to break hearts tonight?"

As we entered the Blanches' drawing room I was determined not to look about the room for him, but when I walked in, there he was: unmissable, unmistakable; a dark, smoldering presence that caught in my throat, took my breath away.

He stood by the fireplace, directly in my line of vision, and we saw each other—eyes locked—instantaneously. I turned away, moved toward our hosts, Davina and Marcus. I took a glass of champagne from a maid holding a tray, stood with my back to him and tried to make conversation, my heart pounding so violently I thought the whole room might feel its rhythm. Then I heard Charlie call out, "Clarissa! Clarissa!

Do come over and say hello to Tom . . . here he is, my dear."

As I crossed the room he watched me, but he didn't smile.

I held out my hand. "Tom . . . how lovely to see you."

His flesh was warm and smooth.

"Clarissa . . . small world."

Charlie laughed, slightly nervously, I thought, and then said, "By Jove, you're right, Tom, it is a small world too. Uncanny really."

He looked the same, and yet different: a little older, more . . . polished, I suppose, and impeccably groomed. His dark hair was slicked back, and I'd forgotten, perhaps intentionally, how handsome he was, how penetrating his gaze, and that in itself threw me. He was smoking, a crystal tumbler in his hand, and when he smiled, lowered his eyes and looked down into his glass for a moment, I realized that he, too, was nervous. But when he raised his eyes and stared back into mine, it was my turn to look away. For there was something about him—his face—that dazzled me, quite literally dazzled me: as though he were a light much too bright to gaze upon directly. And *in* that light I was naked; every sensation amplified; each thought audible.

"You don't look a day older," he said, and I turned to Charlie and smiled, rather than look back into his eyes.

I noticed the girl standing to his side, looking rather uncomfortable, staring at me. "Oh, and this is Penny . . . Penelope Gray, my fiancée. Penny, this is Clarissa Granville—I'm sorry . . . Clarissa *Boyd*. Clarissa grew up at Deyning."

"It's a stunning place," she said, taking my hand, glancing at the diamonds on my neck. "You must have had a heavenly childhood, growing up there."

"Yes, it was . . . idyllic really."

"And Tom lived there too," she added, as though I needed reminding.

I smiled at her. "Yes, yes, he did."

"We were only out on the lake last Sunday," she went on, and I glanced at Tom: *how could you? How could you take someone else out on the lake?* "And Tom said it's simply sublime there on a hot summer's day. Oh, but I imagine you have some wonderful memories!"

"Yes, wonderful memories . . ."

"Well, once Tom's restored the place,

once the renovations are complete, you and your husband must come down and visit. Mustn't they, Tom?"

I turned to him. He'd been watching me, watching me intently, but as I turned he looked away. And for a moment I thought he was ignoring her, pretending he hadn't heard her. Then he looked at me and said, "Yes, yes . . . you must come down. Both of you."

"So, is there a great deal of work to be done?" I asked.

"Good Lord, yes. I don't suppose I'll be in until next year—at the earliest."

"Oh, so you're planning on living there?"

"As opposed to?"

"Well, an investment. I hear you got the place for a song."

"You're right. I bought it at a ridiculous price. The days of those big places are over, I'm afraid."

"Apparently not for some," I said, smiling.

He pulled out his lighter, lit another cigarette, glancing up at me through thick dark lashes.

"No, well, I intend to use it as somewhere to entertain clients. It doesn't need a full-time staff that way, so the costs of running the place will be kept to a minimum. And yes, to be honest, it's an investment as well."

"And I hear you've a place here in London now too."

He smiled. "Yes, I've been fortunate, Clarissa; it's been a good time to be in my line of business."

I still wasn't altogether sure what his *line of business* was, exactly. He'd made money in America, on the stock market, Charlie said, and he seemed to have quickly invested in property in London.

I watched him glance across the room; lift his glass to his mouth. And, already, I wanted to reach out and touch his face. Just to know he was there; that he was real.

"He has a beautiful place down the road, Clarissa," Penny said.

"Oh, really. Where, exactly?"

She replied quickly, "Hyde Park Gate."

"Gosh, not far then," I said, looking back at Tom. "Strange that our paths have never crossed . . . but I suppose you haven't been back here long."

"No, not long," he replied.

"And London's like that, isn't it? You

could be living next door to your own family and not even know it," Penny said, taking hold of his hand. She had a slight Irish accent and I wondered where they'd met, how long they had known each other.

"And so . . . are you back for good?"

"I'm not altogether sure," he said, enigmatically. "What I mean is . . . I'm sure I'll be going back to America—at some stage—but I'm not sure when, or for how long."

I glanced at Penny, wondering how she felt about a transatlantic engagement; she blinked and smiled back at me.

I'd already had a drink before leaving home, and now I felt quite giddy. But it wasn't the alcohol. I'd just discovered that not only did Tom Cuthbert own Deyning, the place that would forever be home to me, but that he was also, for the time being at least, living quite close to me in London. And right at that moment it was too much. I looked for Charlie, who'd moved away and was speaking with Marcus Blanch and another couple, and I wished he'd come and talk to Penny, talk to Tom, rescue me.

"So, you two have already met . . . known each other before," Davina said, appearing at my side, putting her arm around me as though she sensed my discomfort.

"Yes, but quite a few years ago, Davina," I replied.

"How fabulous. I do so love it when paths cross over once again, particularly if there are *old secrets* to be told," she said. And I felt her pinch me.

"No secrets, I'm afraid," Tom said, and then, glancing at me, he added, "Unfortunately Clarissa was always out of my league."

"Aha! But not now," she replied, and then, smiling at Penny, she quickly added, "I mean if you were both single and all that."

I tried to laugh, and so did he.

Later, as we moved through to the dining room, Davina took my arm and whispered, "I've put you next to Mr. Cuthbert, darling. You can reminisce together."

"Oh God, no."

"Why ever not?" she whispered. "He's absolutely divine, darling. Take no notice of the fiancée, she's a little limpet. It won't last."

Davina was right. Penelope Gray was a limpet. All through dinner she watched us, Tom and me, as we spoke. It was tricky.

We sat side by side and spoke mainly of Deyning and what he planned to do with it, without ever looking at each other. Marcus Blanch, sitting to my left, at the head of the table, asked Tom if he and Penny would live there once they were married. "Grand house for a big family, eh?" he said, with a wink at Tom.

"We'll have to see," Tom replied.

"When is the wedding?" I asked.

"I'm not sure . . . perhaps . . . next year," he replied. And I thought, yes, Davina's right: there'll be no wedding.

It wasn't that I didn't want him to be happy. Of course I wanted him to be happy. But it was obvious to me that he wasn't in love. Why he'd become engaged, I don't know. Perhaps because he thought he should, thought it was the right thing to do. But he could do so much better than Penelope Gray. Was I jealous that night? No, because he still didn't belong to anyone. Yes, he was there with someone, but she didn't own his heart. And though I was no longer sure if I ever had, I knew I'd had more, much more of him than Penelope Gray.

Toward the end of dinner, as Charlie,

Marcus and a few others stepped out on to the balcony for a cigar, Tom moved a little closer and asked me, quietly, if I was happy.

"Yes . . . yes, I suppose so," I lied. "And you?"

"I've been too busy to know about happiness," he said.

"I can't believe that you're going to be living at Deyning. It's all so strange . . ." I shook my head. "So strange."

"To be honest, Clarissa, I'm taking a punt, a bit of a gamble—in more ways than one," he added, glancing at me. "The place is a mess, a *big* mess." Suddenly he sounded so American. "It needs a tremendous amount of work—*and* a pile of money, that's why it went for so little. The Fosters, the people who had it after you, they never lived there, didn't do anything to it. And you know the state it was in." He turned to me and smiled. "I don't imagine your mother would recognize her beautiful interior now."

Tom. There he was, once more staring back into my eyes, a smile playing at one side of his mouth. I wanted to say so much. I wanted to say how wonderful it was to see him again; how much I'd missed him; how often I'd thought of him, dreamed of

him. I watched him turn away, lift his cigarette to his lips, and I found myself once
again studying that profile: those cherished features etched on to my heart; that
line of forehead, nose, mouth and chin. I
wanted to raise my hand to his face, trace
its outline and memorize it so that I'd never,
ever forget.

He turned to me, opened his mouth as
though about to say something, then
stopped and held my gaze for a moment,
an impossible moment, where time unrav-
eled and placed us far beyond that room of
strangers. I saw him look to my lips, saw
his eyes move over my face, taking in all
of me; knowing all of me.

"Clarissa . . . Clarissa Granville . . ." he
said.

I could hear his thoughts; feel the rhythm
of his heart in time with my own, the warmth
of his skin against mine. I stared back into
his eyes, into the darkness of the lake,
and I saw us once more under the sweeping boughs of the chestnut tree in the lower
meadow. I saw us walking through the fields,
hand in hand, the honey-hued stone of my
home glistening in the distance, following
a path, dreaming of a future. Together.

I saw him look to my hand, resting on the table, and I immediately thought of that day, so long ago, at the station restaurant. We'd shaken hands then, shaken hands this night. I'll say good-bye and shake his hand, I thought. And I felt a tear, brimming at the very edge of my eyelid, and I knew that if I blinked it would fall, and he would see. Everyone would see. So I struggled to keep my eyes wide open, trying desperately to summon other things, conjuring random images: my engagements for the coming week . . . my diary, lying open on the desk at home . . . the striped wallpaper . . . the old brass lamp that needed fixing . . . and then, out of nowhere, Emily.

Emily.

But I didn't want her to be there, not then, not at that moment; so I tried to blot her out. I picked up a spoon laying on the table in front of me and studied it as though I wasn't entirely sure what it was, as though I'd never seen one before. But I was aware of him watching me, so I turned to him and attempted a smile. "Isn't this all rather queer?" I said, my throat tightening, the room becoming smaller. "You and me . . . here together . . ."

"Queer and wonderful . . . wonderfully queer."

He moved around in his chair, placing his arm along the back of mine.

I felt his hand graze my dress . . . then a finger—a stroke, a single stroke—at the base of my neck, and a frisson, like a small electric shock: reawakening, reigniting. Then the doors opened in a clatter, and Charlie and Marcus stepped back into the room. Davina called down the table, asking everyone—all of her *darlings*—to please go through to the drawing room. "So much more comfortable," she said, rising to her feet—with a shimmy and a twirl. I felt his hand move away, his warmth dissipate.

In the drawing room Marcus put on a record, a medley of piano music: George Gershwin, I think. I sat down on the sofa, and for a moment Tom stood about, looking awkward, one hand in his pocket. Then Charlie appeared and sat down next to me. Tom moved to the other side of the room, sat down in an armchair directly opposite us. And as the others filed through—an overly noisy, overly happy tribe—I avoided his gaze. I looked about the room as though it was an Aladdin's cave of treasure.

And it was. For Davina, like my god-mother, Venetia, had an eye for the exotic and unusual, and the room, littered as it was with souvenirs—a foible of its owner's character—appeared a veritable mishmash of styles: a cornucopia of the places she had visited, or perhaps longed to. Strangely hypnotic tribal masks and primitive art jostled with English pastoral scenes, and Italian marble, Chinese lacquer and French Empire furniture—as well as what my mother would describe as *bric-a-brac*—all vied for the eye.

When Davina finally danced her way into the room and perched herself upon the arm of Tom's chair, I felt a sharp twinge. And I could tell she'd taken something. She waved her hands about over-animatedly, kept sniffing and touching her nose. I watched her as she laid her head upon his shoulder, then lifted it and whispered something in his ear. And when she smiled over at me, I turned and looked away.

Strange though it may seem, I wasn't remotely jealous of Penny that night, but Davina's flirtatious behavior, her physical proximity to Tom, rankled. She was able to reach out and touch him in a way I could not, for I could never play that game with him. We could never pretend. So I tried to smile, join in the peripheral conversation. I laughed when others laughed, lit a cigarette, and glanced from person to person; I nodded, tapped my hand in time to the music, and all the time the only thing I could *feel* was him: his presence.

And all the while I could hear his voice, hear him talking; talking to Davina about America, and American music; telling her how much he loved it, how exciting the jazz scene was, how exciting the whole country was. And though I longed to be able to go and sit with him, to hear about his time there, I was jealous of that country too: jealous of America. A place I didn't know, a place that had taken him and kept him for six years. Suddenly, that loud, brash, big continent, with all her money and modern music, was more of a threat than Davina or Penny, or any other woman in England. I hate America, I thought. And how could he *love* it? How could he love it if it was nothing to do with us?

I think everyone in the room heard Davina say, "So, Tom, do tell—what was Clarissa like when she was a girl? Were you *in love* with her?" I looked away, closed my eyes for a moment. She was teasing, playing, I knew, but it was so inappropriate. When I turned back, he was looking straight at me.

"Of course . . . of course I was, still am," he said, without flinching.

I laughed, and so did Charlie. And then Marcus appeared, handing me another glass of champagne, and said, "You do realize, we're *all* in love with you, Clarissa," and pulled me up on to my feet to dance. I was embarrassed, no one else was dancing, and as he led me across the floor he held on to me a little too tightly.

"Really, darling, we need something with a bit more life to it!" Davina called out, and then she rose to her feet and disappeared from the room. I looked over at Tom, watching me—in contemplative pose, his index finger tapping upon his lips. I raised my eyebrows, smiled at him.

Take me away from here . . .

He stood up, took hold of Penny's hand, and led her across to where Marcus and I were dancing. And for few minutes he danced with Penny as I moved with Marcus. Then he turned to Marcus. "All change!"

He passed Penny's hand to Marcus, took mine, and pulled me to him. I remember the warmth of his hand in mine, the smell of him—his cologne. But then the music changed: louder, faster. Davina had found what she was looking for. As everyone rose to their feet—to *Charleston*—we continued our slow dance, out of time with the music, estranged from the room. He whispered something in my ear. I looked back at him, shook my head. He leaned forward, spoke again, but still I couldn't hear his words. And then Charlie appeared at my side. He smiled at Tom, looked at me and pointed to his wristwatch. It was time to leave. Unable to dance, Charlie couldn't stand to watch others do the things he once enjoyed. So I shrugged at Tom, attempted a smile, released his hand and moved away.

And after bidding our hosts good night, I picked up my bag and followed Charlie across the room. I paused at the doorway and turned. He was dancing with Davina, looking back at me.

Thank you. Thank you for reminding me.

Chapter Twenty-eight

⁓

That night, after Davina's dinner party, Charlie had been in a foul mood. En route home he'd accused me of dancing only to upset and annoy him. He said I was without compassion, had no sensitivity, and that even Tom Cuthbert must have felt sorry for him: having a wife who rubbed her husband's nose in his disability. I didn't say much at all. I apologized, told him that I hadn't meant to upset him, hadn't thought.

"But that's just it. You never think!"

When we reached the house, he went straight to his study, and I to my room. I locked the door and sat down upon the bed. I never quite knew what to expect, how he would be, especially late in the evening. His mood swings had become increasingly erratic, and his anger—always there, just beneath the surface—was exacerbated by alcohol.

And that night, coming home, I'd recognized the signs: the tugging at his collar, the fidgeting and overly bright look in his eyes. I could hear him below me, shouting to himself, slamming doors; and I was frightened. We'd never spoken about that night, the night of the charity dance at the Park Lane Hotel, never acknowledged what had happened. But a few weeks later it had happened again. That time, the second time, I'd put up a fight, or had tried. He didn't strike me, but he was rougher, angrier, more violent, and had held me down by my wrists, which I'd had to keep covered up for days afterward. The third time, as I'd tried to escape from him, out of my room, he'd struck me across my back with his stick. Not as hard as he perhaps could have done, but hard enough. After that, I'd had the broken lock on my bedroom door mended. And afterward I spent most of my evenings there, behind a locked door.

As I sat on the bed listening to his movements downstairs, I wondered what he'd do if he came up to my room and discovered that locked door. Would he break it down? Was he capable? I thought of our cook and maid, both asleep at the top of the house . . . they'd hear, surely they'd hear. Then, at last, I heard the front door slam shut. And I lay back on my bed and cried.

The following morning I realized I'd left my shawl at Davina's, and I telephoned her to ask if I could call in and collect it later that day. Yes, she said, do come over; she had a monstrous headache but would love *a bit of a chat*. I knew immediately that she'd probably want to quiz me about Tom and, sure enough, minutes after I'd arrived there, she said to me, "So . . . come along, darling, do tell."

"About what?"

"Ha! You know! About him, about Tom Cuthbert!"

"Nothing to tell," I replied.

"Oh, come on, I wasn't born yesterday. It's perfectly obvious that you and Tom Cuthbert have had—or even *are* having— an affair . . ."

"We are not having an affair, Davina," I said, and laughed. "I can assure you of that. We had a . . . a friendship . . . a childish infatuation, but it was years ago."

"Well, you could've fooled me," she replied. "It's quite clear to me the man's besotted with you. And you . . . well, really, darling—how could you not be?"

I didn't want to be drawn in and I wasn't about to tell Davina Blanch anything. She was a notorious gossip; someone one only ever told those things one wished to have published without incurring any cost.

"I wonder if he'll get in touch with you . . ." she said, thinking aloud, excited by the possibility of another affair for her to disclose. "Or has he *already* been in touch with you?"

"No, he hasn't. He doesn't have my telephone number, *or* my address. And, to be honest, I doubt he will. I'm married, Davina, and he's engaged . . . engaged to be married."

She leaned back in her chair, rolling her eyes heavenwards. "You really think that stops men when they see something they want? Men like him? The only thing that makes men think is their wallet, darling.

How much it will cost them. And let's face it, Tom Cuthbert might be new money, but he's *big* new money. He doesn't need to think about his goddamn wallet. But you know, it's a mystery to everyone where, exactly, his money's come from. There's talk of speakeasies, bootlegging . . . that sort of thing. Anyway, you know me, I'm not one for gossip, and who cares . . . he's delicious material for an affair," she added, winking at me.

I laughed. "Really, I don't know *where* his money's come from, and to be honest, I'm not interested."

"I don't believe you. I simply don't believe you. No, not for one minute."

"Davina, it won't happen."

"I bet poor little Pen's distraught," she continued. "She must have seen the way he looked at you last night. Poor little limpet. But, darling, what'll I do if he calls me for your number?"

"You can give him my telephone number by all means, and I've no doubt that I'll see him again, at some stage, somewhere. We seem to be moving in the same circle these days. But please, Davina, don't discuss me with him." And as I said that I

realized immediately that I'd made a fun-
damental error: by asking Davina *not* to
talk to Tom about me I'd only fired her cu-
riosity more. Now, she wouldn't be able to
help herself, she'd have to discuss me with
him; in fact, she'd probably think of some
pretext to call him up the very next day.

"Of course not. I wouldn't dream of it,
darling," she said, as we made our way
back downstairs, "but seeing as it was me
who brought you back together, you must
keep me posted."

"Yes, I'll keep you posted," I said, "but
don't hold your breath."

Driving home, I wondered if I'd hear
from Tom. Would he get in touch? Would
he telephone? I crossed Oxford Street,
heading toward home, but I didn't want to
go back. I didn't want to return to that
empty house, my home; and so I turned
right instead of left, toward Hyde Park. And
then I parked the car, walked down the
street, across Park Lane, and into the park.
It was a beautiful summer's evening, not
late, perhaps around six, and I walked in a
southerly direction.

I'm not altogether sure why, but I wanted
to go back to that place, to try to find the

tree: the tree where Tom and I had made love that night, so many years before. I walked quite briskly at first, smiling and nodding at people as I passed them. I imagine they thought I was running late for an engagement, or perhaps a mother rushing home to her children. And for a while I imagined that too. I imagined that I was heading home to a family, a husband and children: Emily and Tom. A house in Belgravia perhaps, with a glossy black-painted front door and an ornate polished brass knocker; three children . . . or even four . . . yes, four: two girls, Emily the eldest, and two boys. They'd be waiting for me in the nursery, bathed and smelling divine; creamy skinned and pink cheeked; dark eyes peering out of a high window, waiting for their mama. He'd anticipate my return too; greet me with outstretched arms, smiling. We'd climb the staircase together, hand in hand, feeling whole once more, feeling complete.

And there she is, Emily, almost ten, the eldest of our offspring . . . standing at the top of the stairs. "Where have you been?" she says. "I've been waiting."

"I'm here now," I reply, wrapping my arms around her. "I'm here now."

As I reached the southernmost point of the park, I stopped.

Somewhere here . . . somewhere here.

But there were so many trees: some huge, old and established; others younger, possibly planted in the intervening years. *Ten years.* I stepped away from the pathway onto the grass, looked back toward Park Lane and tried to remember that night: it had been dark . . . we'd crossed over, entered the park . . . walked upon grit and then grass . . . But where had we crossed? Which path had we taken? A military band played on in the distance, its vaguely familiar melody distracting me, muddling me further, and I sat down upon a bench under the beech trees of Rotten Row.

Once, before I knew about war and death and loss, the earth had drawn me to it, pulling me into its shapes and colors, curling up around me and enveloping me in its warmth. Sometimes, I'd even fancied I could see it trembling, hear it breathing, but not anymore. The earth had no heartbeat, it had stopped, perhaps with mine; for all I could see was what I could see, and nothing more.

I closed my eyes, half listening to the strains of a waltz drifting across the park. *I am a memory, unspoken, unseen. I am but a whisper, a glance. The echo of that other time . . . the rhythm, the dance . . .* Then, through the shuffle and hubbub, through the din of traffic, I recognized the music: "The Blue Danube," my father's favorite.

When, eventually, I returned home, as I stood in the hallway pulling off my gloves, Sonia appeared. She told me that a gentleman had telephoned, twice: a Mr. Cuthbert, she said.

"Was there a message?"

"No, ma'am, but he said he'd try again later."

It was around 8:30 p.m. when the telephone rang out, and though I'd been sitting staring at it, waiting for it to ring, I jumped. I was on my own, had no idea when Charlie would be home and had no wish to see him. "I'll get it!" I called out into the empty hallway, and then I closed the drawing room door and picked up the receiver. And as soon as I heard him, as soon as I heard his voice, I wanted to cry.

There were many pauses, achingly long silences in that conversation, for at times I simply couldn't speak. Words wouldn't come. And so he spoke, and I listened.

"It was wonderful . . . wonderful to see you again, Clarissa. And I'm pleased, pleased if you're happy."

I closed my eyes.

"But I wanted to call you . . ." he continued. "I want you to know that I'm not getting married."

"Oh, I see . . ."

"It's not the reason for my call, of course, but I want you to know that anyway."

"Yes," I said.

"It's over between Penny and me; in fact, it was over before yesterday evening."

Through the crackle on the line I could hear him light a cigarette.

"And the other thing I need to tell you . . . is that I'm going back to America."

I didn't say anything. I could feel myself begin to shake. That wobbling feeling that starts deep inside and then, quite quickly, moves outside—to one's head and hands, and legs and knees. A tremor.

"Clarissa?"

I nodded.

"I really hadn't expected to have to return—at least not yet, not now—but something's cropped up . . . it's difficult. It's not . . . it's not work, it's a personal matter . . . but I wanted you to know, and I . . ."

I heard him suck on his cigarette.

"I don't want you to think I've just disappeared, you see. I don't want you to . . ."

"I understand," I said.

I heard him sigh. "No, you don't understand. I know that. You can't understand. And I wish I could tell you more . . . but I can't."

There was a silence, a long silence. And then I said, "When will you be back?"

"I'm not altogether sure, but hopefully in a few months."

A few months . . . a few months . . .

"I'd like to see you again before I leave." He sighed again, and I could see him running his hand through his hair. "I'm sailing from Southampton next Tuesday . . . and I'll be staying there—at the South Western—the night before."

Another silence.

"Clarissa?"

"Yes. The South Western."

"Next Monday . . . I'll be there on Monday . . . Monday evening. From around six."

I nodded. "Yes, next Monday."

"From around six," he said again.

"Yes, around six," I repeated, smiling.

I can't remember now what we said, if anything, after that.

Chapter Twenty-nine

It was Davina who found me: Davina who unlocked my bedroom door. I'm not sure what I'd intended. But I don't think—no, I can't think—that I'd wished for death. Or had I? I knew he'd sailed that morning, knew that he'd have waited for me the night before. But it had all been so poorly planned; by me, at least.

Charlie said, "I don't think so."

"But it's almost a day trip, Charlie . . . after all, I shall only be staying for one night. I'll be back tomorrow . . . I'll be back tomorrow morning, and Edina," I went on, referring to my cousin, who now lived at

Sevenoaks, "is so looking forward to seeing me. I haven't seen her since she had little Archie. I've never met him."

He lowered his newspaper. "I forbid it," he said, without looking at me. And then he refilled his teacup.

I think that's when I stood up. And as I moved away from the breakfast table, toward the door, and toward him, I said, "I don't care what you say . . . I'm going."

And then, as I passed him, he must have reached out and grabbed hold of my wrist; because I remember him holding on to it and saying, "You will not be going anywhere overnight, and you're certainly not gallivanting off to Kent on your own, Clarissa."

I tried to pull my arm free. I remember that, and his grip, so tight, burning my flesh.

The rest is all a muddle. There was a fight. I picked up his cup of tea, threw it at him. He hit me. I screamed, and then . . . and then I think I screamed again. And I said, "I'm going, Charlie, and I'm never coming back!"

It was he who locked me in my room as I packed. I know that.

And I remember panicking, throwing everything movable, anything throwable—pillows, cushions, ornaments, silver and china—at the door, and shouting for him; shouting for him—or anyone—to let me out.

Mess, mess, mess . . . Everything broken. Me broken.

I remember the tick-tock of minutes and the chime of each hour; and lying on the carpet surrounded by tiny white feathers and slivers of porcelain. I remember daylight fading, darkness descending; barely breathing.

And then the bottle of sleeping pills in my bedside cabinet.

Kiss me; kiss me now . . .

A few days later, my doctor called on me. He spoke to me about something called *neurasthenia*, and prescribed more pills. Of course, he didn't know what I'd done, didn't understand. He told me that these new pills would *help my nerves.* And they did. In the weeks and months that followed I glided through life, moving effortlessly through doorways and rooms, along flagstoned pavements in a dreamy mellow state, smiling. I sat in Hyde Park, lost in the cacophony of the city's traffic: the sound of horns and whistles and motors, and the clippety-clap of hooves. I watched open taxicabs and horse-drawn delivery wagons, men with barrows and street sellers; the organ grinder, surrounded by hordes of children; the ubiquitous war veteran, balanced upon his crutch, a harmonica pressed to his mouth; and the ever-present military band, playing on in the distance. I watched people scurrying, people dawdling; courting couples and windswept picnics. I watched the world pass by, watched people for hours and hours.

At home, I quietly arranged flowers and stared at menus. I tried to read, attempted a few books, but couldn't quite absorb the words or sentences on those pages. I preferred to look at the pictures inside magazines and newspapers, and imagine the stories that went with them. I dined alone most evenings, waited on by the servants; the table set for one, with the very best bone china and crystal. And Charlie didn't bother me. In fact, I hardly saw him. On the few occasions I did, he rarely looked me in the eye, and preferred to speak of mundane matters. If he felt any remorse, he neither showed nor expressed it.

Davina called on me, and quite regularly, but I never told her anything. Luckily, there'd been only enough pills in the bottle for me to knock myself out for a few hours, no more, nothing more sinister. By the time she'd found me I was—to all intents and purposes—lying asleep on my bed. The debris in my room—the result of a huge argument with Charlie, I'd said. Yes, I'd been hysterical. And yes, yes, I'd packed; I'd planned on returning to my mother's, for that night at least, I'd told her.

"Men! They can be such beasts . . . and they're all the same," she said, looking at me, holding on to my hand. "You know, I sometimes feel like running away too . . . but where could I go?" She shrugged. "Where could either of us go? Other than back to our mothers," she added, rolling her eyes. "All marriages are hard work, *bloody* hard work, darling . . . all of them. Don't let anyone tell you otherwise. But the sad truth of the matter is," she went on, "women like you and me . . . we're not meant to be . . . independent, on our own. We'd be no good, no good at all . . ." She looked down into her lap. "Sometimes I think we've simply been bred to be sold, to be *breeding machines* . . . to be owned." She looked up at me with a queer smile. "We'll never be free."

After she left that day, I pondered on her words, for there was more, much more than a grain of truth in them. Had I ever been free? I'd never, not once, had any say in my life, my destiny. It had all been decided long ago, by my parents, and then by Mama, and then, after my marriage, by my husband. I'd always been owned—but never by me.

I think most of that year passed in a blur, for I have no recollection of anything of note, only the solitude and quietness of my life. But I know that it was almost exactly a year—exactly a year after Davina's party—when the by-word-of-mouth invitation came.

He'd contacted Charlie regarding some legal issue to do with his ever-increasing property empire, or that's how Charlie saw it.

"He's very kindly invited us down to Deyning. I think he's having quite a crowd . . . housewarming sort of thing. I said I'd have to check with you, of course, but he said he thought you'd be interested to see what he's done with the place. You quite liked him—when you met him at Davina's—didn't you? Thing is, he's potentially a *very* good client for us . . . and he's looking to break away from Chester and Goring."

I didn't look up at him; didn't say anything.

"Clarissa?"

"I'm not sure," I said.

"You know I had a sneaky feeling you didn't like him; could tell . . . could tell at that party. I saw him trying to win you over, flirting with you."

"He didn't flirt, Charlie. He doesn't flirt."

"Hmm. I think he was a tad starstruck. Understandable, I suppose . . . when one bears in mind his background and yours."

His comment irked me. I looked up at him. "Actually, yes . . . yes, let's go. I rather would like to see the old place again."

"Bravo!" he said, clapping his hands together. "You won't necessarily have to see much of him, you know . . . there'll be quite a houseful. Anyway, I shall let him know."

"Who's the latest girlfriend?" I asked,

flicking through the pages of a magazine; knowing there'd be another.

"Oh, someone called Nancy, I think."

He still hadn't married and I wondered if he ever would; if he would ever commit to someone and live a domesticated life. I'd heard he was back in London, and, according to Davina, and others, he seemed to have the Midas touch. He'd recently acquired a number of central London properties, all at upset prices, and, apparently, planned on converting them into smaller dwellings, flats and new modern offices. Davina predicted that one day Tom Cuthbert would own *great swaths of central London*. She'd told me he didn't attend too many parties, that he spent all of his time working, seemingly in the pursuit of money. But she'd seen him a few of times of late, each time with a different girl on his arm. He'd asked after me, she said, but that was all. "Do tell her I asked after her." And to me it sounded perfunctory, cold.

And hearing his name was wonderful and awful at the same time. For each time I heard it, there he was: Tom. And yet how I longed to be the one to say it, to own it, but now, now it belonged to everyone. *Tom*

Cuthbert. That shining light, the hope, the proof, surely, that someone could emerge from the darkness intact, erect, head high, sane, undamaged, still beautiful, whole. And so each time I heard his name I said nothing.

∽

... But haven't you heard, dear? Oh my, good gracious, the man's the toast of the city! ... and such humble origins ... but of course it's a changed world now ... an unfathomably queer character ... doesn't wear his fortune comfortably ... new money must be such a tremendous burden ... one gets the distinct impression it's rather something of an ordeal for him ...

∽

It was a beautiful midsummer's afternoon when Charlie and I drove through the old white gates of Deyning. As our car motored up the driveway, I asked Charlie to slow down. I wanted to take it all in, I said. I felt as though I was in a dream, as though

I might wake up at any moment. But then what would my reality be? To wake up and discover that I was married to Tom, and not Charlie? To awake and find myself young again, back at Deyning with my family . . . and that Tom had only ever been the figment of a dream? How things had changed. And I suddenly wondered what my father would have made of it all, had he been alive.

My mother, of course, had heard, eventually, through a friend, that a businessman named Tom Cuthbert had bought Deyning. It took her six months to mention it to me, believing, as she did, that she was the initial bearer of this astonishing piece of news.

"Yes, Mama, I know," I'd said to her. "I heard some time ago."

"Really? And you never told me . . ."

"I wasn't sure you'd want to know."

"And do you see him, cross paths with him? He certainly seems to have elevated himself . . . seems to be mixing in rarefied circles these days."

"Yes, I've seen him," I replied.

She stared at me but said nothing.

"He's done very well, Mama."

"Obviously."

It was too much for her. She couldn't bring herself to talk to me about him. It would mean undoing so much, which had, in her mind, been done. After that terse exchange I couldn't bring myself to tell her that Charlie and I were going down to Deyning as Tom's guests. It was easier to lie. We were off to Charlie's sister's place in West Sussex, I'd said.

Tom and his new American fiancée, Nancy, had invited about twenty or so of us to their Saturday to Monday house party, but the only other people I knew who'd be there were the Blanches. I was curious to meet Nancy. Davina had told me she was as rich as she was beautiful—*in that American way*.

When we pulled up outside the house there were quite a few cars, more than I'd ever seen at the place, but I didn't want to go inside. Not yet.

"I think I'll take a stroll," I said to Charlie.

"Is that not rather rude? I think we should announce our arrival, say hello first, don't you?"

"You go and say hello. I need some fresh air," I said. "I shan't be long."

I walked slowly, following the path around the house to the south terrace. I noticed the rose garden, completely replanted. It looked just as it had back in our day. And the parterre too, restored and put back as it was before the army had trampled across it. Then, as I neared the terrace, I could hear voices and laughter, and I turned and headed back toward the stables. I crossed the yard, went quickly through the gate, and as I walked down through the meadow I realized I was walking into a memory, and I felt a great swell of unharnessed emotion rise up in me. Everything looked just as I remembered, just as it had always been, only more beautiful, so much more beautiful. Perhaps it was this, or perhaps it was the sound of my brothers' voices in the distance, but by the time I reached the chestnut tree I was crying. I sat down on a wrought-iron bench, and the certain knowledge that Tom had put it there only brought on more tears.

When I heard my name, I didn't look up. The last person I'd expected to appear was him. I'd imagined he'd be busy entertaining his newly arrived houseguests, but of course he knew where to find me. And I felt embarrassed to be sitting there, alone and crying. He crouched down in front of me.

"Clarissa . . ."

For a moment I couldn't speak. I simply nodded, and tried to smile.

He took hold of my hand. "I knew it would be hard for you—coming back here, but I wanted you to see the place, see what I've done. It's all as it used to be, isn't it?"

I nodded again.

He pulled a handkerchief from his pocket and passed it to me.

I don't know how long we were like that, me sitting on the bench, him crouched in front of me, staring at each other. But words were superfluous, and everything that passed between us in those few silent minutes swept us back, and opened us to each other once more.

"We should go back," I said, eventually. "You're our host, Tom. You've all these people to amuse and entertain."

"But there's only one person I want to be with, and she's right here."

I shook my head. "No, don't say that.

You can't say that. I'm here with Charlie. And you . . . you have Nancy now, and a house full of guests. Please," I said, standing up. "We need to go back. Charlie will be looking for me."

"Yes, there's always someone looking for you, Clarissa."

I said nothing, and we walked through the meadow in silence, then, as we reached the track back to the gate, he stopped. "It's all for you."

I looked at him. I didn't know what to say, wasn't entirely sure what he meant. Then I heard my name and saw Charlie standing at the gate.

"Come along, I want you to show us around the house."

"I wish no one else was here but us. Shall I ask everyone to leave now? Tell them I only invited them all to get you here?"

"Please, Tom. Charlie's watching us." I glanced back at the gate and waved. "Please . . ."

Minutes later, he was guiding Charlie and me through the house; my old home, now his. And he was as attentive to Charlie as he was to me. As we entered each room, I was aware of him watching me, searching my face, waiting for my reaction. And each time I turned to him—to smile—a look of anxiety would melt from his features, and he'd smile back at me. He took time to explain the work carried out in each room, pointing out the detail and craftsmanship. Charlie was impressed. And Tom had done a magnificent job, particularly in the library. There, he'd improved on my father's design. Rather than the former dark wood paneling and shelves, there were now modern pale oak shelves and paneling; unadorned windows, allowing daylight to flood the room; and in the middle, two sofas and an ottoman. As he explained to Charlie what he'd done with the room, the room he now used as his study, I wandered over to his desk in front of the window. I looked out toward the South Downs. This was his view. *This is what he looks out upon; this is what he sees.* I wished Charlie wasn't there, and when I turned and looked back at Tom I knew he was thinking the same: wishing we could be as we once were.

Finally, he showed us to our room: my old room.

"I know this was once Clarissa's room . . .

and I thought you might like to stay here again," he said, glancing at me as he opened the door.

I stared at the twin beds, a panic rising up inside me. I hadn't actually thought about the fact that Charlie and I would have to share a room.

"Still pink," I said, referring to the décor, and moving across the room to the window.

"Yes. I don't suppose it's altered too much since you were last here," he said, sounding awkward for a moment.

"Fit for a princess!" Charlie said, and all three of us laughed.

I stared out through the window, beyond the ha-ha, still dividing the formal gardens from the parkland and fields, to the purple hills in the distance, suffused in midsummer sun. Nothing had changed; nothing had altered. The landscape ahead, windless and still, just as it had been that last summer.

Yes, all the same . . . all the same.

"Well, the view's certainly not changed, but for the electricity cables," I said, and then I turned and looked about the room.

Our bags had already been unpacked,

our clothes put away. I noted the crystal vases of roses on almost every surface, and then, on the table next to one of the beds, a book. I walked over, picked it up: a volume of Emily Brontë's poems. He'd remembered. All those years and he'd remembered. And I wanted to run over to him, wrap my arms around him.

I looked up at him. "Thank you, Tom."

He smiled. "I'd better get back now. But I look forward to seeing you both in a little while," he said and disappeared out of the door.

"Nice chap, eh?" Charlie said, testing one of the twin beds.

"Yes, charming," I replied, returning to the window.

I looked down to the terrace below. I could see Davina, in full flow, and a crowd of people I didn't know. I wondered which one of them was Nancy, but I saw no female who particularly caught my eye, and I heard myself sigh. I saw him emerge. I watched him stride over to a group sitting at a table; watched him run his hands through his hair as he listened to one of them speak, then throw back his head and laugh.

Tom.

He looked so at ease, so confident, and so casual too: dressed in pale trousers, a white open-necked shirt with a dark blue paisley silk cravat. I watched him speaking, wondered what it was he was saying. I lifted my fingers to the pane, ran them down over his shape.

"Right-o then, I think we should go down and be sociable now, don't you?" Charlie said.

"You go. I'll freshen up and follow you down."

He came over to where I stood, and I felt myself freeze. "I do realize that this must be very, very difficult for you. To be back here, I mean; very strange . . . can't imagine." He tried to put his arm around me.

"I'm fine, really I am," I said, moving away from him and looking about the room for my vanity case.

"You don't mind then . . . if I go down?"

"No, Charlie, you go down," I said, placing the small case upon a bed, and wishing he'd leave the room.

"So, how long will you be?" he asked.

"Not long," I said, without looking up at him.

As soon as he left the room I sat down upon the bed. I was going to have to share a room with my husband—for two nights. Oh, he was fine now, perfectly civil, but what about later? I closed my eyes. What was I doing here? Why had I come back?

I rose from the bed, walked over to the window and looked down again. I saw Charlie on the terrace now, leaning on his stick, standing with Tom; and I could almost hear him telling Tom that I was *taking a moment* to myself. Then I saw Tom look up to the window and I quickly moved away.

When I eventually left the room and went downstairs, outside on to the terrace, Tom was nowhere in sight.

"He had to make an important telephone call," Charlie said, by way of explanation, and I immediately felt the light grow dimmer.

I helped myself to a cup of tea and sat down next to Charlie, who was talking to an Austrian couple. He introduced me to them, but I was distracted and uncomfortable, more uncomfortable than I'd anticipated. I looked about for Davina, who was standing by the steps talking to a man. She saw me, raised her hand, but made no attempt to move, and so I sat in silence sipping my tea, smiling from time to time at a stranger, and wishing I were back at home. I wished Tom would reappear and take me off to the lake; wished he'd row us across to the island where we could be alone. And I lost myself in a daydream, remembering that time at the end of the war, when we'd spent so many afternoons there on our own.

It was Davina who interrupted my reverie, standing in front of me with another woman.

I stood up. "Clarissa, this is Nancy, Tom's fiancée," she said.

She was not at all as I'd imagined: handsome rather than pretty, with a strong masculine jaw, and tall and dark, like me. She told me she'd heard a lot about me, but it later transpired that this was from Davina, and not Tom. "How very odd *Tam* never mentioned to me that you once lived here too," she said in her New York drawl.

I shrugged. "Well, perhaps he forgot," I suggested, smiling.

"It's not like him to forget anything," she said, and laughed. "Anyway, I better go see where he's gotten to." She leaned toward me. "He's hopeless," she whispered. "No good at small talk, you know."

I smiled. *Yes, I know, and neither am I.*

Chapter Thirty

Tom never reappeared on the terrace that afternoon and it wasn't until a few hours later, over cocktails in the ballroom, that he emerged, looking more handsome than I'd ever seen him, and with an altogether different demeanor. He was in an irreverent mood, playful and witty. As I watched him with his assembled guests, I tried to remember the shy young man I'd been introduced to in that very same room, so many years earlier. But there was no trace of him, he'd gone, and in his place was someone quite sure of himself, and of his position in the world. Handsome, rich and charming, in control of everything, he enthralled us: each and every one of us.

I was standing by the open casement doors, listening to an unfeasibly tall, good-looking American with one of those ridiculous names: Hudson D. Weiner Junior. He asked me to call him Hud, which struck me as a little familiar at the time, but Americans were very friendly in that way, still are. We were all drinking champagne cocktails and a gramophone was playing some new American jazz music. It was Hud who told me it was American; I really wouldn't have known. When he asked me to dance, I laughed.

"As a rule, Hud, we don't normally dance before dinner," I said. "But perhaps later."

"I bet you say that to all the guys," he replied, leaning over me, his arm against the wall.

"Only the Americans," I said, smiling.

I saw Tom looking over, watching us, and I smiled back at him, but he turned away.

I could hear Charlie on the other side of the room, his voice already a little too loud. And I could see Davina, a cigarette dangling from her painted lips, gesticulating wildly in over-animated enthusiasm. Hud was regaling me with a long and overly detailed story about a bear he'd once shot, and moving closer all the time. I could see Marcus, Davina's husband, sitting at the grand piano with a petite, dizzy-looking blonde—flirting, threatening to play. I glanced back at Tom, leaning against the mantelpiece, smoking, talking to a couple I couldn't recall having seen earlier. He saw me look at him, threw his cigarette down into the fireplace, said something to the couple and walked toward me.

"Weiner!" he called out, stemming the flow. "I hope you're not boring the beautiful Clarissa . . . and not another of your bear stories, eh?"

"Ha! Cuthbert, you old rogue. I thought I was doing rather well there."

Tom looked at me. "I'm afraid I have to steal her away from you now, Weiner." And before the American could say anything, Tom took hold of my hand and led me out through the open doors behind us.

Outside, on the terrace, a few people sat about smoking, and I wondered if he was going to introduce me to one of them.

Someone called out, "Aha! Tom!"

"Back in a jiffy," he replied, without pausing to look at them. So I smiled at them, shrugged as he led me past them. I wasn't sure where he was taking me or why, and I wasn't sure who was watching us. But he must have sensed my apprehension because he said, "Don't panic, Clarissa. I shall return you to your rightful owner in due course."

We descended the stone steps and proceeded across the lawn, then through the parterre. He kept hold of my hand, marching so quickly that I had to run with every few steps. Then I saw something at the end of the pathway, and I stopped, pulling my hand from his.

I turned toward him, my hands over my mouth, incredulous.

"A tent . . . an Arabian tent . . ."

I looked back at the tent, began to walk toward it, slowly. The sides of the canvas were pinned back, a dozen or so flickering lanterns encircling it upon the grass. Standing to one side was the solemn-looking older man I'd seen earlier; Tom's *man*, I presumed, his valet. I noted the bottle of champagne in an ice bucket on a stand to his side.

"Good evening, sir . . . ma'am," the man said, nodding at Tom and then at me.

"Good evening, Walter," Tom replied, and then the man picked up the bottle and released the cork.

I turned to Tom.

"Go on . . ." he said, smiling back at me, "take a look."

I stepped inside the tent, running my hand down the richly colored tapestries draping its interior walls. A vividly colored rug and large cushions lay about the floor, and in the center a brass-topped table with a lantern and two champagne glasses set upon it. I sat down on a cushion and looked up. Above me were hundreds of minuscule, glinting gold stars, sewn into the richest, deepest blue.

I shook my head. "It's beautiful, Tom," I said, staring up at the stars as he stepped inside the tent, holding the bottle. "But what's it for?"

He laughed. "It's for you, of course. I told you, it's all for you."

I turned to him. "Tom . . ."

I was speechless, didn't know what to say. And really, it was all too much.

"But it's perfect . . . perfect, and so beautiful," I said again. "And exactly like the one . . . the one I'd imagined."

He said nothing but glanced over at me as he poured champagne into a glass, smiling. I lay back against a pile of cushions, propped myself on one arm and watched him. How could I not love him? His ingenuity, the romance of him. I took a sip of champagne and stared back at him, unable to stop smiling.

"I can't believe you did this for me . . . can't believe you remembered."

"Of course I remembered. You never did get your Arabian tent, did you? Anyway, it's for you. It's yours."

I laughed. "But, Tom, I have *nowhere* to put a tent. I live in a town house—with a garden not much bigger than this," I said, gesturing. "It would be pointless . . . impossible. But I love it. I love it and I want to sleep here, under these stars." I put down my glass, lay back once again to look up at the stars glistening in the fabric above our heads, and for a few minutes neither one of us spoke.

Then he said, "You didn't come."

And I knew what it was he referred to.

I closed my eyes. "I couldn't . . . I couldn't come, it was impossible," I said.

"I waited for you. I waited all night."

I turned my head, looked up at him. "It wasn't meant to be, Tom."

He shook his head. "It could have been."

And then I saw myself: saw my deranged self, hurling china figurines, scent bottles, silver-framed photographs and brocade cushions at my locked bedroom door. He has no idea, I thought, no idea. "I wanted to come, I wanted to . . ."

"Then please, come here later . . . later tonight," he said.

I'd been no more than a foolish girl when I'd told him I wanted to sleep in an Arabian tent on the lawn, and here we were, so many summers later. He was sitting cross-legged, close to me, staring down at me, and without thinking I reached out to him. He took my hand to his mouth, kissed it. "Tell me you'll come here later . . . please."

"I'll try," I said, my eyes fixed on his. "I'll try."

He kissed my hand again, ran his nose over my wrist. "You smell of my dreams, Clarissa Granville."

Tom.

I had left my moorings, was already adrift, floating out across a lake with him, and nothing else mattered, no one else mattered, to either of us. They were the reeds beneath the water, hampering our crossing to that place where we could be together, and alone.

When we walked back up the steps on to the terrace everyone had disappeared and all was silent.

"Oh dear," he said, with affected solemnity, and we walked on, quickly, through the ballroom, into the lobby and toward the dining room, where people were filing through the doorway in a noisy huddle of smoke and laughter.

"I say! Here they are!" Davina called out. "Darlings! We did rather wonder where you'd disappeared to . . . were about to send out a search party."

Davina, as unsubtle as ever.

"Ha! I was showing Clarissa the new tennis court. Do you play, Davina?" Tom said, moving swiftly ahead of us, with smiles and nods. "We should have a game, tomorrow . . ." he called back to her.

Nancy, standing at the doorway to the dining room, smiled at me as I passed her, but it was a queer sort of smile, and it made me feel guilty. More than guilty, it made me feel wicked.

I was placed next to him, on his right, with Davina directly opposite me, on his left. The meal was an ordeal for me, and I suspect for him too. We'd begun our subterfuge and each time I caught his eye I felt a mix of guilt and longing. I took another glass of champagne rather than wine, and I could feel its effects. Any resolve I'd had was melting fast, and in its place was a yearning; a yearning I'd not known since I was sixteen years old. I watched him as he spoke with Davina, smiling and laughing; I watched him as he stood up and made a toast, and then sat back down and looked immediately to me. Yes, yes, I was proud of him, and yes, I loved him and wanted him. I knew I'd risk my marriage for him. I knew I'd risk everything for him.

Thankfully, Davina was as verbose as ever, but I was aware of her scrutiny, not of one of us, but of us both. And each time Tom turned and spoke to me, no matter how mundane the words, he looked at me in such a way that though I couldn't take my eyes away from his, and though I couldn't see Davina's expression, I could feel her watching us and I knew she'd see that something had passed between us. From time to time I caught Charlie's eye, sitting at the opposite end of the table, a few places away from Nancy, and I tried to smile back at him. He looked happy enough, I thought; he was enjoying himself. And Nancy? I'm not sure what she saw, or what she thought. In his toast Tom had thanked her for her help and complimented her on her "exceptional" organizational skills, but he could have been speaking of an employee, I thought, not the woman he was about to marry.

After dinner, the men adjourned to the smoking room for brandy and cigars, and we ladies removed ourselves to the drawing room for coffee. There, Nancy came and sat down next to me. She asked me about my childhood, and then quizzed me on Tom: if I'd seen much of him growing up at Deyning, and when I'd last seen him. I was vague about the old Deyning days, and very specific on when I'd seen him last. "Oh, golly . . . not for almost a year. In fact, it was at Davina's we last saw each other," I said, and then added, "But we hadn't seen each other for many years before that."

She told me of their wedding plans. It was to take place toward the end of the summer, at the church down the road, and afterward a "small" reception—there, at the house. "Perfect," I said. "And any honeymoon plans?"

"Oh, I don't suppose so. Tom may be marrying me but he's already married—to his work!" she replied.

"And so . . . will you live here?" I asked.

"Between here and the place in London," she said, and then added, "and as and when we have children, Tom wishes them to be brought up here, in the country."

I remember thinking, so they've discussed it; they've made plans. They shall have a family and live here at Deyning. And I could suddenly picture it all, it was so easy. I saw them in years to come: Tom, surrounded by a large brood of dark-haired children, playing with them out on the lawn; up a ladder, decorating a Christmas tree; and Nancy, the matriarch, chatelaine of Deyning Park, Mrs. Tom Cuthbert; reliable and efficient, organizing their lives.

"Do you have children, Clarissa?" she asked.

"No, sadly, I don't," I replied, and for some reason I smiled as I said it.

A few minutes later I excused myself. It was after midnight, and the conversation had turned to babies and children, which I always found difficult. For years I'd practiced smiling inanely as other women spoke of their children. I'd feigned empathy and interest, nodding attentively, and sympathizing with them in their tribulations: oh, the ordeals of raising a family! I'd laughed at their funny stories of little Johnny's antics, sat in silence as they'd discussed schools, and the neatly planned paths for their offspring. But sometimes, sometimes it became too much. And as I climbed the stairs at Deyning that night I struggled to hold back my tears, for I could never join in those conversations. I was a mother, yet I was no one's "Mummy." And I knew, knew the moment I left the room, that Davina would take it upon herself to explain my sad predicament; explain to those straining ears how there were no babies—no children for the Boyds. Not now, and, perhaps, not ever. And in my head I could hear their momentary sighs of sadness.

No, no babies for Clarissa.

It must have been after one when Charlie came to bed. But I pretended to be asleep, and within seconds he was snoring. I lay there for almost an hour wondering what to do. I knew I had a choice: I could remain in my room, or I could go to Tom. But would he be there? And what if someone saw me, saw us? But it was late and everyone had had so much to drink . . . surely they'd all be asleep.

The room was dark but for a strip of light under the door. I reached for my robe, hanging on the back of the door, then opened it and stepped out on to the landing. I stood perfectly still for a moment, struck by a sense of déjà vu. The last time I'd done this was the night before Tom left for war, when my parents had been downstairs and I'd used the back stairway. I could feel my heart pounding, hear Charlie's snoring beyond the closed door, or was it snoring from another room? And somewhere, giggling, and muffled voices. If I met anyone, I'd say I couldn't sleep; that I was going to find a book in the library. I moved quickly down the carpeted staircase, across the marble hallway—tiptoeing on bare feet—and then on, along the polished wood floor to the ballroom. There was a lamp on, and a casement door stood open. I hurried through the door, across the flagstones and down the steps. It was a glorious clear, starry night, and I was seventeen again.

In the distance I could see the lanterns, still flickering around the outside of the tent, a glow inside. He's there, I thought, he's there. I ran along the path through the parterre and across the velvet pile of the lawn, and then, breathless, I pulled back the canvas. A lantern on the table still burned and the smoke of a cigarette lingered. He'd been and gone. While I'd dithered, he'd been waiting for me and now he'd gone. My heart lurched. I stepped back out of the tent unsure of what to do, and then I looked up into the night sky, closed my eyes and made a wish: *make him come back to me, make him come back . . .*

I felt a hand upon my shoulder—and there he was.

"I thought you'd gone," I said, turning to

him, almost in tears. "I thought you'd gone," I said again, wrapping my arms around him.

"Never," he said, lifting my face up to his. "Never," he repeated, leading me back inside the tent.

Chapter Thirty-one

It was light by the time I walked back through the garden toward the house. The air was warm and a cloudless sky stretched out high above me: a transparent wash of pink, pale blue and yellow. I stood on the terrace for a moment, looking back at the tent, and the bucolic vision beyond. Patches of mist hung over the sleepy hollows of the fields and the lake in the distance, and not a leaf stirred. I'm not sure I'd ever looked out upon that cherished landscape at such an early hour before. And it struck me how timeless and ethereal it was in its stillness.

Tom had made me return to the house first, and I tiptoed up the staircase and back to my room, closing the door behind me as quietly as I could. Charlie lay on his back, his mouth open, snoring. And as I climbed into my bed, I heard another door close, and wondered if it was Tom returning to his room. I longed to go back to him, to lie with him and wake up in his arms. Our night together had been so short, and ahead of us—another day of pretense.

I didn't wake until almost midday, stirred by voices—including Charlie's—outside on the terrace beneath the open window. The pink and white floral curtains remained drawn across each of the four tall windows but a very particular light, a bright Sussex morning light, so familiar to my senses, flooded through them and into the room, and I stretched out like a cat, savoring its warmth and energy. And still echoing in my head—my name: a deep, desperate whispering in my ear; against my skin; on my neck, my shoulder. And I stretched out once more, smiling.

I decided to take my time getting ready. I ran a bath and lay in it until the water was almost cold, reliving the events of hours earlier: his words, his touch, his love. When I finally dressed and went downstairs—the book of Emily Brontë's poems clutched in my hand—it was a somewhat depleted group sitting outside under the awning on the terrace. I'd missed breakfast but Nancy kindly organized some coffee for me. Tom was nowhere to be seen, and I chose not to ask where he was. Davina said, "We've all been looking at the Arab tent, Clarissa. Have you seen it? You must go and take a peek, darling . . . it's quite magical. Apparently Tom's only just had it put up—in time for this weekend, so we're quite honored. I think I might even sleep in it tonight!"

"Oh, yes I shall. I'll go and take a look later," I said.

"Sleep well, dear?" Charlie asked, as he sat down next to me.

"Yes, perfect, thank you. And you?"

"Now what do you think? I don't even remember coming to bed! Though I must say, I'm quite astonished that my head doesn't hurt more this morning. Champagne, wine *and* brandy—not a very clever mix . . . but you, you've slept almost twelve hours," and he looked at me, almost tenderly, and patted my hand.

"Yes, I must have been more tired than I realized."

"It's called beauty sleep, Charlie boy. Not that Clarissa needs it—or perhaps that's her secret . . ." Weiner said, from behind sunglasses.

He was sitting next to Davina, in polka dots, and I could tell immediately they had a thing going. Their deck chairs were pushed up together and they spoke in whispers, punctuated by giggles. I looked around for Davina's husband, Marcus, but he was nowhere to be seen. Perhaps he was with Tom, I thought.

It was a perfect day, with a bright blue cloudless sky. I moved away from the table, where Charlie sat reading the newspaper, walked along the terrace and down the steps to a swing-chair set out upon the lawn. I sat back in it, gently rocking myself, and closed my eyes, listening to the conversations behind me. I could hear Nancy, who'd appeared back on the terrace, announcing that we were to have a picnic on the island in the middle of the lake. There were three rowing boats and if we organized ourselves into groups of no more than four we should, she said, be able to do it with each of the three boats making two trips. Those playing tennis would be back soon and we'd set off then, she said. That's where he is, I thought: playing tennis.

A little while later, as people began to assemble, ready to set off to the lake, I heard his voice and looked up from my book. In tennis whites, and looking unbearably handsome, I listened as he told people to go on ahead, he'd catch up. He glanced across to me, turned as if to go inside the house, then turned back again and moved quickly across the terrace, and down the steps toward me.

"Let them all go on ahead," he whispered, standing in front of me, shining with sweat, still breathless from his game.

"But I can't . . . what can I say?"

"I don't know," he replied, smiling at me. "Think of something."

Then he ran back across the lawn, leaped up the steps and disappeared into the house.

"Clarissa!" Charlie shouted. "Do come along, darling, we're off to the lake."

I walked up to the terrace. "I need to put my book away—and fetch my hat . . . you go on," I said to Charlie.

"I'll get it for you, dear," he replied, taking the book from my hand. Minutes later, he was back with my hat. But as we moved along the terrace, a straggling parasol-laden group, I spotted Mrs. Cuthbert, coming through the archway of the walled garden.

"Oh, but there's Mrs. C. I must go and say hello to her," I said to Charlie. "I'll catch up with you." And before he could say anything, I ran down the bank, my hat flying. "Mrs. Cuthbert! Mrs. Cuthbert! It's me . . . Clarissa," I shouted, and I realized I sounded like a child again. She turned to me with a broad smile, put down her trug and stretched out her hands.

"I'm so pleased to see you," I said, taking her hands in mine.

"Miss Clarissa," she said, looking me up and down, smiling and nodding her head. "Tom only told me yesterday that you'd be here. How lovely . . . how lovely to see you again, dear. And my, he's right, you're more beautiful than ever."

"Oh, I don't know about that—a little older, like all of us," I said.

I wanted to put my arms around her, hug her, but it would have been inappropriate, so I purposefully kept hold of her hands as we spoke.

"It's wonderful that you're still here . . . that Deyning's now Tom's. You must be so proud of him," I said.

"Oh yes. Yes, very proud of him, but I was always proud of him, you know that," she said. "And he's so happy that you came, that you came back."

"Yes, I'm pleased that I did. He's done a wonderful job with the place. And it's just perfect, perfect you can continue living here."

"Thirteen years now . . . and over five when the old earl lived here too."

"Gosh, yes, I'd forgotten about that. But that was before Tom was born, wasn't it?"

"Oh yes, before Tom came along. And it feels like a few lifetimes ago to me now, miss."

"I think I know that feeling," I said.

"And so, you're all off for a picnic, are you?"

"We are indeed, and I'd better go and catch up. But I hope I might see you later," I added.

"Well then, why don't you come and

have tea with me? You know I'm in Broughton's cottage now, don't you?"

"Yes, Tom mentioned that you didn't
want to move into the main house."

"No. I like the old cottage. It suits me
fine. And he had it all redone for me, you
know? New roof, electricity, mains water,
a new range . . . even a bathroom." She
laughed, and went on. "And all redeco-
rated as well. He wanted to buy me new
furnishings too, but I told him there's no
need. I like my old things . . . I'm attached
to them. Oh yes, it suits me fine. But come
and see it, come and have a cup of tea
and tell me all your news, and about your
mother too. I'd like to hear how she is."

"I'll do that," I said, releasing her hands.
"I'll come when we get back from the lake."
And then I turned, picked up my hat, and
walked on up the pathway toward the
stable yard.

I stood at the gate for a moment, watching them all in the distance: a meandering
trail of pale linen and straw hats, following
the coterie of servants carrying picnic paraphernalia: umbrellas, rugs and hampers.
I contemplated going back inside the
house, up to his room, but I wasn't sure

where Mrs. Cuthbert had gone, or who else was still about at the house. So I opened the gate and walked on into the field, following the path the others had cut through the long grass. It felt indescribably good to be back there, looking out across that landscape, and I stopped, put my arms up into the air, and then wrapped them around myself with joy.

"You're a vision," he said, appearing by my side, "my perfect vision."

"Are you happy?"

"Happily tormented," he replied, looking into the distance, frowning.

We began to walk, and I reached out, brushed his hand with my fingers. I could already see the three boats, slowly moving across the water toward the island.

"Oh God, Clarissa . . . what are we going to do?"

"Enjoy today . . . look forward to tomorrow."

"Hmm. It's not enough, I'm afraid. I need more than that."

"But I don't think there is more."

"Yes, there is: there's you."

"I'm having tea with your mother later," I said, trying to lighten the conversation.

He turned to me. "Yes, so she said."

"Ah! Here they are!" I heard Charlie say to Nancy, as we approached them.

"Charlie, my man . . . you take Davina and Nancy in this one," Tom said, nodding over at a boat sitting in the sunshine at the end of the jetty. "I'll wait here with Clarissa and Walter for the next one to come back." And he spoke with such authority that no one, least of all Charlie, would have dared suggest an alternative plan. Nancy shot him a glance, and either he didn't notice or he chose to ignore it. A few minutes later, with Charlie at the oars, they were off. Davina's wave and broad smile seemed teasing, but I really didn't care anymore. We stood side by side watching them move away across the water; then he grabbed my hand and led me up the steps, into the boathouse.

"But they'll see us, and Walter's there . . . he's right there."

"Clarissa, you more than anyone should know a loyal servant sees and hears nothing," he said, pressing me against the timber wall. "Let's not go . . . let's go back to the house."

"No, we can't . . ." I said, closing my

eyes, moving my head as he kissed my neck. "We have to go . . ."

But I didn't want to go to the island either, not with all of them. It was *our* place; meant only for us. And so we remained there, in the boathouse, for some time, kissing, holding on to each other, staring back into each other's eyes, unable not to smile. And each long second postponed the agony of letting go, again.

When we finally emerged, Walter was sitting in a boat at the end of the jetty, waiting; the boy who'd helped carry things over to the island and had rowed the boat back—long since disappeared. And so, with his back to Walter and facing me, Tom rowed us across the water. Neither of us uttered a word, and I'm not sure what Walter thought. He'd seen us at the tent the previous evening, been standing guard presumably on Tom's instruction; and now he'd sat and waited for us to come out of the boathouse. But he was elderly, and I imagine he'd seen it all before a thousand times.

Huddled together on that small island there was no escape, no opportunity to disappear and nowhere to disappear *to*, other than by boat. So, we sat about in deck chairs and on rugs, and ate and drank, and whiled away a couple of hours. A few, including Davina and Nancy, strolled off beyond the trees. Charlie fell asleep in his deck chair; and lying close to me, on a rug under the shade of a tree, Tom nodded off too. It was peaceful, heavenly really, if there'd only been Tom and me there. But I began to feel slightly claustrophobic, uncomfortable and hot; and I wanted to go back to the house and freshen up before I had tea with Mrs. Cuthbert. So I quietly asked Walter to row me back across the lake.

I hadn't intended on looking in on his room, I'd already seen it anyway, when he'd shown Charlie and me around the place the previous day. But the door was ajar and it was just too tempting. I walked in, and immediately noticed that his bed was unmade. Shabby, I thought; he needs to have a word with the servants. Then I remembered it was Sunday: most of the servants would have had the day off. I walked over to one of the windows, facing due south, looking out over the terrace and gardens. This had once been Mama's room, and I smiled at that thought: the thought of Tom Cuthbert inhabiting my mother's former bedroom. Out of the window, to the left, was the walled garden, and I wondered if he'd seen me talking to his mother.

I moved away from the window, walked about the room, taking it all in once again and noticing the changes he'd made, and then I wandered through to his dressing room, once Mama's. I opened the doors of his wardrobes, ran my fingers over the rows of shirts and suits on hangers, and then moved on, to his bathroom. His tennis shorts and shirt lay on the floor, his shaving brush and razor by the basin, a damp towel next to them. And I picked it up and held it to my face for a moment. Then I walked back into the bedroom and sat down upon the bed.

A pile of books lay on a bedside table next to a wireless: *The Seven Pillars of Wisdom* by T. E. Lawrence; *Love Among the Artists* by George Bernard Shaw; *Heart of Darkness* by Joseph Conrad. The latter, at the top of the pile, had what I took to be a bookmark poking out from it, and for some reason I picked it up and opened it.

A small, rather badly executed but none-theless lovely watercolor lay on the page in front of me, and I heard myself gasp. *My painting . . . my painting; all these years he's kept it with him . . .*

The paper, once stiff, was now soft and worn like fabric. And it had quite obviously spent a good few years folded and flat-tened. Now heavily creased, frayed at the edges and torn in the middle, it could have been an antique; an ancient scrap of some-thing perhaps once much larger. But as I sat holding it, looking at it, I remembered each stroke of my brush; and each thought that had accompanied each stroke: Tom.

I placed the paper carefully back inside the book, and the book back on top of the pile. And then I lay back, turned my head, and buried my face in white linen.

Chapter Thirty-two

Mrs. Cuthbert opened the door of her cottage looking quite different and altogether prettier than I'd ever seen her, without any apron, and in a navy-blue jersey dress and triple-strand pearl necklace. "Miss Clarissa," she said, smiling at me, "this is such a treat for me." I handed her the flowers I'd picked from the garden and entered the cottage, the place that had once been Broughton's. It was exactly as I'd imagined, and not dissimilar from her previous cottage, but for the freshness of new fitted carpets and wall coverings. She showed me into her parlor, a cozy, immaculately tidy room, with chairs covered in a familiar floral chintz, and a large dark wooden display cabinet filled with glass and china.

She'd already laid out the tea tray, and as she busied herself in the kitchen, boiling the kettle and filling the pot, I glanced around the room. There were two framed photographs sitting side by side upon the mantelshelf—next to a clock, a bible and a palm cross—both of Tom. One of him aged perhaps eleven or twelve, and the other, taken around the time when I'd first met him, in his uniform. I picked up the photograph of him in uniform and moved over to the window.

"Ah, that's how you'll remember him, I expect," Mrs. Cuthbert said, entering the room and putting down the teapot.

"Yes, exactly like this. He was so handsome . . . still is."

She came over to where I stood, looked at the photograph with me for a moment, then took it from me and placed it back upon the mantelshelf.

I sat down as she poured out our tea, and then offered me some of her homemade Madeira cake, saying, "Now, I hope you're not watching your figure. You certainly don't need to and you always liked that particular one, as I recall. I baked it *specially* for you."

We chatted about the old days and she brought me up to speed on the circumstances of those who'd once been a part of Deyning. She kept in touch with almost all of the old staff: told me where they were living, who'd married whom, and who'd had babies. Mr. Broughton still hadn't married, but had returned to his *roots*, she said, and I smiled. He was living somewhere in Devon, she thought, but not gardening.

"Not gardening?" I repeated.

"No, teaching, I think. But you know he was from rather a well-to-do family, don't you?"

I shook my head; I'd had no idea.

"Oh yes," she said emphatically, "he was a very educated man . . . but a bit of a *black sheep*," she added. And I was tempted to tell her that, according to Edna, he'd been more of a *dark horse*. She went on, told me Edna was still in service, working as cook for the new owners of Monkswood, people who owned a London department store, she thought, but she couldn't recall which one. But that place had all changed, she said, because the estate had been divided up after old Mr. Hamilton died. And Mabel? Married, mother to *three boys*, and living in South London.

"And you, no little ones yet?" she asked, her head tilted to one side and smiling.

"No, no little ones, I'm afraid."

She said nothing, but I sensed she was waiting for me to say something more. *Yes, I had a child, your grandchild. But I gave her away one Christmas, many years ago.*

"One sometimes thinks life could be better, that the grass is perhaps greener somewhere, but I'm not altogether sure that it is, Mrs. Cuthbert. And really, I consider myself to be lucky, very lucky, with or without children," I added, looking away and taking a sip of tea.

She asked after Mama, spoke sweetly of my father; said he was "a good man . . . one of the best."

"But you've known such grief," she said. "To lose two of your brothers . . . and so young," she shook her head, "so young."

"We all did," I said. "They were all too young to die." I glanced at the bible on her mantelshelf. "But God spared Tom."

"Yes, he did. He heard my prayers, and there's never a day goes by that I don't feel gratitude and thank Him for that."

Yes, I thought, He kept His side of the bargain; He kept Tom safe.

"And he's done so terribly well, Mrs. Cuthbert."

"He was always going to. He's very bright, you know . . . like his father."

"Oh?" I said, looking back at her, expectantly.

"Yes, like his father . . ." she repeated, glancing away. Then she turned to face me and added, "And now—at last—he's to be *married*!"

"Yes indeed," I said, trying to smile. "It's lovely news. You must be pleased, excited."

"Oh yes, I am. It's not right for him to be on his own . . . not now, not after all these years. He needs to . . ." She looked away and shook her head. "He needs to move on with his life . . . have a wife, a family . . . a proper home."

"Of course."

She began fiddling with the brocade trim on the arm of her chair. "I want to see him settled. I won't be here forever . . . and I'd like to see him happy. We can't always have what we want in life . . . no matter how much money we have. And money isn't everything. It doesn't buy happiness, as he's discovered." She looked across at me. "And I'm sure you'd like to see him settled and happy too . . ."

I heard a latch drop and he appeared, standing in the doorway, smiling.

"Well, this is rather nice," he said.

He moved toward his mother, bent down and kissed her cheek. He towered over her, over us both, his head grazing the ceiling. And it was queer to think he'd once inhabited such a small space, for Mrs. Cuthbert's previous cottage had certainly been no bigger, and very possibly smaller. He picked up a slice of cake, pushed it into his mouth whole. "Mm, that's good," he said, and sat down upon the arm of my chair. Then, in front of his mother—as she looked on, smiling at us—he lifted his hand and stroked my hair. I looked down at the floor, astonished, embarrassed; unsure what to do.

"I'll go and make a fresh pot," Mrs. Cuthbert said, rising to her feet.

"Why on earth did you do that?" I whispered, as the door closed.

He smiled at me. "Do what?"

"Touch me like that . . . in front of your mother?"

"Why not? She knows. She knows everything . . . well, almost everything," he replied, standing up and pulling out his packet of cigarettes.

"No, please, please don't say that. She can't—she mustn't . . ."

"Oh, for God's sake, she's not going to say anything, tell anyone. She's known for years."

"Known *what* for years?"

He lit his cigarette and sat down on the floor by my feet. He felt so comfortable there, in that cottage, I could tell. He reached up, took hold of my hand.

"You mustn't fret. She's my *mother*, not some stranger. She loves me . . . wants for me whatever I want, whatever makes me happy."

I whispered, "She wants you *settled* and married, Tom."

He squeezed my hand, turned to look up at me.

"I can't . . . I can't . . ." I said.

"Can't what, Clarissa? Can't allow me to touch you in front of her? Can't bear me to love you in front of anyone? Is that it?"

"No . . . no," I said, but I knew how it sounded; how he was making it sound. "You don't understand, we've just been talking about—"

"If she was Lady Cuthbert would that make it any easier for you?"

"No! That's not fair, Tom . . . that's not the point at all, and you know it."

"Then prove it to me. Prove to me that you can at least allow me this sanctuary . . . that I can be myself with you here."

When the door opened and his mother walked back into the room, we may as well have been making love; we *were* making love. I pulled my hand away swiftly. It was an automatic response, spontaneous, and without thought. I'd have done the same regardless of where I was, whoever I was with, but I knew and felt Tom's reaction. His intake of breath, his sudden pulling away from me was all part of a chain reaction and no matter what I did or what I said, I couldn't undo that.

We sat there, in Tom's mother's parlor, for a full five minutes without speaking, like a couple who'd had a row—which we were, and had had—as she poured fresh tea, cut Tom another slice of cake and then returned to the kitchen for another plate. I wanted to say something; I wanted to prove to Tom that it wasn't the way he thought. I wanted to say, "Mrs. Cuthbert, I love your son as much as I love life itself." But I didn't. I sat there, frozen, sipping tea, with Tom on the floor, sprawled out like a child at my feet. I wanted to reach out and touch him, but I couldn't do it. Everything I was, everything my upbringing had taught me came together in those few minutes: I was Clarissa Granville once more; taking tea with our former housekeeper. I couldn't let it go, you see. I couldn't reinvent myself in minutes.

And so, eventually, I put down my cup and saucer and rose to my feet. "I must go now. But it's been lovely. Thank you so much, Mrs. Cuthbert."

I didn't look at Tom and he didn't move, didn't even stand up when I left the room. Mrs. Cuthbert saw me to her door.

"Thank you, Clarissa," she said, and I realized immediately that she'd called me Clarissa and not *Miss Clarissa*. I leaned forward and kissed her cheek.

"I love him," I whispered, tears stinging my eyes. "I need you to know, need you to understand."

She frowned, took hold of my hand. "Yes, I understand. I understand more than you know, dear. But you have to let him go. You have to let him move on. Otherwise . . . otherwise he's going to waste his life waiting for something he can never have. And he deserves some happiness."

I nodded. "Yes, yes he does."

Later that evening, at dinner, he was in a peculiar mood, and barely looked at me. Instead, he focused his attention on the petite American blonde, sitting where Davina had been sitting the previous evening. He flirted with her in the most obvious way, and I suspected he simply wanted to annoy me, make me jealous.

"You know, I think I prefer American women," he said, leaning toward her. "I find you all . . . so much less uppity than English *ladies*."

I said nothing.

"I don't suppose all English ladies are uppity, Tom," the blonde replied, glancing at me. "Clarissa's certainly not."

"Ah, Clarissa . . . but you see, I know *Miss Clarissa* slightly better than you, and . . ." He leaned toward her and whispered something in her ear. She looked at me, raised her eyebrows and then giggled.

"Don't you know it's rude to whisper, Tom," I said without looking at him.

"There you go! They're all obsessed with bloody manners!"

"Tom . . ."

He turned to me. "Yes, my love?"

I shook my head.

"No? Is that a no, or a no thank you?"

The blonde laughed again. He refilled her glass, and his own, and then turned to me, straight-backed in his chair, the bottle poised over my glass. "More wine, ma'am?"

I didn't speak.

"Will that be all, ma'am?" He leaned forward, raised an eyebrow. "Or will ye be requirin' me services later?"

I looked across the table, tried to smile.

There were others who'd joined us for dinner that night, neighbors I presumed, and, thankfully, with something in the region of perhaps thirty sitting down to dinner, the room was unbelievably noisy. My mother's dinner parties had been sedate affairs by comparison, I thought, never this riotous. I could hear Hud's booming voice somewhere further down the table, and, from time to time, Davina's shrieks and laughter, but I couldn't make out any conversation, other than Tom's.

"Miss Clarissa . . ." he began, lighting a cigarette, and pulling at his tie, "Miss Clarissa likes the *old ways*, don't you, darling?"

"Please, Tom . . ."

He lifted his cigarette to his lips, staring down the table. "Please, Tom . . . please, Tom," he repeated quietly, imitating my voice, my accent. "Please, Tom . . . I'll wait for you, my darling. I'll wait, I promise," he went on, mimicking a young breathless girl: me.

I leaned toward him and whispered, "You're being unfair . . . and you're being uncouth."

He didn't look at me, but sighed, loudly. "Ah! What it is to be rich and uncouth. Of course, that's why the English don't particularly like Americans, you know?" he continued, turning to the blonde again. She looked nervous, and I wanted to tell him then to stop, but I knew we'd say things, I knew there'd be a scene. "Because you're all so damned rich and uncouth!" He leaned forward, smiling at her now, and her eyes darted from him to me and back to him.

"Oh dear, I do hope not," she said. And as she reached for her wine, she knocked over Tom's glass.

I placed my linen napkin over the wet tablecloth. "Don't worry," I said.

"No, don't worry," he repeated, refilling his glass. "It's only ten pounds a bottle."

"Tom! Please . . ."

He turned to me. "Please what?" And then he moved closer. "Can we leave now? I don't want to be here . . . I want to be with you."

I glanced across the table, tried to laugh, and then looked back at him. "I think you've had enough to drink," I said in a whisper.

He sat back in his chair, surveying the table, his guests; his eyes half closed. And I wondered how much he'd had to drink. It was so unlike him, I thought, to be this angry, this rude.

"I think our host is a tad weary," a voice on my left suddenly said, and I turned to a man I'd barely spoken to all evening, but one who Tom had introduced me to earlier. His name was Oliver Goddard and he was some sort of business adviser to Tom, though I couldn't for the life of me work out what exactly he advised him on.

"Yes . . . perhaps," I replied, knowing that *our host* had had little to no sleep the previous night.

At that moment Tom rose to his feet and excused himself from the table. The blonde looked relieved, and I turned my attention to Mr. Goddard.

"Please, do call me Oliver. Mr. Goddard sometimes sounds to me like the name of an undertaker."

Oliver was unmarried, lived in London, but came down to Deyning quite often. He'd heard from Tom that I'd grown up there and wanted to know more. He seemed particularly impressed by the library, and so I told him of my father's collection of books, how vast it had been, and how many volumes we'd sold at auction for pennies. And we spoke about books—poetry in particular. I failed to notice Tom's return to the table, possibly because Oliver was in the midst of reciting "The Green Eye of the Little Yellow God" to me.

"I love that poem," I said, when he'd finished, "but I'm afraid I don't have the brain to memorize verse like that."

"And I have the brain to memorize, but not analyze," he replied.

"I think women analyze more than men. We like to cogitate and ponder on all things—particularly the human condition . . . and the soul."

Oliver laughed, lifted a match to my cigarette. And perhaps it was that, or perhaps he thought we were flirting, but Tom suddenly interrupted our quiet, civilized conversation and said, in a voice loud enough to silence some of the table, at least, "For God's sake, Goddard, don't try and impress her ladyship with your fucking poetry and intellectual mutterings. If she's out of my league, dear boy, she's sure as hell out of yours!"

I was mortified. And he must have seen something in my face, because all at once he adopted the demeanor of a chastened child, without any word uttered from me—or anyone else. I glanced at Charlie, who gave me a nod, as if to say, it's all right, he's drunk. He was drunk; he didn't know what he was saying. And of course I was the only one there privy to his *torment*.

Davina appeared at my side. She suggested we go through to the drawing room for coffee and, as I rose to my feet, Oliver stood up. I smiled at him, glanced at Tom—who stared down the table with a look of sulky defiance. I wasn't angry for me, I was angry at the way he'd spoken to Oliver, who seemed so pleasant, so harmless.

"I need some fresh air, Davina . . . do you mind?"

"Shall I come with you?"

"You are kind, but can you give me five minutes on my own?"

"Yes . . . yes, of course," she said. "But, Clarissa, you know you can tell me—if there's something you need to share, if you need a confidante."

"Thank you, Davina. But I don't need a confidante, just a breath of fresh air. I'll be back in a moment," I said, and walked off toward the front door.

Outside, a yellow light shone out across the driveway, upon the trees and parkland, creating eerie shadows where there should have been none. Everything has changed, I thought: Deyning—all shiny and bright, with its dazzling electric lights in every room—and me and Tom. We couldn't turn back time; we couldn't go back to how we'd once been. And neither could Deyning.

As I walked down the driveway, I thought of him. I knew he'd feel wretched and my heart ached for him. And though I'd seen it all before—the mood swings, the rage—I wondered how often his anger boiled over, how often he lost control. Everything in his life appeared immaculate and ordered, even the woman he'd chosen to marry. But I'd seen the bottle of pills in his bathroom, prescribed "as and when necessary."

He deserves some happiness . . .

The glow emanating from the house faded, ahead of me blackness; so I stopped and stood for a while, next to the fence where Tom had first told me he was going to leave England. I thought back to that night, remembering my dance with Julian Carter: how I'd grabbed his head in my hands and kissed him. *Oh, stupid, stupid girl . . .* The following year, shortly after Christmas, in his room at a home for disabled servicemen and war veterans, Julian had placed a gun against his temple and put a bullet in his brain. Now I wondered if with that kiss I'd inadvertently reminded him of something; something he'd never again know.

I walked on a little further, distancing

myself from that thought with small steps into the darkness, and then I stopped again, and stared up at the heavens, trying to see the stars. But even the night sky appeared peculiarly illuminated. It was not quite a full moon, and high above me silver-edged clouds moved quickly across her misshapen face, for I'd never seen the man in the moon, only ever *She*: an infinitely patient, nurturing and maternal force. And with such power too: the power to control tides and seasons, fertility and farming, and, perhaps, even sanity. "Oh!" She seemed to be saying to me now, open-mouthed, aghast.

Slowly, stars began to appear, and if I kept my eyes fixed, concentrated, more and more became visible, until the sky was literally filled with them. And then I heard a boyish voice say, "They're all there, you know, if you look hard enough."

"But what shall I do, Georgie? What do I do?"

Let him go . . . let him move on . . .

I heard an owl call out from the top of a tree beside me, and I turned and looked back at Deyning, shining into the darkness like a rampant beacon. Yes, everything has changed, I thought; and I began to walk back toward the house.

Inside, as I crossed the hallway, I could hear the men in the dining room, and Tom's voice: light, back in control, charming. But I didn't want to go and join the women for coffee. I was embarrassed by Tom's outburst, unsure who had heard, and I had no wish to hear about weddings and babies, or flowers and gowns. So I went up to my room, undressed, and lay down upon the bed.

It's impossible, impossible. Soon he'll be married; have a family of his own . . . he deserves some happiness.

I could hear someone clapping; voices and laughter downstairs. My mother had always said that the marble floors—"those blasted floors"—made the house too noisy, and she was right, everything echoed. There would be no rendezvous that night: we'd had our night together. And I reached over and turned off the lamp.

I don't think we exchanged any words the following morning, and his mood was noticeably somber.

"Thank you so much, Tom," I said, shaking his hand as we stood outside the house on the driveway. "It's been splendid . . . really quite splendid."

He stood with Nancy and watched us go, but I didn't wave, and as our car pulled away I didn't look back.

As we headed down the driveway, Charlie said, "Queer sort of outburst last night. What do you suppose brought that on?"

"I've no idea," I replied, turning away, staring out of the car window.

"Hmm. Well, just so you know, he apologized to me after breakfast this morning. Said he hoped he hadn't offended you." And as we pulled out of the driveway, on to the road, he must have seen my face, because he added, "Oh dear, he did upset you."

He reached over and patted my hand. "He'd had a lot to drink, dear . . . and you know, he's a decent enough chap. He'd be mortified if he thought he'd upset you, or any of his guests."

I pulled a handkerchief out from my bag. "He didn't upset me, Charlie, really," I said. "I'm simply sad to be leaving Deyning, again . . . that's all."

I read of his marriage in *The Times* two months later. Charlie had been surprised, even a little piqued that we hadn't been invited. "It wasn't a big affair," I said. "Davina told me that they were only having about a hundred."

"Still, seems jolly rude to have had a wedding there, at Deyning, and not to have invited *you*."

"I wouldn't have gone anyway."

"Really? Why ever not? You love weddings."

"Sometimes," I replied.

There's a one-eyed yellow idol to the north of Kathmandu,
There's a little marble cross below the town;
There a broken-hearted woman tends the grave of Mad Carew,
And the Yellow God forever gazes down.

PART FOUR

Chapter Thirty-three

∽

. . . I never said I "would not," I simply said I wasn't sure, but it really was the most extraordinary and uplifting experience, not at all as I'd imagined, & a tremendous (and unexpected) comfort to me—just to know that they are at peace on the other side, & together. Did I tell you that she was v emphatic that H is alive & well? Across the water, she said, but she couldn't say which water. And I'm still mystified about "the child" . . .

∽

When Charlie told me about the invitation to a drinks reception at the new Cuthbert-Deyning offices in Park Lane, I told him immediately that I didn't wish to go. The thought of seeing Tom again, and with Nancy, was too much.

Tom had recently appointed Charlie's firm as his corporate lawyers, and though Charlie saw him occasionally, in business meetings or at his club, I had not seen him since our weekend at Deyning. Almost another year had passed. During that time there had been a number of events, dinners and the like, occasions where I could have seen him, but I'd managed to wriggle out of them and sent Charlie on his own.

"I don't know for the life of me why you're so reluctant," Charlie said. "He's really a jolly nice chap. Very down-to-earth and quite unlike a lot of these new-moneyed sorts."

"Yes, yes, I know he's very nice. It's not so much him . . . it's his wife," I said, clutching at straws, desperate to find a reason why I might not wish to go.

"Ah yes, the American," he said. "Well, she may not be there. She wasn't with him at the Blanches' last time, and she certainly wasn't with him at the Hyde Park Hotel last week."

"But it's a business thing, Charlie," I said. "Is it really so important that I go along with you?"

"He's invited us both. Look at the invitation," he replied, pointing to our mantelshelf.

"Oh, he'd have had his secretary write that for him," I said, knowing full well it was Tom's handwriting.

"No, darling, that's his hand. I know it."

On the day, Charlie said he'd meet me there; come straight from his office in the city. And all day I felt sick. I toyed with the idea of telephoning Charlie to tell him I was ill, and I tortured myself with the possibilities, how the evening *could* unfold. Would Nancy be there? I wondered. Would they be holding hands as they circumnavigated the room, nodding and smiling at all of Tom's minions and business associates? Would I be standing in line waiting to shake his hand too?

And yet, I wanted to see him; longed to see him again.

I ran a bath, and took a drink with me, even though it wasn't yet six. And as I lay in the bath, looking down at my body, I realized that physically, at least, I hadn't changed much over the preceding decade. My body had produced only one child, when my shape was still young enough to recover quickly. Like Mama, and blessed with her looks, I was naturally slim, and her insistence on good posture and lessons in deportment had paid off. I held myself tall, carried an invisible book upon my head. But I'd recently celebrated my thirtieth birthday and become acutely aware of my age, and of the passing of time. Perhaps that had something to do with Tom. Being displaced, estranged from one's heart served only to make the years more desolate. And I had nothing, nothing at all to show for my life: no children I could talk about; no work or vocation I could speak of.

Clarissa: beautiful, unfulfilled, useless, and childless.

It was a glorious spring evening, and I walked for quite a way before hailing a taxicab. I was no longer nervous. In fact, I felt rather calm and mellow as the cab headed toward Park Lane. I thought of the gardens at Deyning; the rhododendrons would be coming into bloom, the old wisteria too. And then I thought of him. Every unguarded thought led me back to him.

When I arrived at the building, I took the elevator to the top floor, as Charlie had instructed me. It was eight o'clock, half an hour later than the time on the invitation. Charlie was bound to be there, I thought. He would be looking out for me, see me emerge from the elevator.

The room was full of men in suits and, I noticed, a few very glamorous women. I took a glass of champagne from the waiter who greeted me, and then walked on into the crowd, looking for Charlie.

"Clarissa! Over here!"

It was Davina, in crimson satin with matching lips (and teeth).

"But, darling, I'm rather surprised to see you here," she said. "You normally avoid these sorts of things."

"Yes, well . . . *normally* I let Charlie attend these affairs on his own. He receives so many invitations. And you know what he's like. Can't say no."

"But I'm sure Tom'll be pleased you're here," she said, looking at me with a curious smile.

"And where is he?" I asked.

She leaned toward me. "Right behind you," she whispered.

I turned. He'd seen me, was watching me. I smiled at him as he spoke with a huddle of eager people, and then I turned back to Davina. I tried to make small talk, the way one does at those types of gatherings, but I was distracted and Davina was smiling a little too broadly, too obviously for my liking, and so, after a few minutes, I moved away, saying I must look for Charlie. I walked through the room, smiling and excusing myself through strangers, looking for my husband, and for once hoping he was there. But I was aware of someone following in my pathway. I could hear him behind me: "Good to see you . . . thank you for coming." And as I reached the other side of the room, I stepped out on to a balcony, overlooking Park Lane.

"Are you trying to escape from me?"

I looked straight ahead, over Hyde Park. The sun was just beginning to set, slipping down behind the trees, and I didn't turn; I kept my gaze on that pink ball of fire.

"No, not at all. I was looking for Charlie,

actually," I replied, still unable and unready to meet his eyes.

"He telephoned earlier. I'm afraid he's going to be stuck at the office until late . . . at least ten," he said. And I thought, *as flies to wanton boys . . .*

"That's a shame. He was looking forward to being here."

He moved alongside me, placing his hands upon the painted wrought-iron rail, inches from my own. Beautiful hands: hands that had touched me, loved me.

"I suppose you'll just have to make do with me," he said.

I turned to face him. "Yes, it would seem that way," I replied.

"Will you have dinner with me later?"

"And Nancy?"

"She's not here. She's in New York."

I looked away; felt that knot in my stomach, hard and tight from years of longing, years of wanting. Was it always going to be like this? Was I always going to give in to one man?

"Yes. Yes, I'll have dinner with you," I said.

"I'm pleased you came. It's been a while . . ."

"It's always been a while."

"It doesn't have to be. You know that."

I said nothing.

"I have to mingle now, say a few words . . . wait for me," he added, and then he stepped back inside the room.

I stood in the doorway, watching him as he moved through the room: smiling, greeting people, shaking hands. I watched him as he stepped away from the huddle and began his speech. And I looked away as I listened to his voice: so cultured, so assured. I clapped with everyone else, moved further into the room and spoke to a few people. Had I known him long? Had I been at the wedding? Was I a friend of Nancy's? Yes, he was charming—and yes, rather humble with it too. No, I hadn't been at the wedding; I didn't really know Nancy. Yes, it was such a shame she wasn't there.

I could see him on the other side of the room, head bowed, listening intently as someone spoke to him. And he shone. For there was a light that emanated from him, his soul, his substance. I hadn't seen it when I was young, or perhaps I had but had failed to recognize it. But now I saw it, saw it quite clearly, and even at a distance I felt its heat. *Tom*. He looked up, straight at me, as though he'd heard me think his name. Then he turned, said something to the gentlemen he was standing with, and moved over to me. He stood alongside me without uttering a word, and as the fabric of his jacket brushed my arm I felt that current once more: a bolt of electricity traveling through my veins, straight to my heart.

"Right, I'm done. Let's go," he said, taking my arm, and leading me through the room, toward the elevator. As we stepped into it, he sighed, lit a cigarette—the first I'd seen him smoke all evening—then he looked at me and said, "And now, Clarissa . . . now to business."

He was being funny, of course, and I laughed. I was as relieved as he to be away from that ordeal. When we stepped out of the building onto the street, a cream-colored Bentley was waiting—pulled up by the curb. He opened the door, saw me inside, closed it, and said something to the uniformed driver.

"Where are we going?" I asked, as he climbed inside the car.

"Home, of course," he replied.

There was a bottle of already-corked champagne standing in an ice bucket in the back of the car. He lifted the top of the walnut compartment between our seats, pulled out two glasses and poured the champagne.

When he said *home*, I'd presumed he meant *his* home; that he was taking me back to his place in London, though I wasn't entirely sure where that was, and I knew he owned a number of properties in the city. I was nervous and couldn't help but wonder if he kept a place specifically for taking women back to. I wasn't convinced he'd be a faithful husband to Nancy; in fact, I imagined he'd have more than one glamorous girlfriend. After all, he was rich and handsome—what was to stop him? But had he assumed I'd be the same? Was I simply another conquest? As we headed over the river, and then through the streets of Battersea, I began to feel irritated, and mildly alarmed. I pictured some seedy flat in the outer suburbs, and I turned to him and said, "Tom . . . *where*, exactly, are you taking me?"

"Don't worry," he said, turning to me and smiling. "Everything's been sorted."

"No really, I need to know. Charlie will be worried."

"Charlie knows. I have your husband's permission."

"Knows what, exactly? Have his permission for what?"

"Permission to take you out for dinner."

I laughed. "But *where*?"

"Deyning."

"Deyning! And you arranged this with Charlie?"

"Yes, I did. He's working on a rather big deal for me tonight, so I said—I said the least I could do was take you out to dinner."

"But did you tell him *where* you were taking me to dinner?"

He ran a hand through his hair. "No, I'm not sure that I did." He turned to me. "But to be honest, Clarissa, at that point I hadn't decided where I was going to take you."

I'd been kidnapped, albeit politely, and with my husband's approval. How convenient, I thought, that Charlie should be stuck at the office working on Cuthbert-Deyning business. Tom's company was his biggest client, there'd have been no way he could have said anything other than "yes" to whatever Tom Cuthbert suggested. I could hear their telephone conversation in my head, hear Tom telling Charlie not to worry about me; he'd see to it that I was looked after. And of course my husband—oblivious to my feelings, insensitive to any chemistry— no doubt thought it an ideal time for me to get to know what a "jolly nice chap" his rich client, Tom Cuthbert, was.

At that time I hadn't worked out the exact level of Tom's duplicity, but I later realized he'd set the whole thing up so that I'd be on my own. He'd learned from Charlie that we would both be attending his drinks reception, and on the day, late in the afternoon, he'd specifically requested Charlie to handle an *urgent* piece of business. "Work through the night if you have to," he'd said to him. And I suppose Charlie saw the enormous fee he'd be able to invoice Cuthbert-Deyning. It was all too strange, too wonderful for words. There I was, going back to Deyning, with Tom, alone.

Chapter Thirty-four

ᔐ

From the moment we arrived at Deyning I didn't think of Charlie. Not once. Deyning had nothing to do with him and everything to do with Tom and me. In my mind it was sacred, like our love for each other; like all the snatched moments of the preceding years. Stacked together they amounted to so little, and yet I had lived more, felt more alive during those moments than any time in between.

I remember breathing in that soft smoky night air, the scents of pine and cedar-wood so familiar to my senses. And for a split second, as I stepped through the open doorway, time reversed and I was back to that summer: I saw Mama's roses standing in a crystal vase on the hallway table; Caesar, clip-clapping across the marble floor toward me; George, disappearing down the passageway toward the library. Then I saw myself, hat in hand, coming down the staircase, en route to meet Tom.

He stood behind me, in the doorway, leaning against its frame, smoking, watching me. "Home," I said, turning to him, and he smiled.

I walked on, into the lamp-lit drawing room, glanced around, and then went back into the hallway, down the passageway to my father's library, now Tom's study. I walked along the shelves of books and stood by his desk at the window. But for the light from the hallway the room was dark. I could see the lake in the distance, a shimmering mirror, reflecting the vast night sky. Yes, I was home, I was where my heart lived, and I turned and wrapped my arms around him.

There was no dinner, nothing at all prepared and no one about. And I realized that he'd been truthful in the car: he'd decided at the very last minute to take me back to Deyning. In the kitchen, as I looked about, noting all the modern new conveniences, he disappeared down to the cellar, and returned with a bottle of wine, saying, "I've been saving this for a special occasion." And so we ate there, at the table, pulling at a carcass of a cold chicken with our bare hands, and giggling like children at the mess in front of us, and on our faces. Then he picked up the bottle and our glasses and said to me, "Let's go down to the lake."

"But I can't. Look at me."

I was in heels, still dressed for a formal night out in London. He scratched his head, then pulled a "eureka" face. "Come with me."

He led me upstairs to the small room opposite his own bedroom, which I recalled—much to his amusement—as once having been known as "the sewing room." It was Nancy's dressing room.

"No, I don't want to wear her clothes," I said. "I can't wear her clothes."

"Then I'm afraid you'll have to improvise, Miss Clarissa."

"Don't call me that. I hate it."

He took me through his bedroom, turned on the light of his dressing room, stepped back and sat down upon the bed as I moved hangers—looking through his wardrobe for something, anything. As I pulled down my dress, I glanced up through the open door and caught his eye. I pulled on a pair of his trousers, made a point of showing him the rather roomy waist.

"There's a belt in the top drawer, the one on the left," he said.

I chose a pale pink cashmere sweater, and as I pulled it over my head, I breathed him in, wanted to wrap my face in its softness; languish in the feel of it against my skin.

When I emerged through the doorway, he smiled: "You could be seventeen."

"Really, is *this* what I looked like then?" I asked, looking down at myself in mock horror.

We took the back stairs down to the kitchen, grabbing at the cold chicken as we passed by the table, and then we headed through to the garden room. He was still in his dinner suit, minus his tie, and as he bent down to help me into a pair of Wellington boots, he said, "I always said

I'd be a rather good lady's maid to you."
And I giggled.

We walked down through the meadow hand in hand, and as we passed the chestnut tree he glanced over at it. "You know, I often see you there."

"You mean like a ghost?"

"Yes, I suppose so . . ."

At the lake, he brought out two deck chairs from the boathouse, and we sat in silence, side by side, looking across the water—opalescent and vast, and stretching all the way up to the stars. Even if I'd wanted to, I couldn't have spoken; I was in some blissful state beyond words, beyond a here and now. And being there, back there with him, all my years of pain and loneliness evaporated. You see, he was my world, my life: he was my universe.

When he rose from his chair and began to strip off his clothes, I laughed. I watched him run naked along the jetty and dive into the water, and for a few minutes I remained where I was, seated. Then I stood up, pulled off my ridiculous ensemble, all of it, and walked to the end of the jetty.

He called out from the water. "It's perfect. Not cold at all."

I remember the coolness of the water as I dived into it, under it. And I remember emerging, looking up at the stars, and shrieking. As we swam, never too close, we laughed at the memory of that day, after the war, when he'd swum over to me on the island. But there was an almost embarrassed self-consciousness to us both, an invisible barrier, and one that seemed hard to cross. As though we'd both become more aware of the passing of time, the distance between then and now; as if those days which had bound us had slipped further, creating a space, a void.

He climbed out of the water, walked along the jetty to the boathouse, then reappeared, wrapped in a towel, holding another out to me.

"Gosh, such luxury," I said, as I climbed out of the water and grabbed the towel from his hand. "We never kept towels down here in *our* day."

I went to the boathouse, dried myself and put on my clothes, or rather *his* clothes. "Wasn't that glorious?" I said, when I emerged. But he didn't speak, and suddenly I felt apprehensive. Perhaps he'd regretted bringing me back. I moved over to him, placed my hand upon his bare shoulder. "Don't feel guilty," I said.

"I don't feel guilty, Clarissa . . . I feel sad."

He took my hand, pulled me to him, onto his lap, and I laid my head against his cheek, closed my eyes, and once more wished away the life I'd been born into. For even then, it seemed, so many years had passed us by, swallowing up our lives; gulping up our love. I wrapped my arms around his neck, pressed my lips against his skin. I was lost, I was found; I was with him once more.

"I think I owe you an apology," he began, "about my behavior . . . that last night you were here, with Charlie. I was angry, and, I think, quite vile to you." He moved his head closer. "Forgive me."

I ran a finger down the side of his face. "Forgive you? I forgave you that very night."

He took hold of my hand. "And I need to tell you something," he said, closing his eyes, turning away. "Nancy . . ." He paused: "We're having a baby, Clarissa."

We're having a baby . . .

"A baby . . . But how wonderful. Congratulations."

I felt my head begin to spin; the carousel begin to move once more.

A baby . . .

He turned to me, frowning. "I'm sorry."

"Good gracious, don't be sorry," I said, rising to my feet. "It's happy news . . . lovely news."

He shook his head. "You know what I wish? Shall I tell you what I wish?"

"No. Don't tell me," I said quickly.

I moved toward the water, stood with my back to him as I heard him go inside the boathouse to dress. "It's good news . . . happy news," I whispered. "Be happy for him." I closed my eyes. *He deserves some happiness.*

We walked back through the meadow—past our tree—in silence. And as we passed his mother's cottage, I saw him look up at a light still shining from an upstairs window. Inside the house, he took hold of my hand and led me up the stairs, and I said, "I'm tired . . . so tired." In his bedroom, he undressed me, pulled back the covers and helped me into his bed. He got down onto his knees, kissed my forehead and said, "I never, ever want to let you go."

"No, don't let me go. Never let me go."

I'm not sure what woke me, but the room was still quite dark, the house deathly quiet. And for a moment I thought I was at home, in London; thought it was Charlie in my bed, lying next to me with his arms around me. And I was confused. I turned over, and as I did so I remembered where I was: I was with him; I was at Deyning. I reached out, ran my hand over his bare flesh. He sighed, turned onto his back, and I moved with him, wrapping myself into him. I held on to him, listening to his breathing. And I lay there, wide awake, until dawn.

And then I fell asleep.

When I opened my eyes, he was there, watching me; his head propped on one hand. "You've been talking in your sleep."

I reached up to his face. "Oh really, and what was I saying?"

"You were speaking of your *little friend . . .*"

"My little friend?" I had no idea what he meant.

"Emily . . . your imaginary friend."

"Ah . . . yes, Emily."

"She's still with you, isn't she?"

"Yes . . . I suppose she must be. What was I saying?"

He ran a finger along my brow. "I'm not sure . . . couldn't make it out. But you were calling for her." He smiled, shook his head, then lifted my hair, moved his lips slowly down my neck, onto my shoulder. I closed my eyes. I wanted to cry. I wanted to tell him not to take me back to London, to Charlie, to that house, to let me stay there with him. Forever. I pushed my hands through his hair, pulled him to me.

By the time we had breakfast it was almost ten o'clock. And still I didn't think of Charlie: what I would say, what I would tell him. I wanted to walk through the grounds, see the gardens before I left. So we strolled to the bench by the ha-ha, looking out toward the lake, the South Downs in the distance.

"Do you remember when we first sat together here?" he asked, looking straight ahead. "It's when I fell in love with you. You were so beautiful, so innocent."

"*Were*?" I repeated.

"Well, you're certainly no longer innocent . . ." he said, glancing at me with that half-smile. "You were a child then. You believed that everything and everyone was good. Your world was perfect, and I longed to be part of it. Part of the Granville world . . . Clarissa's world."

He leaned forward and lowered his eyes, smiling at a memory.

"What?" I asked, watching him, smiling too.

He shook his head. "I was so consumed by you, so intoxicated . . ." He paused for a moment. "But I've learned to live without you, had to live without you, and yet . . . it never feels *right* . . . nothing ever feels right. Bit like wearing clothes that don't fit, I'd imagine," he added, looking sideways at me.

I reached out, took hold of his hand.

"Do you ever wish we could go back?" I asked.

"No," he replied quickly. "No, I don't. I was no one then . . . I was the housekeeper's son, always looking from the outside in, never quite part of things. Look at me now: the owner of Deyning Park. I've achieved everything I ever wanted, bar one thing . . ." And I closed my eyes, for I knew what was to come. "I don't have you."

"It's impossible . . ."

"Yes, it would seem so," he said, nodding. Then he laughed, but it was a hollow, hard laugh. "Here I am, trapped in the place that belongs to you . . . without you." He looked up to the sky. "Such a waste," he added.

Walter drove us back to London, and I felt as though I was going to a funeral, perhaps my own funeral. That hard knot had returned to my stomach, accompanied by a feeling of dread. We sat in the back of the car holding hands, and from time to time he lifted my hand to his lips, and held it there, pressed to them. But he seemed distant now, preoccupied. As we headed into the sprawl of London I turned to him, but he didn't look at me. He kept his eyes straight ahead, as though concentrating on the road, our journey. And so we passed through the streets of Battersea and Chelsea in silence. And when the car finally came to a standstill outside my home, he turned to me and said, "I need you to understand . . . try to understand—there's a child now." He closed his eyes. "I can't leave her, Clarissa. I can't abandon my child."

I nodded.

He climbed out of the car and moved swiftly to my door, but I'd already stepped out. "Thank you," I said, and I reached up to his face, placed my hand upon his cheek. "I wish only for your happiness, Tom."

I didn't look back; couldn't bear to watch him go. But as I closed my front door I heard another slam shut, then the rumble of an engine, slowly fading as it moved away down the street. I put down my bag, walked through to the drawing room and poured myself something—I'm not sure what—from a decanter, and sat down upon the sofa. It was Sonia who later came into the room and asked me if everything was quite all right; if there was a reason why I'd locked and double-bolted the front door.

That evening, Charlie returned home from work earlier than usual, muttering about the traffic and some ghastly man he'd had to sit next to on the tube. I sat in silence with a book in my hand as he poured us each a drink. And I wondered why he'd come home early: was it to interrogate me, accuse me? I had no plan, no idea what I was going to say, but I wasn't going to say anything until he'd laid the ground, as it were. *Innocent until proven guilty.*

"So, did you have fun last night?" he asked, his back to me, as he replaced the glass stopper in the decanter. "Tom tells me he took a few of you back to Deyning for dinner," he continued. "Must have been a blast."

"Yes, yes, it was. It was fun."

He sat down opposite me. "So . . . who went down there?"

"Oh golly, I really don't know . . . some of his and Nancy's friends. Such a shame you couldn't make it. Did you manage to get your work finished?"

He sniffed, looked away. "Yes, eventually. We finished at three . . . that's why I didn't come home . . . made sense for me to sleep at the office. But what time did you get back?"

I shrugged. "Oh, probably around that same time."

He nodded. "You're not cross then?"

"No, of course not. Not at all."

"It was unfortunate timing, but he's putting so much business our way now . . . well, you know."

"Yes, yes, of course. I understand."

"And he promised me, promised me that he'd make sure you weren't left on your own, and that he'd take you to dinner. You see, I told him, told him how much you hate those sorts of things, how you usually avoid them, and how wretched I felt at having talked you into attending— only to abandon you. Although, I have to say I had no idea he was going to take you back to Deyning . . . and when he told me today, well, I did rather wonder."

"Wonder?"

"Yes, you know, wonder if you'd got caught up in some jamboree you didn't feel part of, and then been forced to go back there with them all. I said to him, 'Oh dear, I do hope my wife isn't going to be cross with me—otherwise I may have to increase your fee, ha!'"

I laughed. "Really, Charlie, it was perfectly fine. I was fine."

"Good. He's a decent enough sort, isn't he?"

"Yes, he is. He's charming."

Later, over dinner, Charlie asked me more about the evening, my trip down to Deyning, and I heard myself lie. We'd eaten in the dining room, I said, had beef—cooked to perfection, and then a wonderful chocolate pudding. Yes, the house had looked the same, and yes, it was his usual driver who'd brought me home. I was vague once more about who'd been there, but as I tried to recall names and describe non-existent people, he'd helped me out, offering me a few to grab on to. Then I said, "Ask Tom. He knows who they all were."

"I can't ask him that," he replied.

"Why ever not?"

"I'm his lawyer, not his bloody mother, Clarissa."

I knew I wouldn't hear from Tom again after that day. He had a proper family now, or the start of one. And anyway, what could we have done from there? We couldn't have had an affair. Secret rendezvous and snatched afternoons in London hotels were not an option for us. We wanted *all* of each other, everything. We both knew it had to be all or nothing; we couldn't share, you see. We couldn't have a part-time stake in each other's lives. To embark upon an affair would have been tantamount to my leaving Charlie, and him abandoning his wife and soon-to-be child. I knew the scandal would ruin him, and kill my mother. And so, my life continued. Ahead of me, years and years of emptiness, stretching as far as the eye can see, like the Sahara Desert.

Chapter Thirty-five

◞

. . . M Zelda almost came up with yr name yesterday. Of course, I feigned confusion, but she would keep on at it, in that way of hers, & insisted that there was something "more." She said she saw a curtain over my life, and behind it a man, & V suggested it was my father. "NO!" said MZ, "this is not a father . . . this is a love, a lover." I nearly fell off my chair.

◞

It's always been something of a mystery to me what exactly motivated her to get in touch with me when she did, but a few weeks—perhaps a month—after I'd seen Tom I received a letter from his mother. My address would have been easy enough for her to find; Charlie and I were listed. She said that she was coming to stay in London with a cousin and would very much like it if I could meet with her, perhaps for tea. Of course, I replied, I'd love to catch up with her over tea. I suggested a time and venue, to which she replied—by way of a postcard—and confirmed our arrangement.

We met in the tearoom at Swan and Edgar, and after ordering afternoon tea for two we settled into predictable, cozy reminiscences of life at Deyning before the war. I wondered if perhaps she was simply lonely, had wanted to see me to go back to a time in her life when she'd been needed. Then she mentioned him, telling me "in the strictest confidence" that his marriage was "not what it ought to be." She said she suspected her son was not a faithful husband; that he was unhappy and that he should never have married "an American."

"Well, Mrs. Cuthbert, I'm certainly no expert on marriage. And, it has to be said,

Tom's a grown man now, a man of the world."

"I don't know why he married her, I really don't." She shook her head. "I wanted him to be settled." I nodded. "I wanted him to have a family. I thought that's what he needed, you see—to make him happy. But it hasn't turned out like that. And perhaps I was being selfish, because I knew . . . I knew at the time he didn't love her, not the way he should've done. And there was me thinking of grandchildren and oh, I don't know what . . ."

"All marriages, it seems to me, are rather hard work," I said.

She shrugged, sighed. "I wouldn't know, and that's part of the problem. You see, I want him to have someone to share his life with . . . not end up like me. But really, what can I do now?"

"Nothing," I replied, refilling her teacup. "You simply can't blame yourself, Mrs. Cuthbert. I know, I know as his mother you only wish for his well-being and happiness, but . . . there's a baby to think of now."

She looked perplexed for a moment. "Oh, you'd heard?"

"Yes, I'd heard . . . I can't recall through whom," I said, quickly, and I wondered if that was why she'd wanted to meet me: to tell me about Tom's baby. "Who knows, perhaps this baby is what he needs, what the marriage needs."

She shook her head again. "I'm not so sure. It's not as straightforward as that with him."

No, I thought, nothing ever is with Tom. "Oh, really?"

"He's like me. Once he's given his heart, he can never give it to another."

I remained silent. She looked so small and vulnerable, and for a moment I thought she was about to cry.

"You see, he fell in love so many years ago, and he's never got over that."

I picked up my cup and saucer. I wasn't sure what to say. What could I say?

"Life's not turned out the way I expected either," I said, looking down into my teacup. "Sometimes it's not easy . . . not for any of us."

"But I think you know . . . I think you know, Miss Clarissa. There's never been another . . ."

I looked up at her and smiled.

"You're *everything* to him. You always have been." She looked down at her lap, twisting a white handkerchief in her hands.

It was awkward. More awkward than I can begin to explain: for there I was, taking tea with Mrs. Cuthbert, hovering on the brink of talking to her intimately about her son. I wasn't sure what, exactly, she knew, what Tom had told her, and I was flummoxed to know what to say to her. And all at once, I felt my mother's presence. I could see her wide-eyed stare; feel her bemusement.

I reached out, placed my hand over hers. "Mrs. Cuthbert, you told me I had to let him go; you said I had to let him move on . . . and I did. And now . . . now . . ." I stopped; I don't really know why, don't know what it was I was going to say from there, but I suddenly thought of Emily, my child, her granddaughter. I stared at her, into her pale gray eyes, and I saw the years of sadness behind them.

"The thing is, Miss Clarissa," she began again, and at that moment I wished she'd stop calling me *Miss Clarissa*. It sounded so . . . subservient, so wrong.

"Please, please—no *Miss*, just Clarissa," I said.

She smiled. "Clarissa, the thing is, I need to explain . . . I want to tell someone . . ." She paused again.

"Yes?

"About Tom's father."

"Mr. Cuthbert?"

"That's just it. You see, there never was a Mr. Cuthbert."

"Oh. Yes, I see," I replied, realizing what my mother had always suspected.

She took a deep breath, looked into my eyes, and then announced, in an unequivocal, clear voice, "Tom's father was the Earl Deyning."

I was silent for a moment. Stunned, and a little shocked by the thought (and concurrent image) of Mrs. C and the old Earl *at it*. But I remember thinking how utterly perfect. And I almost wanted to rush to the public telephone to inform Mama. It had never made an iota of difference to me whether Tom's father was an earl or a pauper, but I'd have liked to have broadcast that particular piece of news to quite a few people, some dead, others still living.

I lit a cigarette. "Does Tom know this?" I asked.

"No, he does not. Oh, I've wanted to tell him, and so many times, but it's so hard . . ."

"But why . . . why did you want to tell me this?"

"Because someone should know. I'm old. My days are running out and I want someone to know the truth. He loves you . . . and I think he believes in his heart that one day . . . one day you'll be with him."

She looked tearful again, and I felt for her. I wanted to tell her that of course I loved her son. I'd always loved him, always would. But I couldn't.

"Don't worry. Your secret is safe with me. I promise you that."

She wiped her nose. "Thing is . . . if anything were to happen to me, if I'd never told him, would you?"

"Do you really wish me to?"

"Yes. I want him to know, and I want him to understand why . . . why I never told him, why I couldn't tell him."

"Then of course I shall. Of course." I put my hand over hers once again. "You have my word, Mrs. Cuthbert."

She smiled. "Please, call me Evelyn. It's

my name . . . and no one ever uses it. No one calls me Evelyn anymore. Not for years."

"Evelyn," I said, gripping her hand.

"You said to me that day—when you came back to Deyning—that you loved him. Do you still love him?" she asked, looking at me beseechingly.

"Perhaps I'm like you and Tom. Once I've given my heart I can never give it to another."

When we emerged from the department store into the London throng that day she looked out of place, quite lost; and I wanted to put my arms around her. I wanted to take her home with me. This was Tom's mother; this was Emily's grandmother. We were connected in love and in blood. As we said good-bye, I held on to her hand, and when I kissed her cheek I was struck by its softness, and the faint fragrance of lily of the valley. But as I walked away up Regent Street, I felt wretched, and all at once sad beyond words, and I turned and began to walk in the opposite direction, toward Piccadilly. I'm not sure why I needed to go back to her, to find her, or what I wanted to say to her, but at that moment my whole life seemed to depend upon it.

I found her, eventually, in the bus queue for Acton, and I wrapped myself around her as though she were my own long-lost mother. What people in the queue must have thought, I really don't know. She said to me, "You're very special, Clarissa, so very special." And I stood there with her, holding on to her hand, until the bus came, and when she climbed on board, I shouted after her, "Evelyn! Evelyn! I'll come and visit you, I'll come down and visit you soon."

I moved along the bus looking in at her through the window and watched her take her seat. She raised her hand, waved at me, and I blew her a kiss. Then the bell rang, and as the bus pulled away I felt the most profound love for her: Tom's mother. I stood and watched it disappear down Piccadilly.

I'm pleased I went back to her that day.

Charlie and I didn't travel, mainly because of his disability. Our life was firmly London based, and so, but for the occasional Saturday to Monday at a familiar house in the country, we rarely ventured far. He did not cope well with unknown, uncharted terrain; could no longer ride or dance, or pursue so many of the activities being a houseguest in the country seemed to entail. I suspect he'd always liked predictability and order in his life. But his time in the army, coupled with the limitations incurred through his injuries, had made him a zealous adherent of routine, and fearful of any spontaneity or disruption to that routine.

We didn't often visit Charlie's sister, but it was a house he knew and could cope with. And the following spring, perhaps six months or so after I'd met Mrs. Cuthbert, we went down to Sussex to stay with Flora and her husband, David. They lived about fifteen miles from Deyning at that time, in a sixteenth-century timber-framed cottage: a hotchpotch, rambling place, and, like so many others, still without electricity or running hot water. Their two sons, my nephews, were both away at school, and they lived a somewhat eccentric, Spartan existence, tucked away there, without any luxuries and with only candlelight at night.

I hadn't planned to drive over to Deyning, but on Sunday, the day after we'd arrived, there was a pause in the day and it seemed the perfect afternoon for a drive. It wasn't long after Easter and the countryside was just beginning to take on the soft, luminous hue of springtime. And of course, being so close to Deyning, I couldn't *not* think of the place; couldn't *not* think of him. The previous evening, over dinner, Flora had mentioned him to me, and I'd immediately felt that momentary sense of loss, a feeling I had each time I heard his name. It was different with my brothers, I'd often thought, because two of them were dead; they had gone and could never return. And Henry? Henry may have disappeared but he was alive somewhere, I knew that, and I also felt sure he would return to us some day. But Tom, Tom had not died, nor had he disappeared. He lived and breathed on the periphery, somewhere on the edge of my life. Flitting in and out of conversation, lurking in the shadows.

Flora told me that she and David had been to a charity fund-raising dinner at Deyning a month or so earlier. "Golly, he is a dish," she said, leaning toward me, as David and Charlie talked business. "But he's not at all at ease with himself. And for all his money, he doesn't strike one as . . . particularly happy."

I smiled but said nothing. I did and didn't

want to talk about him. I wanted to ask questions, but didn't altogether wish to hear the answers. Then she said, quietly, "Of course, there's talk that the marriage has been in trouble from the word go."

"Oh?"

"Mm," she said, taking a sip of wine and glancing at David. "Apparently he's in love with someone else."

I looked at her. "Perhaps he just works hard," I replied.

She smiled, knowingly. "I think there's a little more to it than that, dear." She'd hooked me. I was intrigued.

"And . . ."

"Well, you'll recall Mrs. Wade, who cooks for us?"

"Yes," I said, although I didn't really.

"She sometimes helps out over at Deyning, when they have big dinners there and so forth, and she's been there rather a lot of late." She paused, lit a cigarette from the candle on the table. "She told me it's common knowledge *he's* in love with someone else, someone in London, I think, and that the marriage is in trouble."

"And how does Mrs. Wade know this?"

She laughed. "Clarissa, really, you more

than anyone should understand that servants know *everything*."

"Yes, but they're not meant to tell, Flora," I said.

"I think those days are well and truly gone, darling. We're all exposed now. Anyway, Mrs. Wade says there've been quite a few big arguments and rather a lot of door-slamming going on at Deyning, not that *he's* there much. But when he is . . ."

"But I thought . . . I'd heard that she was . . . that a baby was due?"

She shook her head, shrugged. "No . . . no babies. We saw them only a month ago, and she certainly isn't expecting anything . . . other than perhaps a letter from *his* lawyers," she added, raising her eyebrows. "I think divorce is imminent, dear. And he'll no doubt have his pick for Mrs. Cuthbert number two . . . all that money and those looks, really."

So, as we sat outside after lunch, replete, and enjoying one of those blissful lazy Sundays, rustling newspapers and watching clouds roll across the sky, I said, "I think I might take a drive."

"Oh really? Where to? I might come with you," Flora said.

"I don't know . . . perhaps to Midhurst."

"Darling, there'll be absolutely no one about, nothing at all happening . . . you know it's really terribly dull there."

I managed to get away on my own and took the road back toward Deyning. I had no intention of motoring up the main driveway, but I knew the road that led to the farm, and the track from there toward the woods by the lake. There'd be no one about; no one would see me. I turned off the London road and drove down the narrow lane toward the farm. I drove past two children, waving to them as I crossed in front of the red-brick farmhouse, and then I picked up the track toward the lake, and stopped the car at the gate before the woods.

I stepped out of the car, onto the track where Papa and I had sat and listened to the sounds of guns so many years earlier, and, for a second or two, I thought I could hear them once more. I moved on, opened the gate, and walked into the dappled light of overhanging branches, lifting them up out of my path. The track had narrowed, was overgrown with weeds and thistles, and I caught my skirt on them more than once. I hoisted it up, tucking it into my belt, and walked on again until I came to a clearing and another gate, beyond which was the lower path around the lake; the one Papa had taken me to when I was a child. I wondered if the bench was still there. It was a warm spring day, not hot, and not entirely sunny, but clear and bright. I took off my shoes and my stockings, left them by the gate and headed down toward the lake.

I found the bench, collapsed and rotting; no more than an ancient piece of timber lying on the edge of an overgrown pathway, and I walked on slowly as the house came into view. I couldn't be sure if anyone was there, but there were no obvious signs of life, and it was too tempting not to continue. I kept to the pathway, my head down, picking my way through sharp twigs and the shells of acorns beneath my feet. Then I glanced up and saw the chestnut tree in the lower meadow, the empty bench beneath its branches. When I reached the boathouse I looked up again, toward the house. A number of trees had disappeared, cut down to make the view from the windows on the southeast side of the house more picturesque, I assumed. I could clearly see the gate to the stable yard, but there was no one about, not a sound, so I moved on, along the jetty, and sat down. I dangled my legs over the side, my toes skimming the water, and then leaned back; lifting my face up to a blink of sun between shadows. *Home.*

Was he there? I wondered. Was he sitting yards away, at his desk, staring out toward the water my feet now touched? I remembered Flora's words of the previous evening . . . *no babies . . . an affair . . . a separate life.* I closed my eyes, and for a moment I fancied I could hear his voice in the distance; a memory held and carried back amid the rustling of trees.

"Have you not read the signs, miss? This is private property . . . trespassers *will* be prosecuted."

I turned. A man I'd never seen before was standing at the other end of the jetty.

"I'm terribly sorry," I said, quickly rising to my feet, rearranging my skirt. "I used to live here . . . I grew up here."

He said nothing, didn't move.

"Actually, I happen to know the present owner, Tom Cuthbert, Mr. Cuthbert . . . and

I'm quite sure, quite sure that he wouldn't be in the least bothered by my being here . . ."

"That may be, miss, but I have my job to do. And Mr. Cuthbert'll no doubt already have been informed we have an intruder. You came through the farmyard, didn't you?"

"Yes, that's right, I did. But, as I'm sure you can see, I'm not a poacher . . . not an intruder. I simply wanted to take a walk . . ." I said, moving back along the jetty. "I can go now."

"I'm sure you mean no harm, miss, but I have my job to do," he repeated, as I scurried past him. And as I quickened my pace, back along the path, I could hear voices somewhere. And they were not the voices of ghosts from my past: these voices were male and very much alive. Oh God, I didn't want to be caught looking like a snoop, a spy, and I picked up my skirt and ran.

I ran along the path in agony as my feet crunched on acorn shells, pebbles and holly; my hair tugged and pulled at by newly hostile branches. I stopped by Papa's rotting bench, breathless, and glanced back; I could see three figures, all of them looking in my direction, and I took off again, up the pathway toward the woods, and the gate where I'd left my shoes. When I reached the gate, my shoes and stockings had gone and I yelled out, because I couldn't possibly drive in bare feet. But there was nothing for it, I'd have to try. I passed through the gate, breaking a nail *and* ripping my blouse on its latch, and shouting out again, "No!" I continued back along the track toward the car, in tears, in physical as well as mental anguish. And then I stopped. Why was I running? I'd done nothing wrong . . . I'd simply gone to look at my old home. *My home.* I stood still for a moment, collecting my thoughts, calming my breath. I needed my shoes; I couldn't drive without them. And so I turned and walked back toward the gate I'd just passed through and left ajar. I saw the man from the jetty walking up the bank toward me, carrying something, and I stopped by the gate and waited for him.

"Mi-iss! Miss Larissa!" he called out. And I thought, oh God, he may have my name wrong but he knows who I am, and that meant only one thing: one of the men by the boathouse had been Tom.

"Yes, hello . . . hello again," I answered, closing my eyes as he came toward me, carrying my shoes and stockings.

"I'm sorry, Miss Larissa," he said, huffing and puffing, "but you know how it is . . . we get all sorts here . . . can't be too careful. And being as Mr. Cuthbert has some very valuable antiquities up at the house . . ."

"Oh really," I said, snatching my shoes and stockings from his arms. "It's *Clarissa*, by the way."

He looked confused.

"My name, it's Clarissa—not *Larissa*."

He smiled at me. "A very pretty name too, miss," he said. "And Mr. Cuthbert would like you to know that you're very welcome to . . . to have a paddle in the lake."

I laughed. "I was not paddling, I simply dipped my feet into the water," I replied and then I realized how I sounded, and added, "and I know, you're just doing your job."

I glanced toward the boathouse, but could see no one, and so I looked back at him and said, "And do thank Mr. Cuthbert for his very kind offer of a paddle, but I must get back to . . . to London." And I turned and began to walk back toward the car, knowing full well how I must have looked to the old gamekeeper, with my torn blouse, bare feet and disheveled hair.

Oh God, how I wished I hadn't gone there. To be caught *trespassing*, and then to have run off like that! I pictured him, Tom, standing with his gamekeeper, as the old man explained that he'd chased off a rogue *paddler*. And I could see him, see his smile. I leaned against the bonnet, rolled up my stockings, one by one, and put on my shoes. I got into the car, slammed the door shut and as I started the engine, put the car into reverse, I saw him, Tom, in front of me, hurriedly marching through the grass toward the gate. I saw him raise his hand, shout something, but I pushed my foot down on the accelerator and turned away; and I kept my head turned away until I reached the entrance to the farm, and then I quickly turned the car back toward the main road and my sister-in-law's house.

Why did I rush away from him that day? I suppose because I was embarrassed to have been caught there, trespassing; trespassing on his life. And it only made me feel more desperate, because I wasn't altogether sure whether I'd returned to Deyning to look at the place, or whether I'd gone there in search of him. And so I drove back to Flora's at a ridiculous speed, chastising myself all the way, and crying. When I arrived back at the cottage I went straight to my room, cleaned myself up and changed. Then I went outside into the garden. Charlie and David were both asleep in their deckchairs. Flora glanced up at me. "Nice drive, dear?"

"Yes, heavenly," I said, and I picked up a magazine and sat down.

Chapter Thirty-six

～

Mama moved from her house in Berkeley Square to a flat in Kensington in the summer of 1928. Still proud, she told people that the house was *much too large* for her now, on her own, but in truth it was simply too costly for her to run. She'd grown weary of struggling on with too few servants, was tired of meetings with sympathetic, overly keen young bankers and their talk of *economies*. What did they know? she'd said to me: they had no idea, no idea at all of how things were, before the war. "It was a different world."

And my mother belonged to that different

world; Berkeley Square belonged to that different world: a world slowly fading. Like the Chinese painted silk upon Mama's walls, now discolored and watermarked by damp; like the chipped paintwork on the doors and staircase, and the unseen cobwebs, floating listlessly, clinging to the ornate cornicing of once-busy rooms. The house exuded an ennui reflected in Mama's own lassitude, and even Wilson's devotion to my mother seemed to have taken on a lazy, apathetic air. For Mama herself looked not quite right, as though she *and* her maid had forgotten all about Edina Granville, the woman who'd once presided over so much, and with such innate confidence. Her glossy chestnut hair had faded to a dull, flat gray, its texture altered with its color, and the once-delicate fine curls carefully arranged about her face now replaced by an unruly frizz. Without her garden, without access to that fresh country air, her cheeks, too, had lost their bloom: that luminosity I recalled from my youth. And, perhaps in a bid to restore that vibrancy, she'd taken to wearing makeup. But her powder was a little too pale, her rouge a tad too vivid, and the whole effect, some-how, altogether wrong.

There was a strange shrinking down of my mother at that time. Not just a shrink-ing down of her material world, but of her, her substance. Her life, once commanded on such a grand scale, distilled itself once more, and she seemed to fold herself into that small place; a place of dusty trea-sures, no longer fashionable antiques, and sun-bleached silk brocades.

And something happened to me, too, around this time. I began to change, or per-haps I didn't change so much as begin to know at last who I was, what I wanted and didn't want in my life. For a while I'd con-templated finding a job. I'd looked at ad-vertisements in the newspaper, wondering what, if anything, I could do. I'd gone to an employment bureau on Oxford Street, where I spent ten minutes in a poky up-stairs office, in front of a bespectacled middle-aged man who'd glanced at my wedding ring and asked me if my husband knew where I was. He sat behind a desk, his hands clasped in front of him, smiling at me, and then told me that it really was advisable for me to have my husband's permission before embarking upon *a career*. He'd recently had quite a few young ladies like me through his door, he said, and laughed. "Emboldened by the times, I suppose," he added. But really, why would someone like me want to work? What about charity work? he asked. I told him I already helped my mother with her *district* and various charitable causes, but that I wanted something more. He suggested I take up a new hobby, so I thanked him for his time and left.

At home, I continued to play a part, for I wasn't a wife, not in the real sense, nor had I been for many years. And I was lonely, desperately so. My house was immaculate, my life a tidy, ordered affair. But I was bored of arranging flowers that only I looked upon; bored of approving menus for what I knew would be a solitary supper; bored of shop windows, parks and teas; bored of afternoon card games and matinees, and bored of climbing into my bed each night alone. I'd contemplated an affair, and more than once, but of course there was only ever one man in my dreams: only one man and one fantasy.

And I continued to hear about him . . .

I was in Liberty's, looking at material for a new dress, when Rose tapped me on the shoulder. We tried to remember when we'd last seen each other; had it been at Venetia's New Year's party five years ago? No, I told her, it had been longer than that. And it had. I hadn't seen Rose in almost ten years, not since shortly after the end of the war. I realize now that it was probably a conscious decision on both our parts—to move on, to try to leave those we'd shared a kind of darkness with behind, to be happy. I'd heard that she'd married a major in the army and had moved to Oxfordshire, and she confirmed this that day, telling me she'd been living in the country, raising her own brood.

"I simply can't believe it!" she said, as we sat down together in the tearoom.

She looked more or less the same, a little fuller of face, rounder of figure, and had dyed her short bobbed hair to the Titian red it always promised to be. She talked me through her wedding—"A very quiet affair in the country," she said, looking at me sheepishly—and the births of her children; and she told me how blissfully happy she was. Then she produced a photograph of her three girls from her purse.

"They're beautiful, Rose," I said.

"And you? No babies?"

"No," I replied, with an impeccably rehearsed smile. "I'm afraid not."

"Such a shame. But I suppose we can't have it all, can we? And let's face it, darling, you were blessed with *more* than your fair share of good looks. I remember all those boys, so besotted by you, so in love . . ."

I laughed.

"Strange to think of that time now," she said wistfully, picking up her cup and staring at it. Then, perhaps inevitably, we began the grim roll call of those missing.

"But what about Henry? I heard, of course, through my parents. Still no word?"

I shook my head. "No, nothing."

She stared at me, as though perhaps I knew something more. Then she sighed in an exaggerated fashion. "Well, it's a strange thing, that's for certain, to just disappear—into thin air."

"I don't suppose for one minute that Henry has actually disappeared into *thin air*, Rose," I said, perhaps a little tartly.

"He's somewhere, I know that, and I've no doubt we'll hear from him, eventually."

"Yes, yes of course you will, dear. But it must be simply horrendous for you and your poor mama, simply horrendous." She sighed again, shook her head. "And when I remember poor dear William and George . . . and all the others—seems like only yesterday they were all here."

"Do you really think so? Seems like a lifetime ago to me."

She reached out and placed her gloved hand over mine. "Yes, darling, I imagine it does. You and your family have certainly suffered."

At that moment I didn't want Rose's sympathy. And I didn't want to think about my family. I looked at my wristwatch. "Gracious, I hadn't realized the time, Rose. I'm afraid I'll have to be off in a minute. I have to call in on Mama on the way home."

"And how is she? How is your mama?"

"Oh, she's fine," I said. "Yes, really quite fine."

But I wasn't convinced.

The previous week, I'd called on my mother unexpectedly. It was the middle of the afternoon and I'd found her sitting at her dining room table, surrounded by papers, her traveling jewelry case directly in front of her. She seemed unusually flustered, and had quickly gathered up the papers laying about the table.

"I'm sorry if I'm interrupting you," I said.

"Not at all, I was sorting through old paperwork—to do with Deyning, that's all," she replied, looking up at me, smiling. But I knew this to be a lie; I could see perfectly well that they were letters and postcards: handwritten, personal. And I could tell she'd been crying. I stepped back from her, walked about the room as she finished collecting up the cards and papers, folding pages with trembling hands, placing them back inside the jewelry case.

"There!" she said, closing the lid of the case.

I sat down next to her at the table. She asked me about my day, where I'd been, and I thought her words seemed a little slurred. She's upset, I thought, quite obviously upset. In her hands, resting on the table, she fiddled with the small tasseled key to the case, and I immediately noticed the ring on her wedding finger. It was a ring I vaguely remembered having seen once before, a gentleman's signet ring: gold, and rather heavy looking, but unlike the signet rings of my father and brothers, this one had no crest. It had, instead, initials engraved upon it, overlapping and entwined. Was that an S and an E, or was it a B, and perhaps a D? I couldn't make it out. But she must have seen me staring at it because she swiftly covered it with her other hand. And at that very same moment, as I glanced up and caught her eye, I heard Georgie whisper in my ear. Of course: it was the King's ring, the one *not for playing with*.

Rose frowned. "Oh, but what a shame. I could sit and talk with you for hours and hours. We have so much to catch up on, dear. And I haven't even asked you—how is dear Charlie? And what about the Astley girls? Do you ever see them?"

I opened my mouth, about to tell her that yes, Charlie was well, and that I hadn't seen either Flavia or Lily Astley in some time when she began again. "And what about Tom Cuthbert then?"

I hesitated, wondering what on earth she meant. "What about him?"

"Oh my God, Clarissa, don't you know?

You must know . . . he's worth a fortune, darling. In fact, he now owns your family's old place in the country, *and* half of London!"

"Yes, sorry, of course, I do know that. I'm very much aware of how successful he's been, Rose."

"I should say! And to think we *all* turned our noses up at him, ha! How times have changed. But I must tell you, dear, although I'm not sure when you last saw him . . ." She stopped, looked at me, and I shrugged. She narrowed her eyes for a moment, as though performing some complex internal calculation, and then continued. "Well, anyway, we crossed paths with him at a house party, oh, a few months ago now . . . the Langbournes? Blandford Forum?"

I shook my head.

"He was there with his wife, an *American*." She arched an eyebrow. "Not entirely sure . . . quite haughty and aloof, I thought. Anyway, and more to the point, Mr. Cuthbert is, I can tell you, still as divine as ever. Do you remember how handsome he was?"

"Yes, I do."

"Well, I can tell you he's even *more*

handsome now, darling. Money and impending middle age certainly suit him. Oh, it's too depressing! Handsome men just become better looking as they age, whilst we ladies simply fade." She laughed, raised her eyes heavenward, then turned to me again. "But I must say, you haven't faded at all, Clarissa. But that's probably because you haven't had children. You know they really *do* take such a huge toll on one's body . . . and one's energy."

I blinked, smiled.

She leaned toward me, conspiratorially. "On our second night at the Langbournes' I was placed next to him at dinner . . ." She clasped at her string of pearls. "And he remembered me."

"Ah!"

"Well, I think he did. He didn't mention our little *thing* as such, but he certainly remembered that time . . . the madness, all of us on that dizzy circuit." She paused again, lost in her memory of that time, and perhaps of him. "Anyway," she continued, "I had only recently discovered that he'd bought Deyning Park, and so of course I reminded him that you and I had been dear, dear friends . . . and that I knew the house from way back when. 'Oh really?' he said. 'I never knew that.' And then he said, 'Do you ever see Clarissa?'" She stared at me, waiting for something—I wasn't sure what, perhaps a gasp.

"So I told him," she went on, "that I hadn't seen you for years, which was a shame, because you were on my shortlist as a potential god-mama to Sophia . . . and that I was determined to look you up again soon. It's been too, too long, dear."

I was distracted, doing my own internal calculation. I realized that Rose must have seen him not long after my unfortunate encounter—trespassing.

Rose continued. "And so he said, 'Should you see her, Rose, would you be so kind as to pass on a message?' Of course, I told him, because—really—I was determined to catch up with you, darling. 'Would you tell her that I still have her *tent* . . .'"—she paused, looking at me, wide eyed—"'and that . . .'" She looked away again, struggling to remember the remainder of the message.

"Yes?" I leaned toward her. "And that . . ."

"And that . . ." she repeated, now transfixed by the linen tablecloth. "And that . . .

Oh dear, Clarissa, I'm so sorry, I can't remember. Anyway, he has your tent, dear, and I shan't ask any questions. You know me, I *abhor* indiscretion and gossip."

She sat in silence for a moment, waiting for me to elucidate, but I chose not to say anything. Five minutes later, as I rose to my feet, she said, "But how simply lovely . . . and how fortuitous our meeting like this."

"Yes, it's been so nice, Rose," I said, bending down to kiss her, and then, as I began to walk away, she shouted after me, "An island! He has *your* tent on some island, dear."

I turned and smiled at her. And I continued to smile as I walked down the wooden staircase and out of the shop. I traveled home by bus that day, but I didn't see any street, person, or vehicle. I saw my Arabian tent, on the island at home. And I saw Tom, lying inside it, gazing up at those tiny stars, thinking of me; remembering us.

Trust, Mama once told me, is the cornerstone of a marriage. Without trust, she said, there is nothing: for what can be achieved without it?

But Charlie and I led increasingly separate lives. We occasionally attended dinners, parties and the theater together, smiling, but in private, at home, we avoided each other as best we could, and rarely ate together. When we did, we spoke of mundane matters, trivia. He returned home from the city late most evenings, and often went out again, later still. I asked no questions. I didn't want to know. And I only discovered his affair because he told me. He had to tell me.

Of course it wasn't the first. There had been other liaisons before that, I knew, and I'd chosen to turn a blind eye to them. But this one was different. Madge Parsons had lived with us for over a year, employed as our parlormaid. And Madge had succeeded where I'd failed: she was pregnant with my husband's baby. I went to stay with my mother, leaving him to deal with the debris. I was not heartbroken, but I was humiliated, defeated. And I wasn't sure what to do. I did not love my husband and our marriage was a sham, but it had taken two people, I thought, to create that sham. I was not blameless. And which was better: the sham of respectability or the shame of divorce? Although I'd never told my mother, or anyone else, of the way Charlie *loved* me in private, I knew her thoughts on divorce. It was anathema to her.

Charlie swiftly removed Madge from our home. He begged me to give our marriage another chance. He promised me that he would be different; that he would be a better, more faithful husband. And my mother sat me down and told me once again, "Marriages involve sacrifice and compromise; they're not something one simply abandons at the first hurdle." She took it upon herself to explain to me that men have different needs to women; they require . . . *other things*, she said. And I'd immediately imagined a garment of some type: a hat, a scarf or a pair of mittens. Charlie wrapped up for winter. Then I imagined how she'd react if I told her about the *other things* my husband required. I thought of Mademoiselle, and momentarily wondered where she was; was she still alive, somewhere? Was she explaining to some young housebound girl that men had never evolved properly? And perhaps she was correct; perhaps some men hadn't, but it seemed to me then that Mama and Mademoiselle had more in common than I'd realized.

But I didn't want to resume my unhappy life with Charlie. I could no longer breathe around him, or in that house. I didn't love my husband. We barely spoke. And I yearned to be free, to be able to make my own decisions, to live my own life. Charlie and I were two different people to the idealistic young officer and naive dreamy girl who'd become engaged druing the war. At that time I'd wanted to please my mother; I'd wanted to make her happy again, proud of me. I'd yearned for normality, for some sort of order to be restored to our broken lives, and I'd thought that marriage would deliver that, as well as a sense of security and, perhaps, even happiness. But my marriage to Charlie had not brought me what I'd craved. I could never love him the way he wanted me to, or the way I knew I could love. Despite everything, I still cared about him and would continue to, but not as a husband and certainly not as a lover. I knew the time had come: I had an opportunity to change my life. I owed no explanation to my husband, but I knew my mother would be aghast at my desire for independence. And so, "Trust, Mama, is the cornerstone of a marriage. Without trust, there is nothing. Without trust what can be achieved?"

❧

... I'm delighted. It is the only photograph I had of the two of you together, and quite right that you should have it. As you say, in the blink of an eye. I too have thought of those times, & oh how often! And yes, I remember the boathouse ... I remember it all. But I do believe everything has turned out as it was meant. Time, rightly or wrongly, is a great leveler of emotion, & of ambition also, and certainly we have ALL mellowed ... Yes, my life is different, but it is fine and I am happy, and though this place is small, I must admit—it is rather cozy, & very manageable. In fact, I can say I feel rather liberated to be relieved of the accumulated paraphernalia. But how peculiar to have spent a lifetime collecting it—only to dispose of it!

Chapter Thirty-seven

When spring finally comes she never ceases to surprise me with the lightness and warmth of her touch, her early dawns and frenzied revelry. She is a symphony of rapturous color and vibrant luminosity; she is memory restored, senses reawakened—brought back to life; and I fall in love once more. For is there another season that inspires so many unabashed romantic notions? Is there any other time of the year when we can truly luxuriate in the feeling of being at one with our universe?

I remember this season at Deyning. I remember the cuckoo, the woodpecker and the lark. I remember the blackbird that nested in the tree beyond my bedroom window, and the song thrush upon the roof above my room. I remember looking out on to a never-ending green world. And for a moment I am back there. I feel that soft, breathless air upon my face, hear their song once more.

From the day I moved into my small flat in Kensington, I felt free. I could at last be whoever I wanted to be. I could breathe. For the very first time in my life I was living on my own, making my own decisions and in charge of my destiny. I'd finally taken that leap into the great unknown: independence. Within the space of twenty-four hours my world condensed itself into five rooms, and could easily have fit into what had once been my bedroom and dressing room at Deyning. But I felt no sense of confinement, or that sense of claustrophobia I had lived with for so many years. I looked out on to a bustling street, where buses passed by my window and people once again looked back at me and smiled. London, it suddenly seemed to me, was filled with friendly faces and limitless possibilities.

It was during those first heady days of my late-found independence that I began to make plans: plans for me and about me. I received money each month from Charlie, enough to live on and pay my rent, and I had some savings in a bank account, money left to me by my grandfather. But I still longed to do something with my life, to be fully independent, earn my own money. The man at the employment bureau had succeeded in making me feel something of a joke, unemployable, so I began to think about other avenues, a business, a shop: a flower shop . . . a hat shop . . . a dress shop. Then, for a while, I contemplated a bookshop: an antiquarian bookshop.

What I hadn't anticipated when I embarked upon my new singular life was my own ineptitude. I had never shopped for food, or cooked a meal, either for myself or anyone else; never done any laundry, or sewn or mended clothes; and I had never truly managed a penny, let alone a pound. I'd never uncorked a bottle of wine; never cleaned, or polished or dusted; never disposed of household rubbish; and I'd never used an iron. I could have employed someone, a cleaner, a cook, but it seemed a ridiculous extravagance for one person. So, I purchased a book and set about teaching myself the rudiments of cookery, starting with the basics, such as boiling an egg. I confess I did, however, employ a local service to do my laundry, and, eventually, once the novelty of cleaning and washing up burned pans had worn off, I employed a woman to come in two mornings a week. It was all a new experience, all of it, and I loved it.

Sometimes I shopped for food in Fortnum and Mason or Harrods, mesmerized by the colorful displays and choice, and, perhaps inevitably, returning home with enough food for an army. But usually I patronized the local bakeries, greengrocers and butchers. I became familiar with another world, a place I'd glimpsed once before, beyond the green baize door; the place Edna, Mabel, Stephens and Wilson had come from. At last the world had opened up to me, and it welcomed me with more warmth than I could ever have imagined. And it struck me how queer it was that the smaller, more confined my material world, the more freedom and space I sensed around me; as though God, nature, the universe or whatever it is, is somehow able to balance one's experience—one's lot in life—upon a scale. At Deyning I'd had everything and nothing; now I had nothing—and everything.

I enrolled in an art class and began to paint once more; I met new people, was invited out to new places. I was wooed by a French diplomat, and very nearly fell in love with my art teacher. I realized that I could survive alone, and I enjoyed life in a way I hadn't for years. Then, at a dinner party, I met Antonio Capparelli. Antonio owned a gallery in Mayfair, and he was impressed by my knowledge and love of art, surprised that I'd done nothing with it, with my life. I'd explained to him that I'd had no real education, that girls like me were simply expected to marry and produce children. Something I'd clearly failed at. He suggested I work for him, at his gallery, two or three days a week perhaps, whatever I wanted, and it was tempting, but not enough. And then it came to me: a gallery, I'd set up my *own* gallery.

I used my savings as the down payment

on premises just around the corner from where I lived, on the Fulham Road, and, initially at least, I considered the whole enterprise a type of experiment. If it failed, at least I'd tried. My mother, of course, was mortified; and not just because I'd plundered what little money I had into what she considered to be a reckless business venture. To have a daughter who'd elected to be a *divorcee* was bad enough, but to have a daughter who wanted to work as well was quite beyond her.

And so, "It's a different world, Mama."

I'd been reassured, encouraged, and advised by my new friend, Antonio. It had been his idea that I should only exhibit work by new, undiscovered British artists; that I should focus my attention there, and visit art schools in London and any local exhibitions. And so for those first few months I spent my time getting to know some of the new up-and-coming artists on the scene, visiting Chelsea Art College, the Slade and various other more far-flung institutions. I'd decided early on that any profits from the gallery—once I'd paid myself enough to live on—should go to charities supporting war veterans and families of those killed in the war, in memory of my brothers. I had no need of money, and my motivation to set up a business was never about making money for myself.

I named my gallery the Deyning Gallery. I couldn't think of a better name at the time, and it never occurred to me that there might be any conflict of interest with Tom Cuthbert's burgeoning business empire. Although there were a few people who inquired as to whether the gallery was a "part of Cuthbert-Deyning."

The gallery did well, very well. And I had a number of loyal patrons who seemed keen to invest and purchase new paintings. One collector, who remained nameless, and whom I never actually met, always knew exactly what I was exhibiting. I'd receive a telephone call from a Mr. Pritchard who'd later arrive by taxicab, to pay for and remove the painting, or paintings, his employer had heard of or noticed.

"Does he live locally then, your employer?" I asked, as I wrapped yet another framed canvas for Mr. P.

"No, madam, he does not."

"Are you able to disclose his name to me?"

"No, madam, unfortunately I'm not at liberty to do that."

Of course, he wasn't the only one. There were a few collectors who simply didn't want to be seen to be spending money on something as frivolous as art, particularly modern art. And Antonio had told me it was the norm, even before the war.

I hadn't planned on having an affair with Antonio. He was sixteen years my senior, and I'd always considered his flirting to be something synonymous with his Italian character. We met regularly for lunch and often attended exhibitions, auctions and private views together. And then one night after dinner, he came home with me.

Passionate, handsome, educated, and amusing, Antonio made me feel like a girl of sixteen again. He called me *Clereeza*, and liked me to say certain words so that he could repeat them, mimicking my accent.

"Haughty . . ."

"*Hor-tee*," he repeated.

"Peculiar . . ."

"Pick-u-lee-ar."

"Gorgeous . . ."

"Gor-juz."

Life with Antonio was anything but dull. And, after Charlie, I was once again in the maelstrom of life. We invariably ate out each evening and attended the theater two or three times a week; and I laughed in a way I hadn't for years. I was more than content: I was happy. But things have a habit of creeping up on us when we're least expecting them, or need them.

I'd kept track of Tom, through a grapevine of sorts. I'd heard that he and Nancy had separated and that Deyning stood empty once more. Davina saw him, and reasonably often, and she'd informed me that he'd recently purchased another prime site in central London. "He's unstoppable!" she'd exclaimed, her eyes flashing with excitement. And then she told me of his penchant for beautiful women.

"Oh well, he has the lifestyle, and the money—why not?" I replied. "But it sounds as though he's become everything I wish to escape from," I said, somewhat disingenuously. For of course I had thought of him, and thought of him often.

When I saw him with Venetia in the bar of the Theater Royal that evening—and I saw them before they saw me—I was shocked. And I thought twice about going over to speak to them.

Venetia and Tom.

I panicked, and Antonio must have seen something in my face.

"Whatever's the matter, my darling? Why the frown and look of alarm?" he asked. And so I told him.

"There's an old friend of mine . . . over at the bar, with . . . with my godmother."

He turned to look. "Ah, yes, I see . . . I see. But Venetia, she very much likes the handsome young men."

"Actually, he's not *that* young," I said. "He's rather rapidly approaching forty."

But the irony wasn't lost on me: there I was, with a man almost old enough to be my father, and there was he, with a woman *definitely* old enough to be his mother.

"Shall we say hello?" Antonio asked.

"Let me take a moment, please, Antonio," I said, still not entirely sure whether I wished to step forward and speak to them.

As I deliberated, I watched him. I noticed his skin was tanned, and he had that unmistakable air of success about him. He wore an impeccably cut dark suit, a white shirt and a dark blue tie. And as he moved a bronzed hand through the air, the glinting gold of his wristwatch caught my eye. He looked like a rich playboy, I thought, freshly arrived back from the Riviera. And Venetia appeared spellbound.

He stood with his back half toward me, and I could easily have slipped away; they need never have known I'd been there, standing feet away from them in the crowded bar that night. But I couldn't do it. I had to go and speak to them. I wanted to know more. And that night, like most other nights, it was impossible to miss Venetia. She wore a long red kimono, and a vividly colored scarf wrapped around her head and fastened in place by an enormous diamond butterfly brooch. The Japanese look, I thought, watching her. She seemed to move quite swiftly from continent to continent, in terms of fashion, and was always caught under the spell of some opera. Her husband, Hughie, had not long been dead, but she abhorred black, said it added ten years at least to a woman's face, and she hated the rituals of mourning. The very worst of Englishness, she said: *so passé, and so horribly Victorian!*

"Venetia!" I called out as I approached, sounding a warning shot.

Not surprisingly she looked startled. "Clarissa! *Darling!*"

I saw him turn, but I ignored him and moved toward my godmother, kissing her on both cheeks. "What a surprise," I said, flatly, without any smile.

"Yes . . . well, Tom called on me unexpectedly, and . . . and here we are!"

I turned to him, forced a smile. "Hello, Tom."

His tanned features froze, and for a few seconds he seemed unable to speak.

Then he said, "My God, Clarissa . . . and looking as *divine* as ever." And I thought, no, that's not you; that's not the way you speak. But I continued to smile, and then I introduced Antonio.

He glanced at Antonio, looked to me, then back at Antonio. "Antonio," he said, shaking his hand and elongating the syllables in an unnecessary way. Making a point, I thought. I could tell he was taken aback: he seemed unsure of what to do or say, or even where to look. But as Antonio greeted Venetia, he turned away from them, toward me.

"Fate, eh?" he said, staring at me.

"Coincidence," I replied.

"There's no such thing as coincidence. You of all people should know that."

I couldn't fathom what he meant, but it certainly wasn't the time to embark on any deeper analysis. Trying to keep the conversation lighthearted, the way one would if one had bumped into any old friend, I resorted to the obvious questions: how was he? He looked very well: had he been away? Did he still own Deyning? Still spend time there?

Yes, he was well, very well; life was good. He'd just returned from Monte Carlo, been back only a day. He was thinking of selling Deyning; it cost too much to run, was too big for one person, he said, searching my face.

"Oh . . . I hope not. I hope you don't sell it."

"No . . . no, well, perhaps I shan't," he replied.

And I thought, how easy, what luxury to be able to change one's mind at whim.

He asked after my mother, and then, when I asked—somewhat perfunctorily— after his own, he told me: told me of her death only three months earlier. And I immediately saw her, sitting on board that bus, waving back at me. I'd known then, I think, that I wouldn't see her again, and right at that moment I wondered if she'd come to me knowing that too.

"I'm so sorry," I said, swamped by sadness, the memory of that soft, powdered cheek. *Lily of the valley.* "I only wish I'd gone to see her," I added, looking down at the glass in my hands.

"Well, you saw her; you saw her at Deyning—when you had tea with her, and she very much enjoyed that."

"But I should have gone to visit her," I said, tearfully. "And I told her I would . . . I said to her, as I saw her on to the bus, I'll come and visit you, Evelyn . . . and I never did."

He stared at me, wide eyed. *"Evelyn?"*

I bit my lip, looked away.

"She came to see you . . . my mother came to see you—here in London?"

I glanced back at him, nodded.

"I think we need to talk."

"Yes, I think we do. But not now, not here."

"No, not now."

"And what are you two whispering about?" Venetia asked, stepping toward us.

"Catching up," Tom replied, looking at me.

He sucked hard on his cigarette, staring at me in that way, which always made me feel uneasy, embarrassed. I suppose he knew me so well, knew my secrets. But it was more than that, of course: I felt exposed and vulnerable under his scrutiny; as though he were able to read my mind, see and *feel* my thoughts.

I saw him watching Antonio, looking him up and down out of the corner of his eye, and I wondered what he was thinking. Was he shocked? Jealous? I couldn't tell. But when the bell rang for us to take our seats and Antonio moved over, slipping his arm around my waist and kissing me gently upon my head, I saw him close his eyes and turn away.

"I must say, you're looking quite sensational, darling," Venetia said, smiling at me. "And *so* much happier too . . ."

"Yes, well . . . I am. I am happier," I replied, not looking at any of them.

"And *I* have dedicated my life—my life's purpose—to the happiness of Clarissa,"

Antonio said, with a newly operatic tone to his voice.

Venetia laughed. "To happiness!" she said, raising her glass of water, and as we all clinked glasses I met Tom's eyes, and immediately looked away.

"Let's have dinner together, later, the four of us, eh?" Antonio suggested, and I so wished that he hadn't.

"What an exceedingly good idea! You know, I haven't seen my goddaughter in an absolute age, Antonio. I think you rather like to keep her to yourself, hmm?"

Antonio laughed. "You're right, of course, I have no wish to share her with anyone." He lifted my hand, kissed it. "But perhaps tonight, for a little while, I'll share her with you both," he added, winking at Venetia, who suddenly seemed to find everything hilarious.

I glanced at Tom, forcing a smile. But he didn't smile back. So I said, "Is that agreeable with you, Tom?"

He didn't answer, and Venetia laughed again, and then said, "But of course it's agreeable . . . utterly agreeable."

"Tom?" I repeated. I wanted him to answer me.

"Yes . . . *spiffing*," he said, and then turned away to stub out his cigarette.

When we returned to our seats I was distracted: unhearing, unseeing. Thankfully, we were seated in the dress circle and they in the stalls, and I was relieved; relieved they weren't anywhere near us; relieved I couldn't see him with her. But as the lights dimmed, an image flashed before me: I saw him making love to a turbaned Venetia, saw him draped across her mountainous breast, nuzzling feathers and lace. It had to be an affair, I thought, had to be. Venetia had always preferred younger men as lovers, and there was always someone. Always had been. I wondered how long it had been going on; possibly years, I thought, and closed my eyes. Suddenly it all fit together, all made sense: how Jimmy always knew about Tom's movements; why Venetia had been so interested in my marriage, and my *friendship* with Tom . . .

I shuffled in my seat, and sighed—surprisingly loudly. Antonio reached over, taking hold of my hand and anchoring it just as though I were a fidgeting child. But each time I thought of them a surge of anger rose up in me. *Venetia and Tom* . . . The sense of betrayal—or possible betrayal—was, quite literally, breathtaking. And as the play progressed I wondered if I could somehow fall ill, have an emergency at home . . . How I wished I had a dog, at least, to have to rush back to. I picked up my theater binoculars, leaned forward and peered down into the stalls, scanning along each row. And then I saw them, toward the front, the lights from the stage picking up the brilliant scarlet of Venetia's kimono: the scarlet lady indeed, I thought. How aptly attired.

Later, as I stood in the kerfuffle of the lobby, waiting for Antonio to fetch my coat, they appeared together by my side, Venetia beaming broadly, looking rather pleased with herself, I thought. He mentioned a French restaurant, just around the corner, barely looking at me, and said to follow on—in a somewhat dismissive tone.

"Fine. See you there," I said flatly, and Venetia frowned and shook her head.

It was a strange, uncomfortable meal: strange to be sitting opposite him, looking at him once again. And I don't remember anyone other than Antonio actually eating.

At first Tom seemed inclined to ignore me and talked mainly to Antonio, about art. He knew Antonio's gallery, knew all of the central London galleries, but so many of them sold rubbish, he said. So I pretended to listen to Venetia, and, as she talked, I heard him tell Antonio that he'd recently purchased a painting by Matisse, and was planning on adding another to his collection. I heard Antonio extend an invitation to him, to a private view of a new Italian artist he was particularly excited about.

"And of course Clarissa has a discerning eye, Tom. You may also know her gallery: the Deyning?"

I glanced quickly at Tom, caught his eye, and he smiled at me.

"Really? No, I had no idea."

I knew at that moment he was lying. Perhaps it was his smile, or, and more likely, his rudeness and lack of interest, but he suddenly changed the subject. He picked up the wine bottle in front of him and began to speak—once more to Antonio— about wine: Italian wine. Antonio looked at me, conscious of the snub, and shrugged.

As the evening wore on he became increasingly provocative.

"So, Antonio," he said, looking at me and *not* at Antonio, "how long have you two known each other?"

"I feel as though I've known Clarissa all of my entire life," Antonio replied, effusively, and then placed his hand over mine. "We're soul mates, Clarissa and me."

"Really," he said, still staring at me. "Is that true, *Clereeza*? Have you found your soul mate in Antonio?"

I laughed, looked away.

"And so . . . whereabouts in London do you live, Tom?" Antonio asked.

"Knightsbridge," he replied, slurring the word.

"Oh, Antonio lives in Knightsbridge too," I said.

"Well, what a coincidence," he replied. "My driver can run us all home then. That is, if we're *all* heading that way . . ."

Antonio intervened. "Thank you, Tom, but we'll make our own way. We're going back to Clarissa's," he said.

"Ah, Clarissa's . . . yes, yes of course."

I wanted to leave. I recognized the mood he was in, could tell by the look in his eyes.

"Back to Clarissa's . . ." he repeated,

staring into his glass, then lifting it to his lips.

"Shall we get the bill?" I asked, turning to Antonio.

"Please, allow me," Tom interrupted. "I insist."

When we all stood up, to say good-bye, he reached into his wallet, pulled out a card and scribbled a number onto it.

"I hope you might find time to call me one day, *Clereeza*," he said, handing me the card.

"Thank you, Tom. Yes. I shall. I'll do that."

We didn't kiss, we didn't shake hands, we simply said good night. And then Antonio and I went out on to the street in search of a taxicab.

"I think you broke his heart," Antonio said to me on the way home.

"Why, what makes you say that?"

"He's a wretched man, a tortured soul. He has everything and he has nothing. And I could see . . . I could see."

"But he's with Venetia now."

Antonio laughed. "You are adorable. He may have escorted your god-mama to the theater tonight, but I have a feeling that's as far as it goes."

Later, as we made love, I thought of him. I tried not to, but it was as though he was there, in the room, watching us.

At that time his name was everywhere, the newspapers filled with advertisements for Cuthbert-Deyning's new offices and property developments, and the business papers often quoted their most recent acquisition. Over the next few days I pulled his business card out from my purse any number of times. I looked at it, stared at the number he'd scrawled onto it, and I thought about picking up the telephone and calling him. But what would I say? What would *it* say? No, it was for him to call me, I decided. If he really wanted to see me he could easily find my number.

But of course, eventually, my resolve would waver.

Chapter Thirty-eight

I'd been out to a private view, alone. And I'd been drinking champagne. Someone had mentioned his name, said he was *the* collector, the one to watch out for, the one buying up new modern art. I didn't say anything at the time, didn't let on that I knew him. And yet the mention of his name always capsized me into that well of loneliness, reminding me of my loss.

Later, as I'd lain in bed, unable to sleep and thinking of him, I wondered, as I'd done before, if he was in fact one of my anonymous patrons. And then I wondered if he was with Venetia. Was he lying next to her? Had he made love to her that evening? Was he making love to her *now*? I rose quickly from my bed, agitated and angry with myself for allowing *him* to keep me awake yet again. I went into the kitchen, lit the stove and placed the kettle on top of it.

It had been some weeks since we'd bumped into each other at the theater and I'd recently ended my affair with Antonio, though we remained firm friends. Seeing Tom again had made me realize that there could only ever be one man for me, and, if I couldn't be with *him*, then . . . then I may as well be single. What was the point in pretending? I didn't want a fiancé, or another husband. And they all seemed to want ownership of some kind. No, I'd reasoned, it was probably my destiny to be on my own.

But I wanted to see him. And I needed to see him.

I didn't want to know—didn't want to hear—about him and Venetia, but I had to tell him about his father. After all, I'd promised Evelyn.

"Business," I said, out loud, as I watched the kettle upon the stove. "It's like business, that's all."

But of course it wasn't, because my heart was involved, and because there was more.

I'd recently decided that I had to try to find my daughter. Not to interrupt her life or to try to reclaim her, but to know where she was, what had become of her. I had to know, you see. I had to know that she was cared for and happy. And I wanted Tom to help me find her.

I walked back into the sitting room, pulled my purse from my handbag and pulled out his card. I sat holding the card in my hand for some time; looking from it to the telephone and back at it. Then I picked up the receiver. Minutes away, I thought; he's only minutes away.

"Hello . . ."

It was him: awake and alert. "Hello," he said again.

"Are you busy?" I asked. I'm not sure why I said that. It was half past one in the morning, but I suppose I thought he might have been in the midst of passion with Venetia, or another.

"Clarissa."

"Yes, it's me."

"Let me take this somewhere else," he said, and there was a click.

I immediately felt stupid. Wanted to hang up. I knew the only reason he'd be moving to another room, another telephone, was for reasons of privacy. He was with someone: in bed with someone. Was it Venetia? And already I could see her, lying back in a feathered turban, reciting poetry as he made love to her.

"Hello," he said again, and I wasn't sure what to say. I didn't speak, couldn't speak.

"Don't go silent on me . . . Clarissa? Is everything all right?"

"Yes . . . yes," I said, half laughing, trying to sound blasé. As though I'd called him up simply to compare notes on the weather. "Everything's fine, perfectly fine. I was just wondering . . ." I began, not sure what I was going to say, not sure what I'd been wondering. And I felt myself panic. What on earth was I doing? How could I begin to talk to him about Emily or his father over the telephone?

"I was just wondering . . ." I said again.

"Yes?" he said, and I could hear the smile in his voice.

"I was just wondering how one makes a Singapore Sling," I said quickly.

He laughed. "I don't know. How does one make a Singapore Sling?"

"No, seriously, it's not a joke. I need the list of ingredients . . ."

I could hear him, lighting a cigarette, inhaling.

"You're making cocktails? Really? Now, at . . . one thirty a.m.?"

"No, not at this moment, but later . . . tomorrow."

I closed my eyes, wanted to scream; wanted the ground to swallow me up.

"Please, tell me the truth: you haven't called me up in the middle of the night for a list of cocktail ingredients—have you?"

"No," I replied.

"Shall I come over?"

"No!"

"Old lover-boy still there then?"

"Oh God, look, I'm sorry. I don't know why I called. I couldn't sleep and . . . and for some reason I thought of you."

"Clarissa . . ."

"Is Venetia there?" I asked, and then winced.

I could hear him sigh; almost see him

shake his head. "I could meet you some-where . . . at a hotel . . ."

"Tom! Good grief, do you think I've called you up because . . . because . . ." I faltered, rising to my feet, searching for the cigarette box.

He laughed. "Clarissa, I'm teasing you."

"I'd better go," I said, feeling like a total fool. "I'm not sure why I called you. I'm sorry."

I heard him sigh again. "Don't be sorry . . . never be sorry. Look, I'm leaving for Paris in the morning, but let's meet up when I get back. I'll telephone you."

"Yes, fine. Have a lovely time. And do give my best to Venetia."

He laughed again. "I'm pleased you tele-phoned. I was wondering when you would."

"When?" I repeated, irritated by his pre-sumption.

"You said you would, remember?"

"Yes, I did. I mean, I do remember."

"And Clarissa . . ."

"Yes?"

"Try and be good for me."

"Good night, Tom," I said, and hung up the receiver.

I didn't really expect him to call me upon

his return from Paris, whenever that might be. And I didn't want to wait for disappointment. After all, he'd made no mention of how long he was to be away for, or when he'd be back. It could be a week, a month or longer. I began to regret my ridiculous middle-of-the-night telephone call to him. Upon reflection, his tone had been quite dismissive, I concluded. *I'll call you . . .* What had I been thinking? And did I really want to meet up with him—*alone*? Being newly single, the thought of seeing him again—on my own—filled me with more than a little trepidation. Would I succumb to him, yet again? Or would I feel spurned by his lack of interest? No, I reasoned, it was probably for the best that we didn't see each other again. We could leave it to fate, and perhaps cross paths once every few years.

Then, late one evening, only a few days after my call to him, the telephone rang, and as soon as I heard the voice I smiled. "Hello, Tom."

"Clarissa," he said, again, slightly slurring my name.

"How are you?" I asked.

"I'm very, very well, my darling, and how are you?"

He's drunk, I thought, and immediately stopped smiling. "Yes, I'm well, Tom. About to go to bed, actually. Do you realize what time it is?"

"It's half past Clarissa o'clock," he replied, and laughed. "And I was wondering . . . I was wondering, are you up for cocktails tonight? We could share ingredients . . ."

"Tom, you're drunk. You need to go to bed. And anyway, where are you?"

"Where am I? Where do you want me to be? I can be anywhere you want me to be." There was a clunk at that point and I realized he'd dropped the receiver.

"Hello . . . Clarissa?"

"Yes, I'm here."

"But where is here?"

"Tom, you're not making any sense. I'm going to hang up now."

"No, don't go. I need you. I need to hear your voice."

"And why do you need to hear my voice? Have you no one to keep you company tonight? Is Venetia tired?"

"Clarissa, Clarissa—don't be like that."

"Oh, Tom, really, I think you need to drink some water."

Then the line went dead, and I, too, put down the telephone.

The following morning he called again, apologizing for his late-night call to me. It had been a long day, he said. "Stuck in a bloody meeting."

"I see," I replied, waiting for him to say something.

"I'll be back in London tomorrow—and I wondered, can I take you out to dinner?"

Chapter Thirty-nine

We met for dinner two days later, at the Savoy. He was at the restaurant when I arrived, sitting smoking at the table, and looking rather anxious. As I walked toward him he turned, saw me, and immediately stood up. "Hello, Tom," I said and smiled. He stepped forward as though about to kiss me, then looked down and took my hand. And for a split second he was once again that shy, nervous boy in the ballroom at Deyning, unable to look me in the eye, or smile back at me. He hovered on his feet as the waiter pulled out my chair and I sat down. And then he, too, sat down, and immediately lit another cigarette.

"How's Venetia?" I asked. I couldn't help it. I was still angry.

He closed his eyes, shook his head. "Please, can we not talk about Venetia tonight?"

"Oh yes, if it's private, of course . . ." I replied, looking down at the menu.

He sighed. Loudly. Sounding exasperated already.

We sat at a table tucked away in a corner, next to the window. And I was pleased. I could pretend to be distracted by anything beyond the glass, I thought, turning away from him and catching my own reflection. He didn't ask me what I'd like to drink, but summoned over the sommelier, ordered a glass of champagne and a whisky, and then a bottle of Château Lafite. But there was a particular year he wanted, which he couldn't seem to find on the list. He pulled out a pair of spectacles, perched them on his nose. And as the sommelier, the maître d' and another fluttered about him, I smiled. For they all knew his name, knew exactly who he was: Mr. Cuthbert . . . Mr. Cuthbert, they repeated, seemingly as many times as they could fit into a sentence without completely eliminating all other words. And I could tell he was used to it; long used to it.

When they finally dispersed, having identified and ascertained *Mr. Cuthbert's* choice of wine for that evening, he removed his spectacles, looked over at me, sighed heavily, and smiled. "So, Clarissa," he began, "do you realize how significant this day is?"

I shrugged; wondering if I'd forgotten some feast day or national holiday, then shook my head.

"This is our very first date."

A *date*, I thought: so American. "Oh, really. Is this a date then?"

"You know what I mean," he said, turning his head away in mock exasperation. "It's taken me . . ." He paused, staring at me. "It's taken me sixteen years to get to this point . . . to take you out to dinner."

"Yes, here we are, after all these years."

The waiter appeared, placed our drinks upon the table. We raised our glasses. "So, here's to us: Clarissa and Tom," he said, smiling back at me. And it struck me then, he was in an unusual mood. One I didn't

know, couldn't recall ever having seen before.

"Are we celebrating something?" I asked.

"Yes, we are. We're celebrating us. We're
going to be very selfish this evening, because no one's going to claim either one of
us; no one's waiting for you, or for me. And
we're here. We're here together . . . after
all these years."

It was true enough. Every moment we'd
been together, every single moment we'd
managed to snatch in the preceding sixteen years, there'd always been someone
somewhere, waiting for me, or for him.

I smiled. "Like all our rendezvous," I said.

"Down by the lake . . ."

"In the meadow . . ."

"At the boathouse . . ."

"Under the chestnut tree . . ."

"On the lawn . . ."

"By the ha-ha . . ."

"In the walled garden?"

"No! We never met there," I said. "That
was always Mama's territory."

He stubbed out his cigarette, shook his
head. "I remember the first time I set eyes
on you. Just as though it was yesterday."

"And so do I," I replied quickly. "It was in the ballroom at Deyning."

He looked up at me. "Wrong. *That's* when we were introduced. No, the first time I saw you, the very first time I set eyes on you, you were running through the garden, in the rain." He looked away, remembering. "You were shrieking, laughing, and you looked so completely free . . . a vision." He paused, his eyes half closed, concentrating. "You didn't see me, didn't notice me, but I saw you. I watched you, and I'd never seen anything or anyone as beautiful."

"Yes, well, that was a long time ago . . ."

He shook his head. "Feels like a moment ago."

"You're right, sometimes it does. But then I remember . . . I remember all those who are no longer here. My brothers, my cousins, so many friends . . . and it all seems so long ago. Lifetimes ago."

He stared back at me, into my eyes, and I began to feel that yearning once more: a yearning for another time and place, for him. He looked down at my hand resting on the table. "But when I look at you I go back to that time, and I see you as you were that day."

"Good!" I said, pulling my hand away. "I think I'd far rather you saw me forever sixteen."

He looked up at me. "I see you as you are, Clarissa," he said. "I've always seen *who* you are."

I'd taken a taxicab to the Savoy that evening, quietly practicing my lines, what I wanted to tell him, all the way there; trying to anticipate his reaction and what I would say.

"Yes, Tom, that's right . . . we had a baby. Emily. She'll be almost twelve years old by now, and I need to find her . . . I need you to help me find her . . ."

But after one glass of champagne those rehearsed lines had already muddled themselves. And after another, I felt my edges begin to blur, my anger melt away into something else. Something far removed from the anger I'd carried with me into the Savoy earlier that evening. Each time I looked back into his eyes, that same desperate yearning returned, flooding my senses, drowning me. For he was still the boy I'd stood with by the lake. And I felt overwhelmed by sadness. Sadness at all the days and months and years that had been spent and were gone forever: sadness at the waste.

I noticed his hair, now graying at the temples of his brow; the lines around his eyes, upon his forehead; and as the waiter refilled our glasses, I excused myself and went to the powder room. I sat there for some time trying to remember the order of the words, what it was I had to say. What it was I wanted to tell him.

When I returned to the table his mood was noticeably lighter. He teased me, telling me he'd thought for a moment I'd gone, already bored of his company. But I knew, knew by the slight frown and the look in his eyes that he'd seen my sadness.

"So, how's business? How's the gallery doing?" he asked.

"Doing very well," I replied. "I'm extending it—into the shop next door."

"That's wonderful, Clarissa," he said, and I could tell he was being sincere.

"Tom," I began, emboldened by alcohol, "have you ever *seen* my gallery?"

He hesitated, pondered on that question

for a moment. "Yes," he replied, "yes, I think I do know it."

"And have you purchased anything from me? And by that, I also mean through a third party."

He laughed. "Aha! What a question. What makes you ask that?"

"Because I have a few—or I seem to have a few—anonymous patrons," I replied.

He glanced down at the table. "I might have done."

"Please, Tom, tell me the truth . . ."

"Yes. Yes, I have bought some paintings from you."

"How many?" I asked.

"A few," he replied, holding my gaze. "Does it really matter how many?"

"No . . . no, I suppose not," I said. But in a way it did. Was he one or all of the men who came in taxicabs and private cars to collect paintings?

We moved on. He asked me about Charlie. I spoke of my impending divorce and he talked about his. He said he felt no sadness, no bitterness, and that it had been wrong from the start. Said he'd known the day he was married that it wouldn't last.

"Why did you do it then?"

"Good question. I suppose at the time it seemed the obvious thing to do . . . everyone else was married. You were married."

"But *you* didn't have to marry."

"No, perhaps not, but I was lonely. I wanted to share my life with . . ." He paused, staring at me. "What I wanted I couldn't have, so I compromised. And I've never been much good at compromise."

"I thought you wanted children."

"Yes, I suppose I did for a while, or there was a time when I thought I did. But after I married Nancy, I quickly realized I didn't, or perhaps not with her. And then . . . then we lost a baby. Anyway, it didn't happen, wasn't meant to be." He lifted his glass to his lips and said, "But what about you? You didn't have children either."

And it stung.

"No, it didn't happen for me either," I said looking down at my plate, pushing at a slice of carrot.

"Shame. I've always thought you'd make a wonderful mother."

I looked up at him and smiled, and I pondered for a second or two, wondering what I should say. "Yes, well, we can't have it all," I said, repeating Rose's tidying-up phrase. I could have told him then, perhaps. And perhaps I had an opportunity, but it still didn't *feel* like the right moment. You see, I'd practiced this for so long and in so many different locations, but we'd never been sitting there, in the Savoy— having dinner together. It had never been like that.

"And so . . . what about Venetia?" I asked. I had to. And you know, I really didn't want to. I didn't want to hear.

He leaned back in his chair, smiling.

"Yes?" I said, staring back at him, waiting; blinking.

"You know, I think you ought to speak to Venetia yourself," he said.

I shook my head. "I don't. Quite frankly, Tom, I think it's rather pathetic."

His smile broadened, and I could feel a simmering rising up inside of me again. I stared back at him, resolute, I thought; defiant. "Yes, really rather pathetic," I repeated.

He leaned forward, his arms on the table. "And what, exactly, is *rather pathetic*?"

I realized we were dangerously close to

having a row, and on this, our first proper date, it seemed unfortunate, to say the least. But I had to keep going; I had to persevere. After all, he'd stepped over a line, not me.

"That you and Venetia have been . . ."

"Yes?"

I shook my head, sighed. "That you're carrying on with someone old enough to be your mother, Tom."

He laughed, and continued to laugh for quite a while. "Clarissa," he said at last, reaching over for my hand, but I pulled it away.

"No! Don't. Please don't. I saw you together. I know, Tom."

He sat back in his chair and sighed loudly. "You know, your head's always so *bloody* muddled, Clarissa." And I was really rather astounded, because he suddenly sounded quite angry. "It's not something I wish to talk about with you here, tonight," he continued. "I think *you* need to speak to your godmother; you need to talk to Venetia. And then . . . then perhaps we'll resume this conversation."

I felt more than a little chastened. He

had spoken to me like one of his employees, I thought—one who'd perhaps stepped out of line.

"Fine," I said. "And yes, I shall. I shall do that."

We sat in silence for a while, drinking our wine, each of us staring across the room. *It's a disaster . . . it's a disaster*, I thought. *We have nothing in common anymore. He's turned into a monster; one of those rich playboys Mama loves to hate*. I glanced at him, saw him close his eyes. *He's hating this: he'd rather be with her, Venetia*. Then I caught his eye, and he smiled, but I looked away, across the restaurant floor.

"Please, Clarissa, can we . . . shall we be friends?"

I turned to him. "Yes, of course."

He smiled again, but I could sense something more in his smile: amusement, I thought.

He ordered a brandy, and I wondered how Venetia coped with his drinking. She hardly touched a drop herself. And I saw them again, in her dressing room, upon the daybed: Tom, tie undone; his head to her bosom.

No!

He must have seen me wince, must have seen something in my expression, because he leaned forward at that moment and said, "Please . . . trust me, believe me. There is nothing between Venetia and me . . . other than a mutual interest."

Later, when we left the restaurant, he suggested that we go dancing, but I didn't want to.

"I think I should get home, Tom," I said.

"Then please, at least allow me to see you home."

I wasn't sure. I was still irked by the thought of him and Venetia, and whatever it was going on between them. But I had to tell him about Emily, and I knew it was a conversation we had to have alone, in private.

Chapter Forty

We took a taxicab back to my flat, sitting in silence, side by side, and as we turned into my street, I said, "Would you like to come in for a nightcap . . . a coffee?"

I realized how it sounded, and I was nervous, so much so that I couldn't get my key into the lock, and eventually had to admit defeat and hand it to him. And it felt strange opening the door on to my small, singular world, walking into my home with him. I saw him look about the hallway, taking it all in. In the sitting room, as I took off my coat and shoes, he wandered about the place, glancing up at the paintings on the wall; bending down to view a photograph, picking one up.

"Rather different to Deyning," I said.

"But you've made it beautiful . . . as only you could," he replied, loosening his tie. I turned away from him, walked into the kitchen to fill the kettle, and as I lifted it I heard him collapse into an armchair with a loud sigh. When I returned to the room he'd closed his eyes, and I thought perhaps he was about to leave me, drift off into an alcohol-induced slumber.

No, please, don't fall asleep . . . not now . . .

I sat down on the rug by his feet. Was it the right moment? Would it be a huge shock? Would he be angry, walk out?

"I need to talk to you, Tom," I said, quietly, wondering if he could still hear my words. "I need to tell you something . . ."

And with his eyes still closed, he said, "Yes, I know, and I'm longing to hear."

I was confused. Had he some idea of what it was I was about to tell him? No, it was impossible, surely: the only two people who knew were Mama and myself. But my mind raced on into a freefall of possibilities. Had Mama told Venetia and she in turn told Tom? *A mutual interest*, he'd said.

At that moment the kettle began to whistle, and I jumped to my feet and returned to the kitchen.

That night . . . that night in the park . . . well, we had a baby, Tom . . . yes, that's right, we had a baby.

"We had a baby," I whispered, stirring the coffee.

I walked back into the room, handed him his cup and saucer and sat down on the floor once more. He moved in his chair and I turned to look up at him. He stared back at me, raised his eyebrows expectantly. "So . . . are you going to tell me why my mother came to see you—or not?"

I gasped: a strange mix of surprise, frustration and relief. I'd entirely forgotten about Tom's mother's meeting with me, or the fact that I'd inadvertently mentioned it to him in the theater that evening. And here I was, my heart racing, my mind entirely focused on telling him about his daughter; now forced to tell him of his unknown father.

"Well, that was what you were about to

tell me, wasn't it?" he asked, looking a little bemused by my hesitation.

I turned away. "Yes, of course . . . that's what I was about to tell you."

I closed my eyes for a moment, steadying myself; realizing Emily would have to wait a little longer.

But I wasn't altogether sure how or where to begin about that day, the day his mother came to see me.

Begin at the beginning . . .

"She wanted to talk to me about you," I said, shuffling nearer to his chair, allowing myself to lean against it, against him.

"And?"

Just tell him. Be honest . . .

"She told me you loved me, and that . . ." I paused, unsure how to navigate from there.

"That what?"

"That you'd always loved me."

I was half expecting a shrug, a joke, a witty quip, but he said nothing.

I reached up, took hold of his hand. "And she told me about your father, Tom."

"Ah, my father . . . I see. So she came to see you to tidy up a few loose ends then."

"I suppose she did in a way, yes. She

wanted someone to know the truth; someone who cared, cared about you."

I paused, waiting for him to say something, but he said nothing.

"Your father, Tom . . . your father was the earl, Earl Deyning."

I turned and looked up at him. He stared at me.

"So, I'm the bastard son of the old earl . . ."

"Tom!"

"Well, really, what a lot of codswallop."

"No, it's not . . . it's the truth. Why do you say that?"

"Why do I say it? Because, my darling, what does it matter now?" He shrugged. "I am who I am. I wasn't good enough to marry you . . . wasn't good enough to be part of the Granville family. I think it's rather funny, don't you? I mean funny in an ironic way, of course."

He was right. We'd lost so many years. And really, what did it matter?

"Truly, it means nothing to me, not now," he continued. "Perhaps if someone had told me ten years ago . . . or even before the war, when I needed to know *who* I was, what I was . . . where I fit in, it would have meant something, but no, not now. And anyway, I realized a long, long time ago that I'd probably been born out of wedlock. My mother was never able to furnish me with any information about my father—other than the fact I looked like him—so I assumed they'd been . . ."—he shrugged—"ships in the night, so to speak. And then there was the small matter of who'd paid for my education, where the money had come from to get me through university." He paused, shook his head. "And other monies . . . quite sizable amounts, which my dear mother could never explain. I had my suspicions, of course, and, I imagine, so did quite a few others." He paused again. "I suppose the greatest irony of it all is that I ended up purchasing my birthright, Deyning. Although that was only ever because of you, and nothing to do with any notions of grandeur on my part."

"Because of me?"

He looked down at me. "Yes. I thought if I could buy back Deyning, if I could present you with what you'd lost, what you loved most in the world, I might just win you back. It was a simple enough plan. All

I had to do was make money." He paused, smiling at me, and then added, "And let's face it, I've been rather good at that."

"Yes, you have been rather good at that."

"I didn't—perhaps couldn't—foresee the complications . . . your mother, your marriage, your life with Charlie . . . my inability to be on my own. I thought I'd be able wriggle out of any liaison as soon as I had a sign from you. And then, when you didn't come to Southampton, when you didn't appear—well, I thought that was a pretty clear sign."

"Oh Tom . . ." I looked away. I didn't want to think of that day, that time; my agony, his agony.

"Strange how life turns out, isn't it?" he continued. "And here I am . . . Tom *Deyning*. How very apt that I decided to call my company Cuthbert-Deyning . . . maybe I do have foresight, after all."

For some minutes he remained silent, staring just beyond me with narrowed eyes. As though, despite what he said, despite his somewhat flippant, cynical reaction, he needed a moment's reflection: a moment to cogitate upon the details of his birth, his mother and now, suddenly, his father. He moved his head back, looked up at the ceiling and sighed. "So my mother and the earl, eh? The lord and his servant . . . rather a cliché, don't you agree?"

"She loved him, I think . . . truly loved him."

He moved his head, stared down at me. "True love, it knows no boundaries, does it?"

"No. It knows no boundaries," I repeated. I wasn't sure what he meant, whether he was referring to his parents, or to us, but I could sense his sadness. And as I lifted his hand, still held in mine, I could hear the drift of his thoughts, the word *cliché* echoing.

"Perhaps all love is a cliché, Tom," I said. "Every love . . . apart from ours."

He looked down at me and smiled, and right at that moment my heart sang out for that smile.

"So . . . tell me, did you buy *all* of my paintings?" I said, longing to see him smile again. And he laughed.

"No! I have not bought *all* of your bloody paintings. Though, as you're being so per-sistent, I can tell you I happen to have a fair few."

"And is Pritchard one of your employees?"

"Really, you're impossible," he said, turning away from me for a moment.

"Well?"

"Well what?"

"Is he?"

"Yes, yes he is. Happy now?"

I released his hand, placed my head against his knee, and we sat like that for some time, without either of us uttering a word.

"It's late. I should let you get to your bed," he said at last, and as he rose to his feet, he added, "So . . . dinner, tomorrow night?"

I stood up. "Yes," I said, "sounds lovely."

He put his arms around me, pulled me to him. "Where would you like to go?"

"Oh, I don't know . . . you choose."

We didn't kiss. We walked through to the hallway holding hands, and at the door, he said, "I'll pick you up at seven thirty." He lifted each of my hands to his lips in turn and kissed them. "Sweet dreams, Clarissa."

As he moved through the doorway, he stopped, looked back at me:

"A bientôt."

Chapter Forty-one

I had to know what had taken place between Venetia and Tom. Had they been lovers, or was there something else between them? Was it possible, I wondered, for a passionate yet platonic love to exist between a man and woman; one that needed no expression in physical adoration; one free from all sensual desire? All I'd known was passionate love: a single overwhelming force directing me to one person, one man. And it could never be platonic, never be a friendship. It had shaped my world, consumed my senses.

As I drove to Venetia's house that morning I pondered upon this; and as I passed along the edge of Hyde Park, I realized that my love for Tom was and always had been reflected in everything around me. For every place I knew continued to reverberate and echo with it. As though an imprint—something of *it*—had been left in the atmosphere. And that verdant expanse of central London, the place I'd returned to so often, and for so many years my unlikely refuge, had once again changed its form: the trees had pulled back their shadows, and the road around them—as broad as my vision.

I parked directly outside Venetia's house, walked up the steps and rang the doorbell. I had no recollection of the young maid who answered the door, so I said, "Good morning, I'm Mrs. Cooper's goddaughter, Clarissa Boyd. Is Mrs. Cooper at home?" Of course I knew she would be.

"Is she expecting you, ma'am?"

I smiled. "No, she isn't, but I'm sure she'll be quite happy to receive me."

The maid led me up to the salon on the first floor. Venetia—always fatigued by the commonplace and with a lifelong hankering after the exotic—disliked English words, particularly at home. She could never have tolerated anything so unimaginative as a drawing room in her house. Everything had to be French; the *salon*, the *chambre*, the *hall d'entrée*, *la cave*, and, of course, *never* the lavatory—always the *toilette*.

As I waited for her to come down, for it wasn't quite eleven and I knew she didn't normally rise until around that hour, I perused the invitations propped up around the oversized ormolu clock on the mantelshelf. The room itself was a testament to my godmother's character and style, a European style: a large Louis XV settee, and French Empire chairs upholstered in jewel-colored velvets; an Italian specimen marble table, and an Empire center table adorned with framed miniatures and photographs; against the wall, between the three tall windows, two marble-topped bombe commodes with matching gilt-framed mirrors above each; and opposite, Venetia's escritoire, where she penned her many and various letters, notes, and RSVPs. And an eclectic collection of oil paintings, watercolors and sketches of all sizes hung from picture rails against the dark gold wallpaper.

"Clarissa!"

She was wearing what appeared to be an Arabian costume: a kaftan—of sorts, full length—with a pearl-encrusted headband around her hair, and armfuls of silver bracelets.

I moved over to her, kissing each powdered cheek. "I've been meaning to call on you for so long," I said. "Too long."

"Yes, too long . . . and it's a delight to see you, my dear," she said, as she sat down, "but isn't it rather early for you to be out and about making calls?"

There was no point beating around the bush. I had come on a mission.

I sat down opposite her, cleared my throat. "Yes, it is a little early and I apologize, but I need to speak with you about something . . . something perhaps a little delicate."

She looked worried for a moment. "I see."

"It's about Tom . . . Tom Cuthbert."

"Ah, yes of course. Tom." She smiled, seemed quite relieved as she relaxed back into her chair.

"I know he's been calling on you, Venetia." I looked down, away from her eyes. "I know that you and he have a . . . a friendship, you see, and I need to know . . ." I hesitated, and she immediately spoke.

"You wish to know why he's been to see me?" she said, in a perfectly matter-of-fact manner.

I looked up at her, nodded. "Yes, yes that's right, I do."

She stood up, walked over to the table in the center of the room and opened a silver cigarette box. "And, of course, you have every right to know, dear . . ." She placed a cigarette into a long black holder, lifted it to her lips. "Every right," she said again, tilting her head and blowing a plume of smoke toward the chandelier above her. Then she sat back down, turned to me, and asked, "But first, would you like something . . . tea, coffee?"

"No, no thank you. I have to be at Mama's by twelve," I said. I had promised to call in on my mother to help her select yet another painting to put into auction.

"Tom . . . Tom Cuthbert," she said, staring at me, "came to me for advice, Clarissa."

"Oh really. And advice on what, exactly?"

She smiled. "Well, advice on *you* of course, dear."

"Me?"

She laughed. "Yes. Why on earth else would Tom Cuthbert call on me? And I have to say, I knew the moment he appeared why he'd come!"

"And . . ."

"He wants you!" she said, dramatically. "Wants to win you back *and* have your Mama's blessing."

"But what did he tell you? What did he say?"

"Oh, he told me he'd heard about you and Charlie, but he said he'd always known that you didn't love Charlie because . . . because you love him." She paused, smiling at me rather coquettishly, her eyes twinkling. "He told me that he, too, was getting divorced, and that he had plenty enough money to look after you . . . but one thing, *one thing*," she repeated with emphasis, "still stood in his way."

"Mama."

She nodded. "He wished me to speak with your mother, talk to her, persuade her . . ." She stared at me, her violet eyes brighter than ever, and then she reached out for my hand. "He loves you very much, Clarissa." And as she gripped my hand, I felt a tear make its way slowly down my cheek, into my mouth. "You see, he understands, he knows that you won't—can't—do anything without your mama's approval or blessing. That's why he came to me."

"And . . . and have you . . ."

"Yes, I have. I've spoken with your mother. Oh, she knows nothing of Tom's visit to me, nor can she ever. But I have spoken with her, and at some length, and I think . . . I think she sees things a little differently now. We've all changed, life has changed, and you . . . well, my darling, you deserve to be happy. More than anything else, you deserve to be happy."

I looked down into my lap. "But I wonder if Mama thinks that."

"Of course your mother wants you to be happy! My dear, she loves you . . . you're her daughter, her precious, precious daughter. But she was always so protective of you, so very protective, she *and* your father. They only ever wanted the best for you."

I moved forward in my chair, sat up, straight-backed. "So tell me, what do I do from here?"

"You must speak to your mother. You must have a conversation with her, a difficult conversation perhaps, but one that's long overdue. I can do no more."

"He's a good man, Venetia, but I think you know that."

"Oh yes, I do know that. I most *certainly* know that," she replied, with great emphasis once again. Then she glanced across at me with a new expression, half frowning, quizzical.

"What? What is it?" I asked.

She looked away, her eyes scanning the room, searching for words. "Has he . . . has Tom mentioned anything to you regarding Henry?" she asked, her eyes focused back upon me.

"Henry?" I shook my head. "No, why would he?"

She sighed. "Oh dear." She closed her eyes for a moment. "I do so loathe all this skulking about and subterfuge," she said, shaking her head.

"What subterfuge . . . what is it about Henry? Does Tom know something? Does Tom know where Henry is?"

She stared at me, wide eyed. "My dear,

Tom Cuthbert has been *keeping* your brother these past two years."

"Keeping . . . I don't understand. What do you mean?"

"Henry is in New York, Clarissa, and has been for some time," she said quickly, and then stopped.

"New York?"

"Yes, but I must add—have to add—that I only discovered this myself quite recently. And Tom doesn't wish you to know, or not yet, it would seem. He said he'd tell you all in *good time* . . . once Henry was quite recovered and back on his feet." She paused again, pursing her lips, then continued. "It was Henry who found Tom, not the other way round, of course. At that time Tom had no idea, absolutely no idea that Henry had left England . . . vanished!" She threw her hands in the air with a jangling, tinkling sound. "He simply turned up there one day, at Cuthbert-Deyning's Manhattan office . . . and looking like a hobo, from all accounts."

"I see. And what is it he's recovering from?" I asked. "Obviously not amnesia."

"Oh my dear, you must try not to be

angry, nor must you breathe a word of this to your poor mama. It seems he'd become embroiled in some sort of . . . illegal importation scam. I don't know the details— nor do I wish to—but I do know he was in a mess, a rather frightful mess, but as far as I understand, he's much better now. And he's working, my dear, working for Tom—in his New York office," she added, smiling at me brightly.

I looked down at the floor, closed my eyes.

Henry.

Yes, he'd have known, known immediately when he saw the name Cuthbert-Deyning; known it was Tom, known he'd lend him money . . . *just till I'm sorted, old chap.*

"I knew he'd turn up sooner or later, but I never imagined . . ."

"No."

I explained to Venetia that I'd have to tell Mama something; I had to let her know Henry was alive, and well. She made me promise that I wouldn't mention her name, and that I shouldn't say anything to Tom, but should wait for him to tell me.

I rose from my chair, moved over to her

and kissed her. "Thank you . . . thank you, Venetia."

She began to laugh, tearfully. "Oh, my dear, you have nothing to thank me for, truly. Whatever I've done—whatever I have said—should have been said years ago. But some of us acquire wisdom later than others," she added. "I only wish I could go back upon my life with what I now know." She looked up at me. "Wouldn't that be a marvelous thing?"

Chapter Forty-two

I wasn't sure how to begin that conversation with Mama; that so-long-overdue conversation. And yet I felt no fear, no sense of dread, for I had already determined what I would do, with or without my mother's approval.

We selected not one but two paintings for auction, which Mama then asked Wilson and another maid to remove from the wall and wrap, and we discussed which pictures could be moved, hung in their place. She seemed strangely happy to be relieved of yet more *paraphernalia*—as she'd taken to calling all of her furniture and possessions now. And I suggested to her that she shouldn't sell anything else; not for a while, at least, I said. But the place remained over-furnished. For Mama, Deyning Park and Berkeley Square had all converged there, into a cramped emporium of cluttered surfaces, and antiques much too large and ostentatious for their modest abode.

As we sat down, she said, "And so, are you staying to lunch?"

"No, Mama, I'm afraid I can't today. I've been out all morning . . . at Venetia's."

"Oh, I see," she said, brushing down her skirt and turning to look at me. "I didn't know you'd—"

"And I'm seeing Tom later," I interrupted.

She stared at me. "Tom?"

"Yes, Tom," I replied. "We're going out to dinner."

She looked away, toward the window, and then down into her lap. She lifted a hand to her hair, trying to find a stray curl to twist and tuck back in place. She turned her head to the table next to her, and then up to the wall: a square of bright color where a picture had hung.

"Well," she began, her head still turned

away from me, "I hardly know what to say, Clarissa."

"You don't have to say anything, Mama," I replied, my voice steady, kind.

She turned to me, fluttering her eyes shut for a moment. "So, you . . . you and Tom Cuthbert . . . you're friends once again?"

"Yes, we are. In fact, we've always been friends . . . more than friends." I paused. "We've been lovers, off and on, for years, almost sixteen years, Mama."

She closed her eyes once more, shook her head.

I continued. "And I'm sorry, I'm sorry if it pains you to hear this, to hear me speak about him, but I want you to know. I want to be able to be honest with you, for you to know the truth. I love him, Mama, but you know that. You know I've always loved him."

She raised a hand to her brow.

"I'd like to have your blessing. We'd both like your blessing."

She didn't speak, but kept her hand to her brow, covering her eyes as though dazzled by a very bright light somewhere close to where I sat.

"Mama . . ."

She lowered her hand. "I did what I thought was best, Clarissa," she said, opening her eyes and staring down into her lap. "I did what I thought was right. It was not the way . . . not possible . . ."

I rose from my chair, moved across the room and sat down upon the velvet ottoman in front of her. "I know, I know you did what you thought was right . . . but perhaps, perhaps in hindsight you're able to see that it wasn't right." I reached out, took hold of her hand. "Look at me, look at my life. I've one failed, childless and unhappy marriage behind me. I have nothing, nothing to lose . . . and everything to gain. My heart has been constant, and so has his. And the world . . . the world *is* changed."

She nodded. Then she said, "And does he know? Does he know about . . ."

"Emily. Her name was Emily, Mama," I said. "No, no he doesn't, not yet. But I intend to tell him. He has to know. He has a right to know."

"And then what?"

"*Then* . . . I'm not entirely sure. But I shan't leave him. Not for you, or anyone else."

She didn't look at me and, though I waited for her to speak, she said nothing.

"You once told me that you'd loved someone, someone other than Papa . . ."

She sighed. "That was a long time ago," she replied. "And it was . . . it was impossible . . ."

"Impossible—like Tom and me?"

She looked up at me at last, and my heart ached for her. You see, I no longer felt any anger toward her, none at all, only sadness and regret at all the years we'd lied to each other. Always pretending, bravely hanging on to the idea of what we should be, how we should be, each of us burdened by the knowledge of our hearts.

Then she spoke. "His name was Edward," she said, glancing away from me once more.

"Edward," I repeated.

And I don't know why or how, but at that moment a montage of images suddenly surfaced in my memory: I saw them emerging through the gateway of the walled garden, Mama smiling, turning to look up at him, reluctant to leave his side; I saw them standing together in the hothouse, discussing exhibits for a flower show, looking into each other's eyes as though their lives depended upon some silly rosette; and I saw them once more as they disappeared down the driveway, Mama waving back at me, more animated than ever. Edina and Edward.

Edward Broughton . . .

And in the instant of unraveling, it all fell into place. I remembered the day we left Deyning, when Mama had wept. Her tears had never been about leaving Deyning. I thought of my arrangement with him, regarding Tom's letters: Broughton had been my accomplice, my partner in crime. Had he been the one who'd told Mama? Had he felt duty bound to tell her? Or had he simply seen a pattern of events, a mirroring of situation and circumstance? Something he couldn't have; something she couldn't have.

By the end of the war he'd disappeared from our lives forever, and I couldn't recall my mother ever having mentioned him. But Mrs. Cuthbert had; she'd told me he'd gone back to the West Country, where he had family, and she'd spoken of that family too . . . *rather well-to-do* . . . he'd been the black sheep, she'd said. Now I remembered. But at the time I'd not listened, for my head had been so full of Tom, Tom and me.

"Edward," I said again.

And I saw once more the King's ring upon her finger, her wedding finger, and the initials—quite clearly now: EB. It was his ring, his signet ring. He'd given it to her, a symbol of his identity, just as surely as he'd given her his heart.

She turned to me. "It wasn't sordid, Clarissa. There was nothing tawdry about it."

"No. No, I'm sure."

But at that moment I thought of Papa, and felt a ripple of guilt at my mother's duplicity. Had he known? I wondered. Had he suspected?

"He was different . . ." she continued, wistfully. "And he cared about me, cared about me deeply . . . I was lonely, you see. Your father was away so much, and I . . . well, I enjoyed his company," she added, glancing at me. "He was an educated man . . . without any arrogance at all."

I closed my eyes for a moment. Of course, I thought, of course she'd been lonely. And I had seen it, known it, and then forgotten it. That ineffable, unspeakable sadness about her had been pushed away, denied, and replaced by an enigmatic beauty, unfathomable, unreachable, and simply called *Mama*.

I wanted to say the name Broughton, wanted to say it out loud and see what would happen, but I knew it had to come from her. It would have been somehow altogether wrong and inappropriate for me to speak that name, at that moment, and it seemed to belong to her now. Oh, I could have challenged her, spoken of hypocrisy and double standards, but what was the point? Nothing could alter the past, and I'd made up my mind, she knew that. I imagine that's why she finally allowed herself to say the name. It was her way of holding out the proverbial olive branch. And though she wasn't prepared to give up that secret entirely, she'd finally shared something of herself with me.

She altered tempo and moved on, telling me once again that she had no regrets, that she'd loved my father first and foremost; that life was about compromise, and that we can't always have everything we wish for. "And anyway," she concluded, with a heavy sigh, "I had you to think of. And my children . . . have been my life."

I wanted to tell her about Henry, but I

wasn't sure how she'd receive the news. And yet it had to be, I had to tell her. And in that atmosphere of openness and honesty, it seemed the perfect time. So I took a deep breath, and told her that Henry was alive, and well, living in New York, and working for Tom; that Tom had been looking after him these past two years. Not surprisingly, she was startled by the news at first, and then somewhat confused. She asked me questions: how had Henry found Tom? But *where*, exactly, was he living? Why had he not written? When was he coming home? What did Tom say? I couldn't tell her that it was Venetia, and not Tom, who had told me all of this. And so I said that I really didn't know any more, but I would, of course, speak to Tom and find out Henry's address.

Before I left my mother that day, as I was putting on my coat and hat, she asked me to wait a moment and then left the room. When she reappeared, clutching a small tapestry bag—one with curved faux bamboo handles, which I remembered from when I was young as having been her petit point bag—she simply handed it to me without any words.

"What's this?" I asked, smiling. "You know I don't sew—or embroider . . ."

She didn't reply, but pointed, gesturing for me to open it.

I unclipped the bag, peered inside, then reached into it and lifted out a handful of unopened letters. There must have been twenty or more, each one addressed to Miss C. Granville, c/o E. Broughton, 2 Stable Cottages, Deyning Park; all in Tom's unmistakable hand. And I burst into tears at the sight of my name. For how many days and weeks and months had I waited, longing to see those words: my name and a letter from him?

She came forward, her arms outstretched. "I'm sorry," she said, falteringly. "Forgive me."

We didn't go out to dine that evening. By the time Tom arrived to collect me, I'd read all of the letters, once, twice, some three times. I'd gone back to those dark days, been with him in the trenches, and at Gallipoli, and Passchendaele. And so, that night, when I opened the door to him, saw him standing there, I fell into his arms—weeping.

He held me, asking me over and over

what had happened, then led me back to the sitting room, and sat down with me on the sofa, and I told him about my conversation with Mama, about Broughton, and about his letters—still strewn across the floor. He rose to his feet, took off his jacket and tie, gathered up a few of the letters, and sat back down with me. And with my body curled up to him, my arms wrapped around him, my face pressed against his chest, he glanced through them, and then read some in silence, and some out loud to me: "Last week, another young boy in my battalion was shot. He'd become hysterical, lost his nerve and couldn't face going back into the line. He was tied to what was once a tree . . . a piece of white cloth pinned over his heart . . ."

And though exhausted from that journey back in time, and from weeping, I couldn't seem to stop crying. So he said things like, "Better late than never, eh?" and, "At least you know now that I wrote," and commented upon his spelling and grammar—in a bid to make me smile. But I could see, I could see as he pondered on his own long-forgotten words, that it was difficult for him too; that he was being strong only for me.

"I somehow managed to drag him through the mud and back to the trench, but he'd been hit in the stomach and for almost an hour he lay in my arms—crying for his mother. He'd told them . . . told them he was eighteen, but I very much doubt he was even sixteen . . . *Norton*."

Eventually, he picked me up and carried me through to the bedroom. He lay down next to me on the bed, his head propped in one hand, watching me.

"Don't look at me. I look hideous," I said, for I'd been crying for hours and was exhausted by the emotion of that day, and the previous night.

He shook his head. "You could never look hideous, never," he replied, smiling at me, stroking my cheek. His touch was a balm to my senses: more blissful and calming than any morphia or pills. And for a moment I contemplated telling him then and there about the morphia, about that time, when I'd stood alone at the very edge of the abyss. I wanted him to know, and he had to know—had to know everything, all of me. But not now; I couldn't go back there at that moment. It could wait.

"Please . . . read some more," I said.

And so we lay there, together, and he read out more of his words from that time. I listened to his voice. "Home, it has become an ideal, like heaven, inhabited by angels. A place we dream about . . . and speak of and long for . . ."

I closed my eyes, felt his hand move over my hair . . . felt myself drifting . . .

I looked up at the ceiling. The little dark-haired girl appeared. She said, "I'm not coming down, Clarissa. I have to stay here now."

I opened my eyes, glanced up at him, still reading out loud, quietly.

"Are you going to tell him? Are you going to tell him about me?"

"Yes, yes . . . of course, but not now. A little later."

"You say that all the time . . ."

"But I'm tired . . . so tired. I'll tell him later, I promise."

I felt cold, opened my eyes. "Tom?"

He was on his feet, next to me, undressing me.

"You need to sleep," he said.

"Don't go . . . don't leave me."

He got down on to his knees, his face level with mine, took my head in his hands. "I'm not leaving . . . I'll never leave you."

"No," I said. "Don't ever leave me."

I felt a warmth come up over me, then the tucking in; the sound of water—a tap; a click, darkness; and then his body next to me, his arms around me.

"Tell him about me, Clarissa; you have to tell him about me."

"Come down . . . come down and I'll tell him."

"I can't come down. Not now. I have to stay here now."

And then she moved away, disappeared from view.

Hours later, as daylight crept into the room, I was stirred by the warmth of kisses, along my shoulder, the back of my neck, my spine. I turned, and in the dim light I saw his face and knew it hadn't been a dream. He was there, in my bed; he was with me. And when we kissed, I felt myself pulled back: I was at the boathouse by the lake; I was in the darkness of night in Hyde Park; I was in an Arabian tent, and I was his once more.

"Promise me you'll never leave me . . ."

"I promise. I promise I'll never leave you."

Chapter Forty-three

✍

We'd been to the theater, and afterward dined at the Criterion. And it was he who brought up that night in the park, the night we'd first made love. He was in a provocative mood, playful, trying to embarrass me, I think. But he couldn't, of course. That's one of the few benefits of aging; it becomes almost impossible to be embarrassed by one's misspent youth, simply because we later revel in those early misdemeanors.

"You know, you really were rather wicked," he said, leaning forward, smiling.

"Wicked? No, I don't think so."

"Do you remember what you pushed into my pocket—that night at Jimmy's party?"

I smiled. "Yes . . . yes, I do."

He raised his eyebrows. "I shan't tell you what happened to the garment in question."

"Ha! So you want me to know . . ."

He leaned back in his chair, studying me. Then he lit a cigarette and watched it as it burned in the ashtray.

"Well?" I said. "Are you going to tell me?"

He glanced up at me, his head tilted to one side. Then he bit on his lip, pondering, wondering. "I must have relived that night a thousand times and more in my head."

"Yes, and so have I."

"You know, I still have your glove as well," he said, breaking into a smile.

But all I could think about was her, our daughter; the child conceived that night, in the middle of a war. And I knew I had to tell him. I wanted to tell him. I longed to be able to talk to someone about Emily, to speak her name out loud, at last; for her to be acknowledged by someone; and who better than her own father? But there was no way I could raise this subject in a restaurant, surrounded by people, strangers. So, when we returned to my flat, as we sat together with our nightcaps, I took that leap.

"I need to tell you something, Tom; something about that night."

"Mm, what's that, my darling?" he replied, without turning to look at me.

"After that night, that night in the park . . ."

"Yes . . ."

Here it was at last, my moment. I knew I had to say the words clearly, precisely, slowly, calmly:

"I had a baby."

There, that was it. I'd said it. I'd finally said it. *I had a baby.*

Those four words, locked up for so long, were finally uttered. And I think he thought he'd misheard me.

"What? Who had a baby?"

"I did."

"*You* had a baby?"

"Yes, yes, I did. I had a baby," I said, eagerly, as though I'd been waiting a lifetime to confirm this fact. "We had a baby, Tom."

I was sitting on the very edge of my armchair and he'd been lounging on the floor, his back pressed against it. He sat up, turned onto his knees and faced me, and his confusion, his shock, was palpable and seemed to fill the room.

He looked at me: astonished, dumbstruck. "*We* had a baby?"

"I had a baby," I repeated half laughing, and beginning to cry at the same time.

Perhaps I'd thought I could tell him, talk about it all in a perfunctory way. It had all happened so very long ago. Perhaps I'd thought I'd be able to recite dates, facts, as though I was clearing up something almost akin to a business matter.

"I had a baby," I said again, like a record stuck. And as I said those four words they tore open my heart, and I heard myself say them again. "I had a baby."

"Clarissa . . . what are you telling me? We had a child? We have a child?"

"Yes. We had a child, Tom. I named her Emily . . . after Emily Brontë," I added, remembering. "She was born on November the twelfth, nineteen seventeen . . . in Plymouth. She was born in Devon," I said, trying to remember how I'd planned it; how I'd planned to tell him.

I looked directly at him as I spoke, but as his image blurred, my head began to shake, as though I was telling him something and saying "no" at the same time.

"A *daughter*? You had a *baby*, Clarissa?" he said, repeating words, checking facts, staring at me.

"I had a baby," I said again, his face barely visible. And then I heard myself say it again, and again: *I had a baby . . . I had a baby . . .*

He stood up, moved to the fireplace, his back to me, and I saw him grip the marble mantelshelf. Then, suddenly, he was in front of me, and once more on his knees.

"You had a baby," he said, looking at me, into my eyes. "*We* have a child . . ."

I nodded my head, and I couldn't stop nodding my head. "Yes, yes, we did . . . we do," I said.

He stared at me, searching my face as though he'd find every answer hidden there. Then he took my head in his hands and said, "But why . . . why did I not know? Why did you not tell me this?"

I can't remember now what, exactly, I told him about the events of that year, but I told him everything there was to tell. Everything I could remember. I told him about my mother, Aunt Maude, Edith Collins, St. Anne's—and the moment I'd handed over Emily. And by the time I'd finished he'd covered his face with his hands. And so I lowered myself down onto the floor and held him.

"I'm so sorry," I said. "I'm so very sorry."

He looked up at me, his face contorted. "No . . . No," he shook his head. "I'm sorry . . . I'm sorry that you went through all of this alone, without me. I'm sorry that I was not there for you—for her. I'm sorry that you've carried this with you for so long. That I . . ." and he began to pull at his hair. "That I quizzed you on why you'd never had children." He stared at me, his face crumpled; defeated. "And that's who *Emily* was . . ." he said. "There was no imaginary friend . . . Emily's our child."

I nodded.

That night we lay awake, frozen in each other's arms; each of us searching for that inaccessible moment in our past; the point to which we could return and then perhaps somehow change our now. The point to which we could return, reclaim our child, and from there rewrite our story, her story. How it *could* have been . . . how it should have been. Unlike me, Tom had lived his life without ever knowing he had a child. By withholding that information I'd spared him from the slow and steady stream of loss, a meandering trickle of dates and reminders, only to submerge him in the deluge of one almighty torrent.

The next morning, each of us weakened and spent by grief, he told me that he was going to find her. And it became his consuming passion for the next few weeks. But it proved more difficult than he'd anticipated.

"Perhaps she doesn't want us to find her," I said to him one evening.

"No, we'll find her," he said, turning to me and smiling. "I've already put Goddard onto it."

"But we might not find her, Tom. We might not . . ."

He stared at me, ran a finger across my forehead, down my cheek. "I'll find her, my darling," he repeated. "I'll find her," he said again.

～

. . . Yesterday I sat alone and reread all of your notes & letters to me. I put them all in chronological order, & then jumbled them up again . . . so that one day, they might be a treasure trail of clues— should anyone be interested! We did have such a perfect, heavenly time, didn't we, that last summer?

Chapter Forty-four

~

There's an old white gate at the end of the avenue of my dreams. It's where I sit and watch the world pass by. From there I see my brothers go off to war. From there I see my daughter, playing in a distant field. And from there I see my love, walking back to me.

Unbeknown to me, Tom hadn't just *put Goddard onto it*: he'd put quite a few people onto the task of tracing our daughter. But it was Oliver Goddard who later told me the pieces of the story Tom couldn't bring himself to tell me. It was Oliver who told me that he and Tom had driven down to

Plymouth, to speak with the sisters at St. Anne's. And it was Oliver who'd tell me so many parts of the story Tom would never speak of.

They'd been gone overnight. Tom had told me he had business in Bristol, but he'd telephoned me late in the evening. I'd missed him, and told him so. And he said, "But it's only one night, darling. I think we can cope with one night apart . . ."

It's strange to me, even now, the thought of him retracing my steps; moving through the silent passageways of St. Anne's; glancing out of those narrow windows, so many years after I'd been there. For that time seems more than a lifetime ago, and my recollection of it—and the place itself—is hazy. Like the remembrance of a dream, there are gaps I know I shall never be able to fill. Oh, I can still see a girl, the girl I once was, sitting in a room, staring out through a window, but somehow it's not me, for I was never *really* there. I was always with him.

Oliver told me that St. Anne's had kept records on everyone who'd passed through their doors: the date of arrival, due date of baby, and room assigned. There were no medical notes of course, only the most basic of information. And apparently the place was quite empty of *fallen women*. Different than during the war, one of the sisters had said, by way of explanation. Tom had asked to see my room, and then asked if he could have a moment there on his own. So Oliver and the young sister had waited outside the closed door, in the hallway, in silence. By the time they left St. Anne's they had the name and address of an adoption agency. Mission accomplished, Oliver said. They'd returned to London without stopping, and when Tom came into the flat that evening he'd rushed over to me, to where I was standing in the kitchen, taken me into his arms and said, "I'm never going to leave you again, not even for one night." He pulled me tighter. "I want to see your face each night before I fall asleep, and every morning when I awake. And one day, one day when I take my last breath," he whispered, "I want to be looking into your eyes."

We received a reply from the adoption agency almost one month after Tom's letter to them. They told him that yes, Emily Cuthbert Granville had been adopted, five months after she'd left me, and by a couple from London. At that stage it seemed as though they couldn't or wouldn't give any further information. And all I could think of was those five months . . . those five months she'd been on her own; those five months I'd been tucked up in Berkeley Square, unraveling and in agony. Five months.

And I realized that's when it started, the lie that became my life, for I hadn't been whole, hadn't been complete, since that time. Something of me—a piece of my soul, a sliver of light—had quietly been extinguished at Plymouth in 1917, without any ceremony, mourning, or fuss. And I'd kept it a secret for so long that I'd become *the secret*: unspoken, unsaid, denied. Not-quite-but-almost Clarissa: haunted by nothing more sinister than the truth.

For so many years I'd tried not to think of her. I'd purposefully blurred and blotted out those early years, when she was still a baby, still a small child; when I'd been married to Charlie. I'd celebrated her precious birthdays in oblivion, and when no babies came, I'd accepted it as my punishment. It made sense. And I'd felt relief. The thought of another chance, another child, terrified me. For how could I, a mother already, a mother who had given away a beautiful healthy baby, be expected to love and look after another? I was not worthy of mother-hood. And through my self-hatred I'd almost destroyed myself. And for a while I'd hated my own mother too: the person who'd made me give up my right to mother-hood.

Of course no amount of drugs or alcohol had been able to assuage my guilt, or extinguish my love for my child, Tom's child. I'd thought of her each and every day of my life since the day we'd parted. I'd tried to imagine her, what she looked like, how she spoke, where she lived: who she'd become. Twelve years had passed since I'd handed her into the outstretched arms of a nameless woman in a brown coat at St. Anne's. Did she even know I existed? And if she did, if her adoptive parents had told her the pathetic details of her birth, had she ever thought about me, her mother?

Despite the passing of years, in my dreams she remained a baby. The memory of her soft, clean skin, her tiny finger-nails, her bright blue eyes, her smell; all of her, preserved and held there. But occasionally, every so often, she'd come to me as a child: a miniature version of Tom. She'd speak my name, "Clarissa": a sweet voice, so familiar to me. She'd reach out to me, smiling, and I'd take her into my arms. *Emily*. "But where have you been? I've been waiting," she'd say.

"I'm here . . . I'm here now."

So many years had passed, but I needed to know. And not to absolve myself: for there could be no absolution. All I needed to know was that my daughter was alive and well, and happy; yes, happy.

My heart wobbled as he stood in front of me. And I watched him as he pulled the pages from a large brown envelope. He knew what was coming, of course; he'd already read every word in that envelope, but he had to tell me, had to deliver the news. He dismissed the flimsy covering note, and then looked at me with a strange serious face. And I for some reason laughed. "Yes . . ." I said, extending my hand, "come along then."

He said nothing, handed me the sheet of paper: *a certified copy of an entry of death*.

"Oh, well, this isn't right," I said. "No, no, this isn't right . . ."

I looked at the name: *Elizabeth Rachel Healey . . . Date of death, December the twenty-first, 1919 . . . Cause of death, Influenza . . .*

"No, this is wrong . . . this is definitely wrong. That's not her. That's not her name," I said. "They've obviously made a mistake."

I didn't want to look at it anymore. I put down the sheet of paper and walked about the room. It was a mistake, I said again. *Bloody useless people*. I lit a cigarette, looked out of the window. "It's not her," I said. "It's not her, Tom. They've made a mistake . . . it's the wrong person. That's not her . . . it's not her."

There was no mistake. The people named Healey had adopted our daughter. They'd given her a new name, a life and an identity we could never give her. And for almost eighteen months she'd lived with them, as their child. And then, one night before Christmas, not long after her second birthday, and in the middle of the Spanish flu epidemic, Emily had died.

She had never celebrated a third, fifth,

sixth, or even a tenth birthday; and there would never be any meeting between us. I would never know what she had become, because she had not *become*. I would never hear her voice or know what she looked like, because she had never grown up. My remembrance of her would only ever be as a three-week-old baby.

Grief can be held off for a lifetime, and mine, for the baby I'd given away, took over twelve years to arrive. When it came, it came with the same force of any held-back torrent. It flooded my senses, drowned my perspective. And, though submerged, I occasionally caught my breath long enough to see the debris and driftwood of my life float past me, all pinned with one word: *waste*; the waste of time; the unnecessary waste of love. And the only thing I could hold on to was him, Tom.

Later, he called the number Oliver Goddard had given him, and asked for more information, and someone eventually called him back. Because the child was dead, they said, they were prepared to give a little more information than was usual. They told him that Albert Healey had been a greengrocer, and the family—his wife, and our daughter, Emily—had lived above the shop, in Battersea, London.

And he found her eventually too: in a cemetery at Wandsworth. We drove there together, late one afternoon. The day after he told me of his discovery.

That day, at the cemetery, he seemed to know exactly where to go. And he was remarkably calm, surprisingly in control. He held on to my hand tightly as he led me through row upon row of tombstones, down a pathway to a dank corner, and the name we now knew, chiselled into a lopsided stone: Elizabeth Rachel Healey, 1917–1919.

Emily Cuthbert.

We stood there together in silence, staring at that name. Then I stepped forward and placed the arrangement of white roses I'd had a Sloane Street florist prepare next to the stone. It looked extravagant, expensive, and incongruous: too big for a baby, too pathetic for the circumstances. She'd lain there for over a decade, serenaded only by the rumble of London traffic. Had anyone visited her? I wondered. Had anyone mourned her? Did others come to that place bestowed with memories I would never have? There were no signs of anyone having been, certainly not recently. No fresh or dying flowers; no plants in pots; nothing. And here we were, her parents, standing side by side under an umbrella as a smoky drizzle descended: too late to hold her, too late to know her, too late to explain.

He didn't weep, didn't shed a tear. And even then, through my own tears, I noticed this. How strong and in control he was. But he had been through a war, seen so much, and he was a businessman, I thought. It wasn't until later, much later, that I learned Tom had been on his own to visit Emily's grave before he ever took me.

As I stood in the rain that day, all I could think of was the tiny baby I'd held and nursed; the baby I'd given away: my baby. And I didn't want to leave. Even when the rain became heavier and he pulled on my arm, I didn't want to leave. I didn't want to leave her again, you see.

Eventually, he led me back through the tombstones, up the wet path toward the gate, and I could feel my chest tightening: that wrench, still there. He helped me into our waiting car, carefully tucking in my coat, closing the door, and then he moved to the other side of the vehicle and climbed in himself. And as we pulled away he turned to me, took hold of my hand and said something. Numb, and immersed in my grief, I couldn't hear his words. But as we headed out through the sprawling southern suburbs I realized what he'd said: *I'm taking you home now.*

I turned to him. "Home?"

"Yes, home . . . we're going home, Clarissa."

And as we passed through the old white gate I looked up out of the car window. A pale gray-blue sky stretched out above us, stretched further and illuminated by elongated wavy pink clouds: evensong clouds. And in a split second of déjà vu I finally grasped something: that there is no such thing as the passing of time, only the arc of seasons: a circle and not a line.

Moments can and do come back to us.

Epilogue

∽

London,
May the fifth, 1930

Dearest Ted,

I hope this letter finds you well and that Devonshire is basking in the same blissful sunshine we have been fortunate enough to enjoy here in London these past few weeks. There really is no better time of year, is there? The light, which for some reason I always forget, is altogether different and truly quite heavenly, and the air fresh, & fragrant with new blossom.

I must apologize to you for the tardiness of this letter, but we have had a busy & eventful time of late. C and T were married three weeks ago, on April the fourteenth (six days after her divorce was made final) at the Register Office here in Kensington. It was a very simple, quiet affair, with Venetia Cooper and a business associate of T's—a Mr. Goddard—acting as "witnesses," and afterward, a small luncheon party—including V & the aforementioned Mr. G, Jimmy C (V's son), H and myself—at a favorite restaurant of C & T's on the Fulham Road, all terribly informal—and MODERN.

Unfortunately I was forced to miss the nuptials in order to meet H from the boat train. T had arranged his passage (as a surprise for C) and I had anticipated him being home the day before, but the crossing was delayed due to storms in the mid-Atlantic. As I'm sure you can imagine, it was rather a shock to dear C when I walked in to the restaurant with H on my arm, but the perfect surprise for her on her wedding day. All of us, including me, shed a tear when she rushed into his arms. It was such a happy day, one of the happiest of my life, and I think you would have been very proud.

They are expecting a baby, due early October I think, and so, though T had had all sorts of wonderful ideas & exotic sounding locations planned for their honeymoon, the doctor quite rightly advised against any foreign travel.

She is so happy, Teddy, radiantly happy, and they're quite inseparable, like a couple of children, & utterly content to spend all of their time at Deyning—with T now running & managing the farm, & C the house and gardens. Edna is with them, back as housekeeper and cook, but I have no idea how they manage without servants—& just the one gardener! However, C assures me that this is how they want it.

And I too am to move back there, into the place that was once yours, & ours, at the end of the summer. Oh I can see you smiling now, and yes, it will be queer to be back there—living in THAT cottage. Do you remember, all those years ago, when that was our dream? They are knocking the two cottages (yrs & what was, in yr time, Mrs. C's) into one, so it will be plenty big enough for me now.

I enclose a photograph for you— taken on the day, on the steps of the Register Office. She does look beautiful, and so happy—doesn't she? I know it will make your heart sing to see that face once more. And they make such a handsome couple, don't they? I have no doubt they'll produce rather dashing offspring, and I'm simply longing to be "Grandma."

Do write to me soon and send me your news. In the meantime, & as always, I remain . . .

Yours,
Dina

Acknowledgments

Thanks to Ellen Edwards and to Deborah Schneider, to the teams at New American Library in New York and Headline Publishing in London. Thanks to Sheila Crowley at Curtis Brown, and to Ali Gunn for her passion and faith in me. Special thanks as always to Max, Bella, and Jeremy.

Judith Kinghorn was born in Northumberland, educated in the Lake District, and is a graduate in English and History of Art. She lives in Hampshire with her husband and two children.

THE

Last
Summer

JUDITH KINGHORN

A CONVERSATION WITH
JUDITH KINGHORN

Q: Where did your idea to write The Last Summer *come from? Were you inspired by anything in particular?*

A: I've always enjoyed historical novels, and biographies of unusual and pioneering Victorian and Edwardian women, particularly those who broke rules and pushed boundaries. And I've always been fascinated by old houses and their stories. I live in an old house in the country, and some years ago I researched its history, and discovered some very interesting characters—all women—and quite a few secrets. I think all of these things came together and inspired *The Last Summer.*

I'd wanted to write a first-person narrative for a while, and I wanted to write the sort of novel I like to read, set in a period I was particularly interested in, when there was change and conflict on a huge scale. I also knew it had to be a love story, because I believe all the best stories have that at their heart. And I wanted to create a strong sense of place from the start. I have a very visual mind, and the setting—Deyning—came to me before the characters. That was my starting point, a landscape, an English country house, and a family about to go to war.

Q: In The Last Summer *the cozy Edwardian world of Clarissa's childhood is lost forever with the impact of the First World War. What do you find particularly fascinating about this period in history?*

A: For me, the late-nineteenth and early-twentieth centuries are the most interesting period in history. It was a time of such extraordinary progress and advancement, and—with the advent of mobility—the birth of the modern world. It's also an era that seems vaguely familiar, and accessible; recognizable from old newsreel and sepia-tinged photographs; the world my grandparents and great-grandparents inhabited. But I'm particularly drawn to those years during and subsequent to the First World War, not least because almost an entire generation of young men went off to fight— for King and Country—and didn't return. I was fascinated by the impact of that war on individuals, families, and society as a whole; the speed of change, and collapse of an old order.

Q: You have clearly put a great deal of research into creating the world of The Last Summer. *Were you surprised by anything you discovered in the course of your research?*

A: Before I began my research I'd read only a few books—biographies and novels—set in the First World War. I don't think I'd ever truly thought about or realized—allowed myself to realize—those numbers and statistics, so studying them and that time, I was horrified, appalled by the sheer magnitude and scale of loss. But almost everything about that war is shocking to read and imagine now. It was a cataclysmic, dark time, and yet the days immediately before the war, that long Indian summer we read about and see images of, appear so idyllic; and the years afterward—the Roaring Twenties—so decadent and glamorous. For me, that juxtaposition of heaven and hell, agony and ecstasy, light and darkness, is fascinating, and the perfect backdrop to a novel.

Q: Clarissa's voice is extremely distinctive and, as readers, we feel that we know her intimately by the end of the novel. Why did you decide to write the novel solely from her point of

view? Did you find it easy to get inside her head?

A: Sometime before starting the book I'd reread Daphne du Maurier's *Rebecca*, and afterward, I set myself a challenge: to write a novel in the first person. So that decision came before any actual story! But as soon as I decided to set the novel around the First World War I knew I wanted the voice to be female, a very particular female voice, giving a very particular female perspective. I never wavered in that decision, because I felt writing the novel in the first person offered me the scope to develop a character through a singular, distinctive yet evolving voice. Also, I think—I hope—it lends the narrative greater intimacy.

Clarissa came to me quite slowly at first. And, after I'd written the first few chapters, I wasn't sure if I liked her, which could have been a major problem. She seemed so childlike, almost too naive. But I realized I hadn't gotten to know her, and, as her creator, I knew I had to test her, see what she was made of. So, as the story developed, so did she. And yes, it was very easy—after a while—to be inside her head, know her thoughts, and anticipate her actions and reactions.

I wanted her to be fallible, and sometimes fragile, but not a victim. And she had to be naive at the start, a product of her time and background. Also, I wanted her voice to be authentic, convincing, but at the same time not alienate twenty-first-century readers.

Q: Did your story ever take a direction that surprised you? If so, how?

A: The morphia addiction was a surprise. I'd read about it in my research, but it had never been in the plan, as such. But by the time I'd reached the point where Clarissa had handed over her baby and returned to London, and knowing what was happening in certain circles at that time, I had to make a decision: would she, could she have?

Q: Who is your favorite character in the novel? Is there a character you identify with more than any other?

A: Well, I was definitely in love with Tom. And I had great fun with Mama, whom I think would have loved a much bigger part in the novel. And I grew very fond of some of the minor characters, Edina in particular. But my own favorite has to be Clarissa. Perhaps because I lived inside her head for so long, but also, considering the times and her background, she is in her own way brave, a survivor.

Q: Do you think it would be accurate to say that there are three main characters in your novel: Clarissa, Tom—and Deyning? Is the house based on a real place? What makes it such an important player in The Last Summer?

A: Deyning is central to the novel, possibly the most important character, but it doesn't exist, nor is it based on anywhere. I think it's an amalgamation of places, houses I've seen or visited or read about. And, in a way, it's a figment of all of our imaginations—whatever we wish it to be; a sort of Shangri-La, a mirage of an idyllic world, and a way of life that was once there, for a few, for a while, and is gone.

It represents home, of course, and an old order, but also continuity in a changing world. However, as a symbol of permanence it's not entirely unaffected by the tumultuous events taking place around it. It sees its sons go off to fight, and for a while, at least, it bears its own physical scars. It witnesses changing times and fortunes, and, like Clarissa, endures years of loneliness and neglect. And, also like Clarissa, it is rescued by Tom.

Q: Did you always want to be a writer? What inspired you to start writing?

A: I learned to read and write before starting school, and was writing stories then. Whenever anyone asked me what

I wanted to be, I'd tell them, "A writer." I grew up in Northumberland, in a village drenched in history, where the ruins of a medieval castle—a setting in Shakespeare's *Henry IV*—were my playground, and the thrill of the week was going to the library with my book-obsessed father to select my new book. For a while I attended the same school the Brontë sisters once attended, the inspiration for the school in *Jane Eyre*. Though, I hasten to add, greatly changed by my time! So I suppose from a very young age I was immersed in history and literary influences. And I've written all my life, always kept a journal, and have endless notebooks filled with unfinished stories. But by my late teens it seemed a decidedly uncool thing to say, "I want to be a writer." Other things took over, mainly boyfriends and parties and making enough money to pay my exorbitant London rent. It wasn't until I moved to the country ten years ago that I decided the book in me was long overdue.

Q: Who are the writers you most admire? Is there a book you wish you had written?

A: I'm a voracious reader, of fiction, non-fiction, classics and contemporary. My favorite writers include Edith Wharton, Henry James, Tolstoy, Virginia Woolf, Jane Austen, Emily Brontë, F. Scott Fitzgerald, Ernest Hemingway, E. M. Forster, Daphne du Maurier, Beryl Bainbridge, Jean Rhys, and probably every Virago author I bought as a student. And a book I wish I'd written: *I Capture the Castle* by Dodie Smith. Because it's a book I truly loved, and could read again and again.

FROM BOOKS TO BOARDROOM TO BOOK DEAL

by Judith Kinghorn

When I was ten, twelve, or even fourteen, if anyone ever asked me what I wanted to do with my life, I replied that I wanted to be a writer. I'd learned to read and write long before starting school and words were my passion. But life's full of distractions, and alternative roads, and by the time I reached thirty I'd acquired a rather glamorous albeit adrenaline-fueled career, culminating in my appointment as managing director of a long-established public relations and graduate recruitment company based in

Covent Garden, London, and owned by the late Josephine Hart. Shortly after that I became a director of a corporation.

I've never been much good at pacing myself, tend to hit any deck running, and certainly—as far as my career was concerned—I'd peaked early. For a few years my buzz came from the boardroom, and, bizarrely (because I'd always hated math at school), from figures; namely a profit and loss statement. I drove to work each day, parking my convertible outside my office, lunched at the Ivy (always the fishcakes), and shopped at Prada and Armani. I was nominated for Woman of the Year, became a fellow of the Royal Society of Arts, and by thirty-three years old I seemed to have it all.

But I didn't. I had no time. No time for myself, and very little time for my young son. I spent an inordinate amount of my day in a traffic jam, usually on the phone to work, and always feeling guilty: either about the little boy waiting for me at home or the people I'd left back at the office. I was permanently exhausted and stressed. So, in 1997, pregnant with my second child, I traded in my seemingly glamorous career for the *Teletubbies*, *Tumble Tots . . .* and tantrums. I became a full-time mummy. It was a culture shock: a seismic shift in my life. And, though I loved spending time with my two young children, it took me a couple of years to stop drafting business plans and know how and where I wanted this new life to be.

I suppose I could say I'd given up the corporate world for my children, for us—as a family—to have a simpler, healthier, less stressful life (in theory). But in truth, I'd also yearned for a sense of peace, and space; an environment I thought would unlock my long-dormant creativity. I wanted to paint again, wanted to write (though I wasn't sure about what), and I began to realize that the lifestyle my husband and I both craved wasn't possible in London. The dawn of a new millennium seemed like the perfect time to be brave and pioneering, and so in 2000 my family and I upped sticks, and moved from London to Hampshire, to a mid-Victorian, Arts and Crafts–style house.

I'd never been particularly interested in the history of houses, hadn't thought too much about any of the places I'd lived in growing up, or in London, but my house in Hampshire—its refurbishment—triggered something in me. Discovering solid slate windowsills, hidden under decades of chipped and bubbled gloss paint; tiled hearths, boarded over and long since abandoned as fireplaces; varnished Victorian wallpaper beneath decades of differing fashions and tastes, made me feel like an archaeologist, and I wanted to know more. I wanted to learn the story of the place we now called home. I found myself imagining the house as it had once been, as it had first been; and I wanted to know who'd lived here, who'd chosen that wallpaper. All old houses have secrets, each one has its own story, and I had a hunch that my new home had a tale it was longing to tell.

I knew very little at that time, had no idea who had built the house or when, but

I guessed it had been built by an architect. And I knew the army had been there during the Second World War. And yet, to me, completely inexplicably, the house felt predominantly female. I could only ever picture women having lived there. I'd also reasoned that with so much decorative detail the place must have been built for a woman.

Over the course of two years I managed to piece together the story of my house and its former inhabitants. And I discovered a cast of vibrant, complex women, who'd led fascinating and sometimes scandalous lives. From Charlotte Vincent, an abstemious, God-fearing philanthropist, to Maud Calvert, a would-be writer; from the elderly Viscountess Trafalgar to the duplicitous Countess de Champs l'Anson (for whom the house was built): my home has been home to many interesting women.

And I thought I was stuck for a story.

The history of my home, my research, ended up as a book (published as local history, unedited, and full of typos). Then came a novel: loosely based on the countess's life, and rewritten a dozen times. By the end of 2009, with the book still unfinished, and without any agent or publisher, I felt browbeaten by the countess, her story and my rewrites of it. I needed a break, but not from writing—from her. So I decided to write something else, something completely invented and fictitious, something for myself: the sort of book I'd like to read. . . .

I knew I wanted to write a first-person narrative, and a love story, but perhaps with a dark edge to it. And I decided to set that narrative in the period I'd most recently spent time in (researching). In January 2010—without much planning, and with no idea of my narrative arc—I began writing *The Last Summer*. By July I'd more or less finished the first draft; by the end of summer I'd acquired an agent; a few months later—a publishing deal.

It's taken me almost half a century to get here, to be doing what I know I was born to do, but I think I've had an interesting journey.

QUESTIONS
FOR DISCUSSION

1. The events of *The Last Summer* are seen from the perspective of its heroine, Clarissa. Did you enjoy seeing the story through her eyes?

2. ". . . the end of a belle epoque" is how Clarissa describes that last summer before the outbreak of the First World War. Do you agree with her?

3. How important is the world of Deyning Park to the novel?

4. Which character do you feel undergoes the most dramatic transformation in the novel?

5. Edina does not wish Clarissa to marry Tom because, to her, they are too far apart in social status for their relationship to work. How do you feel about this in light of the revelation of Tom's parentage?

6. The First World War changes society irrevocably. What is the impact on the characters in the novel? How is the class system portrayed?

7. Clarissa and her friends' use of morphine to "produce a pause long enough to obliterate reality, suspending thought and reason" shows a darker side to their Edwardian world than we are perhaps familiar with. What was your reaction to this?

8. Are there parallels between Clarissa and Tom's love affair and that of the anonymous letter writers' in the novel? Did you guess who the correspondents were?

9. Which of Clarissa's relationships do you think has the greatest impact on her life—her relationship with Tom; her mother, Edina; or her baby, Emily?

10. "Moments can and do come back to us." Discuss this final statement in relation to *The Last Summer*.